Fiona McCallum was raised on a cereal and wool farm near Cleve on South Australia's Eyre Peninsula and remained in the area until her mid-twenties, during which time she married and separated. She then moved to Melbourne and on to Sydney a few years later.

An avid reader and writer, Fiona returned to full-time study as a mature-age student and graduated with a Bachelor of Arts in professional writing and editing and a second major in history in 2000. She then began a consultancy providing writing and editing services to the corporate sector. While studying, and then working, Fiona found herself drawn to writing fiction where her keen observation of people and their everyday lives could be combined with her love of storytelling.

Now a full-time novelist, Fiona writes heart-warming stories that draw on her rich and contrasting life experiences, love of animals and fascination with human nature. Her first novel, *Paycheque,* was published in 2011 and became a best-seller. In the nine years since, Fiona has written another ten bestselling novels: *Nowhere Else, Wattle Creek, Saving Grace, Time Will Tell, Meant To Be, Leap of Faith, Standing Strong, Finding Hannah, Making Peace* and *A Life of Her Own. The Long Road Home* is Fiona's twelfth novel. Her new book, *Trick of the Light*, is available in 2021.

Fiona currently resides in suburban Adelaide.

For more information about Fiona and her books, visit her website at fionamccallum.com. She can also be found on Facebook at facebook.com/fionamccallum.author.

Also by Fiona McCallum

Paycheque
Nowhere Else
Leap of Faith

The Wattle Creek series
Wattle Creek
Standing Strong

The Button Jar series
Saving Grace
Time Will Tell
Meant To Be

The Finding Hannah series
Finding Hannah
Making Peace

A Life of Her Own
Trick of the Light

FIONA McCALLUM

The Long Road Home

FICTION
HQ

First Published 2020
Second Australian Paperback Edition 2021
ISBN 9781867208006

THE LONG ROAD HOME
© 2020 by Fiona McCallum
Australian Copyright 2020
New Zealand Copyright 2020

Published by
HQ Fiction
An imprint of Harlequin Enterprises (Australia) Pty Limited (ABN 47 001 180 918), a subsidiary of HarperCollins Publishers Australia Pty Limited (ABN 36 009 913 517)
Level 13, 201 Elizabeth St
SYDNEY NSW 2000
AUSTRALIA

® and TM (apart from those relating to FSC®) are trademarks of Harlequin Enterprises (Australia) Pty Limited or its corporate affiliates. Trademarks indicated with ® are registered in Australia, New Zealand and in other countries.

A catalogue record for this book is available from the National Library of Australia www.librariesaustralia.nla.gov.au

Printed and bound in Australia by McPherson's Printing Group

For all who take a little longer to find themselves and their niche: It's never too late.

PART ONE

PART ONE

Chapter One

It was a quarter to six when Alice's bosses closed and locked the door of the office of the law firm Baker and Associates behind her. They each gave her a hug.

'Are you sure you wouldn't like us to give you and Bill a ride or call a cab?' Peter Baker asked.

'Thank you, but we'll be perfectly fine, won't we, Billy boy?' she said, looking down to the Jack Russell sitting to attention at the end of his lead.

'Okay, if you're sure. Stay safe,' Peter said, surprising Alice with another hug. 'Congratulations again on getting into your course.'

'Yes, we're very proud of you. Walk carefully, now,' Lyn said, also hugging Alice again.

'See you tomorrow at ten at the end of the market, almost-birthday-girl,' Ashley Baker said. And Alice received another hug. She didn't think she'd enjoyed so many platonic hugs in her entire life as she had since moving to Ballarat. It was lovely.

'Yes, you will. Come on, Bill,' she said, and set off down the street with a wave of her hand. As she walked, she marvelled at having forgotten about her birthday amid the excitement.

The early evening sun and fine weather caused the Ballarat central business district streets to glow yellow around the long shadows of the old buildings. Even if it hadn't been a perfect spring evening, Alice would have still been smiling – she hadn't stopped since learning of her acceptance into the Juris Doctor postgraduate law course she'd applied for. Her smile and the warmth in her heart had been increased when her new employers, and now firm friends, had insisted on diverting the phones to message bank a few minutes early and celebrating with champagne. It was further confirmation she'd done the right thing moving to Ballarat from Melbourne when practically everything had gone wrong all at once, just a few months earlier. Now, outside in the fresh air, her legs, actually her whole being really, felt spongy, even heavy, but oddly light and buoyant all at once. She was happy. Though, a little tipsier than she'd realised.

As she walked, with Bill trotting alongside her, Alice tried not to think of the last job where she'd had after-work drinks. But there it was. At least she no longer shuddered at the thought of the awful weeks when she'd been bullied and manipulated almost to madness by the great Carmel Gold of Gold, Taylor and Murphy Real Estate.

A tiny part of Alice was angry that she'd only lasted four weeks and that Carmel had triumphed over her, but an even bigger part knew she had the nasty woman to thank for where she was now and where she was heading. *I'm going to be a lawyer, and a damned good one! I'm going to be one with heart and compassion – there for those who, like me, got bullied out of occupations because management wouldn't do the right thing and put dollars and profit and earning power ahead of common decency*. She hoped one day Carmel would get her come-uppance, though it was doubtful Alice would ever know about it. That was the frustrating thing with karma – it never quite seemed to happen right when you needed it to. Oh well. Alice wasn't a vindictive person.

Of course, that was one of the problems and how she'd come to be a survivor of Carmel at all – and the latest in a long line of executive personal assistants who had left abruptly. Well probably now maybe not even the latest – about two months had passed. For all Alice knew, more had bitten the dust. God, how much must they actually be losing in advertising, interviewing and retraining of staff …?

The great Carmel Gold, indeed, she thought, and actually snorted aloud. And giggled, noticing the sideways look Bill gave her.

'Sorry, Billy boy, too much champagne,' she said.

Her legs were feeling heavier as she stood at the kerb waiting for the buzz and flash of green to tell her she could cross the street. She eased her scarf up and over her chin for more protection against the chilling air before bending down to give Bill a pat. He looked adoringly up at her. Alice's heart surged. He was such a darling, perfectly behaved dog and she was so lucky he'd been there at the RSPCA shelter when she and David decided they would now have a dog along with their new home and sizeable mortgage.

Oh dear. She so didn't want to think about David either. That was the champagne. A slight melancholy was laying itself over her and sapping her buoyancy and contentedness. She'd thought they'd be together forever. Well, she'd hoped.

It had taken her four years to realise how different they were and that they didn't share the same values – the import-ant ones. She'd thought he was everything her husband Rick hadn't been – driven, ambitious, city through-and-through. Alice had now realised she'd run to David from Rick and before that from her mother and family to Rick. Thankfully she'd stopped running now.

This was really the first time in her adult life Alice was truly living a life for her and really felt free at a deep, soul level. On the surface she was almost broke and living alone in a tiny one-bedroom flat in Ballarat, starting all over again at nearly thirty-one. Fear gripped her every now and then until she reminded herself that was just the lifelong conditioning of her mother – aided by her younger sister – poking through her newly acquired armour. No, she didn't need a man and there was so much more she could contribute to the world than as a wife and mother. Thank goodness she'd seen it in time. Thank goodness for Carmel Gold. *Oh dear, I must be more than a little tipsy!*

But it hadn't just been Carmel's illuminating behaviour. It had taken her dear friend from university, Brett – now her best friend Lauren's boyfriend – to open her eyes to what Carmel was doing, what she *was*, and that in turn had made Alice see the truth of her own past.

She still marvelled – more so cringed – at how similar her mother was to Carmel. Alice had spent her life seeking Dawn's love, acceptance, approval. And failed. She'd have settled for the occasional compliment and nod of approval, but even when she'd succeeded in graduating from university with stellar grades, she'd been warned not to get too above herself. Just daring to leave the tiny rural town of Hope Springs on South Australia's Eyre Peninsula meant, they said, she thought herself 'too good for us' and 'all high and mighty'. Now she knew she really *had* spent her life striving and failing in the eyes of her family. Her father, who had been gone for around nine years, would never intentionally have made her feel like that.

She continued to miss him every single day, but she didn't blame him for resorting to suicide. She hadn't ever, but now, with what she'd learnt about narcissists, she had a new appreciation of how hard it would have been for him living with Dawn, who possessed most indicators of the personality disorder: someone who was obsessed with themselves and achieving dominance while disregarding everyone else's wellbeing. Someone who lied, cheated and manipulated in order to receive the adoration they craved. And, perhaps most difficult of all for Alice to come to grips with, was that they weren't capable of having empathy and because of this didn't care who they hurt or destroyed along the way.

Alice shuddered at wondering what gaslighting her dad might have undergone – the feeling that something felt 'off' but you weren't really sure why. Carmel Gold had managed to have Alice questioning her sanity in a matter of days and nearly sent her completely mad in just a few weeks – imagine living with it twenty-four/seven for years, decades … she was so grateful to her father for the neutralising effect he had provided for so long. If she hadn't had that she could quite easily have turned out to be the sort of person who didn't cope at all well with life – an addict or someone with other serious problems – which, apparently, was a common outcome for so many left feeling they'd never be good enough, no matter what, which was the ultimate indoctrination of a narcissist parent.

Goodness only knew what Dawn was doing to Frank – her husband of around seven years. Alice loved Frank to bits and she'd quite recently found an ally in her stepfather after tending to always hold herself back with him. She'd assumed that was because she'd already been an adult when he'd joined their family or because he hadn't had kids himself and she didn't feel he'd understand her. She'd also wondered if perhaps she'd kept him at arm's length as some sort of loyalty to her father. Now, with all she'd learnt this past year, she suspected she'd been subconsciously protecting him. If Dawn knew how much Alice liked and respected Frank, her mother might just turn on him too. Alice couldn't bear it if another kind, gentle man chose to leave her the same way her father had.

Though why did Frank stay with Dawn? She thought about it. For as long as she could remember she'd watched her mother be attentive and super friendly to guests at dinner parties and customers in the shop and then cold and critical to Alice out of sight. She'd thought for years her mother simply didn't like her. She probably didn't, but Alice now understood all too well how the narcissists could switch their charisma on and off at will. Sadly, only their victims saw the truth and were often not believed. Alice hated being referred to as a victim, but she was. But she was also a survivor. What about Frank?

Dear Frank, Alice thought, smiling, remembering how good he'd been to her when she'd made the difficult trip 'home' to her dear friend's funeral. It was probably the most time she'd ever spent alone with him – it was certainly the closest she'd ever felt to him. And she'd seen a glimmer that he too saw some of the truth of what Dawn was.

Alice shook it all aside as she pushed the button on the next pedestrian crossing and then began to cross.

But the thoughts refused to leave. She longed to tell Frank her news about being accepted into law but wasn't prepared to have her bubble burst by one of Dawn's cruel comments – one of her few certainties in life. Alice longed for the time to come when she could laugh off the things her mother and sister said and did. Better yet, shrug them off and not give them any more negative air.

But she wasn't there yet. Her mother's comments and unspoken criticisms, sneers and general lack of support still hurt Alice as much as a knife to her heart would. She knew she shouldn't seek Dawn's approval or love, but still she did to some extent. Sometimes it wasn't intentional – was just a passing comment here or there from the down-to-earth open-book Alice. But always she was swiftly reminded of her place – or lack of – in her mother's heart and affections.

Alice didn't hate her mother. Sometimes she hated what she did and how she treated her, but now with all she'd learnt about narcissism she just pitied Dawn. Apparently, the barbs and mannerisms of a narcissist were deliberate and by all accounts they weren't capable of changing because the ego was so strong that they saw nothing wrong in their behaviour. So it was those around them who had to adjust – usually by resorting to going 'no contact'. Alice wasn't there yet, either, but she felt close. She was currently avoiding her mother's calls as much as she could and keeping her responses confined to text messages. She'd been doing that for around a month. Alice wasn't sure how long she'd be able to keep it up. It was important for her healing. Unfortunately, Dawn had a knack of luring her in thanks, damn it, to all the years of conditioning, especially that family is everything! Brett was so right about *that* being a load of shit.

Alice turned into the small cul-de-sac of five updated and well-maintained single-storey brown brick units. She felt a little surge of something – she still did every time she came home after being away. Excitement? More like peace? Contentment? Maybe a mixture. Freedom? But was that really an emotion? Ah, it didn't matter. What mattered was she liked her little home.

Hello, house, she silently said as she put her key into the lock of the cream gloss painted door. As with the outside, the fully furnished inside was nothing special. It was all neutral tones, but clean and fresh. Alice longed to add some touches of her own colour to the space but was still keeping a tight rein on her spending. She probably always would – she was that sort of person. She was working full time for now, but next year she'd have to cut back her hours to fit in her study. Thank goodness she had employers keen to do everything they could to help her succeed. It would all sort itself out. It had already, she thought, as she stood at the small hall stand inside the front door.

She put her phone and keys in the wooden bowl on top and her handbag on the shelf underneath, and hung her coat and scarf on the hooks above. She'd always been tidy, but now had to be more so because the smallest thing out of place made the flat look cluttered. Bill's bed in the corner of the loungeroom was bad enough. She loved this little ritual of settling herself back in too.

Several times she'd marvelled at how, despite the whiteness around her, it didn't feel at all cold and sterile like the house she and David had bought in Melbourne had. She hadn't realised just how much she hadn't liked that place until she set foot in here for the first time. It was as if the tiny space wrapped itself around Alice in a comforting hug right when she'd needed it and had never let go. Even when she was out she often longed to be back here. For the first time in her life she was alone. Completely alone and free to make all her own decisions – not waiting for her husband Rick to come in from the paddock or the shed or David from a long day at the office or an overseas trip. If she wanted to eat a bowl of cereal for every meal for a week she could and there was no one to comment or scowl.

She knew there were times ahead when she would crave some company. And of course making all the decisions all the time might become stressful. But plenty of other people managed just fine. Alice felt a heady level of exhilaration and pride in herself that she'd finally set herself free.

Yes, I have so much to be thankful for, she thought as she took her phone over to the couch, where Bill was already in position. She smiled and gave him a pat. He loved their home too. He exuded gratitude from every pore. And every *paw*! Alice smiled and then concentrated on reading the well-wishing text messages that had come through in the last hour and a half. All the important people in her life were cheering her on: Lauren, Lauren's parents – Melissa and Charles Finmore – and Brett. Jared and Pip from Gold, Taylor and Murphy – though she felt she was losing touch with them a bit now she was living so far away.

Her heart sank a little. Frank. She brought up his name in her contacts. Her finger hovered over it for a moment. No. She'd update her online profiles instead. Put it off a little longer. Because as much as she wanted to share her news with Frank, she didn't want to with her mother. And she couldn't ask him to keep secrets from his wife. Thankfully, years ago, after complaining about how few people followed them or showed any interest at all in what they had to say on Facebook and Twitter, Dawn and Olivia had both flounced off social media for good. Alice had resisted pointing out they might have to show more of an interest in other people, but there was no telling either of them anything. Alice had blocked them both everywhere and kept an eye out in case they were still lurking about.

Alice updated her social media accounts to say she now lived in Ballarat, had been accepted to the course and worked at the law firm. It all felt good – like she really had stepped in the right direction of putting her life back together. Getting on with it. She felt a surge of pride ... until a little voice inside her said she was getting above herself. A little voice that sounded just like her mother's stern, condescending tone. *No*. What was wrong with feeling silently proud of one's achievement? She'd earnt her place fair and square – her transcript from her Arts Degree with Modern History major was full of high distinctions and distinctions. She'd worked hard to achieve them. She was not boasting. She was stating facts. If her family – or anyone else – felt uncomfortable with it, well that was their problem. Alice Hamilton was done with censoring herself to keep others happy or comfortable in their little boxes. She'd done that for most of her life and it had got her nowhere.

Nonetheless, she was pleased to see a heap of likes and comments appear. Seeing Frank's love heart emoji appear under her Facebook post twisted Alice's heart. She longed to pick up the phone and speak to him. But it must be almost dinner time in the once-Hamilton-now-Roberts household. No doubt he was being told off right then about having his head in his phone and not giving Dawn his undivided attention. Alice had actually forgotten he was on Facebook. She'd accepted his friend request years ago and had never seen him post anything, well, not that she could remember. Wary of becoming addicted and wasting too much time, she'd pulled back while at uni and not been a huge user of any social media for years. But recently she'd got more into it again in an effort to feel not quite so sad and lonely as she'd gone through the turmoil with her last job, leaving David and life in general. There were some things she absolutely loathed about it – the false façades people put up of how absolutely brilliant they and their lives were. And there were things she absolutely loved about it – posts of lost persons and pets being shared and hearing of good outcomes, people's milestones and humour and connections, and valuable information from reputable sources. Since discovering the subject of narcissism, she'd been sharing the posts of several good pages in an effort to help spread the message. She figured if everyone knew the tactics and what to look for in these horrible people, perhaps the predators might eventually be stamped out or at least neutralised. Of course, a certain level of narcissism was supposed to be useful in the world, though Alice didn't see why people couldn't be strong and assertive without being arrogant wankers, which was what she chose to call them – at least to herself.

Chapter Two

Alice's heart seemed to stop momentarily at seeing a notification of an email from David – the de facto partner she'd recently left – with the word 'Settlement' in the subject line. She held her breath as she opened it. She blinked, almost unable to believe what she was seeing. And then she let out a long sigh of relief. There was a bank receipt notification of transfer of payment – the full amount she'd asked for. She felt a pang of guilt. Not that she'd done anything wrong; she'd only asked to be compensated for what she'd actually put into the house deposit and his uni fees. She'd been fair. Ashley at work had told her she was entitled to a lot more. But Alice knew David would struggle as it was with what he had to pay her. He might even have to ask his parents – both civil servants in Sydney – to help, which would just about kill him. Money and reputation were everything to David Green. Alice had briefly thought about walking away without a cent and she might have if it hadn't been for the fact when she left she had no job and no home and very little left in her own bank account.

When she'd left, and was house-sitting for the Finmores, he'd turned up with his version of a settlement and pushed her to sign it on the spot, but she'd been rushed into signing paperwork when her marriage to Rick had ended, only realising later she'd been ripped off. She wasn't making that mistake again. The figure she'd calculated, which was almost twice David's, Ashley had put in a letter on the company letterhead and sent on Alice's behalf. This had prompted a nasty voicemail from David. The man who had always told Alice 'we don't raise our voices; we are adults and will discuss this like adults' was severely pissed off that she'd questioned him and that he might have to fork out more money. As much as Alice didn't want to hurt him – she held him no malice; they were just too different – she had herself and her future to think of. And her own pride, when it came to it. If she were to be a strong, independent woman she had to start standing up for herself to David as she had Carmel Gold. It obviously helped that she had free access to legal advice and correspondence.

She hadn't returned David's call or any of his emails, in turn pathetic and pleading, manipulative and threatening. And now, three weeks later, she'd been paid the full amount she, via Ashley, had asked for. No doubt he'd been to see his own lawyer in that time and told he was damned lucky it was only this amount. She could see it.

Alice took several deep breaths. She was now really free of David. There was no need for them ever to have contact again. How did she feel about that? Sad? Relieved? Both, but mainly sad. She'd been here a month, but suddenly felt for the first time she *was* really here. Really alone. For the rest of the time she'd been avoiding thinking too deeply about her situation, her new circumstances and the abrupt end to her life with David. The end of her Melbourne life, full stop. She'd been kept busy with getting to know Ballarat streets, learning her new job, waiting to hear about her uni application. Settling in. Now as the tears prickled painfully in her eyes, Alice realised she'd been outrunning her feelings or shoving them down inside her.

She was *scared*. Maybe David was right. How was she going to survive on her own financially? Emotionally? Physically? She'd felt abandoned by him in her time of need, when her dear friend Ruth had died suddenly and she'd had to venture back to Hope Springs alone to the funeral. Perhaps, as he'd said, she'd made a hasty decision, been too emotional at the time. Had over-thought it. Could you be both over-thinking and overly emotional at the same time? Wasn't that oxymoronic? Had she made the wrong decision after all? Tears streamed down her face and her insides felt both empty and painfully tight. Oh god. She pulled one of the cushions on the couch to her stomach and held on, hoping the lost, drowning feeling would pass. Maybe her mother was right: she shouldn't be on her own; she'd be lonely.

The tears stopped. Alice blinked. And as her vision became clear again, so did her mind. She would never forget how she'd felt that day standing in the Hope Springs cemetery, surrounded by people she knew but feeling so desolate – sadness the likes of which she hadn't felt since losing her father. She'd felt completely and utterly abandoned. No, she was just feeling sorry for herself. She was allowed such moments. But not too many or at least not for too long!

As her dear friend Lauren was always saying, she had to be kind to herself. She really had been through quite a bit recently and needed to process it in a gentle way. She wasn't selfish and calculating like her mother and sister. She was deeply emotional and super sensitive like she gathered her father must have been. If only men hadn't been raised to believe they couldn't be emotional or shed tears. Oh how she missed him. But she did also like to think she felt him with her – urging her on to find herself, find her way – and soon. Thank Christ she'd left Hope Springs and the narrow-minded family that remained there. She had David to thank, though if she hadn't had some courage of her own she would have said no.

Alice looked at the email from him again and wondered if she should respond. And say what? Thank you? On email it could sound abrupt – like she was being smug or victorious or something. She'd sleep on it.

Alice returned to the Instagram app and smiled at all the well-wishes from her friends and acquaintances. She wasn't alone.

She laughed aloud at Lauren's gif of people waving their arms and cheering. No, she wasn't alone. She might not have blood relatives she could count on, but the Finmores were amazing. If she had a car she could have driven out there for a hug. They would completely understand what she was feeling, even if she couldn't express it herself. They never said, 'Oh, Alice,' in that condescending, sneering tone her mother and Olivia used. And they certainly wouldn't tell her to pull herself together or that she was an embarrassment for being emotional. God, how had she got through her childhood and early adulthood? But at least she was tough and capable.

'Well, when I'm not blubbering like an idiot and feeling sorry for myself, huh, Bill?' she said, ruffling the ears of the dog lying beside her. He turned and licked her hand and flapped his tail. *How do people get through this stuff without a pet in their lives?* She turned back to her phone and felt both affection and apprehension – the latest comment was from Rick, her ex-husband: *Awesome news. Well done! Xx* ♥

She stared at the two Xs and the heart. Oh shit. Perhaps she shouldn't have agreed to connect again with him online after all. He'd asked after Ruth's funeral when she'd been so vulnerable, and she couldn't have said no after he'd been so good to her that day. But oh dear, maybe she'd opened up a connection better left closed. He was single again and vulnerable. So was she. Alice pressed the home key on her phone and turned it over.

As she clicked the TV on she wondered if she should, could, buy herself a house-warming-slash-celebratory gift. Nothing too expensive, but something for herself. Should she think about buying a cheap car too? She didn't like feeling she couldn't just go somewhere for a drive when she wanted to. But she reminded herself she liked the idea of an extra buffer in her bank account more. One of the Finmores was in Ballarat several times a week and their home was really the only place she couldn't easily get to in a cab. And they were only about half an hour away. Charles and Melissa had said plenty of times she was welcome to call them if she wanted to visit. They were both retired and could come and get her. And there was always their farm manager Blair.

Ah, the intriguing, very good-looking Blair … She'd met him at dinner at the Finmores' and he'd brought her in the day she moved into the flat. She'd also thought she'd seen him at the market the other day, but she could have been mistaken. She'd spent time sitting beside him in his ute and at the dinner table, but didn't know anything else about him beyond the fact he seemed friendly, was olive-skinned and muscular, judging by the bulges under the dress and polo shirts she'd so far seen him wearing. She'd had to forcibly avert her gaze from the huge brown eyes, the broad smile and the thick dark hair, which might be wavy but was kept trimmed a little too close to his head to really tell. She'd snuck more than a few covert glances at his rounded backside and long lean legs. Hmm, annoyingly, he'd piqued her curiosity and distracted her far too much, despite her telling herself he was most likely married and she was certainly not looking for a love interest anyway.

Alice brought up her favourite online homewares and gift store and clicked on throw rugs, taking the red sale signs plastered over the site as a good sign. Her mouth practically watered at seeing a magenta wool throw staring back at her. She went into her bedroom and tried to imagine it on her bed and decided it would look perfect on both the navy sofa and the grey waffle quilt cover. Did she even care if it worked or not? She almost pressed the add to cart button at thinking how much David would hate it. He was all about grey and white and everything minimal. It was still very expensive at half price, though … no, she'd sleep on that too. Your ex hating something was probably not a good enough reason to buy it.

She'd also have a look at the stores in the mall tomorrow morning while she was there with Ashley for the weekly market. After that she and Bill were being collected and going out to the Finmores' gorgeous historical home – Toilichte House, which apparently meant happy in Scots Gaelic. They were English and might or might not have Scottish heritage – she'd never asked – but the house had been already named when the Finmores bought it quite a few years back. Speaking of mouth-watering. She just loved being there. She couldn't wait to see Lauren and Brett, too. Then she'd really get stuck into her reading and get a jump on her course. She had a few months yet but figured she could never be too organised or well prepared. The challenge had her fired up. So what if she lived in a tiny rented flat? She had a wonderful life and exciting times ahead. She would make sure of it. She was in charge now. And it was going to be a great birthday.

Chapter Three

Alice waited for Ashley on the corner at the end of the mall in the sun with her coat pulled tight around her. During her walk from home it had been quite chilly, mainly thanks to the brisk wind rushing between the buildings and down the narrow alleys. She almost sighed aloud now at the sun drumming on her back and closed her eyes and lifted her face to the sky to make the most of it.

'Good morning,' Ashley said, startling her a little.

'Good morning,' Alice said, beaming at her new friend, who was almost her height thanks to the tall high-heeled black boots her jeans were tucked into. She loved how confident Ashley was in her skin. The lawyer was plus sized and with straight mouse-brown hair she usually kept pulled back into a ponytail. Alice, sweeping her own long dark locks over one shoulder to keep them out of her friend's face as she bent for a hug, thought Ashley radiated gorgeousness from the inside out thanks to her general effervescence and the huge smile that lit up her round face with its dusting of light freckles and two pronounced dimples. 'Isn't the sun gorgeous?'

'It sure is. Hello, Bill,' Ashley said, bending down to give the dog a pat. But Bill ignored her. He and his new bestie Max, the black miniature poodle, were busy with their own reunion.

'Oh, nearly forgot, happy birthday!' Ashley said, pulling Alice into another hug. 'These are for you,' she said, reaching into her tote bag and bringing out a small box of handmade chocolates from the stall they had admired the week before.

'Yum. Thanks so much. Another year bites the dust,' Alice said, raising her eyebrows.

'Another year wiser,' Ashley said.

'Well, one can hope,' Alice said.

'First things first – I need coffee,' Ashley said, looking around. 'Shall we go where we went last time or try somewhere else?'

'I walked past one just over there and it smelt divine,' Alice said, indicating to her left with her head.

'Perfect!' Ashley said, leading the way. Alice smiled to herself. This was the best way to spend a Saturday – looking over the wares of the clever creative types of Ballarat while grazing on interesting titbits and buying some fresh fruit and veg and meat for the week ahead. And the experience was made so much the better by having the calm but enthusiastic Ashley to wander with, though this was only their third time doing this together. Alice was a little cautious when it came to friendships these days after discovering her childhood best friend, Shannon, had slept with Rick.

Alice accepted she and Ashley might still be in the honeymoon period of their friendship, but hoped not. Deep down she thought their connection deeper and genuine – that they were just easygoing people. There had been a couple of times when Alice had spotted something she wanted to look at and Ashley wasn't all that interested and vice versa. They just caught up again further down the mall.

Ashley was more into homewares and Alice more into the food side of the market, though as she got her finances sorted out – i.e. more dollars all round – she might become more interested in finding a knickknack or two for her little home. Ashley had recently moved into her own townhouse and was in the phase of making it her own. Alice understood – she'd ended up spending hours the night before trawling through several online shopping sites. She'd found two throw rugs she loved and hadn't been able to decide between the plain purple one or the bright multi-coloured check. And no matter how many times she'd told herself she deserved it, she kept hearing her mother's voice telling her she was being silly to spend a hundred dollars on something so frivolous. Though, she'd almost justified, it was still quite chilly in the evenings and early mornings. A throw on her bed and wrapped around her would mean spending less on heating. Lauren would have said she should just do it, but then Lauren had an endless supply of money thanks to incredibly supportive, well-off parents and being an only child. Alice had to keep her wits about her and not be led astray by Lauren's more carefree spending ways. Anyway, Alice had never been a big online shopper. She liked to touch an item, turn it over in her hands and make sure of the colour, size and texture in real life rather than taking a punt on a website's picture and gushing description. Actually, maybe she'd find something at the markets. Something handmade maybe. Alice loved to shop with a purpose.

'Are you okay with us using our own mugs?' Ashley asked the man behind the coffee cart. 'They're clean.'

'Absolutely.'

'Brilliant. I'll have a latte, please,' Ashley said, handing over her travel mug.

Alice pulled her own out of the calico bag she'd dedicated to market use. Her travel mug had been her first Ballarat purchase, spurred on by Ashley at their first market visit together.

'I'll have a latte too, thanks,' she said, handing her mug over.

'Look, quick, a table,' Ashley said, as she turned with her mug after paying. 'I'll just go and grab it.'

'Good idea,' Alice said.

'Ah, that's better. Nectar of the gods,' Ashley said with a long, contented sigh after they'd both taken long sips.

'It sure is,' Alice said.

They took their time, savouring each sip of their creamy, bitter drinks, but before too long they had drained their cups. 'Right, I can get my day started now,' Ashley said, putting her mug back into her bag.

'Yes,' Alice agreed. 'Shall we do the left side and then back up the right?'

'Sounds like a perfect plan to me.' It was how they'd done the circuit each time. They gently tugged on the dogs' leads and got going on their meandering.

'Did your mum call for your birthday?' Ashley asked, pausing while flicking through a rack of knitted jumpers a few minutes later.

'No, she hasn't called yet.' Alice tried to keep the hurt tone out of her voice. She'd received a lovely text message from Frank first thing, but not a peep out of her mother or Olivia. While getting organised she'd wondered if she was being given the silent treatment. They'd had a couple of text message exchanges early in the week, before Alice had received her uni notification. It was odd because Dawn always made a point of getting in first – with everything; she was competitive through and through, even if there was no one to be competitive with. Dawn's birthday phone call had always come at seven a.m. on the dot. Like all narcissists, Dawn had no concept of boundaries; she never thought about what the person on the other end of the call might prefer – or feigned ignorance. Alice was only just starting to realise the truth. So much of what she thought was unconscious or unintended, she now knew was most likely not just conscious but calculated – all about pushing Alice's buttons. She was completely self-absorbed and chose to ignore cues from other people. Several times over the years Alice had let the call go to voicemail on principle, but when she'd called back later Dawn had always been miffed, and her birthday – the reason for the call – was barely mentioned. And Dawn either didn't get or refused to take hints. About anything. Ever. If it wasn't so frustrating it would be hilarious. Maybe when Alice had analysed it and understood it as well as her friend Brett, she'd be better equipped to see the funny side of it.

'I'm actually enjoying the peace, to be honest,' Alice said, more to herself. She'd opened up to Ashley about her family troubles and what she'd discovered in the last six months on a stroll around the lake in the botanical gardens the other Sunday. It had felt good to have it out in the open from almost the beginning. Ashley seemed to be quite up with the scourge of narcissism. Alice had longed to ask her if she'd been a victim, was a survivor too, but had resisted. She didn't want to say or do anything to muddy the waters. And she hoped she'd be friends with Ashley forever – if not working at the family firm forever – so figured there was plenty of time for her new friend to tell her, if there was anything to tell. It might just be that Ashley was more worldly than Alice, which wasn't hard.

As they wandered down the centre of the paved pedestrian mall among stalls decorated with a multitude of colourful umbrellas, Alice kept being drawn to the few outer permanent shops. She stopped outside a window displaying several throws draped across the end of a bed with a charcoal grey quilt cover. Her mouth was all but watering at the rich colours that were so much more vibrant in real life than what she'd seen online.

'It's gorgeous,' Ashley said, stopping beside her.

'Hmm,' Alice said. 'I was looking at this one last night online – if it's pure wool.'

'Come on, let's check,' Ashley urged, pushing the door open. Alice followed her in and discovered it was indeed the same throw. Oh, but there was the multi-coloured check one, too. Oh. And several others. She stood at the rack frowning slightly at the options hanging in front of her.

'They're all lovely,' Ashley said.

'Yes, that's the problem,' Alice said. She turned away. If she was spending that much money she wanted to be sure. And it wasn't as if she needed it.

'Maybe your mum will send one to you,' Ashley said.

'Hmm.' Alice hadn't given Dawn her new address. As far as Dawn knew, Alice was still at the Finmores', which she hoped couldn't easily be found without directions or accessing Google Maps or Whereis, which she didn't think Dawn had discovered yet. Well, she hoped not, anyway. It was another reason she hadn't told Dawn where she was now working. Remaining strong over the phone was one thing …

'What?'

Alice remained silent while she tried to find an answer.

'No?' Ashley said. 'Don't tell me your family doesn't do birth-days, either?' Alice wasn't sure what she meant by 'either' – doesn't do emotion? Doesn't do kindness? All manner of things could be inserted. Alice had opened her heart and mouth; goodness knew just what she'd said. It had been a slightly embarrassing, almost desperate torrent, only the main parts of which she remembered.

'Not really. Well, I've left, so it's different now,' she said, trying to deflect. She didn't want to tell Ashley the whole embarrassing truth – that she had only ever had one planned birthday celebration. Her ninth. And Dawn had somehow managed to forget that too. Well, *pretended* she'd forgotten, perhaps. Alice's younger sister Olivia had hundreds of dollars spent on her every year while Alice had been given merely token gifts – often a top or pair of shoes she didn't like and which ended up being claimed by Olivia anyway. Even when she suggested a new set of pyjamas or towels or a particular book, Dawn would exclaim, 'Oh, Alice, how boring,' and disregard her request. No matter how many times Alice had told her mother and sister casually over the years that she hated the colour red, she was always given this colour. Most likely because it was Olivia's and Dawn's favourite colour – another reason Alice probably hated the colour herself.

These days Alice didn't tend to get too sad about her birthday being neglected, but the blatant favouritism towards Olivia wasn't fine and made her angry when she allowed herself to think of it. God only knew how much Dawn had given Olivia and her useless husband when Alice had been left to fend for herself. But at least she was free. Alice was beginning to really see and appreciate that being the scapegoat in the family dynamic was preferable to being the golden child and essentially locked up in a gilded cage. Comfortable, but trapped nonetheless.

'It's complicated,' she said with a sigh, again more to herself.

'All the more reason to buy your own gifts, then,' Ashley said quietly, her tone sympathetic as she touched Alice on the arm.

'Can I help you?' the woman from behind the nearby counter called.

'Thank you, but I'm just looking. It's a gorgeous shop you have,' Alice said.

'Thank you.'

'I'm going to think about the throws. I haven't decided which colour I like the most. They're all lovely.'

'They are. I can always order more in if the one you want turns out to be sold later when you decide.'

'That's good to know. Thanks.'

'Well, have a great day. I hope to see you again soon,' the woman said as Ashley opened the door and Alice followed her out. Alice felt warmth flood through her despite walking out into the shaded chilly area. She loved how friendly everyone in Ballarat was so far. It might be a city, but it felt like a large country town – with none of the negatives so far like gossip. Hopefully it was too big for that.

They had an early lunch of Thai green chicken curry straight out of the wok at the far end of the mall and then started their slow wander back.

'Alice, fancy seeing you here!'

Alice looked up from where she was inspecting a display of handmade silver jewellery on the table in front of her. Her cheeks were already colouring as she turned around.

'Blair. Hi.' She clasped him as he hugged her and kissed her briefly in one fluid movement before releasing her. 'Ashley, this is Blair.'

'Ha, fancy you already knowing people! You've been in Ballarat two minutes! Blair, it's lovely to meet you.'

Alice watched as they shook hands, willing the heat in her face to disappear. 'Blair is the Finmores' farm manager,' she explained.

'Brilliant. I've been sent in to give you a ride out.'

'Oh. Well, I ...' Alice started, feeling flustered, not just because those incredible big brown eyes with their hard-to-believe-just-how-long lashes were gazing at her intently, but because she wasn't ready. She'd been told she was being collected around three, three-thirty. It was now only twelve.

'Don't worry, Alice, I know I'm way early. I had a few things to do. Hello there, Bill,' he said bending down to pat the dog.

Above him Ashley was staring at Alice with her eyes wide, her eyebrows raised and her mouth formed into an O. Alice gently slapped her arm.

'And you must be Max,' Blair continued below them. 'Aren't you a handsome chap, too. Would he mind a pat, Ashley?'

'Oh no, not at all. He's fine,' Ashley said, clearly a little flustered herself.

Alice laughed. She was glad she wasn't the only one Blair affected like that.

'So, what have we found today? Anything interesting?' Blair said, standing upright again.

'Oh, all sorts,' Alice said, flapping a hand.

'And happy birthday!' he said, pulling Alice to him again and unbalancing her so she fell against his large firm chest, letting out an 'Oh!' as she did.

'Thanks,' she said with a slightly embarrassed laugh.

'You poor thing, I've probably completely upset your routine showing up early like this. I'll leave you guys to it.'

'I should get home, actually,' Ashley said.

'Oh, don't go,' Alice and Blair said together.

'No, no, it's fine. I really should. I've got a heap of reading to do for next week.' She quickly hugged Alice and gave a vague wave in Blair's direction. 'It was lovely to meet you, Blair. I'll see you around. Have fun tonight, Alice, and enjoy the rest of the weekend. See you Monday. See you, Bill. Come on, Maxy.'

Alice watched her leave, feeling an odd sense of being cast adrift, lost. She cursed her heart, which was flickering with excited anticipation. She still didn't know if he was married, gay or anything beyond that he was clearly very close to the Finmores – more than just their farm manager or an employee – more like a member of the family like Alice was.

'God, I'm so sorry,' Blair said.

'What for?' Alice said, frowning slightly, bringing herself back from being lost in staring at his hands.

'I seem to have driven Ashley away,' he said.

'It's fine. Really,' Alice said, shaking off her slightly foggy, mesmerised state.

'I really didn't want to fluster you, Alice. I was in early, had some things to do so came here to kill some time. Sorry, I didn't mean it to be weird.'

'You just took me a bit by surprise, that's all. It really is fine. But I have a couple of things to do at home before we leave, if that's okay.'

'No problem. Will it bother you if I hang there while you do, or would you like me to stay here?'

Yes, you'll bother me, but I can't exactly say that, can I? Alice thought, her face reddening again. *Stop it!*

'Not at all. I just have to fill the mini pavlovas I made for dessert. You can help cut up the strawberries if you like.'

'Brilliant. I think I can manage that. And, yum, I love pavlova.'

'No pressure, then,' Alice said, offering him a cringing grin.

'I'm sure they'll be perfect. Do you have more you want to do here, or shall we go? My ute's just across there,' he said, pointing.

'I'm good to go,' Alice said.

'And, Bill, have you finished?' he said. The Jack Russell gazed up with what looked like a smile on his face. His tail wagged furiously. As they set off side-by-side, Alice thought she could feel sparks zapping across the narrow gap between her and Blair. And then she told herself off for being silly and thought instead of what she had to do once she got home. Alice was glad she'd got up early and got the meringues made. She'd be a disaster with him watching her cook.

'You live in a great spot,' Blair said, as he navigated the traffic and streets.

'Yes, it's perfect – about ten minutes walking distance from work and pretty much everything I need.' They made small-talk until pulling into the driveway outside Alice's flat.

'I just need to bring something, um, large in if you can hold the door open,' Blair called when he was out of the vehicle and Alice and Bill were standing at her door with keys in hand.

'Oh?' Alice turned and looked at him, frowning slightly. As requested, she unlocked the door and pushed it wide open. 'Do you need a hand?'

'No, I'm good. I've just got to …'

Alice watched as he dived into the rear of the immaculate dual-cab ute. When he backed out, she saw he had his arms around something like a big box – the size of a large Esky, she thought.

Inside, he placed the object down in the loungeroom and began unwrapping what must have been a whole roll of grey tape securing an old orange and cream blanket. She stood with arms folded as he worked methodically – tearing, balling up the lines of tape and setting each ball aside then working on the next bit until there was just the blanket covering something hard and oblong, almost square. Bill went over to cautiously investigate the piles of discarded tape.

'Okay. Your turn,' Blair eventually said, sitting back on his heels.

'Sorry?'

'Happy birthday, Alice. It's for you.'

'What is it?'

'Well, for that you'll have to open it,' he said, grinning, and patted the hidden object.

'Oh. Right. Wow. Thank you.'

'You might not like it. Open it.'

Alice was a little discombobulated as she prised apart the folds of blanket. *Why are you giving me a birthday present? We barely know each other. Or does this mean I didn't imagine that we shared a moment – formed a connection?*

'Oh, wow, it's gorgeous? What is it?' She stared at the beautiful polished box in various shades of pale timber ranging from rich yellow to medium brown, unsure what to make of it. It was quite some gift to give a stranger: what had she missed?

'It's a box – a wooden box. With a lid.'

'Yes, I can see that. But what sort of box? I mean, I know it's a wooden box, obviously … And it's lovely, but …'

'Well, you can use it as a side table in here, extra seating at the end of your table, as a blanket box at the end of your bed, some- where to store your study things. When I helped you move in I thought you could do with some hidden storage, since you're in a fully furnished rental. And being all white, I thought a bit of timber might be a nice warm touch – a useful piece of art, if you will …' Blair had become a little flustered.

'Oh my god, did you make it? With your own hands?' Slowly the dots connected inside Alice's head. 'For me?'

'Yup. Just for you.' Blair looked a little uncomfortable now.

She leapt up and threw her arms around him. 'I love it! Thank you. I'll treasure it always.' She kissed him on the cheek.

'Really? You really like it? Because if you don't, I could make you something else ...'

'No way. I love it. I really do,' she said, pulling away again before things had a chance to get awkward. 'Wow, Blair. You really did this?'

'Yup, I really did,' he said with a self-conscious laugh. 'It's my hobby.'

'Well, it's beautiful. You're very talented.' She ran her hands over the silky finish of the timber.

'It's actually made from an old pallet.'

'A pallet?' She lifted the lid and looked inside. It smelt a little like eucalyptus – fresh, clean and earthy.

'Yes, you know, the wooden things that boxes of goods sit on?'

'Wow. I can't believe you've done this. It's amazing.' *You're amazing. And I can't believe you've done this for me.* Alice felt so overwhelmed she thought she could cry if she didn't keep her wits about her.

'Would you like me to put it out of the way? It's not heavy, you'll be able to move it on your own, but since I'm here ...'

'No, just leave it here. I want to look at it and decide where I'd like it best.'

'Okay. Now, what can I do to help with dessert? Or would you prefer to pretend I'm not here? I don't want to completely derail your schedule.'

Pretend you're not here! Yeah, right! she silently scoffed.

'Oh. Yes, I'd better crack on,' Alice said, tearing her gaze away from the beautiful object.

In the kitchen she tried to concentrate but kept looking over at the stunning box. The more she looked at it the more she loved it, but she was also struggling with the fact Blair had made it for her – just for her. She couldn't remember being given such an incredible, thoughtful gift before.

'I got everything packed ready before I headed out, just in case I was caught up. So, it's just finishing the pavs,' she explained, as much to regain her focus as to tell him.

'I love how organised you are. That's going to serve you well as a lawyer, I'm sure.'

'I hope so. Hey, thanks again for your message, too.'

'You're welcome. I hope you didn't mind – that it wasn't weird or anything … But I was with Charles when he got your text and I was so thrilled for you …'

Alice noticed the colour in Blair's cheeks had risen. 'No, not at all. I thought it was lovely of you.'

'Charles didn't think you'd mind since you already had my number. Right, so let's see these famous mini pavlovas of yours,' he said, slapping his thighs.

Did we just have another moment *I didn't understand the meaning of?* Alice wondered as she dragged the platter of small meringues from the cupboard under the bench. She'd put them there in case she got distracted and Bill decided to investigate. As she had, she'd made a mental note to get some plastic ware. The flat didn't have anything big enough. The longer she lived there the more she discovered she didn't have but needed and the more she wished she hadn't left everything with David.

'These do indeed look perfect,' Blair said, casting a gaze over the plate Alice had just placed on the bench.

'Okay, you can whip the cream or cut up the strawberries,' Alice said, finally starting to feel a bit more at ease in his presence.

'I don't mind which.'

'Okay, you can cut the strawberries and I'll do the cream.' Alice wasn't sure she was so relaxed in his company she trusted herself with a knife. 'Oh shit,' she said, her cheeks becoming flushed again. She brought her hands to her face.

'What? What's wrong?'

'I've just realised I meant to buy a small electric beater while I was out. Whipping the egg whites with a hand whisk almost killed me this morning.'

'I can do the whipping, or we can go back out and get some beaters. Your choice. Either way, it's not a problem.'

Alice pondered it, tried to think where she'd get electric beaters from – which store. She couldn't think clearly. It was really something she didn't want to do in a rush with Blair standing by, anyway.

'Or you could take everything out to Charles and Melissa's …'

'I know I can, but …'

'Well, pass me a whisk, then, and I'll get to it.'

'Are you sure you wouldn't mind hand beating?' she said, opening the drawer and pulling out the whisk.

'Not at all. Especially since it's all my fault. You would have remembered them if I hadn't upset everything by turning up early. Come on, hand it over,' he said, smiling at her with his hand outstretched. Alice's heart skipped a beat as she did.

Chapter Four

'You're here! Happy birthday!' Lauren cried after throwing the large front door open. She then raced down the wide stone steps and hugged Alice and then Blair.

'We are indeed here,' Alice said with a laugh. She hadn't seen Lauren for about a month and she'd missed her dear friend's effervescence. That could never be adequately captured in a text, even though Lauren was a gifted writer.

'Hello, Bill, you gorgeous thing,' Lauren said, bending down and picking the dog up and holding him to her. 'I've missed you too, pupper,' she said, kissing his head. 'Oh, so much to celebrate! Come in, come in,' she said with a wave of her hand, and bolted back up the steps with Bill tucked under her arm. Alice and Blair grinned at each other then followed at a slower pace, Blair carrying Alice's overnight bag and Alice the plate of dessert.

'Leave your bag down here – I want you to open your present,' Lauren called, disappearing into the kitchen.

'But I said no presents.'

'It's your birthday, Alice. Your mother might not give a shit, but we, your new family, do. Mum, Dad, Brett, the guest of honour has arrived,' she said, as Alice entered the kitchen, followed by Blair.

Alice's heart swelled. *God I love these guys*, she thought, as she hugged each in turn.

'Dinner's nearly ready, but first things first,' Melissa said, putting down the spoon she'd been using to stir a pot on the stove and wiping her hands down her aproned front. 'Come into the sitting room, everyone.' She stood making shooing movements with her arms in between untying her apron and taking it off. Ordinarily Alice might be embarrassed at all the attention, but the Finmores were kind through and through. At home, attention had gone hand in hand with humiliation, being made fun of. She was still adjusting.

They sat around in the plush seating – Melissa beside a big, beautifully wrapped gift complete with a perfect bow.

'Happy birthday, dear Alice. This is for you,' she said, picking up the gift and handing it to her. To Alice it felt just like Christmas when she'd been a small child and she and her cousins and grandparents were sitting around a Christmas tree eagerly awaiting their gifts. Before her grandparents had died and all her cousins had dispersed to various parts of the country for jobs, marriage or simply a different life and Christmas had been just her, her dad and Dawn and Olivia. Which had been okay – not the same, but okay. And then her dad had died and okay had slipped beyond okay … *God. Stop it.*

'Oh. But …' Alice started and then stopped.

'Uh-uh, we'll have none of that we're not worthy stuff. You are,' Charles said gently.

'Thank you so much,' Alice said, her cheeks starting to flame.

'Just open it, sweetheart,' Melissa said.

'It's almost too beautiful to unwrap.'

'Well, give it here, then,' Lauren said, stretching her hand out.

'Oh, Lauren, leave the poor thing alone,' Melissa said.

Alice carefully undid the knotted bow and placed the black and white polka-dot length of ribbon over the arm of the antique lounge chair and carefully began peeling the first strip of sticky tape off the plain white glossy paper.

'So, what did your mum say about your university news?' Melissa said.

Alice cursed her tightening throat. She paused her picking at the tape and stared down at her fingers. 'I don't know what she thinks,' she said quietly.

'What do you mean?' Charles asked.

'Well, I got a lovely text message and Facebook comment from Frank – my stepfather. But I haven't rung Mum and she hasn't me. Honestly, I don't want her to burst my bubble,' she said, now looking from Melissa to Charles.

'Good idea. You have to protect yourself any way you can,' Brett said, nodding knowingly.

'Wow, you're strong – I wouldn't have been able to not say anything when she rang for your birthday,' Blair said.

Alice dipped her head again.

'They *have* rung for your birthday, haven't they?' Lauren said, staring at Alice with big eyes.

Alice shook her head slowly. Tears prickled, which annoyed her – not because it was a potentially embarrassing display, but because she wished her mother still didn't still have the power to wound her like this.

'Oh, Alice,' Melissa said kindly, putting her arm around Alice's shoulders and pulling her tight to her.

'There's still time. Your birthday isn't over yet,' Blair said.

'Is she giving you the silent treatment again?' Brett asked.

'I'm not entirely sure. Who would know?' Alice said. She tried to laugh, but it came out as more of a gulp. 'Honestly, I don't know why I'm upset. Every phone call feels like a waste of energy, anyway.'

'You don't need to understand why it hurts, Alice. And you certainly don't need to apologise to us. Just know we love you and consider you one of us,' Melissa said.

Alice nodded and smiled weakly. 'You guys have no idea how much you mean to me.'

'Don't get all weepy on us. Come on, just rip it open!' Lauren said, clapping her hands eagerly.

'Manners, manners,' Alice said, forcing herself to grin. She was enormously grateful to Lauren for changing the mood so abruptly. She undid the rest of the sticky tape quickly and pulled the edges of the paper back. 'Oh wow.' There in front of her, the colours clear through the plastic bag, was what looked very much like one of the throw rugs she'd been considering buying herself. She unzipped the bag and brought the multi-coloured checked fabric out and up to her face. It had the wonderful fresh scent of wool. And was so soft.

'How did you know?' she asked, looking around at them with wonder.

'Know what?'

'That I've been looking at throws – and this exact one?'

'We didn't, actually,' Melissa said. 'I just thought you needed something to snuggle up with and you were unlikely to treat yourself. Consider it sort of a house-warming-welcome-to-Ballarat-and-your-new-life present too,' she said. 'It should go with almost anything.'

'Yes, it will. It's just perfect,' Alice said with a long, contented sigh, cuddling the blanket. She didn't want to let it go.

'I'm so pleased,' Melissa said, smiling.

'Hey, is that your phone I hear?' Brett said, interrupting the brief silence. They all cocked their heads to listen.

'I think it is,' Alice said, hearing the distinctive tone coming from the handbag she'd brought in with her out of habit.

'Well, answer it,' Lauren said.

'Yeah, could be best to get it over with, right?' Brett said quietly.

Alice agreed with him. 'Would you mind?' she asked, looking around.

'No. Go ahead,' Charles said.

'If it's Mum, it'll be quick,' Alice said, fossicking in her bag.

'Take all the time you need,' Melissa said. 'It's your birthday – your day – there are no rules for you today. I'll just go and give the gravy a stir,' she added, getting up.

'I'll help,' Charles said, also getting up.

'Yep, speak of the devil,' Alice said, looking at the phone now in her hand and getting up.

'Hi, Mum,' she said as she made her way out of the room and around into the huge foyer behind the front door.

'Alice, what is this I hear about your studying law?'

'Sorry?'

'Is it true?'

'Um. Yes.'

'How do you think it made me feel having to hear about my daughter's plans down the street? And from Gerald at the service station of all places!'

'Mum, it's not really about you. It's my decision. I'm paying for it.' *Well, the government student loan scheme is for now, but still …*

'Not about me? When I'm made to feel like a fool because I apparently don't know what my own daughter is up to? How could you, Alice?'

'A congratulations would be nice, Mum. I earnt my place.'

'So, what, now you've left David you've lost all sense completely. Is that it? Don't you want to get a real job?'

'I have a real job, as you put it, Mum. I'm working for a law firm.'

'Yes, I had to hear about *that* second-hand too,' Dawn said, practically spitting the words out.

Alice stayed silent. There was nothing to say that would help.

'Well, don't come asking for a handout when you realise how difficult being on your own is. How you could have left that lovely David is a mystery to me.'

'Was there anything else, Mum?'

'Don't get surly with me.'

'I'm not.' *I'm genuinely asking. Like perhaps wishing me a happy birthday?* 'So, you're just phoning to tell me off for being second to hear of my plans, which you're not in favour of anyway? Why do you think I don't call, Mum?'

'Oh, Alice. Stop being so childish and prickly. You'd better toughen up if you think you're going to be a lawyer.'

'Thanks for your support, Mum, but I have to go. I'm actually out to dinner.'

'How nice for you. Must be nice to have such a lifestyle. We wouldn't mind such luxuries.' Alice rolled her eyes. 'But some people have jobs and businesses to run.'

'Was there anything else?'

'That's right, Alice, just dismiss your family. We're all well, thanks for asking.'

'So am I. Thank *you* for asking,' Alice said, cursing herself even as she returned the jibe. 'I need to go now. Thanks for calling.'

'Well, just remember where you're from, Alice – your roots – and don't go getting above yourself.'

'Okay, Mum. Bye. Thanks for the pep talk,' Alice muttered to herself after she'd ended the call. Again she cursed her tightening throat and eyes filling with tears. She felt an arm come around her and sank into Melissa's embrace.

'Oh, Alice, I'm so, so sorry,' Melissa said.

'Why is she so horrible?' Alice sobbed.

'I don't know, sweetheart.'

It was a rhetorical question, really. Alice knew exactly why. But it still hurt.

'Come on, dinner is on the table.'

Alice was a little startled to look up and see Lauren, Brett, Blair and Charles hovering nearby, all with concerned expressions on their faces.

'We weren't eavesdropping, we were worried about you,' Lauren said.

'It's okay, Lauren. Anyway, of course you were – you're the nosey writer, remember. Thanks, guys,' Alice said, trying to sound cheerful.

'She didn't wish you a happy birthday, did she?' Lauren said, when they were seated in the dining room.

'No. She was actually calling to tell me off for not telling her I was studying law. Thank goodness I have you guys,' Alice said. 'Now, can we please change the subject?'

'As long as you're sure you're okay,' Brett said.

'I am. Thanks.'

'Good. Because we have a birthday to celebrate! But you have to leave room for the black forest cake Mum and I made.'

'And the lovely mini pavs Alice made,' Blair said.

'And the cream Blair got big guns from whipping,' Alice said.

'Huh?' Lauren said, frowning and looking intently from Alice to Blair and back again.

'Long story,' Alice said.

'Yes, it certainly is,' Blair said.

Chapter Five

Alice woke in her bedroom at the Finmores' feeling unrested. She'd tossed and turned as she'd teetered between pining for her mother's affection, even just an acknowledgement of her birthday – her general existence – and being angry at herself for expecting, hoping, things would change. She'd even checked her phone several times in case her mother had remembered during the night and called her while it was on silent beside the bed. In the dark quietness of the room with the eucalyptus-green walls, she heard the faint tap of Bill's tail wagging, hitting the plush rug beside the bed.

'Good morning, darling boy,' she said. The thumping increased in speed and volume. She smiled. Oh how that simple sound and the dog's gleeful face cheered her. The light behind the curtains told her it wasn't really early. She got out of bed and leant down and picked the dog up and held him to her. She cocked her head to listen for signs of activity, but thick stone walls and lush carpets muffled any sounds from elsewhere in the house. She put Bill down and pulled on her clothes, thinking, as she did, that it was

45

so comforting to know it didn't matter whether the others were up or not; she'd feel at peace. Unlike at her mother's house.

She found herself thinking about how Frank had cooked her a big breakfast – their little secret – the morning after Ruth's funeral, when Dawn and Olivia had been off walking. Bless him. She had never felt she'd known him very well because she'd been married when he met her mother and then joined the family, but she was starting to.

'Good morning, everyone,' Alice said, as she entered the kitchen, where Brett was cooking at the huge bank of burners with Lauren leaning beside him against the stone bench top clutching a mug in both hands.

'Hiya,' Lauren called. 'Coffee?'

'Yes please.'

'Good morning,' Charles said, from behind his laptop at the island.

'Good morning,' Melissa said, looking up from a tablet computer and smiling. 'That was a rather enthusiastic request for coffee – didn't you sleep well?'

'Not really. Too much on my mind,' Alice said with a shrug.

'You weren't snoring, were you, Bill?' Charles said to the dog, who had just run back in after going out the doggy door for a wee.

'No, he was perfectly well behaved, as always,' she said, measuring a scoop of dry food and putting it into his bowl.

'It's your birthday weekend – you're not allowed to be sad,' Lauren said, putting down a mug for her in front of an empty stool.

'Still no acknowledgement of your birthday from your mother? She didn't call back?' Melissa said.

'No.'

'Oh dear.'

'I'm okay. I'll be better after coffee.'

'And pancakes, I hope,' Brett said. 'I've done a spinach frittata type thing, too.'

'Sounds perfect,' Alice said. 'Yum.'

'Here we are.'

'This looks amazing,' she said as a plate was set down in front of her.

'Yes, what a treat,' Melissa said.

'You can stay any time you like, Brett,' Charles said.

'You'd better reserve your comments until you've tasted it – it might be horrible.'

'As if,' Lauren said, settling onto a stool beside Alice.

'It's even better than it looks, darling,' Lauren said a few moments later, leaning over and kissing Brett who was now seated on her other side.

'Yes, top job,' Charles said, sparking off a round of compliments.

'Gotta love a role reversal,' Lauren said with a laugh. 'Get your noses out of those devices, you two,' she said in a mock scolding tone to her parents.

'So, what are you kids planning to do this morning? I'm firing up the pizza oven for a late lunch, early dinner if that suits everyone – say, five? Other than that, you're free as birds, from my point of view,' Charles said.

'Since it's going to be nice weather, what do you think about panning for gold in our creek?' Lauren said.

'Oh, I'd love that,' Alice said.

'I thought you might.'

'But don't go getting too excited: I haven't seen more than a sparkly flake in ages,' Charles said.

'Oh well, it will be nice to just sit with the trickling water.'

***

'I can't believe you remembered I wanted to try panning for gold,' Alice said later when they'd cleared away all signs of breakfast and she, Brett and Lauren were carrying buckets, pans, shovels and tiny specimen vials – just in case – away from the house.

'Come on, it was only a couple of months ago that you said it. I might be an airy-fairy distracted writer, but still ...' Lauren said. 'Anyway, as Dad said, don't get your hopes up. You might be bored in half an hour.'

'The sun's nice,' Alice said as they unloaded everything on the bank and got themselves settled.

'Yes, spring is totally my favourite season – not too hot and not freezing cold,' Lauren said. 'Though the water is! Christ! It's like ice,' she said, pulling her fingers out.

'Listen to you wimps,' Brett said, kneeling and dipping his pan into the clear water.

'Hey, don't worry about your mum. You've got us,' Lauren said, putting her arm around Alice after they'd been silent for a while. The gentleness of her tone almost caused the tears Alice could feel close to the surface again to spill.

'I just wish I didn't let her get to me so much.'

'You've been trying to get her to show you love for as long as you can remember and being disappointed. That's going to take some stopping,' Brett said kindly.

'It's almost worse now I'm aware of it, to be honest,' Alice whispered.

'Of course it is. They don't say blissfully unaware for no reason. At least now you're starting to heal. That's a good thing. Nothing worthwhile is ever easy, remember,' Lauren said.

'Hmm. I just wish I didn't need to heal.'

'I wish you didn't, too. Hang in there. You're doing well,' Brett said.

'Thanks.'

'At least you know why you have to go through all this,' Lauren said.

'I do?'

'Of course, silly. It's so you can be an advocate for others in a legal capacity. I really do think you've found your calling. Your purpose.'

'I hope so.'

'I *know* so. You light up at the very mention of it.'

'Do I?'

'Yup. You do,' Brett said. 'You even look brighter than you did ten seconds ago.'

'I'm really excited, actually, though I know it's going to be hard.'

'It might not be. And you're allowed to be excited, Alice. You don't have to temper it with a negative.'

'I did, didn't I?'

'Yep.'

'It's one of the symptoms of mental and emotional abuse,' Brett said, 'from all the put-downs. You're making sure you don't sound egotistical.'

'Too big for my boots.'

'Yes, and you couldn't be that, ever, Alice. Being happy is allowed.'

'God, I'm a disaster, aren't I?' she said with a laugh.

'Well, half the battle is recognising the problem,' Lauren said, also laughing as she leant in and gave Alice's shoulder a bump. 'Thank goodness you have us to hold you accountable!'

Alice stopped herself just in time from speaking and instead put her arm around Lauren and pulled her tightly to her for a brief moment. She'd been about to say, 'Many tickets on yourself,

Lauren?' While she'd've been joking, and Lauren would get that, it was still criticism. And still mean. And that was not okay. She'd had it her entire life from Dawn and Olivia. She hated never being given credit for anything or being allowed to feel one iota of positivity about herself. And there she was about to do it to her best friend. God, how deep did the damage go? Just how many unconscious tics did she have? Alice blinked hard in order to try to physically banish her next thought: *Who am I, really? What am I?*

She watched Brett with his pan, enjoying the rhythmic sounds of swishing water and the gentle scrape of gravel against the pan and then returned her attention to her phone.

'Look at you,' Lauren said, 'you've got the knack, the perfect action.'

'Maybe, but I haven't found any gold yet.'

'Here, move aside,' Lauren said, shuffling closer to the water. 'I'll show you how it's done.'

'Listen to her,' Brett said, 'one visit to Sovereign Hill several years ago and she reckons she's the expert. Off you go, then.'

Alice smiled and returned to her phone. 'Oh,' she said, a few moments later, pausing in her scrolling at a post by Rick's younger sister, Matilda – one of her two ex-sisters-in-law. She usually scrolled right on by his sisters' posts because they were so often survey results that showed they had genius-level IQs, competitions to win cars and holidays – pretty much everything even the *oldies* online had figured out was bogus. She wasn't sure why she hadn't unfollowed them both ages ago.

'What?' Brett and Lauren both said and turned to look at her.

'Your mother?' Brett said.

'No. Rick. My ex-husband's dad has died suddenly.'

'That would make him your ex-father-in-law, wouldn't it?' Brett said.

A jolt ran through Alice. 'Yes, god, you're right. I didn't mind him, but we haven't kept in touch.'

'Obviously.'

'Do you think you should go back for the funeral? Is that why you're looking so thoughtful?' Lauren said.

'Hmm. Do you think I should?'

'No. It would be a bit weird, wouldn't it, after all this time?' Lauren said.

'Hypocritical, you mean?' Alice said.

'Yes. A bit. Sorry, I don't mean to sound mean.'

'No. You're not.'

'I know it meant a huge amount to you that he – Rick, that is – turned up at your friend Ruth's funeral, but this is a bit different. He didn't have to travel across the country to do that.'

'Hmm, good point.'

'You don't owe him, Alice. Certainly not for that,' Brett said.

'Yeah, you're right. He didn't even really like his father. I don't know if they made peace. I feel bad I didn't ask after his parents at the funeral now. I completely forgot.'

'Hey, go easy on yourself,' Lauren said.

'I feel like I should do something. He sent me a text for my birthday yesterday, actually. But, yeah, you're right, I don't want to look like a hypocrite.'

'Just send him a text, then.'

'It was a little unsettling, weird for him to do that after all these years, wasn't it?'

'Yes. Probably. But not really in the context of this. Maybe he had already gone, and Rick was reaching out for comfort without wanting to say so. They're not going to announce it the minute they find out, or maybe they are,' Alice said.

'Less likely if it was sudden,' Brett said.

'So what should I do? Here, what about this?' she said, not waiting for an answer. '"I saw the post that your dad died. I hope you're okay. Here if you need me",' Alice said, reading what she'd tapped out on her phone. She looked up at Brett and Lauren.

'Hmm. Okay. Just don't add any love hearts or kisses or hugs or anything. You don't want him getting the wrong message,' Lauren said.

'Unless you do,' Brett said.

'No way.' Alice pressed send. She was surprised to hear a signal that she'd received a response before she'd even put her phone down.

'What did he say?' Lauren asked.

'He said "Thanks, I really appreciate it",' Alice said. 'No love hearts or anything else.'

'Right, then. All good.'

Alice continued to stare at the phone until Lauren gently prised it from her fingers.

'No, you don't,' she said and tucked it into the small backpack nearby. 'You're not going to sit and wonder what he might have really meant. He said, "Thanks, I appreciate it." That's what he meant. End of story. Nothing more, nothing less.'

'You know me so well,' Alice said with a laugh. 'Right, show me how this panning thing is done. I can't remember from my visit to Sovereign Hill – it was too long ago.'

After Lauren, assisted by Brett, had given her a demonstration, Alice picked up her own pan to give it a go. She dipped it into the creek, scooped up a mix of silt, fine gravel and small stones and then swirled and swirled and swirled, watching as the water and larger pieces left the vessel until only the finest gravel remained in the bottom. This she then inspected for the glint of gold among the greys and browns, turning the pan this way and that so the sun had an opportunity to highlight any gold specks that might be lurking.

'You know how you tell if it's actually gold and not fool's gold?' Brett said.

'No, how?' Alice said.

'Real gold shines even in the shade, but fool's gold – iron pyrite – doesn't.'

'Well, fancy that. How interesting,' Alice said.

'Yes, thanks for that,' Lauren said.

'No need to be sarky, missy.'

'I wasn't being sarcastic, actually.'

'Just as well.'

Despite knowing finding gold was unlikely, Alice still felt a little surge of excitement every time she saw something of a different, brighter colour.

'Look at you, you're a natural,' Lauren said to Alice, looking over. 'I forgot how hard squatting is. I don't care if I get dirty knees, but I need to change position,' she said, leaning forwards.

At that moment Alice realised she was uncomfortable too. 'I don't know how you can sit like that, either,' she said, falling gently onto her backside.

'You can't pan like that, Alice,' Brett said, 'you're too far away from the water. Wusses.'

'You're right,' Alice said with a laugh.

'No pain, no gain, they say,' Brett said.

'Hmm, I guess when your whole livelihood depends on it, what's a bit of joint ache? Not for me, though.'

'Ah, the young of today – no stamina,' Brett said.

'Oh ha-ha, you're, what, three years older than me and five years older than Lauren?' Alice scoffed. She crossed her legs and continued carefully picking through the bits in the bottom of her pan. Suddenly she could see a speck glinting in the sunlight. *No. Could it be?* Her heart began to beat faster. She stared, frowning. She dipped her finger in and caught the dot on the end. 'Hey, look at this,' she said as she gently took the lid off a vial and dropped the crumb into it. She held the vial up to Brett in the light.

'By Jove, she's done it! Eureka,' he yelled, causing Bill to lift his head off his paws from his position in the nearby grass.

'But, god, it's tiny,' Alice said. It was so small it didn't even make a noise against the glass when shaken.

'Told you,' Lauren said. 'But now you can't wait to get stuck in and find more, huh?' she added knowingly.

'Damned right.' Alice tipped the dregs of her pan out where they'd agreed earlier and resumed her position by the creek, this time on her knees, and dipped her pan back into the chilly water, her determination overtaking her already cramped and uncomfortable position.

As she panned, Alice's mind began to wander. To David. They'd had so much fun panning for gold together that time. He'd been almost maniacal in his sifting and searching. A part of her wished she'd seen it as a sign of just how obsessed with money he'd prove to be – at the expense of them and almost everything else. She found her heart sinking a little.

'Hey, Alice, are you okay?'

'Sorry? What?' Alice looked up and over at Lauren, who had spoken.

'You've been sitting there doing nothing for ages,' Lauren said.

'Have I?'

'Yes. Where were you?'

'Oh. I was just thinking about David.'

'Oh. Well, stop it. It's your birthday weekend and it's meant to be happy.'

'He paid me the money. In full. It's in my bank.'

'Really? But that's great.'

'Yup.'

'So why so sad?' Lauren said, putting her pan down and moving closer to Alice.

'I don't know. You'd think I'd be happy, wouldn't you? But you're right, I feel sad.'

'It's grief,' Brett said, also putting his pan down and coming over to sit beside Alice. 'And disappointment – your future has changed.'

'Hmm,' Alice said.

'Would you go back to him now if he turned up and said you could study and if you had kids be home to raise them?' Brett continued.

'He wouldn't. That was a big part of it.'

'But if he did?' Lauren said. 'If he told you all you'd wanted to hear – and you believed he meant it – would you want him – you two – back?'

Alice thought hard. 'No. The foundations weren't there. I can see that now. Not enough fundamental shared values.'

'There you go then.'

'As if that answers that,' she said, slapping her thighs with her hands. 'So, I'm being pathetic. Look, I'm almost in tears.'

'So?' Lauren said. 'Cry if you want. We don't mind, do we, Brett?'

'Nope, not at all.'

'What would I do without you?'

'You're going to have to stop saying that. We're your friends. We love you and we're here for you. Unconditionally,' Lauren said.

Alice smiled sadly as she tried to blink back the gathering tears and swallow down what felt like a stone lodged in her chest.

'Be grateful you don't have to go to court to get your fair share,' Brett said.

'Yes,' Lauren said. 'It's over now. You can really start to be yourself. No more holding your breath. You know exactly what's what now.'

'Thank goodness for Ashley doing a freebee letter for me.'

'That job was certainly meant to be,' Brett said.

Bill crawled into Alice's lap and she held him close and kissed his head. Doing so almost caused her to completely lose her composure. He always knew just when she needed him close. She'd have paid as much as David had just to keep Bill if it had come to it – and a whole lot more. He was priceless. They sat together, the creak of trees and rustle of leaves overhead in the gentle breeze, the trickle of water and occasional burst of squawking birds flying overhead the soundtrack to their silence. Alice focussed on the rhythmic, soothing flapping of Bill's tail against her leg.

'Do you think he paid it so close to my birthday on purpose to upset me?' Alice said, the thought seeping in.

'Probably,' Brett said. 'But you'll never know. And it doesn't matter, Alice. Don't go there.'

'You're right. I've got the money. It's over. I'm free. You know, I'm really glad he didn't want to get married. Imagine if ...' Alice felt a chill actually run through her.

'God, if you'd had kids together, you'd be forever connected. Forever!' Lauren said, voicing Alice's thoughts.

'Yes. Honestly, I feel like I had a lucky escape there. And with Rick before.'

'Well, I do keep telling you the universe has your back,' Lauren said.

'And I'm beginning to see what you mean. Okay, changing the subject slightly. Do you guys think I need a car?' Alice said. 'It's not really fair for your parents and Blair to have to keep ferrying me about.'

'They honestly don't mind,' Lauren said.

'I know they don't. But …'

'It's up to you,' Brett said.

'Mum and Dad would be happy to lend you one of ours if you want to go somewhere else or on your own.'

'I know. And I really appreciate it. I'll think about it. Please don't say anything to them.'

'Okay, I won't.'

Alice got a whiff of the irony of tying herself to the Finmores further by borrowing a car to become independent. If it wasn't so serious and she wasn't so morose, she might have pointed it out and shared a laugh about it with Lauren and Brett.

'Just remember, Alice,' Brett said, 'not everyone holds you to ransom like your narcissist mother. Normal people give gifts and offer favours all the time without expecting anything in return.'

Alice looked up and over at him, feeling slightly startled. He'd spoken the exact thought just as she'd had it. She'd lived her entire life with everything having a condition attached – that suspicion that everyone else was also like that was something else she needed to shed. She nodded.

'Just don't rush into anything,' Brett added gently. 'Settle into your course. Give it six months or so and then see how you feel.'

'And, honestly, Alice, I'm pretty sure Blair doesn't mind driving you back and forth,' Lauren said. Alice rolled her eyes at Lauren's playful grin. 'And I don't get the impression you mind spending time with him, either.'

'What's his story, anyway?' Alice asked, taking the opportunity she'd been waiting for.

'What do you mean?' Lauren said.

'Married, gay, divorced, a widower, what?'

'Not gay and never been married. A lot has happened in his life, but you'll have to hear about it from him. Sorry, but it's really not my business to talk about.'

'Why are you so interested?' Brett asked.

Alice coloured. 'Just curious. He's such a dark horse.'

'The last thing you need right now is a relationship,' Brett said.

'But she can look,' Lauren said. 'He's not exactly hard on the eye.'

'Oh god, listen to you two,' Brett said, shaking his head. 'Whatever. I've got gold to pan for.'

'Alice has already probably found all there is. Just enough to drive us nuts,' Lauren warned.

Chapter Six

Ashley came into the room where Alice's desk was and dumped a pile of files onto a nearby table. It was late afternoon and she'd been out all day visiting clients and potential clients. 'Hi, how's your day been?'

'Good. And yours?' Alice said.

'Not bad. Not bad at all.'

'That's great. I'm up-to-date. I was just having a look through some files.' Alice stifled a yawn, but not before Ashley noticed.

'How was the rest of the birthday weekend, anyway?'

'Good.'

'Late night last night, then?'

'No, not like that. I stayed up reading. I'm getting a jump on the uni texts.'

'Wow, you're keen. That's brilliant, but remember it's a marathon not a sprint.'

'Yeah, I know. I just want to make the most of it and get it done as soon as I can and get back out into the real world.'

'You *are* back in the real world, Alice. What's this?' she said, expanding her arms to indicate the space around them.

Alice coloured.

'I know what you meant. You'll get there soon enough but, take it from me, if you take on too much too soon you'll lose your love of reading. And believe me when I say it never ends. If you think you're going to devour the course reading to get it over with you'll be disappointed. You'll have to re-read it anyway when you get to it in class. Like most things in life, Alice, slow and steady is the key. And bite-sized pieces. I know you feel like you're coming to this late and you're fired up because you've finally found your calling. But you've got plenty of time. Look at Dad and Mum. They'll be here at least the next ten or even twenty years the rate they're going.'

Alice nodded. 'Thanks. I needed to hear that.' A little of the panic subsided.

'I was hoping you were going to tell me you'd been kept up late by that yummy guy Blair,' Ashley said with a wistful sigh as she pulled open a filing cabinet.

'No. He dropped me off at around eight last night.'

'What's his story, anyway?'

'I've no idea. He's nice, though. A bit like the big brother I wish I'd always had, I guess.'

'Yeah, right. Look at you going all dreamy. You like him. *Like* him.'

'I don't know anything about him. Anyway, it's too soon for me. And I'm pretty sure he's not interested.' Alice thought they'd had another moment when he'd handed her his mug and their fingers had touched and they'd locked gazes for just a moment longer than usual. But then he'd averted his eyes and pulled away.

'Actually, one thing I do know about him is he's creative – good with his hands …'

'I bet he is,' Ashley said with a chuckle, closing the metal drawer with a slight clunk.

'Oh ha-ha. No, as in can build things. He's into woodworking. He made me the most gorgeous trunk out of a pallet. It's incredible.'

'Wow, he must really like you to do that.'

'I don't know about that. He might have already made it before, not necessarily specifically for me.'

'But he gave it to you. That's pretty special.'

'It is. I love it. I can't wait to show you. And you remember how I was looking at throw rugs? Well, the Finmores *gave* me one of them. Gorgeous bright colours. Just what the flat needs. Oh. And I completely forgot to tell you David paid me. The full amount. So, your letter did the trick. Thanks very much.'

'Great. And it was my pleasure. That's fantastic news. I'm so relieved for you.'

Alice picked up her phone at hearing the beep of a new text message. *Uh-oh*, she thought, seeing Rick's name on the screen. He'd already replied to her reply and here he was again. She felt unsure what to do – if she replied again, did that mean she was encouraging an unhealthy relationship? But Alice didn't like not answering messages – it was bad manners and a bit mean. She nibbled on her lip, trying to decide what to do.

Ashley went on putting the files away – opening and shutting the cabinets. 'What is it?' she said, stopping at one point.

'My ex-husband has sent me a text.'

'Oh god, what does he want now?'

'No, not David. He was my de facto.'

'Oh. Yes, right.'

'Keep up, Ash, I'm the queen of romantic stuff-ups, remember,' Alice said with a laugh. 'Thank god we didn't get married and I don't have two divorces under my belt. No, this is Rick.'

'Rick. Right. What's his story?'

'Farmer.'

'And you're friends why?'

Alice coloured again a little.

'Sorry, it's not for me to judge. I'm a slash and burn and leave them in a cloud of dust kind of girl.'

'We weren't friends, but you know how I said I went to my friend Ruth's funeral?'

'Yes?'

'He was there. Did I tell you this already?'

'No, carry on.'

'Well, he turned up. Said he'd come to see me because he knew how sad I'd be. Anyway, we reconnected. I guess enough time had passed.' Alice waved her hand dismissively.

'Or you were vulnerable, and he swooped.'

'Oh god, not you too. He has not swooped.'

'Yet here he is texting you,' Ashley said, pointing to Alice's phone.

'Well, I have to admit I'm wondering if swapping numbers was a good idea, but it's a bit late now. Anyway his dad died and I texted him.'

'Which is fair enough. Are you okay about it – his death, that is?'

'Oh yes. We weren't close and didn't keep in touch once I left.'

'That's sad.'

'We might have kept in touch if Rick had had a better relationship with his parents. Speaking of complicated.'

'Did you like them?'

'I didn't mind his dad and we got on quite well in the beginning.'

'But …? I'm hearing a but.'

'Well, it didn't feel right to be close to him when Rick disliked him so much. I think loyalty's really important, especially when you're married. It is, was, to me, anyway. As it turns out, it's not so much to other people, but that's a different story … He wouldn't talk about it, just dropped a few hints. But I get the impression his dad was mean, a real bully. I think even physically abusive when he was a kid, though I didn't see any signs of that when I was married to him – just some teasing and put-downs. I tried to back him, but I really wish I'd properly stood up for him. I've always got pretty freaked out by any sort of confrontation.'

'And you might have made it worse for him.'

'That's true.'

'Sounds like you guys probably didn't stand much of a chance.'

'No, I'm beginning to see that now. And how similar we might actually have been brought up and behaved as a result. If only we'd stayed as just friends. We were great as friends, before …' Alice became wistful as she thought about the fun she and Rick had had in the early carefree days. 'And then we succumbed to the pressure of getting married and the big look-at-me wedding – all driven by the oh-so-supportive Dawn. Anyway …' she said, waving a hand, suddenly desperate to steer the conversation away. If the subject got onto her mother, she might cry. Still Dawn hadn't acknowledged her birthday. Alice knew it shouldn't matter to her, but it did.

'So is he okay?' Ashley asked. 'Rick?'

'Yes, I think so. He doesn't mince words. So much for the old adage of never speak ill of the dead. He's already thanked me, so clearly he's been thinking about it and wants to get something off his chest. He says: "Thanks, Alice. Your message meant a lot. I know you'll understand when I say it's not a loss. It's a relief. I know it's awful to say, but it's the truth. Now just to get through Thursday. Wish me luck.'"

'Oh god,' Ashley said. 'The poor thing. Does he have other family – siblings?'

'Yes, he still has his mother and two sisters. One older and one younger.'

'What are they like?'

'Okay, I guess … Honestly? I probably shouldn't say this, but they're cold. Especially his mother. Not exactly unfriendly, but …'. Alice shrugged and cringed.

'Not unkind to you but aloof and hard to talk to beyond, say, things like the weather? Is that what you mean?'

'Yes. Exactly. I don't think she means to be, it's just how she is. And we didn't really have anything in common. I wanted to help out on the farm, but she's the quintessential 1950s housewife – I know, insane in this day and age, but there you have it. His sisters aren't quite as frosty as his mother, but I still didn't really warm to them either.'

'Hence why you didn't keep in touch. How does he get along with them?'

'Barely at all when we were together. I'm not sure if that's changed, but we only saw them for the usual obligatory family gatherings. And under sufferance on his part.'

'I'm not surprised if they were mean to him.'

'Yes. Like so many families – mine included – I think they put up a relatively happy show to the outside world. I now realise just how important *looking* good was, to the detriment of other things.'

'Yeah. I'm so grateful for having the parents I do and being an only child. Even we still have our issues occasionally. I think dysfunctional families are more common than functioning ones, to be honest. You wait until you've read through all these files and been practising law for a while. You'll get a sense of just how some families function. Or don't.'

'He always said he never felt like he fitted in or belonged, but I get the sense there's more to it than him not liking them because of any bullying. Like at a deeper level, maybe. Oh, I don't know.'

'You want to go to the funeral to support him, don't you? That's why we're talking about this?'

'Yeah. I kind of do. But I can't.'

'I'm sure Mum and Dad would give you the time off if you needed it.'

'I know. And that's lovely. It's not that. I can't because it would be too weird. It might look like I'm suddenly trying to be part of their family again. As I said, I haven't kept in touch, not properly. I know I could send a card or flowers, but …'

'I get it. Well, at least he knows he has your support – even from a distance. That's the main thing. And I bet it means the world to him.'

'I hope so. Thanks.'

'Don't underestimate how much just knowing you're on his side can mean.'

'I told him to call if he needs me. Though, as I said, I hope I haven't done the wrong thing there.'

'Well, you can always get firm with him later if need be, but for what it's worth, I think you're doing the right thing. You can't not be you. Do what feels right inside.'

'Thanks, Ashley.'

'Ah, I just speak the truth.'

Alice was left marvelling for the umpteenth time recently at just how blessed she was to have found herself in Ballarat and at Baker and Associates.

'I'm parched, as Mum would say. Can I get you a cuppa?' Ashley asked.

'Yes, please.' Alice looked back at her phone and, at the risk of starting a never-ending line of correspondence, tapped out a reply to Rick: 'Hang in there. Thinking of you.'

Chapter Seven

Phew, what an eye-opener, Alice thought as she stood in the sun, leaning against the solid wall of a beautiful old stone building. She had been desperate to get out of the stifling room at the end of the mediation session between a divorcing man and woman. Ashley and Peter must be still having a few moments alone with their client – the woman. Alice was grateful to be given the chance to see the whole process from the beginning. Ashley had said attending court and every other type of legal interaction she could had been really valuable when it came to the mock sessions and role-playing they had to do during her law course. *But, wow*, Alice thought. She blinked a few times and shook her head in wonder. She imagined the warring parties must be feeling completely wrung out. Thank goodness she'd avoided all this stress and palaver in her two failed relationships. She looked up as Ashley and Peter made their way out of the building and down the steps.

'See you back at the office,' Peter said as he moved past Alice and Ashley standing together on the footpath.

'Hey, are you okay?' Ashley said, nudging Alice with her armful of folders after they'd silently watched Peter make his way down the street for a few moments.

'Huh?'

'You look a little shell-shocked.'

'Christ, that was a bit full-on.'

'Yup. Welcome to the world of family law,' Ashley said. 'Hideous, wasn't it?'

'I can't believe your dad stayed so calm. He didn't raise his voice once.'

'It's one of his greatest strengths. And not just professionally, but in life in general. If you refuse to raise your voice and actually answer even more quietly, the person has to stop talking to hear you. It takes some doing at times, but I've had lots of practice growing up with them,' she said, nodding her head in the direction her father had gone.

'In our house, we just shouted until the loudest one won,' Alice said. 'I hate confrontation now.'

'And yet you want to be a lawyer,' Ashley said, tilting her head at Alice.

'Hmm.' Alice grinned back. 'Guess I'd better learn your father's patience. What I don't get is how it gets to that back there – and worse, I guess, in court. I mean, I do get it, I'm not that naïve, but ...'

'I know what you mean. It's sad, isn't it, that those two, particularly, once loved each other enough to declare they'd be together through thick and thin and now six years later they're fighting over who gets to have the kids and the house and cars et cetera? He doesn't even want the kids – he works all the time and hasn't shown much interest in them previously, just wants to punish her.'

'And to pay less child support.'

'Yup.'

'Those poor kids.'

'Yep. At least their mother is trying to bat for them.'

'God, what an arsehole. Sorry, but it just makes me mad that everything boils down to money.'

'And stubbornness.'

'Yes, and that. He doesn't want her to win and him to lose and she wants her kids to win by not going without and not being uprooted from their home and school.'

'God, I'm glad he's not our – your – client.'

'Well, that's another important thing to learn early on – you can pick and choose to a certain extent in a private practice like ours, but everyone deserves representation, a voice, whether you feel they're right or not. Once you get your head around that it makes life a lot less fraught. Also, as callous as it sounds, trying not to get caught up in the emotion is important. It's hard, because you also never want to stop caring. There's a fine line. Thankfully we don't get too many family law cases. We do our best to get them to settle in mediation, but like you've just seen, some people are just arrogant arseholes who insist on making a point, no matter how much it costs and who it hurts. Come on. At least this time he's not our arsehole. That would be worse. I did not just say that out loud. Terribly unprofessional of me.'

'Got it.' Alice smiled. She loved how open and honest Ashley was.

'Anyway, thank goodness our Lena has a wonderful family around her, which is something,' Ashley added.

As they walked on in silence, Alice chewed over what she'd experienced. It hadn't shaken her resolve to be a lawyer, but she did feel a little crestfallen. *Thank goodness I didn't have kids with Rick or David*, she thought, for the second time in as many days.

Fiona McCallum

'Are you okay?' Ashley asked.

'Yeah. Just thinking I probably dodged a bullet in not having kids.'

'Yep, you're tied to the father forever, whether you like it or not, in some way or other. Why do you think I'm never having kids?'

'Seriously?'

'Yes. Deadset serious. What?'

'Wow.'

'Hey, don't look at me like that.'

'Like what?'

'Like I've got two heads or something.'

'Sorry, I didn't mean to. It's just that, well, the idea of having kids being a choice or not. For me, it's always been just a given. Jesus, I need to get out more,' Alice said, wishing she hadn't inadvertently started this line of conversation.

'Because getting married and having babies is all us women are good for, right?' Ashley said knowingly.

'That's the way I was raised. Not that it was discussed as bluntly as that.'

'I hate the way women are put into boxes, put down! Thank Christ I have progressive parents! You know that's why they gave me a unisex name – with unisex spelling? So later when I applied for jobs or anything else in writing I couldn't be discriminated against.'

'Wow. That's awesome. And very forward thinking.'

'Except they shouldn't have had to be.'

'Hmm.' They walked on. Alice was lost in thoughts about kids – rolling it around in her mind. Now she was free to look at the issue objectively and from all angles the question, 'Why do it?' seemed stronger than 'Why not?' Not that she'd ever thought about it this way, but she thought it had always been the other way around in her mind. But why did it have to be something a woman simply did because they possessed reproductive organs? Did she even like kids? Not really. You'd have to, wouldn't you?

'You know,' she said, 'I wonder if maybe I don't actually want kids either.'

'God, don't let me lead you astray.'

'No, I mean it.'

'Anyway, you're recently single and recovering from a break-up, which might be skewing your thinking.'

'I'm not sure I even like children. I've never really thought about it.'

'Do you have nieces and nephews?'

'No; I have the one sister, Olivia, and she's desperate to have kids.'

'Each to their own.'

'It's a touchy subject. Rick's sisters have kids, but as I said, we weren't a close family so I didn't spend much time with them. So, I've not been around small children much ever, really.'

'They do say having your own is different, anyway.'

'Hmm.' Alice felt something large and serious shift inside her, but couldn't place her finger on it and certainly wasn't able to articulate it.

'Just don't use having a career as an excuse not to, because then one day you'll probably resent it. You can have both. Mum and Dad did. But I think you need to decide why – make a calcu-lated decision. I think far too many people have kids to prove something – to themselves or others. I think I'd be a great mother to a human, I just don't feel the need to prove it. And I've had great parents and a wonderful upbringing, so I don't need to prove I can do better. And I'm not an arrogant bloke who needs to prove his manliness or superior genes,' she added, rolling her eyes. 'Oh, please, spare us!'

Alice laughed against the large stone of realisation settling within her. So much of her life was starting to make a lot more sense – not least of which was the fact she had so many more choices than she'd been raised to believe. And that she *could* make choices now and have the strength to stand behind them.

'You're less of a woman, a person, in my opinion if you don't live for yourself, or at least give it a damned good shot. I think people also have children to fix something with themselves – hoping the child will love them when they can't love themselves. Or even to look after them in old age. Well, there are no guarantees with any of it and all of those reasons place a lot of pressure and expectation on both the child and yourself – the parents. Most likely why we end up with situations like we've seen today. If more people understood that we alone are responsible for our happiness, our mistakes, we'd be a lot better off as a society. And simple kindness. It costs nothing to be kind. If you can't manage it, at least be silent and do nothing – don't take out your own unhappiness and insecurities on others. Sorry, here I go getting all soap-boxy.'

'No, you make a lot of sense. And I agree with everything you've said.' Alice thought her father would have said Ashley had an old soul.

'God, what an afternoon,' Ashley suddenly declared.

'Oh. Speaking of which, I wonder how the funeral went,' Alice said, getting her phone out of her bag. 'Thanks for the distraction,' she said to Ashley as she clicked on the icon showing she had a new text message.

'So, what does he say?'

'Oh dear, it's a long one. Here we go: "OMFG, who is this man they're talking about?! What a load of shit. Full of lies. Great that my sisters have such nice memories of our father and their experiences were so clearly different to mine. Mum just looks stoic. I want to spit on the old bastard, not toss a flower in. But of course we don't make a scene out here, do we? Good turnout. Plenty of people gathering their own numbers for their eventual event or just there for the cream puffs and brandy snaps. Fuck I'm angry and disappointed at the hypocrisy. This place. Lucky you getting out. Gotta go and make nice with people." And that's it. With two kisses. Uh-oh.'

'Oh dear. Well, he didn't hold back.'

'No. It's clearly a rough day. But his description had it pretty spot on.'

'It's perhaps not meant to be funny, is it?' Ashley said.

'No, but it is a little.'

'I like the sound of him – his honesty. So many people are horrible during their lives and then get painted as practically worthy of sainthood at their funerals. I bet if that guy today dies tomorrow they'd be saying what a great father he was, how much he loved his children blah, blah, blah, when all he'd been doing just previously was his best to make sure his wife struggled to keep clothes on their backs. Sorry. Do you think Rick's okay? Like, really? It kind of sounds manic.'

'Hmm. Hopefully he's just letting off steam. I'll think about ringing him tonight. I'm just a little cautious.'

'Yes, rightly so. You don't want to become his crutch – that could get awkward later. I do love his honesty though.'

'Poor bloke having to pretend. Put on a happy face – that's practically the mantra of Hope Springs and district. It should be on their stupid welcome sign.'

'I like that he feels he can be honest with you, given all you must have been through.'

'Hmm. It's only because he came and supported me at my friend's funeral. We probably wouldn't have reconnected if it were not for that.'

'I think laying down the swords is nice and shows real maturity.'

'And thank goodness for there being no kids involved,' Alice said.

'Amen to that,' Ashley said as she pushed the door to the office open.

Chapter Eight

Alice led Bill home in a daze. The little dog trotted happily alongside, unaware of the deep thoughts going through his mistress's head. She was so distracted that twice she stood at the pedestrian crossing having forgotten to press the button. The second time someone reached past her and prodded it hard several times, startling her slightly. The afternoon mediation session had changed her. Well, not the session, probably. But she'd changed inside. She could feel it. Her realisation that she didn't want children had settled within her comfortably, a much easier feeling than the many times she'd wondered about the when and where of having a child. And the yuck factor. She'd always felt quite off, queasy even, at the thought of actually giving birth, but dismissed it as something she'd come to grips with if she was meant to be a mother. And she had, of sorts.

Alice let herself into the flat and smiled at seeing her new brightly coloured throw draped diagonally over the back and one arm of the navy-blue sofa. She sat down to take stock for a moment before getting changed and starting dinner. She idly scrolled through her

Instagram feed as she analysed her insides for any flutter of doubt, guilt. Nothing. There was no negative, no unease. Her decision felt comfortable. It was almost as if a piece had cemented itself within her – like the wave of realisation that her destiny lay in law, only stronger. It was impossible to explain succinctly. But that didn't matter – she didn't need to explain it to anyone. She really did have so much to be thankful for. What will be, will be, Lauren was always saying. Alice was beginning to believe it too.

Alice paused her scrolling at a post by Rick's younger sister Matilda and cringed. As she read, her eyes became wider and her disbelief and disappointment more pronounced. *Jesus.*

She brought up Rick's message, quickly read it through again, then clicked on his phone number ready to dial. What harm could her being kind do, reaching out? It might not be the right thing for her, but it felt like the right thing to do for Rick.

He answered before it even started to ring. 'Hey, Alice.'

'Hey, Rick.'

'Thanks so much for calling.' His words came out like a long sigh of relief, causing the slight nervous, apprehensive quiver in Alice to settle.

'I'm so sorry I didn't call earlier when I saw your message. I ...' *I, what? Didn't want to lead you on. Tickets on yourself, much? Lauren would say.* Alice smiled weakly.

'No worries.'

Alice had the strangely disconcerting yet satisfying feeling that she could sit there in silence and Rick would appreciate it. Again, impossible to explain how she knew this or really the right way to describe it, but he sounded so lost. And so far away – a million more kilometres than the eleven hundred or so between them. Right then she just wanted to wrap her arms around him and hold him tight.

'I saw the Instagram post,' she said, suddenly unsure of what else to say. *How was it?* were the words that came to mind, but they were so stupid.

'Yeah. How bloody ghastly. Can you believe it? Honestly, Alice, I don't know these people. I stood there like I was surrounded by strangers. And the things they said about the old man – who the hell were they even talking about? I felt like such a fraud all day nodding and thanking everyone for their condolences and muttering in agreement with their kind words, all the time thinking, *No, you've got the wrong man. Joseph Peterson was a mean old bastard*. It really pisses me off, Alice. Thanks again for calling. At least you get it.'

'Sadly, I do. I think you did well to keep it together.'

'Yeah, just like a trained monkey. Oh, and it gets worse.'

'Huh?'

'Yeah, the Will.'

'Oh. Right. What does it say?' Alice shifted on the couch, feeling a little uncomfortable at what was probably information meant only for family.

'He left everything to Mum.'

'I'm so sorry.' Alice knew Rick was waiting until his father retired to be handed his own farm – the one with the house where she'd lived with him for almost four years.

'Yep, he's managed to still screw me over in death.'

Alice didn't want to appear unsupportive, but thought wasn't it normal for one spouse to leave everything to the other and vice versa in a Will and then things only get divvied up when the last parent died? Her father's Will had left everything to Dawn.

'God, I sound like an arsehole, don't I?'

Yes, a bit, Alice thought, but sure as hell wasn't going to say it. 'You're disappointed. You were expecting something else. I get it,' she said, choosing her words carefully.

'You know, they sat us down around the table to read the Will like on all the American TV shows and movies. It would have been funny if it wasn't so bloody horrible. Basically, it's business as usual. I feel like I've had my prison sentence extended.'

'Walk away, then,' Alice said quietly. She was trying to be supportive, but she also couldn't help pointing out the obvious, or feeling a little frustrated. She knew how satisfying it was to be on the other side having made big, scary, life-changing decisions. But he wouldn't leave. Not now. Because he was like a miner waiting to hit pay dirt – each little step hopefully getting him closer. Not wanting to walk away the moment before it happened. But he'd been in that limbo for years. 'Perhaps it's time to count your losses.'

'Hmm. Mum'll live forever. God, that sounded awful, too.'

'I know what you meant.' Alice was losing patience with him – he was making it purely about money. And that annoyed her – as much as the realisation of how similar he and her most recent ex David were at the core. But to some extent she did agree with Rick's disappointment. Though, had his father even said it in so many words, or had Rick assumed because it's the way it tended to work out there?

'Yeah. Maybe you're right. Maybe it *is* time to walk away. I hate that I'd be starting all over again. With pretty much nothing to show for all these years.'

'Plenty of people have done just that and survived, Rick, thrived even. Me included. We all have to make difficult decisions. I'm sorry if this is hard to hear – and I'm saying it not as your ex-wife, but as your friend who cares about you – but don't sell yourself short. You're smart. You'll always find a way to make more money if you put your mind to it. It might not feel like it right now, but it's true. And in the meantime, there are options, including living frugally.' Alice's thoughts went to the woman from today just fighting to keep a roof over her and her kids' heads. 'Just be grateful it's only you and you don't have a family to provide for. I know I am.'

Shit, have I pushed him too far? Alice wondered as the silence stretched. She was about to apologise for being too harsh when he finally spoke.

'Christ. I'm being a victim, aren't I – a spoilt brat?'

'Sorry, but you are a bit. Things could be a lot worse, Rick. Think about that.' *Oh god, could I sound any more like Dawn?* she thought, rolling her eyes. 'Just don't make any rash decisions, especially while you're so emotional. Let the dust settle,' she said, softening.

'Hmm. You're right. On both counts. I'll play it by ear. Jesus, enough about me. It's really good to hear your voice, Alice. How's things with you? Congrats again on the new job and getting into law.'

'Thanks. It's all going well.' She tried to dampen her enthusiasm. Now was not the time to shout her joy from the rooftops.

'What's Ballarat like?'

'Awesome. You'd love it. It has the feel of a big country town, but without everyone knowing you or your business. You should visit.' Shit, the words were out of her mouth before she could stop them. 'But I don't have a sofa bed or anything. My place is tiny – a shoebox really,' she raced on, scrambling to undo her offer.

'Maybe I will. It might be good to have a break before harvest starts. Jesus, I hope Mum doesn't suddenly forget she's never been hands-on and starts throwing her weight around. That'll be the end of me.'

'Hmm. Rick, why couldn't you ask her if she'd sell you your place? If it's all hers now, maybe she'd …'

'I don't have any money to buy it with, remember?'

Alice felt a tug of guilt. Was that a stab over having had to pay her out all those years ago? Her divorce settlement had been meagre – and he'd hidden assets until after they signed, too, which meant it was less than her entitlement. It took all her will to ride out the silence, not take the bait.

'I guess I could ask,' he eventually said, sounding deflated. 'Maybe she'd transfer it into my name, just because. On the same day pigs start to fly. I'd have more chance if it weren't for Matilda and Danni. Sorry, I'm being such a guts ache. I really do appreciate the call.'

'It's okay. You've just lost your father.'

'Who I hated, or at least could barely stand the sight of most of the time.'

'Regardless, you're going through a big upheaval. Maybe speaking to your counsellor would help you get some perspective,' Alice said, remembering the secret he'd sworn her to that day at Ruth's funeral.

'Yeah. I'd better go. We're having a family dinner at the pub with a few hangers-on from the funeral. I'm not sure what category I'm in there, really,' he said with a hint of a laugh.

'Well, hang in there.'

Alice hung up. She'd thought he might have evolved a bit more if he was seeing a counsellor. But then remonstrated with herself. Who was she to judge? The reality was she was disappointed in herself when it came to him – that she'd chosen a textbook guy as dictated by her upbringing. Despite all she'd learnt, she still sometimes got annoyed with herself for being so manipulated for so long. Also, she could see she'd have to be careful to not get too preachy. She was well on the way to finding herself. Not everyone was so fortunate, and those who hadn't been, like Rick, couldn't be shown until they were ready to see. At least he was seeing someone neutral and outside the family and district. And even if the call had left her feeling a little frustrated, she was glad she'd made the effort. It had clearly meant a lot to Rick. And that's what really mattered on a day when he'd lost his father and his life had been turned upside down.

Chapter Nine

Alice put the finishing touches on her plate of scones, jam and cream by dotting some fresh strawberries around. She checked her watch. As usual she was ahead of schedule. She didn't want to get to the park early because she didn't know any of Ashley's friends. The other week when she'd taken a stroll through the gardens there had been several groups lolling about. How embarrassing it would be to join the wrong one! She explained to Bill that he couldn't come because she didn't know if the people she was meeting were generally dog-friendly or not. Alice hated leaving him behind. Thankfully Bill merely flapped his tail at hearing his name, lifted his head, and then settled back down to sleep again.

Alice was a little anxious. She always was when meeting new people. One day she hoped she'd learn to not give a toss. She was getting there. One step at a time. She was idly scrolling through her Instagram feed to fill in time when her phone began to vibrate and then ring in her hand. She almost dropped it. Bill groaned his disapproval at being disturbed and rolled over. Alice stared at Rick's name lit up on the screen for a moment before answering.

'Hey, Rick, how are you doing?'

'I'm okay. How are you?'

Something in his tone piqued her interest. 'Why? Shouldn't I be?' she said with a tight, awkward laugh.

'Oh. Not at all. Well, um, I just thought you might be, um …'

'What? Spit it out. What's on your mind?'

'You didn't mention your lot was selling the shop.'

'What?' Alice felt her heart slow. 'Don't be ridiculous. Who told you that?'

'I've just been in and got the weekend papers. Everyone in the newsagent was talking about it. And then … Oh my god, Alice … You didn't know, did you?'

'No.' She felt as if a large rock had settled painfully deep within her. 'You know what rumours are like in that place,' she said quickly.

'It's actually in the paper, Alice. There's an ad.'

'Seriously?'

'Alice, I wouldn't lie to you.'

Alice put a hand behind her and felt for the arm of the sofa and lowered herself onto it. 'Why wouldn't they tell me?'

'I don't know.'

'Why would they be selling – why now? I know things are tough, but they've always been tough.' Alice felt a little light-headed.

'Jesus. I'm so sorry, Alice, that you had to find out like this.'

'No, don't be. It's just a shock. And it's not your fault. So, what are you doing looking at the commercial property ads, anyway?' she said, trying to lighten the mood and take the spotlight off her. *There must be an explanation*, she thought. But her next thought was, *Whose chain is my mother pulling now? Who is being punished? Everything to do with Dawn is calculated. Calculated to wound or manipulate.* Alice could see it clearly these days. *At least this time it isn't about me, because it couldn't be, could it? That wouldn't make sense.*

'Are you seriously thinking of walking away from the farm now?'

'Hmm. Maybe. Not really. I wish. Hey, do you want to run a business together?'

'The shop, you mean?' Alice glowed a little. It had once been her dream to work alongside her dad. And then after his death a brief moment of dreaming of running it alone with her husband. 'Was that a serious question?' she asked when Rick hadn't continued speaking – no quip or snide comment.

'I didn't intend it to be, but … We always made a good team.'

When we weren't fighting. 'Rick, you hated me wanting to know, asking questions, offering different ideas on the farm, remember? Oh, how quickly we forget,' she added with a laugh.

'Ouch,' he said. 'I remember. I was an arsehole, and I'm getting help with that. But back to the question at hand. Pretend I'm being serious, hypothetical, if you like.'

Alice's heart fluttered and all the ideas she'd had over the years flooded her mind like a moving montage. Oh, how she loved the store building with its bay windows either side of the door. She'd given up on it when her mother had declared Olivia would be running the shop with her. Alice had married Rick to escape the torture and sink her teeth into a new totally different life. And to connect with her father whose people had been farmers and graziers.

'I think the ship has well and truly sailed on that dream, Rick,' she finally said. 'I don't have any money to buy it and there's no way I'd be given any concessions by my mother. Anyway, I'm really excited about being a lawyer. I really think I've found my groove here. But there's no reason *you* shouldn't do it. If you did, I'd come and consult – give you all my ideas. Anyway, I hate the place now – Hope Springs – remember? There's nothing for me there now.' But she could feel the coals being fanned inside her.

'Nah, you're right.'

'They've always struggled. You might be inheriting a nightmare. And you'd be forever coming up against people saying, "That's not how the Hamiltons did it." Just remember how much that place *loves* change. But don't let me talk you out of it.'

'Yeah, you're right, though. It was just a romantic notion. I can see that.'

'Rick Peterson, romantic! You're getting soft in your old age.'

'Yup. But I prefer "in touch with my emotions". Real men don't cry, my arse. I've howled these last few days. Don't tell anyone.'

'I won't.'

'I don't know why, though.'

'Maybe relief, Rick?'

'Hmm. Glad you said it, not me. Hey, I'm really sorry to blindside you with the stuff about the shop.'

'That's okay. I'm glad it was you who told me. I wonder why Frank hasn't.'

'Maybe he's been blindsided too.'

'No. Surely not. Surely his wife wouldn't keep something like that a secret.' But as she said the words, the knowledge that that could indeed be the case settled upon her. Who would know with Dawn? 'She is a control freak, after all. And the rest,' Alice mused aloud. 'Maybe she's turfed him out or something. I'd better ring him.' She got up off the couch and began pacing. 'Actually, do you mind if I go?' she said.

'No, not at all. Call me if there's anything I can do.'

'Thanks.'

'And, again, sorry.'

'Don't be. I was clearly meant to know.'

Alice rang Frank but hung up on his voicemail message.

Despite knowing she was probably playing right into her mother's hands, like she'd successfully done all these years and was trying to stop, Alice, with quivering finger and pounding heart, brought up Dawn's number on her mobile. She took a few deep breaths to steady her nerves, cursed that it didn't help and then held her breath as the phone began to ring. Maybe Frank would answer. The thought lifted her ever so slightly. She started the mantra, *Frank, please answer, Frank, please answer* ... She was so fixated that she almost gasped when Dawn's voice came on the line.

'Alice, what can I do for you?' Crisp and sharp.

'Mum. Hi.' Alice cursed herself for feeling like a chastised ten-year-old and hoicked her shoulders up and back. 'Are you selling the shop?'

'Unfortunately, it looks like we have to,' Dawn said, the defence clear in her tone. 'Why do you ask?'

'Well, it might have been nice to be told.' Alice shook her head at how much she sounded like her mother. Damn it, this was not going well. She was not sounding strong and in control. 'Why, Mum?' And there it was – the ten-year-old pleading with her mother for a scrap of comradery, affection, anything positive.

'What business is it of yours, Alice? You have your life away from here. You've made it very clear how little you think of us.'

'What? Because I dared leave and get an education after you made it clear I wasn't a part of the family?'

'Oh, for goodness' sake, Alice. Stop being melodramatic. Not part of the family. Oh dear, you really do say the most ridiculous things.'

'You said the business can only support so many mouths and that you'd chosen Olivia as your partner, Mum. Remember? You couldn't have made it much clearer.'

'Well, as it turns out it can't support even that many mouths,' Dawn said haughtily.

Alice knew how hard it must be for her mother to admit to a failing. But no doubt there was a higher purpose to doing so ...

'So, what are you going to do?'

'Sell, Alice, I imagine. Are you dense?'

'Well, it would have been fair to be told.' *And offered the opportunity*. These words remained unspoken.

'Don't tell me you want to come back here and run it, Alice,' Dawn scoffed.

Alice could picture the sneer on her face and wanted to reach through the phone and slap her.

'Oh come now, you're going to be a fancy lawyer, remember? Or have you changed your mind about that now too? Anyway, ask Frank since you're so close to him.'

'I'm going to go, Mum. I hope everything works out okay for you,' Alice said, dangerously close to tears.

'Not that you care. Why would you? You turned your back on us years ago.'

Alice hung up. Dawn always had to have the final word. And what had she meant about asking Frank – or was it just a barb?

The building and small supermarket had been in Dawn's family. Alice was connected, but not as much as she might have been. She'd loved her maternal grandparents, but they'd died a long time ago and had been old. Their deaths had not been as shocking as losing her father. She was glad her father wasn't around to see how Dawn had treated Alice compared to Olivia. It had been less obvious before he'd died. Hadn't it? Alice was only now seeing it – she'd been too close to it, so no doubt he'd been unaware too. He'd clearly been very troubled, and about a lot more than her relationship with Dawn. But Alice didn't want to think about it. Not now. It made her too sad and disappointed.

Her phone began to ring. She brightened a little when she saw Frank's name on the screen.

'Hi, Frank.'

'Hi, Alice. I'm sorry I missed your call. I suppose you've heard, then?'

'About the shop being for sale? Yes.'

'Sorry you didn't hear it direct from me. Things have been a little hectic of late.'

'What's going on? Are you okay?'

'Oh, I'm fine.' But he didn't sound fine to Alice. He sounded tired and broken. Her heart went out to him.

'Are you sure?'

'No. Not really. No,' he said with a slight laugh. 'It's all come as a bit of a shock. But, sweetheart, it's complicated and I still need to get my head around a few things. Can I tell you another time? Are you okay? That's what's important to me right now.'

'Thanks, but I'm fine, Frank, honestly. Just a little shocked at the news.'

'Yes, I imagine. Sorry to cut this short, but I need to go now. I promise I'll be back in touch soon.'

'Okay. Look after yourself.'

'You too.'

Chapter Ten

There was a knock at the door. 'Stay. Good boy, Bill.' Alice checked her watch as she went to answer it. She hoped it wasn't one of her neighbours, all of whom she'd met, wanting a chat.

'Ash. Hi. I thought I was meeting you there.'

'You were, but I decided I didn't feel like turning up alone.'

'Is something wrong?'

'No.'

'Well, great minds and all that. I'm feeling the same. I'm all ready to go. I'm leaving Bill here.'

'I've left Max at home with Mum and Dad.'

'Okay, I'm good to go,' Alice said, after doing her quick inventory aloud as she got the plate of scones out of the fridge.

'Ooh, these look good. Bringing out the country girl in you.'

'Hope Springs is a town. I was a townie and married to a farmer for about three minutes, Ashley, I don't think that quite qualifies me for CWA baker of the year.'

'Oh, don't shatter my rural delusions. Anyway, they look good to me.'

'Thanks,' Alice said, realising she might have sounded snippy when she'd been going for charming and witty. 'It's a gorgeous day,' she said, changing the subject. Now she cursed Rick for plaguing her thoughts again, along with Frank, her mother and the whole shop business. Alice paused at the car before getting in, trying to banish her crappy mood. She felt like staying at the flat on her own and not being sociable with people she didn't know. She'd been looking forward to chatting with 'the girls' as Ashley referred to them. The last time they'd met had been in a noisy pub and decent conversation had been a nightmare. She just hoped she'd remember everyone's names.

'Hey, are you okay?' Ashley asked, looking at Alice while they were stopped at a red traffic light.

'Yeah. Sorry, I just had a run-in with Mum.'

'Oh no. What did the witch do now?'

'Nothing really, just being her usual self. And as usual I fell for it and took the bait.'

'Oh dear. Tell me. If it will help.'

Alice relayed to Ashley the whole conversation with Rick, her mother and about her brief, cryptic chat with Frank.

'Wow, you must be exhausted after all that. What a morning you've had!'

'Yes, I am a bit.'

'So, other than tired, how do you feel about it all?'

'A bit sad and disappointed. I know lots of people shop at the bigger supermarkets, but I still think they should have been able to make it work. Though, I wasn't allowed to be involved, so what would I know? I am a bit chuffed that Rick would think of me like he did, though. It's the disloyalty of my mother that hurts the most. But I'm kind of getting used to that. Now I see it for what it is.'

'That's good.'

'And, you know, it's almost funny if you think about it and if it weren't so bloody annoying, but it's exactly what I got told off for on my birthday – well, not exactly the same situation, but you know what I mean.'

'I do. Do you think perhaps that's rather the point?'

'Sorry?'

'Well, perhaps it's payback – the not telling you. I don't think for a second they'd go so far as to pay for advertising, engage a real estate agent, which they clearly have, but …'

'Oh, I wouldn't put anything past my mother. She's often doing stupid things that end up being pretty much her cutting her nose off to spite her face. I'm curious about what Frank has to say. Meanwhile, I'm just really annoyed with myself that, one, I rang her and, two, I engaged and didn't just say, "Well, thanks for the update, Mother, whatever you want to do, see you later."'

'Oh well, it's done now. You just have to do your best to shake it off. Today will be fun,' Ashley said, pulling into a parking spot.

Happy face, happy face, Alice told herself, as she went to the boot of the Peugeot coupe where Ashley was getting out their food.

'Here, you put this over your shoulder, your plate on top of this and I'll carry the chairs and the picnic rug. I brought both to give us options.'

'Perfect. A great idea,' Alice said.

'I think Tamsin is bringing a folding table for the food.'

After they'd got settled and the greetings and new introductions made, the large group broke into smaller clusters to chat. They all agreed to eat first since the flies had started to show an interest and there wasn't enough room in the Eskies for all the plates of food. Anyway, they all complained that the smell of the nearby barbeques was making them ravenous. A few of the children had sidled up to their mothers and were also complaining that they were hungry.

As she stared at her plate of small morsels of food – sausage roll, mini quiche, and a ribbon sandwich – Alice felt a longing grip her deep within. Oh how she missed Ruth, and this spread – 'A mighty fine spread!' her dear friend would have cried – reminded her of her funeral. Where had that come from? Damn it. Her eyes were suddenly glistening. Not now. Please. Thank goodness she was wearing sunglasses. She ignored the hollow ache in her stomach and picked up the mini quiche and concentrated on tasting its flavour and then joining in with the chorus of murmurings of 'yum' and other compliments.

Alice found her mind wandering to why this morning had happened. Maybe it was a test, she thought with a start. That's what Lauren would have said: perhaps the universe is testing your resolve, since your law course hasn't started yet, by suggesting other options. A sense of calm came over Alice. *No, I'm where I'm meant to be, and on the path I'm meant to be on.* No matter how small the flat was, it could never be as stifling as living back in Hope Springs. God, wasn't that the truth? *Universe, if I'm meant to be somewhere else, doing something different, then you'd better send me a decent sign.*

Alice was pleased to get through lunch without needing to engage in much chatter. They packed the left-overs away for later and then sat back in their chairs complaining for a few minutes that they'd eaten too much and watching the kids burning off energy by running around squealing and throwing Frisbees and chasing balls.

The shadows were long and the light became far richer, softer, more yellow around them. They'd played a few sessions of Frisbee, gently kicked the ball around, taken a stroll along the pathway around the lake and back again and the group – minus those off attending to children – lounged around on picnic rugs or leant back into their deck chairs laughing and talking.

A knot of sadness gripped Alice again as she watched Brittany and her mother laughing together. She pushed aside the twinge of jealousy. How lovely to have such a relationship with your mother that you invite her to your girls' catch-up. Alice had been surprised when Brittany had introduced her mother as Angela before adding – her arm threaded through Angela's – 'and my best friend'. Alice's heart had been stretched to its fullest by indulging in a brief fantasy of imagining that being herself and Ruth.

'Sorry?' she said, thrown from her current reverie by a nudge to her elbow.

'Penny for your thoughts?' Ashley said.

'Oh. I was just snoozing,' Alice said, trying to deflect attention. She didn't want to say what was really on her mind.

'You were not. Your eyes weren't even closed. You were looking at Brittany.'

'Was I? In my own little world. Just thinking.'

'You do far too much of that, Alice.'

'I know. It's a habit I'm trying to break,' she said, turning to Ashley, a smile plastered on her face.

'So …? Penny for your thoughts,' Ashley persisted.

'I was just thinking …'

'Yes, we've established that.'

'Ash?'

'Yup?'

'Do you think you might change your mind about not having kids?'

'Maybe. Probably. Probably not. I have no idea. I'll see what the universe has planned. But I do know I'm not keen on the single mother path. Are you feeling clucky being around all these kids? Has the hunky Rick or Blair got you all broody?'

'Stop it.'

'Sorry. Serious,' Ashley said, running a hand over her face to indicate changing expression.

Alice looked around her to check who was nearby before speaking. 'I don't think I like children. Like *really* don't like children,' she whispered, leaning closer to Ashley.

'And that's okay.'

'But is it?'

'Of course.'

'I don't think they're cute at all. And, oh my god …' There was a slow thudding deep within Alice that she recognised as realisation. Like destiny-changing realisation.

'What? What is it? You've gone all pale.'

'Oh. My. God. If I have kids, I'm tied to Dawn forever too. I have such wonderful memories of my grandparents. It would be hard to deny a child their grandparents. And grandparents have legal rights now, too, don't they?'

'Um. Yes and no. The legal side of it is mainly around arrangements going forwards after separation and divorce. And it's actually the *grandchild's* right to continue to have access to their grandparent, not the other way around, if they've had a close relationship prior. But it's certainly not about making parents expose their children to toxic family members,' Ashley said.

'Hmm. You know, Ashley, I'm so close to going no contact with my mother.' She stared at Ashley.

'Wow. That's huge. But from what you've told me, I'm not really surprised.'

Alice felt hollow, but it was not a cold emptiness – it was a light feeling. Freedom. There it was again. Another piece of freedom.

'I can't pretend to know what you're going through, Alice, or what your life has been like. If you feel that, then it's real and you have to go with that.'

'I thought the whole point of family – well, it's what has been drummed into me, my whole life – is that they're there for support. They're your roots – not just in a biological sense. But there is no support in mine. And I'm just so tired of all the angst, all the tiptoeing around. Aren't your family members the ones you're meant to be able to really be yourself around – warts and all?'

'Yep. That's certainly how I feel.'

'I don't want a child of mine feeling even a smidgeon of what I have.'

'And a parent's first role is to protect their child,' Ashley said.

'Exactly.' Alice felt the unspoken declaration settle within her and settle with a gentle ease of acceptance. *I, Alice Hamilton, am not going to have kids while my mother is alive.*

Alice shuddered against a gust of icy breeze. Suddenly there was a flurry of activity around her. The day was being packed up – the decision to leave made. Alice smiled to herself, thinking it was probably what her ovaries were doing right now, too. Shutting up shop. She hoped so. And for a brief moment she longed to be beyond childbearing age and have the decision taken out of her hands altogether.

Chapter Eleven

Alice had spent a wonderful solitary Sunday. After a long walk with Bill she'd done some reading and then put a batch of lamb shanks into the oven. Even though she was alone, she still cooked large amounts, portioning them out for freezing. Alice loved to cook and loved to be organised. She'd often spent Sundays alone while David went off to play golf or for a long bike ride. Initially she'd joined him, but soon saw that his competitive streak meant it wasn't her company he enjoyed but having someone to beat. They didn't chat or attempt to solve the world's problems – he always shushed her and told her to focus or concentrate.

Out of the corner of her eye, she noticed Bill was suddenly at attention beside the couch. 'What is it, Billy boy?' She cocked her ear to listen, mirroring the dog's pose. There was a knock on the door.

'Who's this visiting us?' she muttered. 'Stay, Bill, there's a good boy.' She quickly dried her hands and made her way to the door. 'Sit, Bill. Stay,' she said again for good measure as she opened the door. 'Frank! What are you doing here? Oh my god! How did you get my address?' Alice was annoyed at the fear galloping through her.

'Surprise,' Frank said, opening his arms out wide.

'Well, it's certainly that,' she said, hugging him a little tensely and looking past him to the driveway.

'It's okay, it's just me,' he said cheerfully, releasing her. And then the grin fell from his face and Alice cringed inside, right through to her soul. 'Oh, Alice, I'm so sorry. I didn't think. I got caught up in wanting to surprise you without considering how you might feel about it. I used the White Pages and called the Finmores and spoke with Charles. Oh god. Please don't be upset with him. In his defence, I did have to be very persuasive. They clearly care deeply for you and are very protective. He only agreed when I said it was for a birthday surprise – which is partly true. I also assured him I wouldn't tell your mother your address. And I promise I won't. Can you please forgive this old man his stupidity and thoughtlessness?'

Alice nodded, stopping an involuntary apology before she could make it. 'Of course. Come in,' she said, stepping aside. 'Welcome. But before we go any further, can we start over with another hug?' She closed the door behind them and held her arms out.

'Yes please!' Frank said, gathering her to him and holding her tighter than she'd ever felt him do before. *He really does give the best hugs*, she thought, as her remaining tension fell away.

'Oh, it's so good to see you,' she said.

'I'm glad. You look much better than when I last saw you,' he said, holding her out at arm's length and smiling warmly at her.

'Yes, it was a very difficult time.'

'And how are you doing now – okay on your own?'

'Oh my god, Frank, I love it. I didn't realise how stifled I felt, but I'm loving having my own space, no one quizzing me about where I'm going, what I'm doing – not that David ever really did that, but still … Enough about me, what the hell are you doing here? And I hope you don't take this the wrong way, but you look terrible – exhausted. I'm not surprised if you've been driving for hours.'

'I am a bit weary, actually. I've driven from Adelaide. But I'm not disturbing you, am I?'

'No, not at all. Plonk yourself down and I'll get you a cup of tea. Or would you prefer coffee?' Now she'd got over the shock, Alice longed to ask him about the shop-slash-Hope Springs shenanigans, but she stopped herself as she realised that's exactly what Dawn would have done. *Enjoy alone time with Frank; there's no rush*, she counselled herself.

'I could murder a tea, thanks. And a glass of water.'

'Coming right up.'

'And this must be the lovely Bill.'

'It sure is.'

'Hello there, aren't you a handsome fellow?' Frank said, bending down to pat Bill, who had positioned himself right in front of Frank and was looking up expectantly, his tail wagging.

'Come over here, Bill, I need to sit down,' Frank said, pulling the nearest chair out from the table.

'I hope you don't mind dog hair – I'm sure there's plenty around, despite my best efforts,' Alice said as she put a glass of water on the table in front of Frank. She returned to the kitchen to wait for the kettle to boil.

'Oh no, not at all,' Frank said. 'I love dogs and cats. I've actually missed having a pet. Your mother …'

'Yes, Dawn doesn't *do* pets. I know,' Alice said. Alice's father had been a huge animal lover; and now she thought about it, Alice felt a surge of hatred towards Dawn for rehoming her dad's kelpie after he died. She'd completely forgotten about that.

'You're going to stay for dinner, aren't you? I have lamb shanks on – there's plenty for both of us.'

'Oh, that sounds wonderful. I didn't want to presume, but I did want to say something smells good. I'd love to stay if I'm not putting you out.'

'Not at all. I'd love you to. And I did offer. I was out all day yesterday with friends and so stayed in and cooked today.'

'I'm so pleased you've made some friends, Alice.'

'Don't start,' she said, with a grin and rolling her eyes. 'You sound like my mother. "You need to make friends, Alice, you can't be locking yourself away reading all the time",' she said.

'Sorry, I just meant I'm really happy that you've settled in so well.'

'And I'm sorry, that wasn't fair of me. She just … Anyway, are we going to address that particular elephant in the room and get it out of the way, or just keep ignoring it?' she said more gently now, as she put his mug down and took a chair herself.

'Thanks. Ahh, that's just the ticket,' he said, taking a long sip.

Alice sat looking at Frank expectantly. He clasped his hands in front of him on the table and let out a long sigh. Alice itched to fill the growing silence, but she forced herself to wait it out, grateful she had her own mug to wrap her hands around and focus on.

'I've left your mother, Alice,' he eventually said.

'Oh, Frank, I'm so sorry.' Alice wasn't really. She wanted to tell him that it was about bloody time. She wanted to cheer.

'Thanks. Unfortunately, I don't feel devastated. Like you, I feel a sense of freedom. I wanted to tell you in person, because … well … because Dawn will skew the truth. But … Oh. Now I'm here, it doesn't feel right to be discussing any of this with you.'

Alice put her hand over Frank's arm. 'Frank, I am fully aware of what my mother is. I may have only just realised the truth about her and my upbringing, but I can assure you I now have my eyes wide open. If you'd like to talk about it, I doubt anything you could say will come as a surprise to me. But, equally, if you don't want to talk about it, that's perfectly fine too. Honestly though, Frank, I have wondered recently why you stayed so long,' she added kindly.

'Like you, I didn't fully realise the truth or the damage. The manipulation. The gaslighting. It was your social media shares about it all that made it click for me. It's the forest for the trees – you can't fully see until you start looking for it through a different lens. I'm not telling you anything you don't already know. But there really do seem to be two quite different Dawns.'

'Yep, I think she's definitely a covert narcissist.'

'She was so charming when we met, so easy-going and kind, even really quite amusing and fun at times. She seemed interested *and* interesting, and managed to keep that façade up until we got married. And then as if a dimmer light switch was slowly turned, she began revealing the real, the dark, Dawn – the mean, bullying woman. Maybe I just didn't want to see it earlier. I do know in the beginning I put plenty of things down to us settling into married life – the honeymoon being over, as they say – and even menopause hormones. I was understanding about that: I know some women really struggle. But it was her treatment of you that made me really question what I'd got myself into. Oh, Alice, I'm so sorry I didn't stand up for you more in those early days, but I just …'

'Frank, it's okay. I get it. You were feeling your way, getting to know us, too. Go on. You've been married for years. Why now? And, actually, why get married at all, especially when you'd spent your life on your own?'

Frank sighed again. 'It was the thought that I was maybe missing out. And perhaps a bit of the fear of growing old alone, wanting to have someone take care of me, to some extent, I'm ashamed to admit. And to answer your question of why now – I couldn't bear the lack of empathy towards you or even her own loss over Ruth. Ruth was supposed to have been one of her best friends. But she didn't shed a tear. Not a scrap of emotion. Nothing. And the way she treated you when you'd come all that way alone was just too much for me. I almost went home and packed my bags after taking you to the airport. But making rash decisions is never wise. And then her refusal to acknowledge your birthday ...' he said, shaking his head. 'She remembered all right, Alice, she just wanted to hurt you.'

'Well, she did,' Alice said quietly. 'I know it shouldn't matter, but it still does. I want to not care, but I can't seem to help it,' she said, blinking back a wash of sudden tears.

'I know,' Frank said, putting a warm hand over hers. 'You're a good person. Of course it hurts. That's one of the things that makes you so wonderful – that you *feel*. After seeing that, I couldn't take it any more. I told her I knew what she was doing. After being given a few days of silent treatment, I packed up my things and got in the car. And here I am.'

'I'm so sorry, but I don't have anywhere for you to stay,' Alice said, looking around her and suddenly feeling frantic.

'Darling, I didn't come here to impose. I've already checked into a motel.'

Alice's tension eased. She really needed to find a way to deal with this constant need to please and learn to say no, or at least stop offering things she didn't necessarily want to give. And the truth was she didn't want another person in her space. Not right now. No matter how much she loved Frank. Bless him for knowing that and respecting her.

'That's a lovely wooden box,' he said.

'Oh. Yes. That was a birthday present. It's not part of the place – I'm renting fully furnished. I'd give you a tour,' she said with a laugh, 'but you can pretty much see everything from here. My bedroom is just down the end of that little hall. The bathroom is that door there, when you need it,' she said, pointing. 'First on the left.'

'So what's the story with the box – is it from the Finmores?'

'No, they gave me the lovely throw over there. Blair – the Finmores' farm manager – gave the box to me. He made it.'

'Wow, that's some birthday gift.'

Alice detected the ever so slight tilt to his eyebrows. 'He's just a friend, Frank.'

'Are you sure about that?'

'Yep. He's like a brother I never had. He hasn't shown any interest in me beyond the purely platonic.' She almost told Frank about the *moments* she thought they'd shared, but even in her mind they seemed lame.

'And would you like him to?'

'Honestly, I'm not sure. I think I need to be on my own for a while.'

'Fair enough. Well, maybe he'll make the right move when the time's right. Or not if it isn't.'

'Yeah.'

'But I do sense you want him to.'

'Hmm, probably. I just don't want to rush into anything. Especially now I know about all the damage having a narcissist for a mother has done and that I've chosen the wrong relationships because of it in the past and now understand why – you've read the narcissist posts, you said. Right?'

'I have. Probably all of them.'

'So, you understand what I'm saying?'

'I do,' Frank said thoughtfully. 'I understand your need to feel your way and take it slowly. But don't use it as an excuse to steer clear completely unless that's what you truly feel inside. I made the mistake of not wanting to be hurt again and spent far too long on my own.'

'And yet here you are – again.'

'Yes, true. But not in the same way … Just remember, knowledge is power. Maybe I didn't truly love your mother as much as I should have – didn't let myself because of the past – but I'm not shattered. Bruised and cut up a little, but I'll heal,' he said, smiling sadly.

'I'm sorry, Frank.'

'Me too, Alice.'

'So, who was she?'

'Sorry? There's no one else. I'd never be unfaithful, no matter what.'

'No, I know that. Before Dawn. Who kept you single all those years, Frank?'

Frank examined his mug for what seemed an age. And just as Alice was about to tell him he didn't need to tell her and ask him to forgive her nosiness, he took a deep breath and began to speak.

'Raelene. The first girl I ever kissed, ever loved. She died after an allergic reaction to a bee sting when she was eighteen and I was twenty-one.'

'Oh god, Frank, I'm so sorry. That's awful.'

'Thanks, Alice. It was a long time ago. But like you with your dad, you're left to wonder. Make up fantasies in your head of the perfect life together. Maybe it wouldn't have worked out,' he added with a shrug. 'But I would have liked the opportunity to know.'

'Yes.'

'Come on, I didn't come here to get you all depressed. You know too well what it's all about. I do just want to say, Alice, that I'm really proud of how you've made your way.'

Alice looked at Frank with a slight frown on her face. She felt he wanted to say something more. And she wasn't quite sure what he meant.

'I know how your mother must have put you down out of anyone's hearing or knowledge and I think you've done well to climb out from under that oppression and do something with your life.'

'Thanks, Frank. I'm determined to be happy.'

'Good girl. You deserve to be.'

'Speaking of Olivia, which we weren't, but … Do you have any more news about the shop being for sale?'

'I'm sorry I wasn't completely open when I called you back. I was on the road, as you've probably now guessed. Since we're being upfront about things, and again, I wanted to tell you properly in person. To put it bluntly, it's an attempt by your mother to manipulate me.'

'Into staying?'

'Yes. And pouring money into the business.'

'Oh?'

'I don't know what you know about our finances – I'm guessing pretty much nothing … Anyway, to put it simply, we've always kept separate what we had before we met.'

'So, she's got a real estate agent involved and paid for advertising of the business all purely to manipulate you?' If Alice didn't know all she did about her mother's personality now, she wouldn't have believed it.

'Oh yes. As I've recently realised, Dawn really will go to any lengths in order to manipulate and get what she wants. I know this sounds cold, and I apologise for that, Alice, but Olivia and Trevor having a business to run is not my responsibility. And perhaps if Dawn had been more fiscally responsible with her inheritance she wouldn't be in this position.'

'So, they do need to sell or is it just manipulation? Sorry, I'm a little confused.'

'Join the club. I think it's a bit of both. You know your mother. She doesn't really look at the big picture. And I've never been privy to the books or running of the business despite doing quite well on my own over the years.'

'Right, but hang on. If you divorce, wouldn't she get your money anyway, or at least half?'

'Probably. But money isn't the right reason to stay. It's a bit complicated with the business, but we had a Binding Financial Agreement – a prenup if you will – drawn up before we got married. It's all a bit early for me to have nutted out exactly where we stand.'

'But I thought prenups weren't legally binding in Australia.' Alice felt a little embarrassed at not knowing this for sure, but at least she wasn't a qualified lawyer yet.

'They can be tricky. There are strict guidelines and they have been known to not hold up to scrutiny when it came to the crunch ... Look I don't want to bother you with all of that. Just, please know I'd never do anything underhanded.'

'So, she really has cut her nose off to spite her face, then?'

'Yes, you could say that.'

'I shouldn't be so gleeful, and I'm not, but I can't help being glad some karma is coming her way. And to Olivia.'

'Your sister really is a chip off the old block. She's going to be very disappointed if she thinks the world will keep on giving her everything.'

'Hmm.' She stared into her mug, sorting through her conflicting emotions and piecing everything together.

'Alice, if you had the choice, the chance, would you want your family property?'

'Not you too!' she said, the words escaping before she could stop them.

'Sorry?'

'Rick. Rick Peterson phoned – that's how I knew about the shop being for sale in the first place. He's thinking of leaving the farm and asked if I wanted to go into business with him.'

'And?'

'No way. It would be too weird.'

'Yes, I imagine it would be.'

'Anyway, I think his offer might have just been out of guilt or something.'

'Alice, I'm sorry I didn't check properly how you were during the divorce. I wasn't aware of everything going on.'

'That's okay, Frank. I didn't ask you and I could have.' The truth was Alice had always liked her stepfather, but she hadn't really known him very well. That day he'd taken her to the airport after Ruth's funeral had been a real turning point in their relationship. She thought about how she'd seen the black clouds part to let a beam of bright sunlight through and had felt it was a sign Ruth was watching and wishing her well.

'So, the shop. What about on your own? Alice, I know you had dreams, plans for the business. So, I'm asking – forget about how I'd do it or any of that; there's always more than one way to skin a rabbit. Using your heart not your head, would you want me to buy it for you? If it came with none of the encumbrances currently attached? You wouldn't have to run the same business there – that would be entirely up to you.'

She opened her mouth. *You'd do that for me?* But the words didn't come out – there was a large lump in the way.

It had felt so good to know she was believed about her mother. That was the biggest of healing that all the survivors of narcissists wanted and what seemed to stop a lot of them moving on. And now this.

'No pressure. Honestly. I know you have a new life. But I wanted you to have the opportunity.'

'It means the absolute world to me that you would even think it, Frank, but why? Why me? Please don't say to stick it to my soon-to-be-ex-wife.'

'Oh, no, never, Alice, that's not in my nature. Because I believe in you. You will be brilliant at whatever you turn your hand to.'

Tears prickled in Alice's eyes. She'd wanted to hear words like those – she had waited to hear them from her mother her entire life. 'Oh, Frank,' she said, getting up and wrapping her arms around him. He hugged her back for a long moment.

Eventually she let him go and returned to her seat.

'Well ...?'

'Well,' she said. 'You just making the offer means so much to me – you'll never know how much – but I don't want anything handed to me on a plate. Honestly, as much as I love the building and think I'd run a good and successful business – whatever I decided to do – going back to Hope Springs would be a big backwards step for me.' *Although if my mother and Olivia left ...* 'I feel like

I'm on the right track now. And as much as Hope Springs needs legal services, it won't be from me. I'll be sad to see the building sold, but that's the way things go. I think my sentimentality lies more in my memories there and when my dad was still alive. He's in my heart and that's enough. Well, it should be. Thank you. But seriously, if you're keen to run it as a business – carry on as it is – maybe it's worth talking to Rick.'

'I always liked him, but wouldn't it be a bit, oh, I don't know, disloyal to you? He *is* your ex-husband after all. I know you seem to get along okay now, but still … Anyway, I thought you said once he was lazy. Or am I remembering incorrectly?'

'Yes, I did say that,' Alice said, colouring. 'And at the time I thought it. But I'm wondering if maybe like me he hadn't completely found what was in his heart. He's never felt a strong connection with his family and maybe he was trying to be loyal to his upbringing and gain his parents' approval, like I spent so long doing. I wouldn't be surprised if now his dad has gone he starts to properly find his feet. I just think that people can summon a lot of drive to do something they're truly passionate about, when it comes down to it. Anyway, it's just something to think about,' she added with a shrug. 'Although, I'm not sure quite where his head is at right now – he's a bit too angry at not being left his farm by his father.'

'Well, it's never a good idea to make decisions when emotions are high, as I've said. I'm certainly not making any more right now. But I will keep him in mind while I'm deciding what to do going forwards. Now, let's change the subject. Do you fancy a glass of wine – I got a bottle along the way in case I could convince you to come out for dinner with me.'

'Yes, I think I need a drink after all that,' Alice said with a laugh. 'And are you happy to stay in and eat?'

'Oh yes, please. I can't resist your lamb shanks now I've been smelling them. I'll be back in a jiffy,' he said, getting up.

'I'm so glad you're here, Frank. I really am,' Alice said, turning and smiling up at him.

'I'm glad,' he said, laying a hand on her shoulder briefly before making his way out.

'How lucky are we, Bill?' Alice said, lifting the dog up and giving him a cuddle while she waited for Frank to return.

Chapter Twelve

Frank returned a minute or so later with a bottle of wine tucked under his arm. He was also carrying a large brown paper carry bag, which he put beside his chair, and a small box-shaped object wrapped in pink and silver gift wrap.

'Happy belated birthday, Alice,' he said, handing her the parcel.

'Oh, wow, Frank. Thanks so much,' she said, sliding her finger under the first piece of sticky tape.

'No card, I'm afraid. I couldn't find the perfect one.'

'I don't mind one little bit. Ooh, this is intriguing,' she said, peeling off the pieces of tape. She bit her lip and looked at Frank and then back to the oblong dark blue box with Waterman printed on it in gold. 'Oh, Frank.'

'Open it.'

Alice opened the hinged lid. Inside was a pair of pens in glossy black and purple swirling marbled lacquer. 'Oh. My. God. They're beautiful.' She picked one up and turned it over in her hand. It was cool to the touch and heavy, but the weight felt good. Well balanced. She'd only ever used ordinary plastic pens before. She looked for the clicker to bring the nib out.

'You have to twist the top,' Frank said, pointing. 'I'm not sure if that's the mechanical pencil or the ballpoint you have there.'

'Oh wow,' Alice said as she scribbled on the underside of the discarded gift wrap. 'It's amazing to write with, too – so smooth and silky.'

'You wait until you see all the different colours you can refill it with.'

'Brilliant! Oh, Frank, I love them and will treasure them always.'

'I'm so pleased,' he said, beaming.

'I'm sure having the most stunning writing instruments will help keep me focussed when the study gets hard, too.' She was feeling a little overwhelmed. She had to swallow the lump rising in her throat. 'Thanks, Frank. Best birthday ever!' she cried.

'My pleasure. You deserve it. And, now, this is for you,' he said, bending down and bringing up the paper bag and carefully putting it on the table.

'What is it?' Alice said as she placed the pen back into its box and closed the lid.

'I just hope I've done the right thing in taking it, but I didn't want to leave it in case ...'

'Why? What do you mean?' she said, frowning.

'They've started going through everything in preparation for open houses – or just spring cleaning if they're not going to go through with selling. Anyway, I grabbed this because I figured it must have been your dad's. We both know how unsentimental your mother is, and Olivia, and ...'

Alice didn't hear any more words as he brought out a large book and placed it in front of her. She stared at it, unable to speak, as a multitude of intense memories and emotions swamped her.

'Do you know it?' Frank asked, clearly unable to read her expression.

Alice managed to nod. She brought her hands to her face and then picked up the large tome and held it close, hugging it to her chest, breathing in its old paper and leather scents. She felt a twinge of guilt as she remembered deliberately leaving it behind when she moved in with Rick – in a momentary show of anger and disappointment with her father for leaving her, she had taken it from her shelf in her room and put it into the one in the loungeroom. Dawn might not have liked to read, but she liked having a full bookshelf in her home for anyone who visited. The books had all belonged to Alice's father.

'Thanks so much for this, Frank.'

Frank visibly relaxed. 'I hope I'm not bringing up painful memories for you.'

'No, not at all,' she said, running a hand over the embossed gold title and surrounding decoration – *Library Atlas*.

'It's actually quite valuable. I looked it up on the internet. So, if you don't want it for sentimental reasons …'

'I used to sit on Dad's lap when I was little and then beside him on the couch when I got too big and we'd look at this book together. Nearly every night. Once I could probably have told you the order of the chapters and the old names of countries and places on the maps. I haven't opened it since he died,' she said, sadly, guilt tugging at her. She swallowed back the lump forming in her throat and pushed on. 'It was our thing. Mum thought we were silly going on about places we'd never visit and re-reading about them over and over.'

'She was probably jealous of your relationship with your dad.'

'Yes, I know that now. I'm actually surprised she didn't burn it. I feel terrible that I'd forgotten about it for so long. I should have taken it with me.'

'She probably wouldn't have let you.'

'No, probably not.'

One of the things about Dawn was that if you showed an interest in something she'd want it when she'd never been interested in the object before.

As Alice sat there, with the book clutched to her, it all came flooding back. 'Oh,' she said.

'What?'

Alice let out a laugh as she started flicking through the book. 'Do you remember when they changed two- and one-dollar notes for coins? It was before I was born, I think.'

'I do,' Frank said.

'Dad got a couple of new notes and kept them in here to keep them safe and in perfect condition – he reckoned they'd be worth something one day. He made me promise not to touch them. Hmm, I wonder where we put them, and if they're still here.'

'Somewhere logical, I'm guessing, knowing you,' Frank said.

'Or just in the middle so they had the weight around them, if I'm remembering correctly. Oh, look. Here's one! Oh, wow.' She was overcome again. She put the open book down and pushed her chair back a bit from the table, feeling the need to be away from Frank's scrutinising gaze.

'See if there are any others in there. I just need the loo,' she said, getting up quickly and leaving.

Alice sat on the loo trying to take deep breaths and compose herself. But she couldn't breathe properly and she was gasping, taking quick short gulps. She pulled at her T-shirt, which was suddenly feeling too tight. She wanted to take it off, but her hands and arms weren't working properly.

Suddenly Bill was there in front of her – she mustn't have clicked the door shut properly in her haste. He peered up at her between her knees and put his paws up and then licked her chin when she bent down to stroke his head.

'Oh, Bill,' she said, rubbing his ears. 'Mummy's a bit sad and freaked out. But I'll be okay. I just need a minute.' The tight atmosphere started to dissipate and her breathing became easier. The dog licked her again and then sat down, curling up at her feet. Oh how she loved him. He ordinarily didn't lick much, but thank goodness he'd brought her back. Had that been a panic attack? She looked around and pulled a length of toilet paper from the roll and wiped her eyes and blew her nose. She was being silly. No, not silly, that's what her mother would say. No, she was just having a moment, which was perfectly okay. She'd never stop missing her dad or get over losing him. You didn't get *over* grief, Alice now understood, you got *through* it, but became a different person as a result. Having moved away from her cold mother's constant influence, she'd become more sentimental and more sensitive, which she'd always known herself to be but had just stamped down. And now she was free to be herself, her true character was coming out. She just had to learn not to be so shocked by the depth of her feelings and reaction to things. Her dad wasn't there, but he was watching over her and helping to guide her. She couldn't explain it beyond just knowing it to be true. She wasn't religious and didn't believe in there being a god – a lifeforce, yes, but not a bloke with a beard pulling all the strings. Her dad was a big part of that lifeforce. At last she'd started listening to it – acknowledging her intuition.

'Good dog, Bill. You're a good, good boy,' she said, ruffling his ears again before getting up. 'Come on.' She gave her eyes a final wipe, washed and dried her hands and left the small room. Sorry about that, Frank,' she said, patting his shoulder as she retook her seat at the table. 'I just needed a moment.'

'I'm sorry I upset you. It wasn't my intention.'

'It's okay. I'm happy sad. Sort of.'

'You be whatever you need to be. As long as you're okay. If you want me to go …'

'No, no. I'm fine. I just got overwhelmed for a moment. I'm okay now. Honestly.' Alice liked that she could be so truthful with Frank. He'd never tell her she was being silly, overly sensitive, embarrassing.

'You know, it was probably because of all those years sitting with Dad and this book that I ended up studying History at uni. Which is what got me to where I am now. So, there you go,' she said.

'I think it was all definitely meant to be.'

'And if Dad hadn't died, I wouldn't be exactly where I am and who I am now,' Alice said slowly. 'Perhaps with death it just takes longer to see the connection.'

'Maybe it does. You know, Alice, he'd be very proud of you – your resilience, your generosity of spirit. I know I am.'

'If he hadn't died, I wouldn't have met you, either, Frank, and I'm really glad I did,' Alice said quietly, and put a hand on his arm.

Frank put a hand over hers and smiled while looking into her eyes for a moment before looking away. 'God, look at me getting all emotional now,' he said, wiping his eyes with the back of his hand. He cleared his throat. 'There are two other two-dollar notes in there and a couple of ones too – a bit further on. But I found this,' he added, holding out a piece of folded A4 white paper.

'What is it?' Alice asked as she accepted it.

'See for yourself.'

Alice unfolded it and blinked several times, trying to make sense of what she was seeing.

'Is it yours?'

'No, I've never seen it before. It must have been Dad's.' Alice's heart fluttered, then settled into a slow deep rhythm. What she was looking at was an acceptance to study by correspondence through TAFE – Introduction to Law. *What?* 'Oh. My. God. He was going to study law?' She looked up at Frank, holding the paper out for him to read. She wasn't sure how closely he'd already looked at it before handing it over.

'It looks like it.'

'Wow.' Alice stared at the date, trying to register it and then reconcile it with other dates around that time.

'This was about a month before he died. Killed himself,' she said quietly, when it had become clear. 'Why would he …?' The words fell off her tongue. She looked at Frank again, sadly this time. Of course she knew why. Because Dawn had probably said no, had probably manipulated him by threatening divorce or something, and he'd given in. Alice had begun to realise how hard a life married to Dawn might have been for her dad. Now it was practically there in her hand, written in black ink on white paper. This was as good as the final nail in his coffin – or the final knot in the rope he'd put around his neck. Alice's heart sank. If only they'd left together. If only he'd had the courage to leave Dawn and take Alice with him. But, of course, what would Dawn have said and done about that?

'Wow,' Alice said again, and sat back in her chair. She took a deep breath and let it out loudly. How would she feel if the letter had been about medicine or something else? Would that make a difference to how she was feeling? But it wasn't, was it – it was for law.

'Well, clearly you're exactly where you're meant to be. He'd be so proud, Alice.'

She had a strange sense of being apart from her body – like that this was not her, not her decision, that Dad was pulling her strings. Was he in control? But, no. They were in it together. She felt a renewed energy about her path and the strong feeling that had been with her since deciding – the urgency to get it done as quickly as possible – left her. She felt it as a calmness overtaking her. If she could have seen it, she thought it would have been a waft of smoke floating up to the window and out.

'Jesus,' Alice said, looking at Frank with wide eyes.

'Yes. Indeed. I wouldn't have believed it if I hadn't seen it for myself. Obviously Dawn has never mentioned it to me,' Frank said.

'Truth seriously is stranger than fiction sometimes, as my writer friend Lauren would say.'

'It certainly is.'

'I just wish it hadn't taken me this long to figure all this stuff out.'

'Perhaps you missed other, more subtle signs or weren't deemed ready – emotionally or psychologically or something,' he said with a shrug. 'I think timing is important too.'

'Hmm.'

They sat in silence for a few moments until Alice broke it. 'I'm exhausted. And I really do need that drink now,' she said with a laugh. 'I feel like all the stuffing has been taken out of me then shoved back in roughly and in the wrong order!'

'I'm not surprised. I'm feeling much the same way myself. That's a good description for it.'

'Speaking of hollowed out. I'm suddenly hungry, too. How about you?'

'Yes, I could certainly eat. I had an early lunch. I'm ravenous.'

'Why didn't you say?'

'I wasn't before. It's smelling your food that's to blame.'

They'd just finished off dinner with mugs of peppermint tea when Frank said he needed to head off.

She hugged him tightly at the door, after reminding him to come by her office the next day at noon to meet her work family and go out for lunch together. She waved as he backed out of her paved driveway and into the street before going back inside.

Alice went to bed, but she couldn't sleep. She was both exhausted and wide awake. She'd brought the book in with her, unable to let it out of her sight again. She opened it to where she'd left the letter poking out. She took it out and stared at the book. Was there anything else hidden between its pages? Frank had gone through it to find this and the one- and two-dollar notes. There was probably nothing else, but she needed to know for sure. The book was precious, so she carefully flicked through each page, unfolded each map and refolded it. She dared not look at the clock. She paused several times to rub her tired eyes, so she knew it was getting late. But she persisted until she'd gone through all the pages.

She sat back feeling shattered at finding no further clues from her father – or direct correspondence. She closed the heavy book, hugged it to her and began to sob. She'd felt so sure her dad had left her a letter – a suicide note, or at least an explanation. For her eyes only. She thought they'd been really that in tune with each other. Now she felt as if she were losing him all over again. And then there was such a rush of anger and frustration passing through her that she came very close to throwing the book across the room. She might have if it was actually her room and not a rental. Alice had never been a violent person, but Carmel Gold had brought her close – had undone something within her. Thankfully she had been able to breathe through it and resist the urges.

She got up and began pacing the room. Bill sat up in his bed in the corner. 'Sorry, Billy boy. It's okay, I'm okay. Stay.' Alice did a lap of the small flat, stopping at the sink and pouring herself a glass of water. She stood looking out the kitchen window to the tiny courtyard garden while she sipped her water, trying to rein in her emotions. Gradually she felt her insides uncoil and the tension sliding off her shoulders and neck. And then she felt guilty. *I'm sorry, Dad*, she said silently to the air around her. She went back to her room, settled herself cross-legged on the carpet beside Bill and began running her hands along the velvety belly he presented. Stroking him always calmed her.

'Why didn't he leave me a note, Bill?' she asked. Bill twisted himself, practically inside out, in order to lick her hand. Gradually clarity returned to her. *If he had something to tell me, something I need to know, he would have, wouldn't he?* The thought rolled around in her and settled. She knew everything about his death that she was clearly meant to. While a part of her was disappointed, she also realised she was a little relieved. If she'd learnt something different, it might have opened up that old wound again that she'd worked hard to heal. She was still frustrated that she didn't know why he decided to study law but had to accept she never would now. She couldn't ask her mother and risk Dawn saying it wasn't true or putting him down.

She so badly wanted to talk all this over with Lauren or Ashley – she was always able to succinctly put emotional things into perspective with them. But it was too late. Lauren would be in bed. Anyway, she knew what Lauren would say. Most likely, that her dad was clearly a good man because he didn't burden Alice with knowing more about what he'd gone through to take the drastic action he had. He was protecting her, she'd have said. And Ashley would have gently said, 'It's not about you, Alice. Perhaps he couldn't find the words. If he had then he probably wouldn't have done what he did. It's not about sharing it with you, it's about protecting you. Saving you from the burden of knowing why.'

As Alice kissed Bill on his head and said good night, slipped into bed and turned out her bedside lamp, she decided she was glad to have the book and its couple of relatively benign secrets, but relieved that nothing major regarding her dad had been revealed and she wasn't having to grapple with her memories and thoughts of him being completely unravelled. She wasn't sure she could deal with that after everything else this year. But she was mighty glad to have Frank. While a stab of guilt accompanied the thought, she admitted to herself she was glad he'd left Dawn. Not for her or out of any malice towards her mother, but for Frank. He was too good a man to be reduced to a husk – or worse – by her mother, like her father had been.

Finally Alice felt calm enough to go to sleep and turned over and pulled the quilt around her. She really looked forward to getting to know Frank properly without the larger-than-life control freak Dawn overseeing everything. *Bless him.*

***

The following morning Alice was feeling tired and bleary-eyed from lack of sleep. She'd slept, but tossed and turned and had strange dreams – mainly fragments that didn't complete coherent sequences or even really fully form. Alice wasn't really someone who dreamt much at all, so when she did she noticed and tried to make sense of the details. She lay in bed for a few moments trying to remember what she'd dreamt before giving up and pushing the covers back. Bill was still in his bed on the floor, but only just. He was sitting to attention, waiting for her. If she hadn't had him demanding her, needing her, sometimes in these past months she might have pulled the covers back over her and sunk into a lasting depression. Pets really were the best medicine.

'Come on, then, mister. Breakfast time.' Thankfully she didn't have a headache from the red wine she'd consumed with Frank – she must have had enough water and food as well. She smiled: it had been so good to see Frank standing there alone on her doorstep.

Alice was just eating her toast, with liberal butter and a thin layer of Vegemite, when her phone rang. 'Lauren, hi. How's things?'

'Good. Great. Have I got you at a bad time?'

'No, I'm just having breakfast. It's a bit of a slow morning here.'

'I won't keep you long. I want to get on with writing. I just wanted to let you know Brett and I are coming back again this weekend. Lunch at Mum and Dad's on Saturday if you're free.'

'Oh.'

'What?'

'Well, I …'

'Don't tell me you've got a hot date!'

'Oh ha-ha. No, but you'll never guess what … But of course you probably already know, you …'

'Alice, you're not making sense.'

'Frank – my stepdad – turned up last night. He said your dad gave him my address.'

'There? Turned up *there*? Oh, god. Shit. That must have given you a real fright, given … Your mum wasn't with him, was she?'

'No. He's alone.'

'Thank goodness for that. Dad mentioned Frank had rung, but I'm pretty sure he didn't realise he was planning to show up. I think he thought he wanted to send you a birthday present. And after the disappointment of that, well ... Shit. I'm so sorry. Please don't be cross with him – or me.'

'I'm not. It did freak me out a bit – well, a lot – but I'm okay. I'm glad he told him. It was a wonderful surprise.'

'Oh, thank goodness for that. So, what's he doing there?'

'He's left Dawn. Shit, did I just sound pleased?'

'A little bit,' Lauren said with a laugh.

'Oops.'

'Oh well, you can't help what you feel. So, is he okay?'

'He's great. Oh, Lauren, we had the best time. I've always liked him, but do you know, I've realised I can count on one hand the times I've had a chance to talk to him one-on-one.'

'Wow, that's crazy. But, as we know, narcissists make everything about them. So, I'm guessing he wasn't weeping on your shoulder, then.'

'No. A part of me feels like I should call Mum and tell her he's here – commiserate. At least acknowledge what's going on. But I'm quite enjoying the silence. And she'll either think I'm gloating ...'

'Which you kind of might be, just a little.'

'Hmm. But I do know what it's like to go through a break-up. Maybe it's an opportunity to reach out, bond a little, maybe.'

'Well, that's up to you, but just remember you can't win with a narcissist. And I bet she'll just upset you all over again.'

'Yeah. God. You're right. What was I thinking?'

'You're just being you. Personally, if you're still getting the silent treatment, I'd leave it all alone.'

'Hmm. You're right. Oh.' Alice stopped speaking. She'd just realised something.

'What?'

'I've just realised that me wanting to ring her is probably the programming – the need to please and always be the one to smooth things over, regardless of how many times I'm rejected. God, it's still sort of seeking her approval or affection, isn't it?'

'Yep, probably. You haven't done anything wrong, Alice. You're not the one who should be holding out an olive branch.'

'You're right. Thank goodness I have you to make me see sense.'

'Well, you always will, but remember, you just realised what you were about to do all on your own. That's progress.'

'Yes, right. And Frank can see it all too, now. He knows what she's like. It was seeing how she treated me and how she reacted to Ruth's death, or didn't, that opened his eyes. And he's pieced it together after seeing the posts I've shared about psychology. I think it was the one on the family dynamic showing the golden child and the scapegoat that was the clincher. Actually, I feel a little bad about thinking ill of him in staying and being clueless now. There's so much more to him. He's a lot smarter than I'd realised. I'll tell you all about it later. I know I'm going on, sounding a bit manic, but, oh, Lauren, it's so good to have someone who's seen it with their own eyes in my corner. You've no idea.'

'I get it, Alice. I do. And I know it's really rare. Think yourself very lucky.'

'Oh, I do. I really do. Shit, I'd better get cracking else I'll be late. And, sorry, you want to get on with your writing. How's it going?'

'Slowly but surely. So, Saturday. Frank's welcome too. I can't wait to meet him, and I know Mum and Dad will feel the same.'

'Well, if you're sure? I don't like to intrude.'

'Don't be ridiculous, Alice, you're family. And Frank is, too. Mum and Dad will love a new person to get to know – you know what they're like. But, yes, I know your impeccable manners prevent you from actually calling and asking. So, I will call Mum and, yes, if there's any doubt at all, I will let you know and you can gracefully withdraw and put in an apology. But it will be fine. Better than fine – brilliant.'

'You know, in the shower before I was actually trying to work out how to have you all around here with my limited space.'

'Well, now that can be a game of Tetris for playing another day.'

'And, guess what? I won't even need to be collected. Frank has a car!'

'You're so funny. It really is no problem to collect you, Alice.'

Alice smiled to herself. It was all very well for Lauren to make such declarations – she wasn't the one doing the driving back and forth.

'Okay, gotta run.'

'Shit, sorry to keep you.'

'Stop apologising, Alice, it's fine. Have a good day. See you soon.'

'Bye. Have a good week.'

'You too.'

Alice quickly finished getting ready, hooked Bill's lead on, grabbed her stuff and left for work.

She was still feeling slow and bleary-eyed but a little lighter thanks to Lauren's call. She smiled at thinking how retro it was that they actually often called each other instead of messaging all the time. It was nice. They'd been just like everyone else with their communication before all the palaver with Alice's previous job that had nearly caused her to lose her mind, Ruth's death and then leaving David. Her friendship with Lauren had deepened significantly. And what had previously been the odd text message trail had turned into Lauren calling to hear Alice's voice and check up on her. She was very perceptive, and Alice knew she couldn't fob her off with a text message saying she was okay when emotionally she really wasn't. Alice didn't call Lauren nearly as much as Lauren did her, and vowed to herself, now that her life was calming down, that she would right this balance. Thinking about Lauren and the Finmores, and how their love had helped her change her life, made her almost skip a few steps.

It occurred to her to hope Frank wouldn't find emancipation too hard and go back into the web. That happened a lot, according to what she'd read online. And she could see how easily it did.

'Oops, Bill, we'd better pick up the pace before we're late,' Alice said, checking her watch and increasing her stride.

She heard her phone ringing inside her bag. She itched to answer it but had a rule of not being on the phone when out walking, especially when she had Bill. Beside the door to the office she leant against the wall to collect her breath. She had two minutes before her official start time: just long enough to listen to the voicemail that had arrived with a ding earlier.

'Alice, it's Melissa. Lauren said she called you. No need to return my call. I'm just confirming we'd love to see you and meet Frank on Saturday for lunch. Come whenever you like after, say, ten. Just yourselves. Oh, and the lovely Bill, of course, that goes without saying. Can't wait to see you. Have a great week. Bye for now.'

Chapter Thirteen

Alice called the directions while Frank drove. She was in a particularly buoyant mood, which she tried to tell herself was about spending time with Frank and catching up with Lauren, Brett, Melissa and Charles and nothing to do with Blair.

'Ooh, ahh,' Frank said, slowing the car as they came out from under the canopy of the tree-lined driveway and saw the stately home looming large ahead. 'Cripes. I feel a little underdressed,' he said, shooting Alice a slightly stricken look.

'Don't. They're awesome. And very casual and laid back.'

On the doorstep moments later Alice had just finished the introductions and handed over the bottles of wine – one red and one white – she and Frank had taken nearly an age to choose at the bottle shop when they heard the sound of a vehicle approaching. They all turned or lifted their heads to look. Alice's heart skipped a beat as she recognised Blair's ute.

'Howdy,' he said, striding across to them on his long legs. Another introduction was made to Frank – thankfully by Charles as Alice's throat was suddenly dry and she found herself unable to speak. She swallowed, nodded to Blair and managed a croaked, 'Hello.'

Blair shook hands with Frank and Charles and pecked Melissa and Alice on their cheeks. Alice wondered if he had felt the heat in her face. She longed to put her hands up to feel how bad it was and cool herself down. Her heart was going at a ridiculous rate.

'I'm not here yet – well, obviously I am,' Blair said with a laugh, 'but …' Alice wondered if it was she who had him so unsettled '… just wanted to check you didn't need anything on my way through.'

'You are a saint,' Melissa said. 'But no, we're all good, I think, thanks.'

'I thought you would be.'

'Why don't you take Alice with you for a drive, since Lauren and Brett aren't here yet? I'm sure she'd love to see your workshop, if she hasn't already,' Melissa said.

'No, she hasn't. Good idea,' Blair said cheerfully.

'Maybe Frank would like to, too,' Charles said.

'Oh I want to keep Frank here, dear – get to know him,' Melissa said.

'Yes, you're right. You kids go along,' Charles said.

'Bill, you stay with Aunt Melissa,' she said, picking up the little dog.

'Okay. See you later,' Alice said, hesitating before getting into the passenger side of Blair's dual cab.

'It's okay, we'll take good care of both of them,' Charles said, clasping Frank on the shoulder.

There was silence in the cabin of the vehicle as they did a U-turn and then turned right instead of back the way Alice and

Frank had just come. She looked out the window at the passing scenery – neat, even crops, which were starting to turn from green to yellow; ripening.

'Wheat. That's a wheat crop,' Blair said.

'It looks good. Nice and healthy. I'm not sure if you know, but I was married to a farmer.'

'Well, there you go. No, I didn't know that.'

'Though I still probably couldn't tell you the difference between a barley and a wheat crop, even when they're ripe.'

Alice's thoughts turned to Rick and how he'd look at a crop anywhere and be able to tell the difference straight away. 'I do know they're nice-looking sheep,' she said as they drove on to where a large flock grazed. She guessed they were Merino, but it was only a stab in the dark.

'Yes. They're beauties. White Dorpers.'

Blair pointed things out both sides of the vehicle as they made their way slowly, and Alice experienced a wave of unsettling yet also comforting déjà vu pass through her. This was just like the day Rick had first taken her to the farm where she would later live. What she now knew was that he'd been pointing out features, crops, livestock et cetera, not with love and pride, like Blair now, but as a list of what was what. To Rick, she'd been on a farm inspection as was a common outing for country folk – usually with an Esky of beer in the back and drink in hand. She loved hearing the enthusiasm in Blair's voice.

'It's turning out to be a good year after a slow start. Fingers crossed it finishes off well. Here we are,' he said, turning into a small, orderly yard with a variety of sheds, which they drove between up to the side of a small weatherboard house painted dark periwinkle blue – nearly purple. 'We've come in the back way,' he explained, driving around to what was clearly the front of the house, complete with garden fence made from old-fashioned woven wire.

'It's gorgeous,' Alice said, admiring the brightly blooming flowers dotted around in clumps of colour. There had to be a woman seriously involved at some point, she thought, feeling her heart sink a little, while at the same time remonstrating with herself for her sexist assumption. He was clearly creative – she'd seen his handiwork in her wooden box for herself – why couldn't he also be a gardener who enjoyed the bright English look? And Lauren had said when Alice house sat that they had someone prune the roses – maybe that was Blair's work.

'Well, it will be in a few months when the roses flower. Come in while I put my milk and things away and grab a bottle of wine, and then I'll show you my favourite place to work,' he said, getting out of the ute and retrieving a bag from the back seat. 'Welcome,' he said, holding the gate open for her.

'Thanks,' she said, trying not to swoon at the rich warm scent coming off him as she passed close by. She told herself to stop with the fantasising and just settle down. If he was interested in her in any way beyond platonic, he'd have just kissed her when she'd paused and their heads had been level.

As Blair opened the door to the house their eyes locked briefly. Alice held his gaze until he looked away. *And there it is*, she thought. She was disappointed, but also a little relieved to have the cards on the table. She felt her shoulders relax and then her whole being, and she started to properly take in her surroundings. Again déjà vu passed through her – when Rick had shown her into the house and where they'd live together if things went that way. Not *my* house, he'd explained – part of the family company. He'd gone on to open each door and point out the spaces with all the enthusiasm of a real estate agent who wasn't very good at their job.

'Wow, what gorgeous furniture,' Alice said, running a hand over the golden shining streaky tones of the hall table.

'Thanks.'

'Did you make this, too?'

'I did. Most of the furniture is mine – or at least restored by me.'

'That's amazing.'

'Man's gotta have a hobby,' he said with a shrug.

He seemed a little uncomfortable with the praise, or perhaps it was just having her in his space. Or maybe he was preoccupied. She couldn't tell. 'I know what you mean. I've become obsessed with reading to get ready for my course. I've got a few months yet before I start.'

'Well, you can't be too organised.'

'Is this your family?' she asked, moving closer to a large framed photo on the wall above.

'Yep, that's our motley lot,' he said, moving close to her side. She fought to keep her breath steady. 'Mum and Dad and my grandparents – Mum's side on the left and Dad's side on the right. They're all retired and living in Ballarat – part of the reason I'm in town so often. And my siblings – both far too smart to stay here and be farmers! Tom, my older brother. He's an engineer high up in mining in WA. And that's my younger sister, Katie, a superbly talented costume designer in New York. Last year she worked on her first big Broadway show,' he said, proudly. 'We all went over and surprised her, including the grandparents. Poor old New York will never be the same again after our rowdy mob stormed the place. We kept forgetting to tip and which way was uptown and downtown on the subway. Utter chaos, I tell you! But it was awesome. *They're* awesome. I'm very blessed,' he added, touching a finger to the glass briefly before turning away. Alice ached with envy as they moved through to the kitchen.

'Oh, hello,' Alice said, brightening, as two dogs appeared in front of her – one a stocky red kelpie and the other a large short-haired black and white dog, which she took to be a border collie-kelpie cross. Rick's family had similar-looking dogs. They stood politely in front of her, waving their tails back and forth. As she gave them both a pat, she briefly thought she was glad she'd left Bill with the Finmores. He might be intimidated by the sheer size of these creatures. Though they might all get on very well – Bill had been friendly with every other dog he'd come across while out. She found herself liking the idea that he had dogs. Though, he had sheep, so it stood to reason.

'Alice, meet Eric and Ruby,' he said.

'Cute names. They're well-behaved.'

'They're okay,' he said as he placed the carry bag on the bench beside a turned wooden fruit bowl filled with apples and oranges.

'Can I help with anything?'

'No, you're good. I won't be a sec. Can I get you anything?'

'No, I'm all good, too, thanks.'

'It's a work in progress,' he said, turning back from the fridge and noticing her looking around at the neat and tidy if dated kitchen. 'Right, that's the milk and butter saved and the bottle of wine not forgotten. Come and see where it all happens,' he said, leading the way through the kitchen onto a small back porch and then out into a back garden. This space was dedicated to a few large trees, which Alice recognised as fruit trees, and some neat raised beds, which she assumed were for vegetables. She let out a sigh of awe at the order of the space as she looked around her. Where the front garden was beautiful and relaxing because of its charm and colour, this was enchanting because of its clean lines and tidy order.

'I don't do haphazard,' he said from beside her.

'I can see that.'

'I may be a little obsessive.'

'Oh no, I love it,' she said before catching herself and reining in her enthusiasm. At Rick's, the yard hadn't even been fully fenced. It was dirt, with the only green being weeds. When Alice had broached the subject of planning a garden, she'd been swiftly told it was a waste of water and something to the effect of, 'Why would I want to farm on my time off?' She'd thought at the time he had a point. She wasn't a born and bred farmer. What would she know? But here was Blair.

'Have you always been on the land?' she ventured.

'Yup. I'm the third generation,' he said proudly.

Again, there was none of the burden that Rick had seemed to carry; only pride. To be fair, it sounded as though he'd had much better luck in the family department than poor old Rick – it would be easier for him to like farming life.

'It certainly is a beautiful spot,' she said, shielding her eyes against the late afternoon sunshine and looking to the large gum trees and the blue hills further away. There was not a car body or broken piece of machinery or rusted hunk of metal in sight, she noted as she followed him down a red-brick herringbone-patterned path and out a wire gate, which she carefully clicked closed behind her.

He smiled back at her from where he'd paused just beyond the gate. 'Yep, I know – rule number one; leave every gate as you found it,' she said.

'You're a keeper,' he said, leading the way forwards again, leaving Alice to catch her breath and ask her stomach to stop somersaulting. She hurried to catch up. 'Can you hold this?' he said, handing her the bottle of wine before she had a chance to respond. 'And the piece de resistance.' He used both hands to pull

Fiona McCallum

back a huge corrugated iron sliding door and then flicked a light switch just inside. There were a few buzzes and clicking sounds as a series of fluorescent lights sprung into life and lit the centre of the cavernous space. In the darkness in the other bays, Alice could see machinery lined up.

'My happy place,' Blair said, walking over and pulling white sheets off pieces of machinery and projects in various states of progress – like a magician, though, unlike a magician, who might have tossed the fabric coverings aside for dramatic effect, he carefully balled them up against his stomach.

'God, it's so neat. I love it,' Alice marvelled. She felt a whole new wave of lust for him. The only sign that this was a working woodwork studio was a small pile of shavings on the floor below the lathe.

'I'm guessing your farmer was one of the other types,' he said.

'Not too bad, but certainly not this well laid out. This is a whole other level of tidy,' she said, moving around the space. She'd almost cried, 'Oh, you have no idea' and rolled her eyes, but had stopped herself in time. She didn't want to be disloyal to Rick, and he hadn't exactly been allowed to be his own man, from what she'd seen. She'd tried plenty of times in the early days to help him clean up, pleading safety, and 'tidy life, tidy mind', but he had seen it as a waste of time and had made it clear he didn't want to spend time in the shed full stop. While she knew lots of farmers tinkered in their down times, Rick preferred to stay in the house watching TV. She'd longed to ask him what his issue with the shed – and the place generally – was, but Rick back then didn't do calm and rational discussions if her questions held even the slightest hint of criticism. She hoped he was different now he'd been having counselling.

Alice jumped slightly at finding Blair suddenly right beside her. 'It's a beautiful grain, isn't it?' he said. Alice looked down. She hadn't realised she was stroking the shiny surface of a small table. Blair's fingers touched hers before he snatched his hand back. This time she hadn't imagined it. He put his arm around her shoulder, drawing her to him. 'Thanks for appreciating it; it means a lot,' he said, kissing her on the side of her head and releasing her.

That's it? What the hell! Alice felt hopes that had suddenly risen slide away again and her molten insides harden. *What was that about? What's his story? Is he interested, or isn't he?* She moved away and pretended to look at and caress other pieces, then made a show of checking the time. What she wanted to do was pick up the small sanding block and throw it at him.

'We'd better get back. Lauren and Brett should be there by now,' she added lamely.

She hoped she didn't sound as petulant as she felt. She wasn't sure how bothered she was either way – if he wanted romance with her or not – but she didn't like feeling confused. Was he playing games with her, deliberately messing with her, pulling her strings?

'Okay, then. Yeah, you're right.'

In the ute, Alice tried to appear as buoyant as before, but knew she was failing when instead of putting the vehicle in gear after turning on the ignition, he turned to her and with a frown said, 'Are you okay? Have I done something to upset you.'

'No, sorry, it's just me. This has brought up a lot of stuff for me,' she said, scrabbling to give an excuse, no matter how lame, for her deflated mood.

'Fair enough. Sorry, I didn't mean to …' He put the vehicle into gear and began driving slowly away from his place back the way they'd come.

Alice chewed the inside of her cheek, feeling annoyed with herself – for, one, letting such a silly thing get under her skin and, two, saying everything was okay when it wasn't. She cursed the years of conditioning. She was doing what she was programmed to do: be meek and mild; do and say the right thing for everyone else; make sure no one felt uncomfortable. Suddenly she was gnawing her cheek more ferociously, not to remonstrate with herself, but to find the words, literally chewing on them, rolling them around to find the right ones and their order to say what was on her mind. She took a deep breath before speaking.

'Blair, can I talk to you about something?'

'Sure.'

'Um, could you stop the car?' Alice said, surprising herself.

Without a word, Blair eased the vehicle to a stop, put the hand-brake on and turned to face her. 'What's up? Are you okay?'

She almost lost her nerve at seeing the concern written on his face. 'I'm not car sick, if that's what you mean.'

'Oh. Okay.' He turned the ignition off and turned more towards her.

'Blair, why did you pull away back there? Because I didn't imagine it, did I?'

'No,' he said, looking away.

'Did you realise I was interested – I mean, I guess I could have made it clearer, but …'

'No, that's cool. I know it's harder for women to be really upfront. I knew, anyway. There *is* a connection, for both of us.'

'Then why?'

Blair took a deep breath – so deep his solid, wide chest visibly became larger. He rubbed both hands across his face before turning back to her and speaking. 'I like you, Alice. I really do.'

'But not in that way?' *God, am I twelve?*

'No. Yes. Well …'

'Oh god. Right.'

'It's just … Look, you've just come out of a serious relationship. I'm guessing the last thing you need is a man making moves while you're sorting yourself out. I'm sorry if I've sent mixed messages. I tried not to, but I do like you. And, yes, in *that* way. But …'

Was that a but? Alice wasn't sure if she'd heard it or not. I mustn't have, she thought, because nothing followed it. Relief flooded through her.

'I'm sorry, too, Blair, for putting you on the spot – I …' Ugh – she was meant to be stopping the automatic apologies.

'Hey, there's nothing wrong with wanting to get things straight.' He seemed to relax, and Alice felt her shoulders drop a little in response.

'I can understand you thinking I need time but, I assure you, I'm not heartbroken. That sounds awful, like I don't care. I do, it's just that, well, he never felt like *the one*,' she said, using air quotes.

'You don't need to explain, Alice, I get it.'

But clearly *I do, because you obviously* don't *get it. Otherwise you'd be kissing me now. Oh god.* Suddenly Alice's throat was too dry for words and any boldness she'd gathered seeped away. She undid her seatbelt and turned towards him more, edging a bit closer as she did. Her heart was hammering again. She wanted to say, *Blair, please just kiss me.* But she couldn't make herself. She reached across and clasped his hand. And then she watched, stunned, her eyes growing wider, as he slowly pulled it away – as if in slow motion.

'I'm sorry, Alice, I can't.'

'But you just said you liked me.' *Oh god, how much like a whiny teenager do I sound? Jesus, can it get any more humiliating?*

'I do like you, Alice, more than I have anyone for ages. More than I want to.'

'What's that supposed to mean?' Alice said, her frustration and humiliation crossing into anger.

'I can't have kids, Alice.'

She looked at him, perplexed. 'What's that got to do with anything, Blair? I'm not asking you to marry me. Or have kids. Oh. Are you religious, as in you don't believe in sex before marriage?' God, she had him pegged all wrong.

'No,' he said with a laugh. 'I'm actually anti–organised religion.'

'Right. Good to know. Me too, for the record. So, what is it?'

He took another deep breath and let it out loudly. 'I like you too much, Alice, that's the problem. If we got serious, I'd break your heart because I don't want kids and you'd break mine because then you'd leave.'

'Um, hang on. What?' Alice blinked. She was genuinely confused, had got a little caught up with the words 'I like you too much, Alice' and had almost missed what had followed. Perhaps she *had* missed something. 'Did you say you can't have or don't want kids?'

'Both. And does it matter which?'

'Huh?' Alice's head began to pound.

'I've had cancer and I wouldn't want to see any kid of mine go through it, especially knowing there's a chance I've passed on the gene.'

Cancer. 'God, you poor thing.'

'I don't want your pity, Alice.'

'No, sorry. I didn't mean … What sort of cancer?'

'Does it matter?'

'Oh god. No, you're right. It doesn't … I didn't …' *I'm just freaking out here.*

'Breast. I know, it's weird for a bloke. Just don't laugh.'

'Why would I laugh? Jesus, Blair, what do you think I am?' Alice stared at him.

'People have. Blokes, though.'

She shook her head slowly. 'What the hell is wrong with people?'

'I know, right?'

Gradually his issue came clear in Alice's brain. 'But ...' She paused as she struggled to replace the words that had immediately come to mind. *But, this is good*, was so the wrong thing to begin with, especially when they were on such shaky ground already.

'Please don't say, "But there's no guarantee" and "They might have found a cure by then", or any of the other buts,' Blair said, cutting her off.

'I wasn't. And it hurts that you'd think I might be that shallow or thoughtless, I was going to say. *But* you're making the assumption I want kids. And I'm pretty sure I don't, actually. Just because I'm a woman does not mean I have the desire to procreate.' Alice wrapped her arms around herself. It felt so good to speak her decision out loud – hell, to feel free to make such choices. She knew countless people did this every minute of every day, but it was different for survivors of abuse. She unfolded her arms in case Blair thought she was annoyed.

'But ...'

'There's that word again, Blair,' she said, smiling at him.

'When did you decide?'

'I've never felt maternal, but always assumed I would some day. It's what we women are supposed to do. But with all I've known turned upside down recently – that's a whole other long story that I won't bore you with now – I realised I can choose not to. And I have!'

'But you're young. You might change your mind.'

'I might. I don't know what the future holds. I *can* tell you that right now I don't even like children and have absolutely no desire to have any.'

'I'm sorry, Alice. I ...'

'Oh.' As she studied him more closely, she felt her heart sink slowly and painfully. He looked troubled, torn. And sad. 'But you're not prepared to take that risk, are you? Because you've been here before, haven't you?'

He nodded in response.

'Our timing's all wrong, isn't it?' She blinked back the tears.

'I think it is,' he said, and looked away. 'Please don't let this ruin our friendship. Please, Alice,' he said in barely more than a whisper.

'Of course it won't. We're okay.' She smiled to reassure him. *I'm okay*, she told herself, but she was heavy with sadness and disappointment.

'We'd better get back,' he said, sounding a little brighter. He turned the key in the ignition, put the vehicle in gear and slowly got back up to speed.

'Yeah.'

'I'm really sorry,' Blair said, again.

'I know. So am I. But it's okay. I understand.' Alice turned to face the window. Overwhelming sadness hung all around her and inside she was numb. She wished she could be angry with him – that might hurt less – but she couldn't. His honesty and his selflessness in wanting to protect a child from illness endeared him to her all the more. And oh how she so badly longed for him to take her in his arms and hold her tight – hold this pain until it went away.

With nothing left to say, they travelled in silence. To Alice the trip back seemed to take an extraordinarily long time, despite the whooshing by of the scenery outside in a blur of dotted fenceposts and strips of green punctuated by the grey of large tree trunks. By the time they pulled up beside Frank's sedan at the front of Toilichte House, she had managed to blink back all the tears and was calm.

'Again, I'm really sorry, Alice,' Blair said, putting his hand on her knee as she had hers on the door handle and was about to get out.

'I know. So am I,' she said. 'But I understand. It is what it is.' She smiled in an attempt to reassure him and convince herself further. The sag of disappointment was still there as she got down out of the vehicle and closed the door. *Okay, Alice, bright, normal. Happy face*, she commanded. But it didn't work. Her tread was slow and laborious as she made her way to the steps and up to the house she'd once marvelled at for being stately and graceful, but which now seemed mountainous.

'Hello, anyone here?' Alice called out when she got inside. She could hear voices coming from several directions. Blair had caught up and was right behind her.

'Through here,' Melissa called.

'There you are,' Lauren cried, appearing from a room to Alice's right and gathering her to her.

'Oh god, it's good to see you,' Alice said, holding onto her friend hard.

'My turn,' Brett said, materialising beside them.

'Hey there,' Alice said, reluctantly letting go of Lauren and sinking into Brett's embrace and trying to focus on how good it felt to be wrapped up in his huge arms. She didn't want to let go, but suddenly she was dangerously close to a flood of tears. She could feel it rising in her, her eyes beginning to burn. She eased herself away from him as casually as she could. 'Excuse me. Back in a sec. I just need the loo,' she managed, and bolted upstairs.

Chapter Fourteen

In the small en suite off the room they'd christened as hers – the green room – Alice sat down on the toilet seat. She let the tears flow freely in the hope of getting it all out so she'd be able to face everyone downstairs and at least pretend to be her usual bubbly self again. She wished the tears would hurry up and stop, so she could wash and dry her face and look presentable again. *You're being ridiculous. Stop feeling sorry for yourself*, she told her reflection in the mirror. *Pull yourself together. Suck it up, Princess.* But while the tears finally stopped, the sadness and ache deep inside her remained. *Oh, Bill, I need you. Where are you?* He could always distract her. Just the thought of him made her smile. She felt her heart expand and the pain recede.

'Knock, knock.'

'Coming,' Alice called back to Lauren. She got up, flushed the toilet, straightened her clothes, washed and dried her hands and wiped her face over. She took a deep breath and gave her reflection a final look before stepping out. 'Hey.'

'I thought you might be needing this,' Lauren said, smiling kindly and handing Bill over.

'Bill, there you are! Thanks.' Alice cuddled the dog so hard he began to squirm. She put him down and he trotted away. She wanted to cry all over again. 'So, what's up?' she said, trying to look away from Lauren's piercing gaze as she made her way into the bedroom.

'I'm here to ask you the same thing,' Lauren said, frowning with concern at Alice.

'Nothing. I'm good. It's all good. Have you met Frank – isn't he lovely?'

'Yep. He's great. We arrived just after you and Blair left. Stop trying to deflect. Did something happen with Blair?'

'Why, why do you ask?'

Lauren laughed. 'You're kidding, right? He looks like he's just run over his dog and you raced up here like a stair-climbing athlete. And, actually, he said quietly – don't worry, not so anyone else heard – that I should check on you.'

'Of course he would.' *Could he be any more perfect?* Alice thought, tears prickling again.

'Huh? So, what gives?'

Alice sighed. 'Nothing. Everything. It's silly. I'm being ridiculous. I don't know why it's hit me so hard.'

'Er, maybe because you've pretty much been emotionally abused your whole life and you're finally seeing the consequences and starting to heal? Despite what you've been taught by your horrible mother, there is nothing wrong with being sensitive. It's a good something to be. You'll be reacting just as much as you're meant to, for you. Just be grateful that this pain you're feeling means you're nothing like her. So, sit. Spill,' Lauren said, sitting on the edge of the bed and patting the space beside her.

Alice sat and took a deep breath before speaking. 'I sort of might have made a move on him and got rejected.' She picked idly at the edge of her top.

'Oh. Shit. That's gotta hurt.'

'Yeah. Exactly.'

'But, hang on a sec, what does *sort of* mean? Was he maybe being a typical clueless male and missed a hint or something?'

'No. Definitely not. We talked about it. He's not interested in me because he thinks I might want kids.'

'And you don't?'

'No. I'll tell you about that another time. But he just assumed I would. And we haven't even kissed or anything. Anyway, his issue is he's worried I might change my mind. I'm pretty sure I won't.'

'Perhaps it's for the best. It's quite soon after David, and not so long ago you thought you probably *did* want kids. Maybe you do need time. Please don't think I'm taking sides or anything, but I can see where Blair's coming from, too.'

'Oh, so can I. Totally. He was lovely about it. I told you I'm being ridiculous.'

'Please stop staying that. Be kind to you, Alice. Carry on.'

'I'm not wanting to get married or anything, but I thought I was ready to at least dip my toe back in.'

'Maybe you are and maybe you're not.'

'Huh?'

'Maybe what you're feeling and your reaction to whatever's happened isn't about you and David or you and Blair. Maybe you've just had too much going on recently and it's a gentle reminder that you need to take things slowly.'

'So why do I like him so much, Lauren?'

'Because he's lovely. There's nothing not to like. But you don't want to go there with him if you'd be on the rebound.'

'How long until it's not a rebound?'

'About as long as a piece of string.'

'Brilliant. Just brilliant.'

'I imagine if I'd lost one of my best and dearest friends, moved house twice – including to a whole new city – got a new job and was in the process of a completely new career direction, the last thing I'd be wanting is a new romantic relationship. And you're going through some heavy stuff to do with your mother and family, too, remember? Christ, Alice, give yourself a break. And just stop and breathe.'

'When you put it like that …'

'Exactly. Take some time to enjoy where you are right now.'

'Oh. My. God. I'm repeating a pattern, aren't I?'

'Quite possibly.'

'I'm trying to get Blair to be my knight in shining armour, aren't I?'

'Maybe. Just a little bit. So, tell me what actually happened.'

Alice told Lauren in as much detail as she could remember about what had gone on.

'For what it's worth, I do think he was a bit of a dick for assuming you want kids. But you can't blame him for trying to protect himself, too.'

'I know. And I feel really bad. The look on his face …'

'Ah, yes, those big, beautiful puppy-dog eyes. They'll get you every time. It'll all work itself out, Alice, you'll see. I know I keep saying that.'

'All part of the grand plan, right?' Alice said.

'Exactly. Another wonderful life lesson.'

'I just wish they didn't hurt so bloody much.'

'You might think you're being a needy hot mess right now–'

'Thanks a lot.'

'–but you did actually stand up and demand to know what was up with him when you could have – and the old you probably would have – just accepted the mixed signals and internalised it instead.'

'Hmm. You're probably right.'

'I'm always right!'

'Oh ha-ha. I'm so s–'

'Don't you dare say you're sorry, Alice. You're meant to be deprogramming yourself, remember? You have nothing to be sorry for.'

'But you keep having to tell me the same old crap.'

'If I minded, I would tell you so. But don't be surprised if you one day recognise yourself in a character or two in my writing. Come on, before a full search party gets dispatched,' Lauren said, getting up.

'So, changing the subject completely, well, only a bit – what's all this about kids?' Lauren asked as they slowly made their way along the hallway towards the staircase.

'I'll tell you another time, but right now can we please stop talking about me? It's always bloody well about me. What are you doing back so soon, anyway?'

'One day it might be all about me and you'll step up. I know that.'

'But you have Brett. How're things with you two?'

'Brilliant. All progresses smoothly. Actually, we're thinking of moving back – well, here – you know what I mean.'

'Oh wow. Really?'

'Yup. Brett's looking at jobs and I'm going to talk to Mum and Dad about running writing workshops. Oh, and I've just handed in my thesis. So, fingers crossed, I'll be finished soon. And I want to start earning some money – not that Mum and Dad would ever pressure me.'

'You'd be a great teacher.'

'I think it's something I'd really enjoy. While I'm waiting for the perfect idea for a novel to write, that is.'

'You'll do both brilliantly. God, how am I going to face Blair?' Alice said, as they carefully negotiated the stairs.

'Don't worry about it. It's just a little blip.'

'Being a human is hard and regularly sucks.'

'Yep. I concur. Come on. I *really* like Frank, by the way,' Lauren said, tucking her arm through Alice's.

'So do I.' Just the thought of Frank made Alice feel warm inside and helped push aside all the negative feelings. 'I'd love to be a fly on the wall back at Hope Springs right about now.'

'So, you haven't heard from that side?'

'Nope. Still getting the silent treatment, I think. Or maybe it's transferred from that to them waiting for me to call and offer my commiserations, or something. Who would know? I also reckon the last thing she'll want to do is admit that her husband has left her, knowing Dawn. Either way, I'm not calling. The silence is a bit too golden.'

'Yeah. You'll never win – it'll somehow be your fault. Avoid that as long as you can, I say.'

***

Alice enjoyed the evening and gradually her and Blair's awkwardness dissolved and they shared a laugh together. It helped that Lauren insisted on a round of charades after dinner and put Alice, Frank and Blair on a team of three.

As they said good night and Blair held her and briefly kissed her forehead, she didn't feel her heart skip a beat, but she did feel tranquillity come over her. If nothing more happened between them ever again, he was a good friend to have. As she got into the car beside Frank, she was both relieved and a little disappointed it wasn't Blair driving her home.

'They're lovely. What a really lovely evening,' Frank said.

'Yes,' Alice said. 'It was. They are. Very.'

'While you were away, they even offered for me to stay, rather than at the motel. I won't, of course, but it was still very good of them.'

'Hmm. Yes, they're very generous,' Alice said.

'Anyway, I'm going to head off and see a bit more of the area – definitely check out Castlemaine and Bendigo.'

'Sounds good.'

'Did something happen with Blair earlier, Alice?' Frank asked after they'd been driving in silence for a few minutes. She hadn't meant to be so quiet; she was just tired. 'If you don't want to tell me, that's fine. And if you do, that's fine, too. I just want you to know, I'm here for you.'

'Thanks, Frank, I appreciate it. We did have a bit of a, um, misunderstanding, but it's okay now.'

'Well, that's all right then. I like him.'

'Me too,' Alice said wistfully.

'A little too much, huh?'

'Yep. Probably.'

'Take it from an old bloke who's been around the block and done a dance or two – there's no need to rush into anything.'

'I do like being on my own.'

'Yes, it's important to know who you really are and you can only do that alone. Then when you realise just how disappointing people can be, you bounce back much faster. At the end of the day, Alice, we're responsible for our own happiness and wellbeing. Once you realise that, life becomes a lot easier to manage.'

Alice nodded in the darkness. Sadness engulfed her as she thought his quiet, gentle tone sounded like her dad's, and she could imagine something like that coming out of his mouth.

'I love you, Frank,' she said, and patted his leg.

'I love you too, Alice,' he said, gripping her hand. 'Now, is that ABBA I hear?' he said, cocking his head.

'It might just be.'

'Let's crank it up then.'

Chapter Fifteen

Alice had briefly felt a little lost when Frank had left Ballarat to travel further afield, but was also happy to return to her routine. It had been nice having him around and going out to dinner. She had also, however, felt a bit disloyal towards her blood family, who she still hadn't heard from.

She'd just finished her chicken stir-fry with Singapore noodles and settled in front of the TV with her wad of sticky notes, mechanical pencil, notebook and current textbook. Alice was taking a scattergun approach to preparing for her studies in order to keep it interesting and avoid burn-out. She had several textbooks she dipped in and out of rather than reading one from cover to cover. A couple of times she'd tried that and found it was a better remedy for insomnia than adding to her bank of knowledge. The case studies were her favourite parts. Bill was beside her taking zero interest in her task, more interested in the antics of the world's most adorable cats – or whatever the show was playing in front of them.

Frank had promised to keep in touch. Alice had wondered several times if he was in denial, since he didn't seem at all upset over the demise of his marriage. But then she realised she didn't appear distraught over her split with David, either. Perhaps, like her, he had the odd wobbly moment in private and had carefully honed his 'put on a happy face' act like she had. Years spent living with Dawn would do that.

Alice's phone rang just as she had paused her reading to consider her views of the arguments being put forward and the possible verdict. She cursed not putting it on silent after Frank had called earlier. *Uh-oh*, she thought as she leant towards the coffee table, where her phone sat with 'Mum Home' lit up on the screen. Bill groaned and put a paw over his eyes. *Exactly, Billy boy*, she thought, and would have laughed if she weren't too busy grappling with which option would be worse – leaving it or dealing with Dawn now. She took a deep breath and pressed the green spot.

'Hello, Alice speaking.' Her chest was tight.

'Alice, it's me,' Olivia said.

Alice's anxiety reduced a notch. 'What's up?'

'Are you going to phone your mother?'

'Why? Have I missed her birthday?' She checked the date square on her watch – nope. Dawn's birthday was in a little over a week and she'd carefully calculated the date and placed a note on the fridge stating when she had to have a parcel in the post in order for it to get back to Hope Springs in time. She had to buy a different gift now, too. Weeks ago she'd found some gorgeous handkerchiefs, but in light of Frank's defection, that seemed a perhaps slightly cruel gift. And, of course, Dawn would say something snide, whether Alice meant it that way or not.

'No. But you haven't called Mum.'

'Right …?' Alice didn't want to fall into the trap of digging herself into a hole by assuming she knew what she was in trouble for – that had happened too many times in the past.

'Well, she's upset you haven't called. Disappointed.'

Alice heard her mother correct Olivia in the background.

'But her birthday isn't until next week.' Not that Alice was planning to call even then. A gift would be enough. Alice was learning how to play the game.

'Not about her birthday.'

Uh-oh. Alice was close to having to lie in order to not be drawn into this conversation, which she knew could only go one way – downhill.

Thankfully Olivia filled the silent void. 'Oh, god, haven't you heard?'

'Heard what?' Alice cringed as she played along. 'That the business is for sale?'

'No, not that, we know you know that, Alice; stop being dense. Frank's left Mum. She's having to sell the business.'

'What? Why?' Alice congratulated herself on her acting skills. 'Why what?'

Alice stayed silent, hoping Olivia would carry on.

'God, Alice! Don't you care at all? We're going broke over here because Frank's left us in the lurch. And now we have to sell.'

Oh please. 'Olivia, the business was going broke years ago – well before Frank came on the scene. Why do you have to sell now if you didn't then? And, anyway, you and Trevor were meant to be taking it over, weren't you?' Alice tried to keep the sneer out of her voice but failed.

'It's all just a mess. Some sympathy or support would be nice,' Olivia said, sounding just like their mother.

'I'm sorry you're going through some stuff, Olivia, but I'm not sure what you want me to do about it,' she said curtly, and was annoyed that she sounded just like Dawn, too.

'So, do you know?' Olivia said.

Uh-oh. 'About what?'

'Frank leaving, for a start.'

'Yes.'

'How? Did he call you?'

Um. Alice deliberated over saying no, in order to stop the interrogation. She sighed. 'Yes.'

'Do you know where he is? Mum's beside herself.'

'On his way to Canberra now, I imagine. He was here. He has his mobile ...'

'Well. That's just typical! Thanks a bloody lot.'

'It's not my fault if she's in denial. I've heard the whole story, Olivia.'

'Yes, only Frank's side.'

'Well, I know who's more trustworthy.' Alice hit her head with her palm. *Just shut up and stop taking the bait, will you!?*

'So you've chosen him over your own family, then? Nice, Alice, real nice.'

'Olivia, I haven't chosen anyone over anyone. Frank turned up here. I heard him out, end of story. And, anyway, he *is* family, since Dawn married him.'

'Why are you being so horrible?'

'Sorry, how am I being horrible?'

'Well, you could have called Mum.'

'And said what?'

'You could have said you're sorry, for a start.'

'Why, what have I done?' Alice almost laughed out loud. This was the nonsensical arguing narcissists did that all the people on the forums talked about. Now she could see it, it was a bit amusing. *And here we are back at the start – full bloody circle. You people are fucking unbelievable.* 'Olivia, I don't recall getting any sympathy from Mum – or you, for that matter – over my recent separation. Or the one before that.' Against all her better judgement and the advice she'd read on the subject, Alice wanted to educate these people – make them see.

'Two wrongs don't make a right, Alice. So stop being mean. Don't you care that the family business is being put up for sale?' Olivia said, a little gentler.

'I do, as a matter of fact. But if you want sympathy, if Mum wants sympathy, perhaps you should have considered discussing it with me, behaving as if I'm actually part of the family.'

'Okay, so here's the woe-is-me, I didn't get the business rant again.'

'I'm not ranting, and I never do. Perhaps if I had ...'

'What? So, it's my fault Frank left and we're losing the business?'

'Olivia. Frank has not taken the business. And none of this has anything to do with me. So, if there was nothing else, I'm busy.'

'Well, thanks a bloody lot. Jesus, you're being so cold – such an arsehole.'

'If there's something Mum wants, I suggest she ask me herself. And if there's something you specifically want me to do, Olivia, then tell me. And if I sound cold, that's because I've had years of training. I know the business is probably only for sale because Mum is being manipulative.'

'Don't be ridiculous.'

'You're being played, Olivia. Think about it. For a start, why are you calling me and not Mum? Start thinking for yourself, and stop being her puppet. It's all about Dawn, it always has been. She doesn't care about anyone but herself.' *Although you are the golden child ...* 'Perhaps this is karma.'

'God, Alice, what a horrible thing to say.'

'Sorry if the truth hurts, Olivia. That's not my fault. I've had to get a job and put a roof over my own head. Maybe you'll have to start facing reality, too, soon.'

'So, you're not coming home to help us?'

'Help you? What? Why?' Alice wasn't expecting this, and it pulled her up quickly.

'To help us stop losing the business.'

'What are you saying? Help you how?' This was as close as Olivia kneeling in front of her and begging. That didn't happen. Ever.

'Mum's really upset,' Olivia said in a whisper, softening.

But Alice wasn't falling for it, not this time. 'Really upset over what people might be thinking, the perceived humility of having to move into another house?'

'You've just left David.'

'Yes, so I know what she's going through. And, as I said, I'm sympathetic about that …' Suddenly the tone of Olivia's words caught up with Alice. 'What? You have something you want to say? Come on, then, say it, Olivia.'

'Well …'

'Well, what?'

'You've left David who had shitloads of money, and …'

'Oh. My. God. Are you being serious right now?! You want me to invest in the shop?'

'We really need the money.'

'That's not my fault. You've both made it very clear plenty of times that my input is not welcome. Maybe if you listened to some of my ideas you wouldn't be in this position, Olivia.'

'Don't be like that.'

'Like what? You can't have it both ways, Olivia.'

'But we're going to lose the shop. Everything Dad and Mum worked for. And me and Trevor,' Olivia said, whining now. A year ago this would have worked on Alice – especially the string that was her father.

'It has nothing to do with me. Look, Olivia, we're going around in circles here. I have no money and even if I did ... I have to think about my own future.' Alice cringed at her choice of words and the reason she gave.

'That's right, don't think about anyone but yourself. Thanks a lot, Alice. You could at least come back and help pack up,' Olivia added, sounding a little desperate.

'I left, remember? I don't have anything there. It's not my problem.' Alice found herself staring at the red button on her phone. *Dare I?* Her finger hovered. *Yes.* Alice ended the call.

As she sat concentrating on her breathing, the thought came to her that she wouldn't have minded going through the shed in case there were some long-forgotten dust-covered remnants once belonging to her father. But then she let it go. It wasn't worth it to check. And, anyway, she realised, if she showed an interest in something, it would be suddenly found to be of vital importance to Dawn or Olivia or Trevor.

Alice stared at her phone.

Of course, she wasn't surprised at how the conversation had gone, or the reason for the call. And she wasn't all that sad. It was what it was. But what was interesting was just how true to form they were – the projection, the not taking responsibility ... Yep, no matter what Alice did or didn't do, she'd be branded as difficult, the one who wasn't loyal to her family. The thing that did bother her – and oh how she wished with all her being that it didn't, but no doubt it would take a long time to work out of her system – was concern over how she would be now be spoken about at home. And, worse, to others outside the family. As someone who was raised in the glare of everyone knowing everyone's business and by a mother who was paranoid about others' perceptions of her and did all she could to control the narrative, Alice didn't like this situation at all. How long until they embarked on the smear campaign to assassinate Alice's character now they knew they couldn't pull her strings any more? How long until she was being painted as too up herself to help her family back in little old Hope Springs and people started tut-tutting about how terribly selfish she was for not returning to her family in their time of need. Leaving out, of course, the unsavoury matter of their expectation of Alice contributing financially. Narcissists never played fair or truthfully. And she wouldn't have her dear friend Ruth over there to defend her name and set people straight.

Her grief had settled into a dull throb deep within her. Now it suddenly rose up and stabbed her painfully, causing her to gasp and her eyes prickle with tears. She concentrated on her breathing. Both Ruth and Lauren would say she was not there for a reason. All she could do was stay well out of the way. Not engage and thus not make the mistake of looking like the crazy person so many on the forums spoke of.

With a jolt of fear, Alice saw that a year ago she wouldn't have hesitated to get on a plane home to be by her mother's side, though, as David would never have let her put money into a business as badly run as Dawn's, it might only have been to say, 'It'll be okay, you'll get through this' – all the things she wished her mother and Olivia had said to her through her own ups and downs. *God, I have come a long way*, she thought. She looked over at the gift of beautiful handkerchiefs on the shelf below the TV. It was almost worth sending them – she was already in trouble; it wouldn't make any difference. And they were lovely. And had been ridiculously expensive. Alice used tissues because she refused to iron, but should she keep them for herself? No, they'd be a constant reminder of her mother. Maybe Dawn wouldn't see anything more than them being a lovely gift and if she did, did Alice actually really care?

'I'm the worst person in the world right now, apparently, Bill,' she said. 'What do you think?' The dog turned over and presented his belly to her for a rub. 'Yep. That's what I thought.'

As Alice tried to return to her case study, she did begin to feel annoyed at the expectation that she invest in the business. But it summed up quite succinctly what the family was about, where their loyalties and priorities lay. Oh how she missed her dad. And Frank. She picked up her phone again and sent him a text. She deliberated over saying *I love you* and adding a heart emoticon, but thought that might cause him to worry about her. Instead, she wrote: *Just had Olivia calling to tell me how horrible I am. Oh and they want money.* Then she deleted it and put the phone down. He knew what was what and what their tactics would be – they'd discussed it over dinner several times. She briefly thought to call Rick. He'd understand and commiserate with her. As would Lauren. And Ashley. And Melissa. But she pulled herself up. *You're just looking for attention. Leave it. Be strong. Stand on your own two feet. Don't buy into it. No. Maybe I won't even send a gift. Or call. Maybe I'm done with all this shit …*

PART TWO

PART TWO

Chapter Sixteen

Rick glanced at the order of service from his father's funeral still sitting on top of the pile of bills, statements and other stuff at the end of the large wooden farmhouse kitchen table. He was a little surprised to see it there – had thought several times to just throw it in the bin. Thought he had, actually. He reached across and drew it towards him. What did he feel when he looked at the old man's image?

Rick was anticipating the question from his counsellor, Anthea Gibbons, next visit. Nothing much. Not now. While probably true, it wasn't very helpful. He stared at the image, forcing himself to look into those cold, green eyes, study the lines, the slightly bulbous nose. *Why did you have to be such a prick? What was your bloody problem?*

Such good things had been said about Joseph Peterson at his funeral and afterwards while people had been mingling. Rick had nibbled on the inside of his lower cheeks – first one, then the other, and back again in an effort not to interject and give his thoughts on the matter. How would they feel about knowing there'd been a couple of times before Rick was eleven when the fine upstanding father, regular churchgoer, great community man and all-round awesome bloke had lashed out at his young son with something close to hand – a piece of a hose or fencing wire or rope. It didn't take Rick long to become quick on his feet and read the signs boiling point was approaching. Thankfully any red welts were confined to his upper legs and backside where no one could ever see. Maybe if he had visible signs as a constant reminder, he might hate the bloke still, but mostly now just thought he was a stupid old fuckwit.

His mother had always been quiet and calm, but distant – all the relatives on the Vandenberg side were or had been – and if she knew or noticed that he had trouble sitting down at the dinner table those few times, she never said. And it would have hurt him worse to have her not believe him if he told – so he didn't. Ever. Maybe his mother had put an end to it or all the messaging in the media about abuse had finally sunk in. Or maybe they'd had a better season one year and the old prick simply hadn't had enough frustration to release and lost the habit. But the occasional bouts of ranting and regular snide comments and taunts had only now ended with his death.

Relief. That's what I feel.

Rick had tried to be a good son, but in Joseph Peterson's eyes, he'd been useless and a disappointment from the get-go, because there were some things he just couldn't make himself be a part of – like the use of guns and the killing that were such a normal, and at times critical, part of life on the land. When he was ten, he'd been taken out to learn to shoot. He'd so badly wanted to bond with his father over *something*. But he hadn't been comfortable even holding the gun. And he hated how loud they were, even with earplugs in. He'd rather have endured almost any other punishment than being called namby-pamby by his father, glared at with disdain and then not spoken to the whole way home or for the rest of the day. What made it a million times worse was that his sisters loved shooting and were good at it.

Not every moment of every day of his life with his father had been bad, but he couldn't easily bring up any outstandingly good or fun memories. There were plenty he could call up where his two sisters had been doted on, but nothing where he was the centre of his father's universe or recipient of his kind attention. He hadn't been a naughty or mischievous kid, but he'd been too gentle – 'a sissy'. The titles of sullen and lazy were quite reasonable at times, too. But what did Joseph Peterson expect? Joseph didn't teach, he ordered. And Rick couldn't help it if he wasn't as interested in farming as he should have been. It might run through his veins, but nothing had been done so that it excited him. He was the only son. Out there they were still usually automatically the favourite – to be revered and nurtured and trained to one day take over. So why hadn't it been like that for him?

Their farm set-up was probably different from most. He wasn't much more than a well-paid employee. He and Joseph had worked together across both properties – the 'home place' and the second property, where Rick lived, fifty kilometres away on the other side of the district – but Joseph made all the decisions. The machinery and sheep were owned by the business and Rick was paid a salary in lump sums after harvest and shearing. In the good times he was also given a bonus, which he really appreciated. Obviously. But he hated the way it came to him. Joseph Peterson, who had adopted internet banking without complaint when encouraged by the bank, insisted on handing Rick a physical cheque in person.

Rick wished he could give more of a shit about all the ins and outs of it all. He'd tried to force himself to show interest and ask questions, but had given up ages ago, after years of the questions being mocked or ignored. And so, while his peer group spoke fondly of the virtues of the rural lifestyle, for Rick it had become all about the money.

Though, one thing he'd always enjoyed was driving a tractor or header – being left alone for hour upon hour with his thoughts and daydreams as he drove. He'd always thought there was something quite beautiful and magical about the pale earth turning dark and the way the light changed among the mounds and furrows of a freshly turned paddock and the soft waving crop of cereal became stiff, sharp stalks behind the header. He was regularly mesmerised. With all the technology in the cab there wasn't a whole lot for him to do but look around and ponder his place in the world. Perhaps that was the problem.

He wished he'd confided in Alice about everything. But he couldn't have stood having her laugh at him or put him down too. Or worse, tell him to stop feeling sorry for himself, like she as good as had the other day. He'd have exploded. She'd been the first person he'd loved. Of course he'd spectacularly fucked that up. He now knew why, thanks to Anthea's help: because he'd been an insensitive, uncommunicative jerk, just like his father. Well, she hadn't actually said it like *that*. But it was the truth and Rick had hated himself for a long time for it and was trying to be different. Shedding some of his destructive behaviours, as well as, hopefully, figuring out who he really was inside. Why he didn't seem to share any characteristics with anyone else in his immediate family and why he didn't fit in where he was meant to. Why he didn't *feel* like a farmer.

A big part of why he was seeing Anthea was because he was hoping for a lightbulb moment – to suddenly know what else he was meant to do with his life. He might have set his expectations too high, but he knew this life wasn't for him and he didn't know what to do about it.

So why was he still doing the farming thing? It wasn't a question Anthea had asked, but he thought he'd seen it in her eyes and on her pursed lips. At the time, he'd thought, *That's a very good question, and another one I don't have the answer to. Habit? Fear of change?*

But he'd been kidding himself. He knew damned well why: it had always been out of fear and hope. Fear of his old man – of the repercussions of standing up to him and disappointing him further, fear of being cast out of the family and of course, but to a lesser extent, fear over how he would be spoken of in the small community. And then there was hope that kept him there: hope that something inside him would click and he'd suddenly love this life on the land and with that the hope that his father would suddenly like him and trust him enough to set him up on his own farm. Rick had always thought being self-employed was the key to him really clicking with this career that he was born to. While he hated to admit it, there was quite possibly some of Joseph Peterson's stubbornness in him, too – an unwillingness to admit defeat and give up. Ingrained was a certain level of obligation to the family, too, being the only son. He liked to think it was loyalty, but wasn't entirely sure about that.

If Anthea had asked the question back then, he'd have lied rather than admit to it or blunder about trying to find the right words to articulate it. He felt bad about that, but also thought she'd have understood. She was all about taking small steps. If only he'd been able to completely open up and trust her from the start, he probably would have got to the point Alice made the other day much sooner and would've been well and truly out of here. God it helped to talk to someone neutral, who assured him he wouldn't be judged – well, helped in the sense that he quite liked it. He always left feeling a little lighter. But then on the hour and a half drive home he'd always start to feel heavy, shit, again, starting with disappointment over wishing he'd been able to tell all this to Alice.

Of course, there had been other women since his marriage. But, and, oh god, he was so ashamed about this, none that had come close to Alice. He could see that now. Now he could see she'd had her own flaws in the love department – actually knew it because she'd told him about all the stuff with her family that he'd been completely clueless about. He'd begun to recognise them thanks to Anthea diagnosing his own problems.

Unlike Rick's way of shutting down, becoming silent – sullen, if you will – Alice became brittle. It's the only word he'd found. She'd purse her lips, her face would become tight-looking and she'd make clipped, critical comments. Since they'd split up and he'd seen her mother a few times, he now knew where it came from. Dawn had a way of cutting you down with just a few words and a look. He'd been so shocked to finally see it very clearly the other month at Ruth Stanley's funeral. The meanness – in some ways subtle and covert like his father, but also very different.

And now he'd seen what Alice had shared online about narcissism it made a lot more sense. He was a little ashamed to say he'd gone back through her timeline and checked what she'd been up to before they'd reconciled that day and then reconnected online. He'd read all the articles she'd shared about psychology in the hope of finding the clue to him and his family, too. Though she never actually said anything specific about her own family while sharing the information – he'd just connected a few dots. He could see you might come to that conclusion about Dawn. And Alice's sister, Olivia. He'd never really quite warmed to her. To either of them, actually, though he'd made an extra effort with his mother-in-law. Because that's what one did. Trevor, Olivia's husband, was a fuckwit. There was no other way to describe him. And as far as Rick was concerned, they deserved each other.

Yup. Alice fitted with her family almost as badly as he felt he fitted with his. Just perhaps in a different way. Because Rick hadn't found that his father was a narcissist. He was just a mean bastard. Though, just like they said about narcissistic parents, he did feel that his father didn't like him. His mother to some extent too. But he suspected her view was more about siding with her husband than anything else. One thing he had to admit he preferred about his situation over Alice's was that Joseph told it like it was and didn't tend to fuck with your mind. Other than the general stress of it all, of course. Rick always knew when he'd done the wrong thing in the old man's eyes and why he was pissed at him.

Rick sighed. Crazy thought, but right about now he wished his mother was more like that. Maureen didn't seem to have any thoughts of her own, or at least didn't voice them. He and she were alike in that, he supposed. What a fucked-up family they were. He felt sad to think she might have had the potential to be a more vibrant woman before marrying Joseph and being silenced, controlled. Though, what would he know? A few times Rick had wondered if Joseph had ever hit her, especially all those years ago when he'd laid into him. But then he always came back to the look she bestowed on her husband when placing his plate down on the table in front of him, when she looked up from the chair in the loungeroom when he came in. Unless he was wrong, Maureen looked at Joseph with utter devotion.

He sighed again. Enough of the stalling and thinking – he had his mother to go and see. Get the lie of the land, so to speak … She'd been struggling with the loss – had seemed completely lost. In a daze. Perfectly understandable, but Rick didn't have a clue what to say or do to help – about her or the farm. It was his duty to at least try to keep things going for her, but he was clueless, and not only because he wasn't all that interested. Nope. The grip Joseph Peterson had kept on things was vice-like. Rick had always been too embarrassed to tell anyone how in the dark he'd been. One of the worst things had been hearing about big decisions Joseph had made from someone in the street outside the post office or the bakery and having to nod along as if he knew. As the only beneficiary and Executor of the Will, Maureen was now in charge. And if she didn't start making some decisions, they'd be really in the shit. One of their busiest times, harvest, was mere weeks away.

God, he wished Alice was here for moral support. Too late he'd realised her value, her smarts. He was damned lucky to have her back in his life at all. He knew he didn't want her – them – to be how they were; too much water had passed under the bridge for that. But at least she'd obviously forgiven him. He hadn't forgiven himself. That was what Anthea was helping him with. He was learning to love himself. And didn't that make him sound like a complete wanker?

That day in the cemetery when he'd told her about seeing a counsellor and she'd shared her own secret – that she'd chucked her job in and couldn't bring herself to tell Dawn – was an oddly great memory. Right then, with them trusting each other properly for the first time, he'd wished he'd let her into his world – his soul – properly. And oh, how he wished he hadn't ruined her friendship with Shannon – her best friend of over twenty years. Because, god, how Rick now knew the value of true friends. He'd seen how their own group had shunned her at the time of their split and he'd been grateful – pleased even. He'd been hurting.

It was the old tradition of the farmer being higher up the pecking order of a place like their district than townies. But now he thought he felt a little of that abandonment. It wasn't the same, of course, and not nearly as pronounced, but while he'd had a couple of text messages right after his father's death and the funeral, no one had answered his calls or phoned back after he'd left a message. He so badly just wanted to talk to someone – not even about deep stuff, just to hear a friendly voice. He'd be fine with talking about the weather or the latest stock prices. But since he'd stopped drinking to excess several months back, things had been different. Out here, mates still showed mates support by getting pissed together. To be different was to be viewed with suspicion. They didn't know how to commiserate without booze, so they just weren't doing it at all.

Rick got up and dropped the order of service in the bin. Why would he keep it?

Maybe his mum might hand over control to him. There wasn't much you couldn't teach yourself online these days. He could catch up. But whatever happened going forwards, everything was already so much better now his father wasn't there.

He chucked the newspaper cutting of the ad for the Hamilton shop into the bin, too. He felt bad about dropping that particular grenade on Alice. He wasn't the only one being kept in the dark.

He hadn't really been serious about buying the shop and running it with her. He didn't have any way to finance it. He wasn't sure he wanted to be in a business dealing with the picky public every day, anyway. And Rick thought if he was going to do something different, he'd probably be better off anywhere but this district with its gossip. And he'd certainly never expect Alice to come back here after escaping to the bright lights and big ideas of the city. Oh how he envied her that. *So why don't you leave, gutless prick?* Indeed. Gutless for sure. And duty-bound to the family farm, wasn't he?

Farm life was all he knew so while Rick regularly daydreamt of doing something else with his life – though he had no idea what – he'd continue to work on the family farm. He longed for the day he owned his own land – possibly so he could sell it. Rick had pleaded with his dad plenty of times, using the argument that he'd be more committed, more passionate, more everything, if his patch was in his own name. Part of him believed it. But Joseph had scoffed that he couldn't be trusted. That he was lazy. Wasn't being answerable to a 'boss' rather than self-employment the answer to his lack of interest? Where was the incentive to do well in the current situation? Rick knew Alice had thought him lazy, too. Well, he was. As well as a bit lost and disinterested.

Anthea had suggested he might be depressed. Could you be depressed for your entire life? Well, as long as you can remember? Was his whole family, and he'd inherited it? He hadn't asked the questions. It had felt like a can of worms he wasn't ready to open. Of course he'd had good times, things he'd been interested in. He'd loved school. But his dad had pulled him out after year ten to work on the farm. What point was the extra two years when he wouldn't be going on to further study? Rick had thought he'd be shown how to run the farming enterprise, but no. It was to escape some of it that he'd married Alice, just as he knew she had her family. He'd gone in with such hope for their future, only to stuff it up.

Rick was a little ashamed to admit – and wouldn't out loud – that his first thought at hearing his old man was dead was the hope that he'd been left the farms – or at least his own. But, no. He then told himself that the structure of the Will leaving everything to his wife made sense for someone of Joseph's age – it was mere formality. He wouldn't have thought for a second that he'd be dead at sixty-one.

God, he envied Alice with her new and exciting life. He still felt guilty about ripping her off in their financial settlement, more so now he'd reconnected with her. He'd deliberately not included the value of the pigs he'd raised as a side-line and, so much worse, the bonus cheque from his father, which he'd held off banking until she signed. He'd been greedy and fearful of losing what little he had. His whole life had been governed by fear. He could see that now, thanks to Anthea.

The night he'd phoned his parents to say he and Alice were separating, Joseph had said, 'Don't expect me to fund your divorce if you've been stupid with your money.' It was such a ridiculous comment Rick was now amazed it had hurt so much. The lack of support had stung, but it hadn't exactly been a surprise. His mother had simply said, 'Oh, Rick, I'm sorry to hear that. Alice was a lovely girl.' His sisters had been a little more sympathetic and at least invited him over for a pity feed occasionally.

He knew Alice knew she'd been ripped off. And still she'd forgiven him. He shook his head with slight wonder.

Rick wasn't sure he liked the idea of the university study that Alice apparently loved. He'd enjoyed school but hadn't been a particularly good student. Well, except art. He'd loved that. But it had been short-lived. His father had insisted he do tech studies – wood work and metal work – instead as elective subjects. He hadn't minded so much – he enjoyed building things.

His heart sank now as he remembered his father's reaction to the first major free project he'd brought home – a small side table with wrought iron base and legs and lacquered pale timber top. He'd been so proud to present it to his parents.

'That's lovely, dear,' his mother had said, looking a little stunned. Or perhaps her expression had been more well-what-am-I-meant-to-do-with-this? He hadn't been able to tell, but he'd pondered what had seemed a strange reaction for ages before giving up. He hadn't wanted to ask and look like he was fishing for more compliments.

His father had given a harrumph-like sound and walked out of the room, muttering something like, 'Bloody waste of time.' Rick had got the hint. He'd taken the little table to his room, where it lived until he brought it with him when he moved into the house with Alice. He still loved it, but he'd never made anything decorative since – had kept his projects to more practical items so as not to disappoint anyone further on that front. He hadn't told them he'd got such high marks that he'd been taken by his teacher to the principal to be praised. Sitting in his room that night, Rick had been devastated. He thought now he'd never actually recovered from it, or that it was the beginning of a downward spiral that ended after about seventeen years with his first visit to Anthea.

He still didn't like thinking about how bad he'd got to have made the call to book that first appointment – one too many close calls in his car. He must have fallen asleep at the wheel because he'd looked up to see a massive gum tree lit up in his headlights. He'd swerved hard just in time and ended up facing the wrong way on the dirt road. He hadn't rung Anthea's office for help with his alcoholism – he wasn't that bad; could go a day or so without a drink. No, he'd rung in a desperate effort to end the dark thoughts and questions that refused to go away: was he glad or not that he'd turned that wheel and survived? And, a little quieter, should I try that again, get it right this time? Thank Christ he'd found her.

Oh god, why do I keep thinking of all this stuff? he thought, swiping away a tear. That was something else that counselling had brought up – crying. He'd always been pushed to tears easily, which had been one of the banes of his existence – both at home and at school. More fell as quickly as he wiped them away. *For fuck's sake*, he told himself, ignoring all the work he'd done with Anthea. And then he softened a little. If he was ever allowed a few tears, it was now.

Rick left the house and walked across to the shed where he kept his car and the farm ute. As he paused to blow his nose, he felt a glimmer of hope – a tiny flicker of inspiration. *Why don't you leave? Or even go visit Alice in Ballarat for a week – not stay with her, that would be weird – have a change of scenery?*

It was something Anthea had said several times. And each time he'd said, 'But where would I go?' And now he had somewhere. Of course there was an infinite number of other places he could go, but he couldn't just go driving aimlessly around or go to the airport and get on a plane to some random destination. He thought plenty of people probably did just that, but not him. Then he slumped in response to his next thought: *If I couldn't have before, I certainly can't go now. Mum needs me. Someone has to keep things going.*

Right, here we go, he told himself as he took a deep breath and turned the key in the ignition.

Rick barely noticed the surroundings that whizzed past the ute in a blur of various colours and tones. *You chose a good time to bugger off, Joseph*, he thought. The sheep had been shorn and they were now pretty much just waiting for the crops to ripen before the stress and chaos of harvest started up.

He wondered if his mother was still holding on tight to her tears. She'd been stoic and steely at the funeral, and since. Though she'd sounded choked up on the phone last night, but said she was fine when he'd asked if there was anything she needed him to do or get on his way through town. He didn't think he'd ever seen her cry.

He drove over the steel cattle grid, the shudder going right through his bones. He always felt a jolt of anxiety when he drove over it and entered the home place – as the main and original Peterson property was referred to – and drove up to the old stone homestead. Today it was worse than normal. He parked at the usual spot at the back near the kitchen, which as with most farmhouses was the main door used. He sat enjoying the sun through the ute's window for a moment while looking around, checking, feeling for anything to be different. Nope. Nothing.

When he didn't hear any answer to his knock, he slowly opened the door. The kitchen was silent, which was odd. Usually his mother would be there pottering around getting a hot lunch ready or a batch of scones for morning tea or something else hand baked.

'Mum, you here?' he called. He cocked his head. The house was eerily silent. He walked through the kitchen and paused at the door into the hall. Dare he open the door to his father's office and enter the room that had been off limits his entire life? Or go outside and look for his mother? His heart rate increased as he looked at the door to his left. His hand shook as he put it out and placed it on the old steel handle. He called out to his mum again. And waited a few moments. And then with his heart hammering loudly in his chest and ears, he slowly turned the handle. He stood at the threshold of the tidy room staring at the old plain wooden desk with its drawers each side and neat stack of document trays on top. Behind it was a large high-backed modern chair in black leather or faux leather, he wasn't sure which. Two three-drawer beige metal filing cabinets stood against a wall. An old timber wardrobe stood on the only other empty wall, opposite the filing cabinets. Rick took a step forwards and took in the space. Had he ever been this far into this room? He didn't think so. Whenever he'd come to get his father for a meal, the door had always been closed and he'd called from the other side.

Chapter Seventeen

'You won't find anything useful in there.'

Rick spun around at the sound of his mother's voice and cleared his throat. 'How are you doing?' he asked.

'I'm fine,' she said, reaching past him to pull the door closed, forcing Rick to step aside. He tried to get a good look at her and answer the question for himself. It was too dark in the hall to read her expression, but not so that he couldn't see how upright and tense she was, as usual. He could also feel it. He had the sudden urge to stand in her way, make her stumble into his chest so he could wrap his arms around her, hold onto her until she stopped being so bloody proud, or whatever it was she was being, and let down her defences.

But they didn't hug. They weren't that sort of family. They didn't do any air kisses or anything physically affectionate. Never had. Sometimes Rick had wondered if it was normal or if there was something wrong, broken, about them, but he always concluded or told himself that at least they didn't pretend to be something they weren't. With the help of years' worth of church on Sundays they'd been raised to believe that family was everything and that they could count on each other for anything and everything.

Only as Rick now knew, again thanks to his work with Anthea, there were caveats, some things that you couldn't ask for and some things that you wouldn't get from a family that literally kept you at arm's length.

Somewhere along the line someone had decided – no doubt before he'd been born – that impersonal was the way to go. And it had contributed a lot, he'd recently realised, to his relationship with Alice failing. He'd done things for her to show his love – filled the car with fuel so she didn't have to before work, and he put it out the front ready so she didn't have to open the big shed doors and risk getting dirty – because that's the way he thought it was done. But she'd wanted affection – words and touching that didn't lead to sex every time; she'd wanted him to tell her he loved her, speak the words.

But back then he didn't have those words in him. How he'd longed to phone Alice and tell her he understood now. He'd been meaning to the other night, but it hadn't felt right. He'd also learnt to listen to his instincts – not just bluster forwards without any thought to the consequences. Read the room or the air as had been the case. He'd been shocked and fascinated by what he read in Alice's posts about the children of narcissists, and especially realising how it connected so many of the dots of Alice. She'd needed him to say he loved her a lot, reassure her, because she hadn't heard it, or even felt it, from her mother – it was the same with expressing approval or gratitude. He'd spent most of his last session with Anthea discussing it. He'd left feeling really sad. And angry at his parents for not instilling in him the language of love and affection, and angry at himself for taking their word for granted.

'Sorry I wasn't here. I went for a walk with the dogs. I'll put the kettle on,' she said as they made their way back to the kitchen. 'Get the milk out, will you? And the biscuit barrel — there are some melting moments in there from Bev Shackleton next door.'

'Yum,' Rick said and did as he'd been asked, glad to be relieved of his useless hovering.

Seated back at the table, he watched her filling the kettle, her back to him. When he heard the water hitting the sink, he got up and went over. He reached past her and turned off the tap. She looked across at him, frowning slightly as if not sure who he was or how he happened to be there. He tried to gently prise the kettle from her grasp, but she suddenly pulled it tight to her, spilling water down her front, and wrapped both arms around it protectively.

She looked up at him with such a pained, helpless expression he could no longer do nothing. He wrapped his arms around her from behind and held her and the kettle. Gradually he felt the tightness leave her. Her shoulders wobbled and then shuddered violently, and hot tears spilt onto his bare arms. He laid his head against the side of her face.

'It's okay, Mum,' he whispered, 'let it out,' choking on the lump in his throat. He thought he felt her nod.

Finally, his mother's tears subsided and she became still again. He released her and moved back a little but stayed beside her. She put the kettle down in the sink and dragged a hanky from inside the sleeve of her jumper and stared out the window while she sniffled and dabbed at her tears and then blew her nose. She put the kettle on its stand and it began hissing to life.

Rick sat back down at the table and took the white lid off the ancient plastic biscuit barrel. He stared in at a mound of small yellow perfect little homemade biscuits joined together with white icing for a moment before putting his hand in. He wasn't hungry, but wanted to stay busy.

'Yum,' he said again as he bit into the biscuit, while watching his mum who was still staring at the kettle. He noticed her shoulders were back and tight again and felt a bit mean at being relieved that that meant she wasn't going to open up any further.

And then she turned around. Her mouth opened a little as if she was about to ask something. But she didn't. Her chin wobbled. He rose in his chair to go to her. But she put her hand up to stop him and he sat back down.

'Look at me. I'm a mess,' she said, looking down at herself.

'It's okay, Mum. It'll dry.'

'Here you go,' his mother finally said, as she put his mug in front of him with a thump. She returned to the bench and wiped it down and then stood with her back to the sink twisting the tea towel in her hands. Was she trying to keep busy like him or looking for the right words to speak?

'Aren't you having one?'

'No. I've got too much to do.'

'Like what? And, anyway, five minutes won't hurt.' *Please, just sit down.*

'Yum,' he said again, as the lemony icing in the centre joined the buttery richness in his mouth. He was on his second when his mother finally brought her own mug over and sat down in her usual place at the end closest to the sink and stove. She stared at the mug and sighed, wrapped her hands around it. But instead of lifting it to take a sip, she stayed as she was and looked up at him.

'I don't have a clue what to do, Rick,' she said quietly. 'He's left us in the lurch. The stupid, pig-headed old fool,' she added in barely more than a whisper. But while the words were a criticism, the tone was gentle.

'You can talk to me, Mum. What can I do?' he said quietly.

'He didn't tell you his plans, did he? I can't believe he didn't write anything down. I mean, well, he always said that, but I thought it was just ...' She removed a hand from her mug and waved it helplessly. *Him being an arrogant arsehole?*

'He didn't? Like, seriously?' Rick had to tell himself to close his gaping mouth. He had often marvelled at how Joseph knew everything about every crop that had been planted in every paddock – the yield, protein rating. Everything – and could recall it when asked. If there was one thing Rick had admired about him, then that was it – his memory.

Rick looked back at his mother now twisting the tea towel in her hands again. He'd always seen her, thought of her, as strong. Now he saw what little substance there was. She'd truly been Joseph Peterson's shadow. Now she was his widow. He'd always assumed his father had discussed everything with her. He'd pictured them doing just that while sitting up in bed at night together or late at the kitchen table.

Wow. Christ. His mother, to the best of his knowledge, had never set foot in a sheep yard or climbed into the cab of a tractor beyond taking a meal out or collecting the dishes.

'It'll be okay. *We'll* be okay, Mum. I can take over.'

'But you don't know what he wanted.'

'I'll figure it out. I'll learn.'

'You don't happen to have the passwords for the internet banking, do you?' his mother now said, ignoring him.

'No. Sorry.' *Jesus, can this get any worse?* He'd thought she might have been doing the books behind the scenes with Joseph taking the credit there, too. But, no, clearly not. 'What about the computer? Maybe he has everything on there.'

Rick's mother shook her head. 'No, nothing. I've checked. That password is on a slip of paper stuck to the side. I did Sudoko on there for a while, so … I might get back into that when things settle down.'

She'd said it in a relatively matter-of-fact tone. Was she coming unhinged? No, just terrified and trying to hold it back, he thought. She should be. Not only were they a huge ship without either a rudder or a captain, she was now hanging over the side and being dragged along. *Christ*. Selfish, controlling old bastard. Rick rubbed his hands over his face. Where the hell to start?

'It's okay, Rick. It will all be fine. I'm seeing Steve at the bank in the morning. I'm sure he'll sort me out and help me organise a new password. And I've spoken to Jessica at the accountants.'

The accountant. How much must he have made off a man whose only contribution to preparing the taxes had apparently been the presentation of a large box of loose receipts, statements and other paperwork. That was the rumour. Rick used the same accountant, but at least he presented his figures on an Excel spreadsheet. It was strange that Joseph had never put his figures into a spreadsheet and fully embraced computing and all its many advantages yet had adopted GPS guidance for the tractors and header. Though maybe that was because that was something he could brag about with the neighbours.

'Well, I guess all we need to worry about right now is getting through harvest in a few weeks,' he said, more to himself. 'We'll need to organise someone to drive Dad's header or a contractor.'

'Yes, I suppose so,' she said and concentrated on sipping her tea.

'Do you want me to make some calls?'

'No, Warren Smith called offering. I'll call him back.'

Rick felt the sting of rejection but pushed it aside. *It's not about me: she needs to do what's right for her. But I have my answer, don't I? She doesn't want me to take over. She is. And she's not going to be transferring any land, is she?* He tried not to react to his disappointment. Was he disappointed not to be tied there, though? He could go away for a week or so, try out leaving, if he wasn't needed.

'Another biscuit?' She picked up the plastic barrel and leant it towards him.

'No thanks. What's for lunch?' he ventured, as something to say. For the first time he could ever remember, there were no cooking smells or sounds. It was usually a hot lunch in the Peterson house – meat and three veg presented in about six different ways rotated during the week, and then a roast on Sunday. Even Monday's cold meat and salad meals were always accompanied with potatoes boiled on the stove and drizzled with butter.

'I have no idea, Rick,' Maureen said, wearily. 'I haven't given it any thought.'

'Oh. Okay.' *Good for you, Mum*, he thought. Perhaps she hadn't enjoyed all the meal preparation all these years, after all, but had felt obligated.

'There's plenty of stuff in the fridge if you're hungry. The neighbours and everyone have been dropping meals off left, right and centre,' she said.

'That's good of them.'

'Well, it's the way it's done, Rick.'

The return to stoicism was starting to feel oppressive again. He needed to get out of there. But he also didn't want to leave her. 'I'm thinking of visiting Ballarat. Before harvest,' he said to ease the mood.

'What? Why?' Her head lifted suddenly and she was looking directly at him.

He had trouble reading her expression. 'Don't worry, I won't go for long – just a change of scenery. And I'd definitely be back in time for harvest.'

'What about the sheep?'

'There's plenty of feed at the moment, so it's just a matter of keeping an eye on the water – making sure there's plenty and it's clean enough. You could call Warren.' He hadn't meant to sound prickly, but he might have a little.

'But if you're not here … and there's a pipe leak or something …'

Ugh. 'It's okay, Mum, I won't go anywhere. Actually, I'd better go and do a check of all the troughs now.' Anything to get out of there – though he still hadn't found out what he really wanted to know.

'That's a good idea.'

'Would you like to come for a drive with me?'

'No. I'm going to start sorting through your father's clothes.'

'There's no rush for that, Mum.'

'Well, there's no point putting it off, either, is there?'

'No, I suppose not. You need to do what's right for you.'

'Yes. I need to keep busy. I've got Matilda and Danni coming over later to help load everything into the car for the op shop.'

Rick shuddered at the thought of seeing someone else in the small town walking around dressed in his father's clothing, but then reminded himself that like most farmers there was nothing distinctive about anything Joseph had worn. He'd always been in blue or brown for special occasions and khaki workwear the other ninety-five per cent of his time. Rick tried to push back the rising thought that he was being ousted from the folds of the family. But it grew.

His sisters had no interest and no involvement with the operation and hadn't married farmers. The four of them were professionals – Matilda and her husband Matt were teachers and Danni and Owen were nurses. Maybe Maureen was going to ask them to run it with her – they'd be coming at it with about as much knowledge as Rick had right at the moment.

Rick said goodbye to his mother and got back into his vehicle, pleased to be away from the kitchen, where grief was being pushed down deep and not dealt with. She waved him off from the back step, which was a little unusual, he thought, as he waved back, having caught sight of her out of the corner of his eye while reversing. He'd check all was well with the sheep and head back home.

Rick slowed the ute as he passed the compound with the three large black and white kelpie-border-collie-cross dogs snoozing in the sun. His heart panged at seeing them like this. They had everything they needed – food, water, shelter and room to stretch their legs – but still every time he saw them, he longed to bring them inside. He loved dogs and wasn't sure why he'd never bought his parents' view that dogs were for working sheep and they belonged outside. Rick didn't see why they couldn't be pets too – what harm could it do? But his father had been firm all those years ago, and it *was* a popular position among farmers. None of his friends growing up or now had their dogs inside. It didn't help that work dogs loved to roll in sheep shit and the decaying corpses of whatever animal they could find, the results of which were putrid.

After he'd split from Alice he'd half-seriously considered getting a house dog before deciding he couldn't deal with the teasing his father would dish out about him having a wussy dog. And if he had to go away overnight there was no way his parents would take care of it.

He shoved the gear stick into first and carried on. After a few minutes he pulled up on the top of the main rise at the edge of the paddock to survey the large open space below him. The sheep were scattered around grazing, lambs in tow. He got the binoculars out of the glove box and scanned them more closely. There had been stock thefts lately in the district, so everyone was a bit on edge. Rick did a rough count. It was one thing he was good at that his father hadn't been able to ridicule him for.

He knew the old man had pushed them through the raceway in the yards quickly in order to unseat Rick's counting, but Rick always managed to keep up and come up with an accurate number.

Out there in the paddock he could tell by looking if twenty or so were missing. He reckoned everything seemed in order.

Rick drove over to the trough. He emptied it out and gave it a quick clean with the brush kept attached to the ute – more to give him something to do to feel useful than the trough being too grubby.

Back in the ute he found himself picking up his phone and bringing up his younger sister's number. He and Matilda got along better than he did with his older sister Danni. He wasn't as close as he'd have liked to be or thought he should be to either of them. He'd tried over the years, but had come to the conclusion that you could only do so much.

Anthea had said he couldn't make someone bend to his wishes. Rick hadn't wanted to chew up their time together and his money on things that weren't directly relevant, but he thought it might have something to do with their birth order. No doubt Danni had got her nose out of joint when he'd arrived on the scene and she no longer had her parents' undivided attention. Though that didn't explain Matilda's dislike of him ... Rick-the-odd-one-out might as well have been the tagline to his life, he thought as he waited for the call to connect.

'Hey, what's up?' Matilda said.

'Hi. How are you?'

'Okay. Doing okay, I guess, all things considered. What's going on?'

'You're seeing Mum later today, right?'

'Yep. Why?'

'I've just left and she seemed … oh, I don't know … sad.'

Rick had searched his mind for the right words to say without being disloyal to his mother. It wasn't his place to tell anyone she'd fallen apart in front of him, or anything else for that matter. He needed her being upset at him like a hole in the head. And, anyway, when he'd left, that's exactly how she'd been.

'You're kidding, right?'

'What?' Rick knew exactly what, but he sure as hell wasn't digging his hole any deeper.

'She's just lost her husband of thirty-six years, who she adored and who was her entire world, Rick, of course she's bloody going to be sad. He's only been gone a week. She's probably still in a state of shock. We all are. Well, *I* am.'

'I know, but …'

'Rick, just because you hated the old man doesn't mean the rest of us aren't upset. It might be business as usual for you, some kind of relief maybe, but it's not for us! Are you being serious right now? Don't be a heartless prick. Not now. Please.'

Jeez. Thanks a lot. But she was right. What would he know about grieving for a person he was glad was gone?

'I'm sorry,' Matilda said, breaking into his thoughts. 'It's just a lot to deal with.'

'I know. I'm sorry, too. I don't know what to say that's right.'

'No one does, Rick, that's part of the problem,' she said.

Ah, Rick thought, *she's referring to Matt. I'm being put into the all-men-are-dickheads pile because he's said something insensitive.*

'I've got to go, but thanks for calling.'

'Let me know if there's anything I can do.'

'Okay. Will do.'

While he was proving useless for moral support and buoying words, Rick Peterson was good with his hands and could fix or build practically anything with a roll of fencing wire and a pair of pliers. He'd been called on a couple of times by Matilda and Danni to do things around the house because their husbands were a bit useless – gifted in other areas Rick wasn't aware of, apparently. Both couples had met at boarding school or uni, he couldn't remember which. Joseph had been adamant about the girls being sent to private school for their last few years. Rick had heard his sisters say several times while swapping stories – always with pretentious accents, and he hoped tongue in cheek – that they were not only getting a good education but also being schooled in how to find a decent husband. Decent being more about the size of his bank account or earning capacity than the size of his heart and good character, as far as he could tell. Plenty of sons in the district and all those of the families the Petersons had always been close to had been sent to boarding school, too, before getting stuck into learning the ropes on the family farm and then set up on their own property or took over the management in time. Rick wished he'd got to go away – he might have never come back from the city if he had. It was another reason he figured he felt he didn't fit into the family or his peer group. He didn't have the same stories to swap.

Rick put his phone down and the vehicle back into gear and drove on. He was pleased to see how well the crops were doing. Would it turn out to be good enough for a bonus on his salary? *No. I'm meant to be learning to be more assertive without getting angry and frustrated. I'll ask when the time comes*, he told himself firmly and nodded.

Chapter Eighteen

On his way back home, Rick rounded a bend and saw a silver vehicle pulled over on a long straight stretch ahead. There was no dust hanging in the still air behind, so they must have been there a little while. He slowed, ready to stop if someone jumped out in front to flag him down. As he drew closer, he realised he knew the silver dual cab. The number plate BILKO81 was a giveaway. His heart sank a little – here was probably his group of mates who he'd wanted to be on a crop inspection with. He checked his mirrors and pulled alongside. A part of him wanted to keep going, but he was committed now. And his vehicle was recognisable, too. Somehow everyone could tell all the similar models of silver and white utes in the district apart.

'Hey,' Rick said, as cheerfully as he could.

'Hey,' Bilko said, and literally squirmed in his seat. Rick noticed Tommo and Steve in the passenger's side with their heads turned towards the windows looking out at the crop.

'How's things?' Tommo called from the back seat. 'Pretty shit, I guess.'

'Yeah.' Rick didn't fancy trying to explain how he really felt.

'How's your mum doing? Just been out to see her?' Steve said.

'Yeah. You know, as well as can be expected, I guess,' he said with a shrug.

He checked in his rear-vision mirror. A vehicle was approaching, leaving a bank of dust in its wake. Still a decent way off, but a good excuse to keep moving.

'Well, better be off. Catch ya.'

'Righto. Look after yourself,' they all said at once, the passengers holding up their beers in a farewell salute.

Rick's heart was heavy as he pushed the gear stick forwards and then waved as he drove off. He couldn't really blame them for not wanting to risk him being a dampener on their day, but it still hurt. He'd as good as ruined his relationship with these guys when he'd stopped going to the pub.

The first time he'd gone and said he wasn't drinking – sticking with water – they'd looked at him sideways all night – like they no longer trusted him. It was the strangest thing and he hadn't wanted to believe just how shallow his friends were – that the extent of their friendship really was just getting pissed together and playing pool while shooting the breeze. He'd got such a shock: like he was suddenly standing on the outside looking in on his life or from above it. They were uncouth, pissed dickheads – and probably technically alcoholics, if they couldn't enjoy a night out or go a day without alcohol.

This had been another revelation of Anthea's. Well, not exactly a revelation – she'd simply guided him to make the connection. He'd come to realise that drinking didn't actually block out his problems after all, just clouded his judgement and made him feel shittier the next day, which brought back with a sudden rush all he'd been avoiding, anyway, and with the added burden of feeling crook. He'd also been forced to agree with this father that drinking so much alcohol was a waste of money. Perhaps if he'd told him he'd realised he was right their relationship might have got better. Rick almost snorted. As if! He'd tried plenty of times over the years to suck up to his old man only to be told not to be so weak, so *namby-pamby*. It was one of Joseph's favourite words. Fuck he wished he could remove it from his vocabulary, erase it from his mind completely, along with the condescending tone it was uttered in.

Rick thought back to the guys in the ute. It wasn't their fault they hadn't known what to say, had chosen to avoid him in order to not have to face anything too deep. That was them – it was probably why they drank so much. Anthea hadn't said it in so many words, but she'd made Rick realise that all the jibes about country people being 'hicks' were pretty much true. He'd only recently seen the irony himself of how they all drove home drunk, running the gauntlet of the district's only police officer, after getting shitfaced as some stupid ritual to send off a local who had died as a result of drink driving. For fuck's sake!

God, he wished he could talk to Anthea right now – not because he needed to, but because he wanted to. He'd had to cancel his last appointment because of his father's funeral. That had hurt more than anything else recently, he realised. They had a standing fortnightly slot. He was lucky to get that – she was booked out months in advance. He'd love to have seen her every week, but he couldn't afford the time or petrol to be driving up to Whyalla and back – a three-hour round trip. Also, he knew he was already addicted to her – dependent.

Rick was surprised to find a tear gathering at the corner of his eye at the thought of how completely alone he felt – abandoned by his friends and unloved and misunderstood by his family. He bit down on his lip to stop his chin from wobbling and his throat from exploding. Real men didn't cry. He knew it was bullshit, but still you didn't want to be seen doing it around here.

He cursed his vision becoming blurred. He pulled over and allowed himself to sob. He couldn't help it. Too bad. And anyone who stopped and saw him might allow him this leeway. He blew his nose loudly. *Get it together, Ricky boy, and stop feeling sorry for yourself.*

He sighed.

It'll all sort itself out, he told himself. He wasn't sure he really believed it would, but he badly wanted to. He did feel a little better, though, calmer at least. He really could see why they said shedding tears was physically good for you. And it wasn't just a myth – he'd looked it up after Anthea's initial attempts at deprogramming him. He put on his indicator, checked his mirrors and pulled back onto the road.

Rick slowed right down as he approached the pub on his way through town, checking for any cars or utes he knew. It didn't really matter if there weren't any. The few old timers who got there on foot would be inside on their usual barstools, shooting the breeze. Maybe just sitting beside them would be enough. He had his indicator on to pull into the carpark before reluctantly deciding it wouldn't help. His stomach growled and his mouth began to water. A schnitzel would be good. But then he realised everyone in there would be offering their sympathies and talking about Joseph, spouting their own eulogies. Rick didn't need that.

He flicked his indicator off again, checked his mirrors and offered a wave and a grimace to the patient person sitting in their navy-blue sedan behind him while he'd been stopped deliberating in the middle of the main street. No road rage or honking here. Some people might have zero patience and get hot under the collar dealing with sheep, but when it came to patience on the road, they had it in spades. Rick stuck his arm out the window and waved again for good measure. Goodness only knew how long he'd been idling there. It felt like it could have been days.

Rick drove out the main highway home, ignoring the road-house with its offering of assorted takeaway options. He'd just suddenly felt the need to get to his house – not unlike the feeling of running inside to escape the dark closing in behind him after feeding the dogs or chooks when he was a kid. He'd always had a fear of the dark. He didn't know why. He'd throw the offering through the gate and then race back into the light of the verandah as fast as he could with his heart in his chest and barely able to breathe so as not to cop a teasing from his old man or one of his sisters. He knew his dad sent him out into the night more than his sisters as a strategy to toughen him up. Sometimes he'd resorted to turning off the verandah light and forcing Rick to stand outside in the dark alone.

Nothing had worked. Even these days as an adult whenever he came home alone after dark – and let's face it, alone was the status quo now – he'd park his ute out by the house so he didn't have to face the black in the shed or the walk back across. And he wasn't allowed to waste electricity by leaving lights on. Joseph paid the electricity bill for both properties because most of it was a business expense and therefore tax deductible. That was another reason he wanted self-sufficiency – to be able to make the choices that suited him.

He wasn't sure if he'd ever shared his fear with Alice. Perhaps she'd guessed. She would never have teased or ridiculed him. It wasn't in her nature – even when he'd been so cruel to her.

Rick's heart ached as he now wished he'd confided this to her. Talking about your issues didn't make you weak at all! He'd been taken for a ride his whole life.

That had been so earth-shattering to him that he'd been left feeling physically shaken. He'd sat in the car outside Anthea's office collecting his thoughts and taking an inventory of how he felt for ages. It had been their second session and after he'd beaten around the bush and spoken bullshit for one session and then ten minutes into the second one, she'd gently said she was more than happy to take his money and listen to him talking about nothing, but really preferred to help with whatever had caused him to seek her out in the first place. Reluctantly he'd seen he had to start trusting her and opening up. And he had. At first it had been a drip, then a trickle.

Now he'd let loose with a torrent of words and she could barely get one of her own in. But it didn't matter – just getting his thoughts and frustrations out helped more than he'd ever thought possible. Especially to someone who would keep it to themselves and not criticise him, no matter how ridiculous he sounded. He reckoned his parents would be horrified if they knew what he'd been saying.

Occasionally in the past few days he'd wondered if his father might send a bolt of lightning or some other ethereal message to express his disapproval from above? Heaven! What was he thinking? His parents might still believe in heaven and hell and all that religious crap, but he hadn't for a bloody long time. Though he did occasionally lift his eyes upwards and ask for stuff, usually rain or for the wind to piss off. That was just a habit. No doubt if it were all true, god would have been charmed by his old man, too, and sent him in the wrong direction.

Rick was a little hesitant to initially be too forthcoming with Anthea – he didn't want his negative thoughts to come back at him in the form of some kind of karmic payback. Or maybe they had, he suddenly realised as he pulled into his shed. Maybe he hadn't been given the farm or responsibility for it because of all his whining to Anthea.

No, he hadn't done anything wrong. Anthea hadn't said it in as many words, but she seemed to not believe in the karma payback theory. Though she did encourage him to be kind and hold back from unleashing any frustration. Same thing, really. Treat others as you'd like to be treated.

He'd just turned the ignition off when his phone rang. His older sister's name was on the screen. *Okay, here we go*, he said to himself and took a fortifying deep breath against the knot of tension that had just tied itself inside his stomach.

'Hi, Danni.'

'Rick. Hi.'

'What's up?'

'Why did you have to go and upset Mum?'

'What do you mean? She's a bit in shock and sad, but …'

'Of course she's sad and in shock. We all are – well those of us who are mourning our father.'

'Danni, what am I meant to have done wrong? I went out to check on her and the sheep.'

'What's the point in quizzing her? The farm's your department. You've been doing it for long enough.'

'Well, I don't know, *actually*, Danni, he didn't tell me – I'm in the dark as much as the rest of you.' *Didn't Mum tell you that? What has she said?*

'Don't be ridiculous.'

'It's true. The control-freak old bastard would only ever tell me what to do on a daily basis – weekly if I was lucky.'

'But that's insane.'

That's one word for it, Rick thought. *Maybe now you're starting to see what the old man was really like. Maybe the pedestal is starting to sway.*

'You've been working together for more than a decade. Surely you … No … Really?'

'I'm not sure what you want me to say or what Mum told you, but when I was there, she was clearly across the fact that she's in charge now. And she *is* the sole beneficiary and executor, remember.'

'But Mum's never even so much as … counted a mob of sheep.'

'I know that. I offered to at least try to organise a contract harvester or someone to drive Dad's header, but she said she would. She'll have to do it soon – before everyone gets booked up. I've told her I'll continue to look after the sheep.' *Because I'm not such a heartless bastard that I'd leave their welfare in the hands of complete incompetents.* 'But beyond that, I'm just a salaried employee waiting for instructions.'

'Fuck,' Danni eventually said after a long pause.

Fuck, indeed. So, she's human after all. He could picture her running her left hand through her hair over and over, her phone in her right hand. If the situation hadn't been so scary and serious, Rick might have laughed. He'd have given up one of his pinkies to see her face. He didn't think he should feel such pleasure over her discomfort. Danni Peterson – always in control.

'I could just walk away, you know. I wouldn't mind even a short break before harvest, but when I mentioned that, Mum clearly wasn't keen. So, of course I wouldn't do that to her.' He hadn't been able to resist digging the knife in at least a little. Maybe they might start being nice to him.

'Sorry. I didn't know. Jesus, what a shitshow.'

'Yup. It's a shitshow all right. And a kick in the guts.' Rick hadn't meant to say those last words out loud.

'I know you didn't get along with him, but I'm sure he didn't hate you.'

Rick wanted to say, 'We'll have to agree to disagree on that, Danni. And, no, I'm not feeling sorry for myself. It's the truth. You've never liked me either.' But what was the point? He'd just sound like he *was* feeling sorry for himself. He had to remember that while he felt a certain sense of relief – farming circumstances excluded – in his father's demise, his sisters were clearly upset and grieving their version of the man – no doubt fun, supportive, possibly perfect.

'I'd better go. I need to talk to Matilda and Mum and figure some things out.'

Well, don't take too long. 'Yeah, let me know what you need from me.'

'Thanks.'

Rick sat staring at the phone in his hand for a moment before getting out and locking the vehicle and then pulling the heavy iron shed door to behind him. As he made his way over to the house, he shook his head at what an absolute disaster the great Peterson empire was. The old him might have been ranting and raving and completely lost the plot. The new Rick was calm. Soon he might even start to see the situation as amusing. Not my monkeys, not my circus, he thought, remembering a funny meme he'd seen recently online. Even the thought of everyone else in the district thinking him a useless dick for not being all over the running of the farm didn't bother him. It was what it was.

Chapter Nineteen

The following morning Rick sat at the kitchen table fidgeting with the handle of his mug. He needed to keep himself busy – he knew that – but how? Watching TV wasn't the answer. He knew that. What else? He'd always been busy on a weekday, even these quiet times between major jobs on the farm. But what had he done? Driving back and forth between farms – often just to arrive at his parents' and be told to go back again or into town to pick up or deliver this or that. When he could have done it on his way through.

He was beginning to see what a waste of time his father's control-freakishness had been as well as completely doing Rick's head in. He'd accepted it. How would he know any different? And he'd been happy – well, happy was too strong a word – he'd gone along with it with his eyes firmly on the prize. His prize being his own farm.

It seemed ridiculous when he looked at it critically beyond the here and now. Had he ever really wanted the farm – a farm? Probably not, though he did like the idea of owning where he lived. He supposed it was ingrained in him – and of course owning land around here, especially the best dirt and large parcels of it, put you in the upper echelons of society. It harked back to the notion of the landed gentry, didn't it? Arrogance. But Rick liked belonging somewhere. Having four walls around him, if not land to work and making a living from. But in his world those came hand in hand. Also, to own one's own farm was what a farmer's son aspired to. It was in the DNA.

And by *own*, of course he meant in partnership with the bank. A lot of farmers were obsessed with getting bigger and bigger, buying more land and having newer machinery, too, regardless of the huge debt and never actually being free from the bank. Of course, it was pretty impossible to buy land without borrowing. That was one thing. But after a good season, a lot around here upgraded their machinery and utes and four-wheel-drives, even if the old stuff was in good nick and working perfectly fine. It was all about minimising tax. And of course the loan repayment amount was tax deductible too. Rick thought it was short-sighted and arse-about, given you didn't get dollar for dollar back on what you spent. He'd come to the conclusion that it also probably had a lot to do with ego, too – looking like you were doing well, even if you weren't. Keeping up with the Joneses, greed – all of that. To so many, impressions seemed to be pretty much the be-all-and-end-all of everything around here. He thought that glove had fitted Joseph Peterson well, but he knew nothing about how the books were run and the old man didn't discuss it with him, so what would he know?

He looked up and around him at the kitchen. The thought of losing this house didn't really bother him, if it came down to it, but the idea of not having a place to call home did. He drained the remainder of his coffee and got up, rinsed his mug and put it in the sink. He needed to stretch his legs, move, get some of this frustration out of his system – try not to think about how he'd lost one master and pretty much gained three more, and what that meant down the track. He hated this limbo. He thought fleetingly of going into town with the guise of checking the mail and buying the paper, but he knew he might end up in the pub. And the last thing he needed was to get caught for drink driving and lose his licence. And the way he was feeling …

He grabbed his battered work Akubra and oilskin coat off the hooks by the back door and headed outside. The mornings were still a bit chilly. Outside he paused at the gate at the end of the concrete path. Today he needed a change. Since he'd begun walking, another suggestion from Anthea, he'd been going left and out to the road, telling himself he was checking the crops. Today he went straight down past the two large implement sheds and the shearing shed towards the old dump, where the bodies of broken-down cars and assorted discarded steel and wire were strewn about in a haphazard group. He'd spent ages fossicking there when he'd first moved in, investigating the site they'd inherited along with the arable land and improvements, until his father had told him off for wasting time and his mother had tut-tutted about how low class it was to be doing such a thing. It wasn't like the council-run land-fill full of rotting food and plastic and all the other modern yuck that humans these days disposed of. That was in a hole further away. The worst here would be bottles and cans. Rick loved finding old bottles – he'd gathered quite a collection, which he kept hidden away in a cupboard. Some dated back to the nineteen twenties – he knew because he'd looked them up online. The most recent he'd found was from the sixties.

As Rick stood staring at the pile of bent, discarded metal and wire, he felt a calm he hadn't since his father's death had turned things on their head. He sat down on an upturned enamel drum from inside an old washing machine and grabbed hold of the end of a piece of rusty wire. As he pulled, he began to bend it, gently so it didn't snap, and turn it around and around into a coil. He enjoyed the repetitive, relaxing nature of it. Before he knew what he'd set out to do, he realised he'd made something. He didn't know what it was – a bowl-shaped sculpture. He liked the colour of the rust – it was sort of earthy but also showed its manufactured nature. But new wire would be more flexible and shiny. Did he dare? His father would throw a fit – even probably somehow from the grave – about him wasting fencing wire. Did Rick dare defy him? Yes. But as he looked at the random yet neatly formed object in his hands, he realised he really liked the idea of creating something out of something discarded. Cleaning up the dump was something he was meant to have been doing over the years. But every time Rick had come down here it had felt sacrilegious to destroy this relic of the past.

Rick sat back, closed his eyes and lifted his face to the sun. When had he last felt like this – this at peace? It was the kind of feeling you got after the first drink had gone down and seeped into your system. The ahh …

With a slight start, Rick realised this is what art had once done to him, *for* him – before his father had decreed it was nonsense and a waste of time.

Anthea said he would benefit from having a hobby – one that wasn't drinking in the pub. He hadn't wanted to be rude and laugh at her. Farming took up enough of his time. He could now see what she'd meant about finding a way to gain happiness – not happiness in the sense of being drunk and cheerful, but happiness in the sense of contentment. Peace. No, not TV, either. He smiled now as he remembered how she'd skirted around a lot before using the word 'meditation'. She'd got the measure of him very quickly. Once she'd said it and he'd lowered his raised eyebrows, she'd gone on to explain that it didn't have to be anything formal – just staring at a candle in order to stop the outside worries and let the subconscious do its work might help. He'd raised his eyebrows again. He didn't do candles. Or just sitting quietly with no distractions and staring at a spot on the wall, she'd been quick to add. He'd given it a shot. He liked how calm it made him feel – almost like he'd had an afternoon nap. Not that he told anyone else about it, and he'd struggled to remember to do it once back at home. But now, looking back down at the object in his hands, he thought he might have just found the happiness, contentment, she spoke of. A sort of warmth flooded through him. Like being in love – not the heady days of infatuation when your heart raced and other parts of you ached and tingled. No, that wasn't love, that was lust …

His attention was drawn back to the present by the sound of an approaching car. He opened his eyes and saw his mother pulling up at the gate and Maureen getting out. He put his wire creation aside and got up. As he strode towards the house, he wiped his rust-dust streaked hands on his jeans-clad legs. He probably should jog and make sure he caught her before she gave up on him and left, but he didn't feel like breaking the spell of his pleasant mood to that extent. She'd probably go inside and do his dishes before she departed, anyway. Maybe even put on a load of washing. The house wasn't locked, and if it had been his parents had a key – they'd always come and gone as they pleased, barely giving the door a tap before entering. They'd almost caught him enjoying afternoon delight sex with Alice, and several other women, on plenty of occasions over the years. You'd think they might have learnt. But it was part of the control, maybe. Rick's contentment seeped away and his annoyance returned.

'Oh. There you are,' his mother said, turning from filling the kettle. She began wiping the already spotless bench tops. He'd long ago given up being annoyed that she didn't think him capable of being clean and orderly; he took it as one of her tics – her need to be constantly busy, doing. Mothering, he supposed. Moving things around on the bench and rearranging his cupboards. Just for something to do. Rick was a little shocked at how pale and tired she looked – like she'd aged ten years overnight, twenty in the last few days. There were bags under her red-rimmed eyes.

'Cuppa?'

'Thanks. I'll have coffee,' he said, pulling out a chair and sitting down heavily. He was now on edge – tense. She was back to the way she'd been before her breakdown yesterday. He hoped she wasn't embarrassed. He flicked through the paper she'd put in his place on the table, pretending to read it. But nothing was going in – the headlines forgotten as soon as they'd been read, the lines underneath a blur.

'How are you?' he ventured. She was standing at the kitchen sink looking out as if in her own world. 'Mum?'

'Oh, you know …' she said, turning slowly, her words floating away like the steam from the nearby kettle.

'You can talk to me, Mum, you know. You know, about how you feel.' He almost laughed at his ridiculous boldness.

'Thanks, Rick, but if I start, I might not stop,' she said with a sigh. 'And where would that get us, eh?' she continued, offering him a wan smile before putting two mugs down on the table. As she flopped into a chair, he felt the spell, if there had been one, broken. He'd thought maybe she was here to finally open up a little, but clearly, he'd been wrong about that. Perhaps she just needed to be out of the house for a bit. He sipped on his coffee.

'I'm really sorry about everything, Rick – about the way your father has left things. What he's done.'

Well, do something about it – put me in charge. Sign over a farm. 'I don't think it's for you to apologise, Mum. He made his choice.'

'But if I'd been stronger, stood up to him back then …'

Back when? Hang on, what are we talking about here? He itched to ask, but forced himself to stay silent, waiting, like Anthea did.

'I'm sorry, too, that I haven't been a very … Well, warm, maternal mother to you. I know it's caused you some pain – a lot of pain.'

'You can't help what you feel, Mum,' he said, parroting Anthea's words. Sort of. 'If you don't feel it, you don't feel it.' He added a shrug in the hope it might look like he didn't mind all this. He probably failed. But he wasn't feeling full of self-pity. After all, she was confirming what he'd felt his whole life. He probably should be glad to know it hadn't been all in his mind, but it did hurt a little to hear it confirmed. He stared into his mug.

'It's not that I don't …' She lifted her hands and dropped them again in a helpless motion, but she didn't continue. The silence stretched on and on. He was keen to hear her out, so he let it. *If you use the L word – love – I'll lose it. Not now. Not like this.*

'I'm sorry, Rick. I … I … just wanted to say I'm sorry.'

For what? Not loving me? He couldn't make himself say the words. Berating himself for being gutless didn't help either. 'Okay. Thanks.' He picked up his mug and took a sip.

'I'm so annoyed with Joe for leaving things in such a mess.'

'I'm happy to take over, if that's what you want.' *Am I, though?* Suddenly apprehension gripped him. 'You just have to say the word, Mum …'

'It's all happening so fast, too quickly. I just … I feel like I'm drowning … Lost.'

Well, I'm here as good as holding out a life preserver ring … You're the one refusing to take it. Rick felt the anger and frustration rise in him. *Damn it. She's not sorry; well, maybe she is, sorry for screwing me further.*

'I know you want the farm, Rick, but that's clearly not what your father wanted.'

'But it's up to you now, Mum. He's not here. The controlling old bastard is not here!' *Jesus, what must he have done to her that she still didn't feel free to speak her mind or do something for herself?*

'Rick!'

'Sorry, but are you listening to yourself? You came in here saying sorry and admitting that you haven't been a warm, loving mother. You're saying you feel like you're drowning and lost. Well, how do you think I feel? I've been as good as kicked in the teeth. You said you didn't want me to go away. Well, what am I staying for? What do you want me to do?'

'You can't be angry with him for not leaving you the farm. He was protecting me, my future.'

'I know. I get it. I just feel like my whole life is a waste of time. What have I been doing all these years? What about *my* future?'

'Do you even want to be a farmer, Rick? Are you really happy here? You could do any number of things.'

Since when has being happy come into it and having a choice, for that matter? If he wasn't so confused and worried about upsetting her, he'd probably have laughed. 'What's that supposed to mean? What are you saying?' *Oh my god. You're chucking me out completely? Fuck. No.*

'Nothing. I didn't mean anything by it,' she said. But Rick had seen a flicker of something, her tone had suddenly been a little different – almost like she'd suddenly realised she'd said too much and pulled back. If he were being paranoid … But no matter how much he told himself he'd imagined it, he couldn't shake the feeling that she was here to say something new. If only she'd stop going around in circles. But he also knew he had to be gentle, the woman was grief-stricken – fragile and probably not thinking clearly. *Oh my god. This is doing me in*, he thought as the tense silence stretched on. And then he had another thought. *Assertive, Rick, you don't need to be cold and hard, like the old man, but maybe she needs you to ease her burden without her losing face or something.*

'I've said I can take over. But if I do, I'd need free rein.'

'Are you giving me an ultimatum?'

'No. I didn't mean to. But you can't have it both ways. Or the way it is. Because it's clearly stressing you out.'

'That's not it.'

'Well, then what *is it*?'

'Nothing. It's all such a mess, that's all. *Everything* is,' she said with a long sigh and put her head in her hands.

'Yes, it is.' *Thanks to the stupid old bastard you were married to.* 'You can't just bury your head in the sand, Mum.'

Rick watched as his mother traced the pattern on the mug with her finger. She seemed to be chewing something over in her mind, formulating something to say. A decision? But the silence stretched on. He ignored the increasing desire to fill it. What else could he say? His position was clear – well, clear-ish.

'I've never really felt you enjoyed being a farmer,' she eventually said.

Christ, we're back here again? Have you forgotten we had this conversation just before and didn't get anywhere? 'Well, perhaps if I had some certainty like everyone else.'

'Perhaps there's something else you want to do?'

Shit. Had Alice said something to someone about the shop and it had got around? No, he trusted her completely. He waited her out. *What's she saying? Where is she going with this?*

'What are you saying, Mum? Just spit it out.'

'Nothing, Rick, just thinking aloud. I'm sorry you and your father never really got along and that we weren't better parents to you. We tried. You weren't always easy, either, you know,' she said, getting up and taking their mugs to the sink and rinsing them out.

Don't put this back on me, Mum. He bit down on his lower lip so he didn't say the words out loud. Arguing and defending himself wouldn't help.

'Well, I'll continue keeping an eye on the stock, then,' he said, and got up to walk her out. He wasn't angry, he was disappointed. He reminded himself it was hard for her because she'd loved her husband – or had been very controlled by him, or both. But still …

'I'm sorry, Rick – for everything,' she said, pausing with her hand on the gate. And then she almost knocked him over – with both the shock and the force – as she grabbed him into a tight, uncomfortable hug. It was brief, and as she drove off, he was left staring after her car wondering if he'd imagined it. Sure, they'd hugged yesterday, but that had been him responding to her falling apart. This felt very different.

And then he started to wonder when she'd last hugged him. His wedding day, as they'd come out of the church after the ceremony? He frowned. What had she really been trying to say? Because he couldn't believe she'd driven down just to say nothing different from what had already been said. She had plenty of neighbours and friends in the district who would welcome her with open arms if she'd simply needed some company. Had he stopped her saying something new? He went back over the conversation for answers to his questions. No idea. And, no. He was glad he'd at least stood up for himself a bit – or at least not completely taken the bait and got angry.

Should he ring his sisters? And say what? Be reminded that they were grieving? No. He couldn't bear any more of their barbed, patronising comments. And until they made some decisions about the farm going forwards, there wasn't much else to say, or for him to do. He felt a tiny niggle of guilt over not being more helpful but was also a little relieved that it really wasn't his problem.

He made his way back down to the old dump. He might as well be sitting there thinking about things as up here in the house. Maybe he might make something worth selling, even. He stopped mid-stride. Shit. Where had that come from? He laughed. As if.

Settling on the drum again, he started to relax. As he sat bending wire randomly, just to do something with his hands, Rick felt the tension that had regathered start to seep away again. As he made random shapes, he felt content. More than that, he felt himself opening up, the shadow of his father disappearing. He wasn't going to let them govern his future, keep him jailed, grounded. He'd been treading water for the last few weeks, and for what? Damn it, if he wanted to go away, he would. *Maybe I will do something different. I can be whatever I want.* The idea of what that was didn't come. It didn't matter. It would in time. It had for Alice, and all the other people who had been changing their lives completely since time began.

Rick felt as if he were a house and all the blinds were being opened after winter and the sun was streaming in – warm and comforting, sanitising. It was the strangest, but also one of the loveliest feelings he thought he'd ever had. He tried to not let his mind move to what was next for him. He'd sit here for as long as he could and then think beyond that later.

Chapter Twenty

It was the morning after his mother's visit and Rick was just leaving his farm when his phone rang. He hadn't put it in the hands-free cradle so he pulled over to answer it. 'Danni Mobile' was lit up on the screen. *Uh-oh. No doubt I'm in trouble for upsetting Mum again.* 'Danni, hi.'

'Where are you?'

'On my way out to the home place to check the sheep and take a general look around.' *Being the good son that I am ... Why? Where should I be?*

Then he realised there'd been something odd about her tone. Danni was a nurse, she didn't get panicky, but that's just what she sounded like.

'Why? What's up?'

'Mum's gone.'

'Huh? What do you mean, Mum's gone?'

'Dead, Rick.'

'What?' A strange calmness came over him. 'How? When?'

217

'I think she committed suicide.'

Oh my god. No. Surely not. 'Shit. What do you need me to do?'

'Just get here. I've called the police and ambulance. They should be here soon.'

'What about Matilda?'

'She's on her way.' Rick stamped down the niggle of annoyance of being, as usual, the last to know. 'And of all the times for Owen and Matt to be away with the kids on a school camp. Look, I'd better go.'

'I'm not far away.' He put his vehicle into gear and spun his wheels in the loose gravel edge of the road before he got back onto the firm surface. *Jesus. But drive carefully.* He felt a little guilty at being relieved he'd gone for a walk, dawdled over breakfast and then checked the sheep on his place first and hadn't been the one to find her. Danni's work meant she was much better equipped.

How did she do it? Is there a big pool of blood somewhere? The thought made him feel queasy. He swallowed. *Or is there now a rope hanging in the shed – its frayed end swinging in the breeze?* He shuddered. He was afraid of what he might soon see. He took a deep breath against his racing heart. And then the guilt cut in again, slicing through his fear and other uncomfortable thoughts. He should have made his mother say what she'd wanted to yesterday. But he hadn't stopped her, had he? You couldn't make someone say something they didn't want to, just like you couldn't make someone stay alive if they didn't want to, could you?

Unfortunately, suicide was not an uncommon occurrence out here. Rick knew plenty who had chosen to end their lives, including Alice's dad. He didn't judge them. They had their reasons. But why his mother? She'd seemed sad and lost, a bit overwhelmed by where to start with running the farm and putting her life back together, but it had only been a bit over a week. Where was the woman who always said you had to give something a damned good shot before deciding it wasn't for you and giving up? She'd usually said this about trying new foods, mainly vegetables, when he'd been a kid, but still … *Wow. Fuck.* He rubbed his hand across his face.

After a journey that both took forever and went much too quickly, he rounded the corner and drove up to the main entrance of the house. He was relieved to see the ambulance and police car there. Adrian, the local cop, was talking to the two green-uniformed ambulance volunteers. Rick turned his vehicle off, paused to take a deep, steadying breath and got out.

'Hi, Moira. Hi, Ron,' he said. 'Thanks for being here.' He wasn't sure if shaking hands was the right thing to do or not, so kept his arms by his side. They were a husband and wife team he'd known for practically his whole life. *How hard must this be for them?*

'Hi, Rick, we're so sorry for your loss,' Moira said.

Ron's greeting was a nod and a mumble.

'Sorry, mate,' Adrian said.

Rick felt for these three and what they must have seen and had to do. He suddenly wasn't sure what *he* was meant to do. Had they just arrived, too? He was anxious to get inside and provide some support to Danni – she must be in there, right? – and also stay out here in the sunshine of the perfect spring day and not face what had gone on.

'Um. Where is … um … she?'

'Around the back. In the pool. We have to wait until CIB have been before we can move her. It's technically a crime scene until then,' Adrian said.

Rick nodded, though he was struggling to process what he'd just heard.

His confusion and concern must have shown. 'It's standard procedure. Every death not in a hospital needs to be treated as a crime until we know otherwise,' Adrian explained. 'A report needs to be prepared for the coroner. Unfortunately, we can't move your mum until photographs have been taken and evidence collected. We can't make any assumptions. Sorry to sound cold and unfeeling, but I – we – need to follow procedure. I'm afraid we'll be here for a little while yet, too – CIB has to come down from Whyalla. They're on their way.'

'It's okay. I understand. Thanks.' Rick wasn't really sure he did, but still … 'Where's Danni – she's here, isn't she?'

'Yes. She's in the kitchen. I've just spoken to her. I'd rather you didn't go in, or talk to her, until I've taken a statement from you, if you don't mind.'

Oh. 'A what?' Am I a suspect? Suspect for what?

'We need to establish the facts, a timeline,' Adrian explained, 'of who saw your mother and when, the last person to see her, how she was, her state of mind … It won't take long.'

'Right. Okay.'

'Shall we sit over here and get it over with?' Adrian said, pointing to the old wooden bench under the weeping pepper tree.

Rick nodded and made his way over.

'Okay, just in your own words.'

'Where do you want me to start?'

'When did you last see her? How was her state of mind, do you think?'

'She came down to see me yesterday. She's been lost, overwhelmed – said she was, was worried about what to do with the farm. Dad didn't leave any instructions, you see. But I don't think she was depressed – well, you know, not any more than someone probably would be after losing their life partner so suddenly. I guess. Although, I got the feeling she was trying to tell me something yesterday, but decided against it, or something … Is this the sort of thing you're looking for?'

'Yes, go on, you're doing well. What time was she there, when did she leave, try and remember exactly what she said, if you can.'

'Okay. Well …'

Rick did his best. She really hadn't seemed suicidal to him, not *that* depressed. He guessed that was the point – if people could actually talk about how they were feeling, that they were thinking such dark thoughts, then they probably wouldn't be in that dark a place anyway.

'Thanks, Rick. That's all for now. I might need to ask you more later, if that's okay.'

'No problem. I'm not going anywhere.' *Where do things stand now with the farm?*

'Well, I've got your mobile number if you do.'

Rick now wanted to ask a few questions of his own, get some idea of what to expect, prepare himself. But just as he opened his mouth, there was the sound of another vehicle coming. They both turned to see and then got up as Matilda's car came around the corner and skidded to a stop in the gravel back a bit from them.

'Oh god,' Matilda cried, running over towards them, clearly on her way to the house. Adrian and Rick both stepped forwards. Rick reached out and grabbed his younger sister by the arm. 'Matilda, stop. Adrian doesn't want you going in until he's taken a statement.'

'What? Why?'

As Adrian explained everything, just as he had to Rick a few minutes ago, and most likely to Danni not long before that, he found himself thinking how patient he was and that this was not at all like the fast pace of the American crime shows he loved to watch on TV. On them, everyone bustled about, always busy. There was none of this standing around. Out of the corner of his eye he noticed Moira and Ron sitting in the back of the ambulance pouring liquid from a Thermos into mugs. They were clearly used to the waiting around and had come prepared.

'So, how did it happen – what did she do?' Rick heard Matilda ask. He turned back to listen to Adrian's answer. This is what he'd wanted to know.

'Are you sure you want to know the details?'

'Well, we'll find out eventually, won't we? And I'd rather know before Don in the butcher's tells me. Sorry, I didn't mean to snap, but I … You know what it's like out here – with the gossip.'

'It's okay. I understand. And, yes, I do. Okay. It will take a few months to know the cause of death. I don't want to speculate, but I can tell you, it's not gruesome, as far as scenes go. She was found in the swimming pool. In her bathers. Danni said that wasn't unusual – that your mother swam even when it's quite chilly?'

'Yes, that's right,' Rick said. 'Whenever the temperature got above ten degrees, she swam.' That might be the only thing considered unusual about Maureen, he thought now.

'So there's no blood?' Matilda asked.

'No.'

'Oh, thank goodness for that.'

'Hang on, you asked about medication before,' Rick said. 'Did she take a heap of pills or something? Is that why Danni told me she thought it was suicide?'

'We did find some packets and bottles, yes. I need to phone the doctors to see what she was prescribed.'

'Oh. I don't know what she would have been taking,' Matilda said. 'Mum didn't discuss anything too personal, really.'

'It's okay, phoning the doctors and pharmacists is part of the investigation. Once I've taken your statement, I'll get onto that.'

'Oh. Right. Okay. Should we do mine now?'

'If that's okay with you? Rick, sorry, but I'll need you to move away. Perhaps go in and check on Danni? Though, again, as I said earlier, please don't go out to the pool.'

Rick made his way into the kitchen. Danni was sitting at the table doing something on her phone. She stood up as he entered. Her face was red and there were glistening lines down both of her cheeks. He moved towards her. If there was a time in their lives for a hug, this would be it, he thought. But she held up her phone as if to put a physical barrier between them.

'Did you know she was taking sleeping pills?' Danni said.

'No. Did you?'

'Of course not. God, why didn't she talk to me, or at least one of us? If she was ...?' *Because we don't talk, not like that, remember, we never have?*

'Have you spoken to Adrian?'

'Yes. Matilda's out there now doing her statement.'

'Did you see ... um ... Mum's ... um?'

'Body?'

Rick nodded.

'Of course I did, Rick, I'm the one who found her, remember?'

'Oh. Yeah. Of course. Sorry.'

So, this was going to be his fault, too. He softened a little. She was upset. He couldn't take it personally.

'Poor Moira and Ron having to wait around out there.'

'I did offer them a cup of tea and to wait inside,' Danni said.

'I guess they're used to waiting around,' Rick said with a shrug. He wished he was outside with them. The house felt oppressive, the large kitchen tiny.

'She left a note,' she said quietly, almost in a whisper. 'But I'm not sure if it's a suicide note or not.'

'Oh. Right. Wow.' He hadn't thought to ask Adrian. *Would he have told me, anyway?*

'Adrian has the original, but I took a photo of it while I was waiting.'

'Okay.' Rick cursed his suddenly very limited vocabulary.

'It's okay, I told Adrian I had. I don't know what it means, though. Here.' She brought it up on her phone and handed it to Rick. He frowned as he read. He could see what she meant. It was odd and left more questions than provided answers.

Dear Rick,

I'm sorry. I wanted to tell you yesterday, about everything. I tried to, I really did. But I should have told you a long time ago. Your father didn't want me to. And I'm sorry I wasn't strong enough to do it myself. It was all so long ago, and I agonised over whether it was best to let sleeping dogs lie or not. I'm sorry we failed you – Joseph and I. We thought we were doing the right thing by you. But we didn't let you be you. Perhaps we shouldn't have …

The handwriting was firm, neat and straight on the unlined page and then stopped abruptly.

'Why just you? What do you think she's on about?' Danni asked.

'I'm stuffed if I know.'

'Jesus, damn it – could she be more cryptic?'

'And she's not apologising to *us*. Thanks a lot, Mum.'

'Danni, I don't think it's a suicide note. Well, it could be, but …'

It's to me; not everything is about you, Danni. God, why couldn't she have finished the damned letter or just bloody well said whatever it was to him yesterday?

He knew Alice didn't think her dad selfish for committing suicide, but right then he did think his mother was. How could she have left it like this? He felt the anger building up in him. You bloody coward! He took a deep breath. Ranting and raving – even if he managed to keep it inside his head – wouldn't help anything. She'd done her best, and she hadn't been able to make herself do any more. He had to have empathy for the pain she must have been in, even if he didn't understand what she was on about. He racked his brain for some answers, looking for a fragment of memory of something – a part conversation started long ago, a hint … But there was nothing.

Maybe Mum's Will has some answers, he thought, but didn't want to look like the greedy gold-digger by being the first to mention it, so kept the comment to himself. Though, did it matter? Something told him whatever she was trying to say – whatever secret had been hidden – was bigger than the farms. A slow, uneasy feeling roamed around inside of him. *What had she been trying to say?*

'Perhaps we should start going through the office,' he said. 'I don't want to sit around doing nothing.' *I've been doing that since Dad died.* 'And Adrian said it's only the pool that's off-limits.'

'Don't you think we should just wait until Adrian and the CIB people have been and gone? Just to make sure?'

'I'm sure Adrian would have said. Hang on, I think I can hear a vehicle.' They both tilted their heads. Seconds later a young woman and an older man in black suits came in, dragging latex gloves onto their hands as they did.

'This is Rick Peterson and Danni Smith,' Adrian said from behind the newcomers. 'Rick, Danni, this is Detective Sergeant Ros Makin and Senior Sergeant Gary Hill from Whyalla CIB.'

'We're sorry for your loss,' they said together.

'Thank you.'

'We won't take too long and then be out of your way,' Detective Makin said, clearly itching to get on with things. Senior Sergeant Hill was taking photos of the kitchen.

'Just through there and then down the hall all the way, out the door, and then to your right,' Adrian said. When the other officers remained where they were, he led the way out of the kitchen and into the hall. Rick listened as their voices and heavy footsteps became fainter and then the clunk as the front door was pulled closed behind them.

'I don't know about you two, but I need a cup of tea,' Danni said, putting on the kettle.

'I need something stronger than tea,' Rick said with a sigh as he sat down.

'Yeah, me too,' Matilda said, also taking a seat at the table. 'God, how horrible.'

'Yeah.'

'So, did you know about the big secret?' Danni said, looking at Matilda from where she leant back against the edge of the Laminex bench top.

'What big secret?' she asked, looking from Rick to Danni.

Rick shrugged. 'She left a note. Danni has a photo of it.'

'Well, hand it over. What's it say?'

Danni handed her phone over.

'It's not exactly a suicide note, is it? Not *clearly* a suicide note, I mean.'

'No,' Rick and Danni said in unison.

'Nope, not a clue. It makes no sense to me,' she said, frowning, staring at the picture, clearly reading the contents of the note several times. 'She must have gone and had a swim to figure out the next bit,' she said. 'That's what it looks like to me,' she said with a decisive nod, and handed the phone back to Danni.

No shit, Sherlock, Rick thought. He wanted to leave. Just walk away. Get in his car and drive to Ballarat. Another funeral to organise. A house full of shit to go through. He didn't want to face any of it. Right now, he felt he could even walk away without finding out the contents of her Will – find out if he was finally going to be treated in the usual way the only sons of farmers were treated and inherit the farm, farms plural. His head felt over-full. There wasn't enough air or space in the room for him to fully catch his breath or clear his mind, but he knew he'd feel the same outside, so he stayed put. At least here, like this, he didn't need to worry about his legs letting him down.

They sat mainly in silence. It was about an hour during which Rick couldn't even have told anyone what he'd been thinking, other than reminding himself to sip the tea that he'd dumped several large teaspoons of sugar into, prompted by Danni. It was too sweet when it hit his tongue, sickly almost, but he drank it, and as he did, started to feel a little better, less fraught. When Matilda got up and stood by the kettle and held out her hands for their mugs for a second cup he complied. Doing something was good. Rick tried not to think about what was going on outside by the pool. He figured they all were.

Suddenly Adrian appeared in the doorway from the hall. 'Just letting you know we're just finishing up now. Then we'll be out of your hair,' he said.

'Can we go out there now?' Danni asked.

'Yes, we've finished our investigation. The house is yours again, to do with as you wish.'

'What about Mum's body?' Matilda asked, frowning. 'Can we see her?'

'If you like. She's just being taken out and put into the ambulance now. I'll get them to wait – go out to where they were parked before,' he said, and walked back out into the hall. Rick glanced at the kitchen clock and was surprised an hour had passed – a little over two since he'd left home.

Just then they heard the recognisable voices of Moira and Ron talking to each other, working together, and the metallic rattle, creak and thump of a stretcher outside the kitchen window. They must have come right around the house.

'Rick?' Matilda and Danni said, prompting him from his stupor. They were standing by the door, looking like they were about to walk through it.

'Sorry?'

'Do you want to say goodbye to Mum?'

'No. I think I'd rather remember her how she was,' he said. He remembered someone once telling him they'd seen their grandparent after they were dead and then could never get the image out of their head or remember what they'd looked like before when they were alive. Rick didn't want that to happen to him. He couldn't think of a reason why you'd want to see a dead body – what purpose would it serve?

Chapter Twenty-one

'I can't believe Mum would do this to us,' Matilda said, sniffling, as she sat down in the huge plush chair behind the desk.

'Well, even if she didn't, she's gone. So we'll have to just get used to it,' Danni said, surveying the office with her hands on her hips. Rick stood just inside the door taking in the space, waiting for instructions from Danni, who had always been the one to take charge.

'Thanks a lot. Aren't I allowed to be upset?'

'We're all upset, Matilda. Go home if you want or roll yourself into a ball and lie in the corner – it's your choice. But I for one am going to try and sort through some of the mess and keep busy,' Danni said.

'Jeez, cold much,' Matilda said, a fresh batch of tears running down her red face.

'I care, Matilda, I just don't see much point in falling apart.'

'I can't help it, can I?' Matilda said, sniffling and gulping.

Rick looked from one to the other. *Should I be intervening? No, then they'll gang up on me like they always do.* He put a hand on Matilda's shoulder, to at least do something.

'I'm sorry, Matilda, but if I stop, let myself cry, I might never stop,' Danni said gently. Rick looked at his older sister. Her eyes were full and glistening. She cleared her throat and dragged her sleeve roughly across her face. 'Let's at least find Mum's Will and see if she left us any instructions.' She went over to the filing cabinet and pulled the top drawer out.

'The kids are going to be devastated. They're only just coming to terms with losing their grandfather,' Matilda said.

'Hmm,' Danni said. 'Here, go through these,' she said, handing a pile of files from the metal cabinet to Rick. He sat down on the floor and opened the first one. He was a little scared. A part of him was keen to go through the office that had been out of bounds his whole life. Another part of him didn't want to know what was in his mother's Will – if it cut him out or didn't acknowledge him fully or handed everything over to him. Either way had a downside. A selfish part of him wished he'd gone to Ballarat after all. He sighed. He was here and he had to do this. He sat on the floor and opened the file. He let out a sigh of relief at seeing what looked like a heap of articles about farming torn out of magazines and newspapers. *Didn't do paperwork, my arse.* It probably wasn't worth going through, but he would in case there was something important slipped in between the pages. And at least he was doing something that didn't require too much brain power.

'Did Adrian tell you Mum came to see me yesterday?' Rick said, turning each piece of paper over slowly.

'No. How was she?' Matilda said.

'She seemed weird. She said pretty much the same as what she wrote in the letter – sort of. And made about as much sense.'

'Why didn't you call me?' Danni said.

'Or me?' Matilda said, going through a file of her own.

'I didn't see the point. It wasn't really anything all that new. And I told you when I saw her out here the other day that she was a bit off and you said she was just grieving.' *And you weren't exactly nice about it, either.* He tried to keep the accusatory tone out of his voice, though a part of him wanted to snap that both his sisters had shut him down. But this was all hard enough. He hadn't figured out how he felt yet. Just figured he was in a state of shock. He kept thinking about his mother lying in the back of the ambulance on the way into town to the hospital. Someone – who? Or was he imagining it? – had said she'd then be flown to Adelaide for the autopsy. He really hoped Moira and Ron wouldn't blame themselves for not checking up on Maureen more this past week or so. No doubt that's where Danni's anger was coming from, and Matilda's overwhelming sadness – each thinking that if she'd had a better, different, relationship with her mother they might not be here, doing this. Rick felt numb. And, if he was being honest, a little bit antsy about what his future held.

'This place is a lot more ordered than I would have thought, given Dad reckoned he didn't write anything down,' Rick said.

'Well, he spent enough time in here,' Matilda said.

'Lots of these files are in Mum's handwriting,' Danni said, 'so she must have been allowed to be involved at some point.'

'Yeah, about thirty years ago I'd say. When they were first married,' Matilda said. Rick felt the hot creep of shame making its way up his neck. He'd done the same with Alice, let her set up his filing system and then basically cut her out of everything to do with anything. He'd been an arsehole on so many levels – and to his detriment. Beyond the obvious one of losing her completely. Too late he'd realised how clever and capable she was. But even if he'd realised soon enough, he probably still wouldn't have found the strength to admit it out loud. Anthea had helped him see he'd been threatened by Alice.

They'd been there for ages when suddenly Matilda called out from the hallway, having got up to stretch her legs, Rick supposed. He'd heard the floorboards under the carpet creaking as she walked slowly up and down. Most likely she was avoiding being in the claustrophobic office or was already bored with their task. 'Hey, don't you think it's weird that there are no baby photos of Rick? Like *baby* baby. There's none of him before he's walking. That's weird. How come I've never noticed that before? Have you guys?'

'Don't be ridiculous,' Danni said, getting up.

Rick stayed seated on the floor. He'd noticed it years back and had asked his mum. He knew the photos and their exact positions on the walls on each side of the hall by heart – he'd spent a lot of time waiting outside his father's office as a child, so badly wanting to be invited in and to form an attachment with his old man. Part of a memory was tugging at him. He froze as it dissolved again in an attempt to stop it going. He couldn't now remember what his mother had said the reason was. But he could picture her – the quick, nervous flick of her head, twisted mouth, offhand laugh.

'Further proof they never liked me,' he called now, trying to sound light, but failing.

'Oh, stop with your neglected-middle-child crap. I'm sure there are plenty and they just didn't bother putting them up. Or took them down to make space for the ones of the grandkids. Or maybe they didn't have a camera when they had you,' Danni said.

'Well, they had a camera when they had you – you're everywhere. And Matilda.'

'It's not a competition, Rick. Or whatever. God, we're going to have to divvy up the family photos. What a nightmare,' Danni said.

He could hear the creaking again as Danni and Matilda moved around. He pictured them peering at each of the dozens of framed images.

'See,' Matilda said, sounding triumphant.

'You're right. There's not one baby photo of him. That is weird.'

Rick tried to ignore them. He finished the folder, put it aside and grabbed another one. This one seemed to be insurance product disclosure statements. He didn't read anything, just flicked through and tried to concentrate on finding the Will. He suspected he was on a fool's errand, because the papers in the files seemed to be reasonably well ordered and subjects adequately grouped together. But he was okay with sitting with his thoughts and looking like he was doing something, contributing somehow.

He could hear the girls muttering, still moving around out in the hall – no doubt Danni trying to prove Matilda wrong.

He felt a sudden tug of annoyance at himself for not pressing his mother again more recently about the whereabouts of his baby photos – especially in the days since Joseph's death. Maybe it had something to do with what she'd been trying to say yesterday, and in the letter. He pushed the frustration away, got to the end of the file and put it aside.

The girls came back into the room.

'What if he's not even related to us?' Matilda said with a laugh. 'That would explain a lot. The alien child.'

'Don't be stupid,' Danni said.

'Don't call me stupid.'

'Well, it was a pretty stupid thing to say.'

'I was only joking.'

'It's not really the time to be joking, is it?'

'Stop fighting, you two. It won't help anything,' Rick said.

'Shut up, Rick.'

'Yeah, alien child.'

'What are you, twelve? And what do you two care that there are no photos of me, anyway? I'm the one who should be upset.'

'Are you?' Matilda said.

Rick shrugged so he didn't have to answer. *Not really. Yes.*

'You've been watching too many episodes of *Midsomer Murders* or *Criminal Minds*, or whatever,' Danni said. 'Come on, focus. I want to at least find Mum's Will. I have to get to work by six,' she said, checking her watch.

'You're not going to work after …?' Matilda said, staring at Danni.

'Of course. Me staying at home or here moping isn't going to help anyone. And Mum's dead, remember?'

Rick was a little shocked at Danni's tone. She was ordinarily a bit cold and aloof, but she'd practically just spat the words out.

'We don't need reminding, Danni,' Matilda said. 'I'm sorry if I'm being nosey, but I want to know why there are no photos of Rick as a baby. Ridicule me all you want, but something doesn't feel right about it.'

'Hey, I'm right here.' Rick attempted to laugh to provide a circuit breaker.

'Miss Marple,' Danni said, ignoring Rick, 'how about you put your detection skills to the test and help us?'

'I'm a little overwhelmed, to be honest. Sorry, Danni, but I think I'm just going to sit here for a bit. I feel sad.'

'We all feel sad, Matilda, but giving in to it won't help,' Danni said, a little gentler this time.

'Well, being stoic and not crying isn't helping, either. And it clearly didn't help Mum, did it?' Matilda said, slumping into the chair further and crossing her arms over her chest.

'I don't like being an orphan,' she said after a few minutes when the only sounds were the turning over of papers and the metallic thump and slide of the opening and closing of the filing cabinet.

'Well, you'd better get used to it. Anyway, you're twenty-eight and have two kids of your own. If anyone should feel sad and lonely, it's Rick,' Danni said.

'Why me?' Rick looked up suddenly. *Does she know something about the missing photos, after all?* He still couldn't shake the feeling that something was going on that was bigger than farms and the missing photos.

'Because you're single and childless. Duh,' Danni said.

'Hey, did you see Alice's single again now, too?' Matilda said.

'I did. We connected online again. And I spoke to her last week, actually.'

'Don't go getting any ideas. Never going to happen,' Matilda said.

'Yeah. She's too good for you,' Danni said.

'Jeez, thanks a lot.'

'Sorry, that's not what I meant. I *meant* she's clearly moved on. Bright lights, big city, and all. She's certainly no longer little Alice from Hope Springs.'

'I don't think she's changed a bit – well, not who she is inside. I spoke to her at Ruth Stanley's funeral as well.'

'Yes, ooh, that got tongues wagging,' Matilda said.

'As if I give a shit,' he said, rolling his eyes. 'This place … What they don't know, they make up.'

'What's the deal with all the stuff about narcissism and toxic families she's plastering all over the place online?' Danni asked.

'You'd have to ask her,' Rick said.

'Just because someone shares something doesn't mean it's directly relevant to them – they might be doing it just because,' Matilda said.

'It could have something to do with what she studied at uni or something, I suppose,' Danni said.

'Yeah, because her mum and sister are both really nice,' Matilda said.

It was on the tip of Rick's tongue to give his view on the discrepancy between public perceptions and actual lived experience – case in point being the eulogy they'd done for their father ... It also crossed his mind to remind them of this morning and why they were here. He was surprised Danni hadn't already. It was probably the most time they'd ever sat together in such a confined space without being at each other's throats. The reality would come crashing back in before too long. Who was he to disturb the peace?

'I was actually thinking of going to visit her in Ballarat,' Rick said. 'I would have been there now ...' *I wish I was* '... but Mum didn't want me to go.' *Oops.* He cringed. He hadn't meant to mention their mother – it had just slipped out.

'Ooh,' Matilda said.

'Not what you're thinking.'

'God, there's so much to go through. And this is just one room,' Matilda said, looking around.

'Well, if you'd actually do something, Matilda, instead of sitting there swivelling around on the chair,' Danni said.

With a sigh, Matilda started to open the first of the left set of three desk drawers, rifled through, shut it with a clunk, and moved on to the next one. Rick abandoned his pile of boring files and moved to beside her and, kneeling, began going through the drawers to the right side of the desk. The top contained books, a scattering of business cards and notes from his mother of who had phoned and why. *Why would he keep these and not just toss them in the bin at his feet?* Though there were so many strange things his father had done over the years that Rick had learnt to quickly dismiss. *Who would know?* had become a mantra in his head early on. He scanned the rest of the items – letter openers, bulldog clips, pens and pencils, random rubber bands and batteries, and assorted bits and pieces – before closing the drawer and opening the second.

It was brimming with stationery items branded with the different logos of stock firms and banks and insurance companies they dealt with or that attended the field days – pocket-sized notebooks, pads of paper, rulers, calculators – Joseph had been a cheapskate, so loved nothing more than getting a freebie, whether he would make use of it or not. In his pocket he'd always kept a small red notebook with a mini pencil tucked in the gap against its spine, and he used it to jot down prices stock had been sold for at markets and other notes. Plenty of instructions had been written for Rick and torn out and handed to him, accompanied with a sigh of frustration or a snide comment about him having the memory of a sieve.

'Speaking of Ballarat,' Matilda said. 'Here's a letter from there. Mum clearly knew someone there. How spooky is that?'

'Who?' Rick said.

'I don't know. I'm not opening it – it's addressed to Mum. Cute envelope, though. Someone's hand decorated it.' She absent-mindedly passed it to Rick, who turned it over. Whoever had drawn the series of mice running along the bottom, in various poses, had some artistic talent. He put it down beside him. Rather than being curious about what the letter contained, he was more interested in knowing who had written it and if who had written it was the person with the deft artist's hand. He found himself thinking about the sculpture he'd made yesterday and allowed himself to feel a little proud.

It suddenly struck him that there was no one now to comment on what they found in his shed and that maybe he'd do more of it. It all depended on what his mother's Will said. Or did it? Maybe he'd just leave this farming caper. Walk away. Maybe this was his opportunity to get out. Did he have the guts? That was the question. He felt himself deflate a little. Nope. Probably not.

'Who are these people, do you think?' Matilda said, looking up from the same drawer she'd taken the letter out of. Rick looked. She was holding up a framed picture of a couple.

Danni came over. 'No idea. Ancient ancestors?' she suggested with a shrug.

'They're in colour, Danni, so they can't be *that* old.'

'No, good point. They kind of look familiar, but then I think everyone can look a little familiar if you stare long and hard enough. The woman's about to give birth. Look at her – you don't get much more heavily pregnant than that.'

Rick held out his hand and then looked at the couple in the picture he now held and smiled. Both had hair sticking up and wore colourful clothes.

'How much fun do they look?' he said. When he studied it more closely, he saw their colourful clothes were paint splattered as well. The couple was standing in front of what looked like the gaping entry to a warehouse-style building made of corrugated iron – two-storey and with windows. Rick imagined by their slightly perplexed expressions – or mischievous, maybe; he couldn't tell which – they'd been unprepared to have their photo taken. It seemed an odd sort of picture to be framed. All the others chosen for display were more formal looking – posed. And this had clearly been chosen for display at some point – even if it was tucked away upside down in a drawer now – because it was framed. Someone had gone to the trouble and expense of putting it in a frame. And just like all the photos in the hall portrait gallery, it was framed in simple white painted timber. Maybe it had something to do with the fact the woman was not far away from giving birth.

He noticed Danni looked particularly thoughtful.

'What?' he and Matilda said at the same time.

'It looks familiar. No, not them, the brown floppy monkey-looking thing the woman has tucked under her arm.'

'You probably had one the same – you had *everything*,' Matilda said.

'Oh ha-ha. I did not. And, anyway, how would you know; you weren't even born until I was at school.'

'Well, you would have – seeing as you were always the favourite.'

'So says the youngest, most spoilt of all of us.'

Rick stayed silent. He was jealous they could banter and go close to crossing the line into insults, when he'd never been able to get away with anything near it. Must be a girl thing, was a phrase that ran through his mind at times like this.

'Say whatever you like, but that squishy toy is familiar. I've seen it before. And I'm pretty sure I never had one. I always had a small blanket, as far as I know, that I carried around everywhere. It's in plenty of those photos out there,' Danni said, handing the picture back to Rick.

Rick stared at it. Something about the people really was familiar. 'Long-lost relations or friends,' he said, and put the photo down.

'How weird, that all there is in this whole drawer is the letter and that photo,' Matilda said, pulling the drawer right out and inspecting it.

Rick's gaze kept going to the photo.

'You know, that bloke could be Dad – look at the ears. And the nose. They're quite like mine,' he said. 'See.' He handed the photo back to the girls, who were both now standing together on the other side of the desk.

'God, you're right. Though Dad would never have been seen dead in those clothes,' Matilda said. 'Shit, sorry, that's ... I didn't mean to ...' she lumbered before stopping and covering her mouth.

'It's true, though, he wouldn't have. Other than that, it could be him. Must be his doppelganger,' Danni said.

'You don't think he had another family, do you?' Matilda said, wide-eyed. 'You hear about that sort of thing all the time these days.'

'Online, right?' Danni said, with her eyebrows raised.

'Yeah,' Matilda said quietly. 'I know, not all you read online is true, blah, blah, blah.'

'Anyway, that man is around thirty, which is when we have photos of Dad with us. And I don't remember him being away *ever*, let alone regularly or for long periods of time, Miss Marple,' Danni said.

'Yeah,' Matilda said, sounding disappointed. 'Maybe Dad had a brother.'

'I'm sure we'd know if he did, Matilda,' Danni said.

'Maybe he died or they had a massive falling out before we were born.'

'I think we'd still have heard *something* about him.'

'Well, Mum and Dad weren't exactly warm and fuzzy,' Matilda said.

Glad it's you not me pointing that out, Matilda! Understatement of the century!

'Are you about to bring up them picking on you for your weight over the years?' Danni asked.

'No. I wasn't, actually. Why would I do that? Now of all times? Chill, Danni! I was just stating a fact. They never talked about the past or reminisced much at all. I never noticed, but now I think about it, they didn't. And, for the record, I've never been *fat* – not even very chubby, *actually*. I've looked at the photos. My husband loves my curves.'

'You chill. No need to get so defensive.'

'Well, you never got picked on, so what would you know?'

I did. I know all too well. And I stuck up for you, remember? Rick opened his mouth and then closed it again. He wanted to say he thought Matilda looked great the way she was, and always had, that it wasn't men who wanted women to be stick figures who were afraid of food – well, certainly not him. But he wasn't sure how to without sounding creepy or patronising, or both. And he'd never been anything but tall and lean without any effort, so what would he know? Yes, best he stayed well out of their spat.

'It was years ago – you were a teenager. It was just some gentle teasing to stop you from getting fat. Build a bridge.'

Stop being mean, Danni. It was mean of them. They were mean. A lot.

And then he had the strangest wave of realisation slowly make its way through him: could it be that the girls didn't feel like they fitted in either, that they didn't feel loved in this family, too – especially Matilda? Was all the social media posting she did that looked like – and he was ashamed to think this, but he had – blatant attention-seeking Matilda's way of feeling loved and included in a different family? Was she lonely and trying to be part of a bigger, kinder family while not causing ripples in this one?

It might be laughable to think what went on online might be less dysfunctional than the Petersons of Hope Springs, but maybe that was the sad truth. But now was certainly not the time to be bringing it up – anything for that matter.

'Maybe easy for you, *ice queen*. Well, I put money on him being a long-lost relative,' she added, defiantly.

'Unfortunately, we'll never know now,' Danni said. She'd returned to the filing cabinet and was flicking through files.

'Rick, do you want a copy of your birth certificate?' she said after a few moments. 'You may as well have it,' she said, holding out a clear, plastic pocket with a cream piece of paper inside.

'May as well, I guess,' he said, holding out his hand. Though he didn't see much point. He had the original back at his place. He glanced at it as he put it to his left to start a pile of things to keep. As he did, the word Ballarat caught his attention. He almost laughed at the coincidence before the puzzlement and then the truth caught up with him. *What? Why does it have my place of birth as Ballarat?* He felt his whole insides tighten. *How come I've never noticed this before?* And then he almost laughed at himself for being jumpy like Matilda. He *had* noticed it – when he'd gone to get his Ls maybe? Going for the first part of his driver's licence would have been the first time he'd needed it, wouldn't it? He remembered Maureen making some vague comment when he asked, but not what she'd said. Most likely he'd been too excited about getting his driver's licence and eventually being able to escape the farm on his own when he wanted.

He thought about other times he'd needed his birth certificate – ah, his marriage licence. He mustn't have really looked closely at it again. Well, he hadn't needed to, had he? He knew his date of birth by heart. But surely he'd needed to give his place of birth somewhere along the line too? He vaguely remembered the minister who officiated at his and Alice's wedding had copied details from their birth certificates into a book or onto a form. And he'd signed the marriage certificate. But he had been too nervous that day to read anything too closely. He studied the document further. *Huh? What?*

'Something weird's going on here,' he said quietly, frowning.

'Finally. Mum's Will,' Matilda said.

Rick looked up, relieved to have the distraction from trying to figure out his birth certificate, the details on which didn't make sense at all. It was starting to do his head in. Matilda was holding up an envelope and then handing it over to Danni, who slid open the flap and prised out the stapled contents. She read silently, with Matilda standing nearby. Rick watched: he was holding his breath. This was it, he suddenly realised. His whole future rested in their hands – literally.

'Okay. Hang on. Oh.' Danni's eyes were wide and she now had her bottom lip between her teeth.

'What?' Matilda and Rick said.

'Um ….'

'What is it?' Matilda said. By the way Danni was looking at him, Rick suddenly realised he didn't want to know. He was sure the look was pity.

'I'm so sorry, Rick.'

'Why? What's she done?' Matilda demanded, snatching the paper from Danni.

'She's left the farms and everything equally to us and just a hundred thousand to Rick,' Danni said with a sigh. Rick was glad he was sitting down. 'I'm so sorry, Rick.'

'What? But that's not fair,' Matilda said. 'But how can she have …? After all …'

'It's okay,' Rick managed to mumble. Though he felt anything but okay. He felt sad, completely deflated and hurt. Completely mortified, really – that was the term, wasn't it? He untangled his crossed legs and slowly stood up. 'I, um, just need some air,' he said, stumbling a little.

'Don't worry, Rick, we'll look after you. Won't we, Danni?' Matilda said.

But Rick didn't wait to hear the answer. He didn't want their pity, their charity. And, anyway, people said all sorts of things in the heat of the moment, especially while under scrutiny, that they changed their minds about later when it came to the crunch or after the dust had settled. He found himself having the inane thought as he left the room that he was glad the police had gone. He almost laughed at his next thought: *How much worse, or stranger, could this day get?* God, he wished he'd been halfway to Ballarat and blissfully unaware.

Chapter Twenty-two

Rick went outside and around past the cackling, fossicking chickens towards the dogs, not sure why. He found himself undoing the latch on the gate to the dogs' compound. The three large dogs gathered around him, half-leaping, scrabbling for his attention, licking, yapping. He patted their heads, ran his hands down their sleek coats. Gradually they moved away, realising no food was forthcoming. They weren't interested in him. This realisation hit Rick hard and his eyes filled with tears. He stood there looking around him. Why had he come out here? He'd had to get out of the house, away from the truth, but why here? He frowned. At least he could breathe again. He should probably go back. Instead, he went into the old chicken coop that was now the dogs' kennel and sat down in the corner on the bedding. Danni's voice saying what was in his mother's Will came back.

He felt a renewed surge of disappointment with his mother – not even what he'd been left, not much, in the scheme of things, but the fact that it showed her as being so under the thumb of her deceased husband. Would she have done things differently if she'd had time to make a new Will? He'd like to think so, but it didn't help him now. His whole being ached.

He found himself rolling into the foetal position, hugging his knees to him, in an attempt to ease the physical pain. His surroundings were quite putrid – smelling of dirty, musty dog, the meaty smell of dog biscuit crumbs. He ignored the inner voice – not unlike his father's – saying he'd get fleas. He should move. He'd end up stinking. One of the dogs – the female named Jess – came in and sniffed him. He patted her. She curled up next to him, with a harrumph, her back leaning against him. He took his hands from around his knees and put one under her neck and one over her. He could have imagined it, but he thought she snuggled closer. It felt nice. He stroked the dog in front of him. Jess. She let out a contented groan. He could feel her warmth against him. Right then it was the most comforting feeling in the world – like sitting in a car, safe and sound, in the sunshine during winter when it was cold outside. Rick felt himself relaxing inside and his curled position outside easing a little, a few pieces of his smashed heart and soul starting to piece themselves back together again. He was still sad and hurt and confused, and he ached physically, but it felt a little better. Sure, when he returned to the house, he'd have to face the ashes of the life he'd known, but for now he felt safe. He could think.

A memory tugged slowly and then revealed itself, as if someone had pulled the end from the middle of a ball of wool – pulling, pulling, pulling. It was like déjà vu. His breath slowed. The thudding in his chest almost disappeared.

Then he experienced a really strange feeling – both unsettling but comforting all at once – pass through him like a wave. Almost like he was having an out of body experience – not that he knew what that was like – someone else was doing this, sitting there, and he was seeing and feeling it. Was it a memory or just his brain playing tricks on him? Was he having a seizure or breakdown? Whatever it was, he felt so strongly that he had been here before – well not *here* – but somewhere like it: lying on a dusty, dirty floor, snuggling with a large dog, underneath something. In the darkness. He'd put money on it or swear to it in a court of law. It felt that real. Jesus. What did it mean? Was his subconscious trying to tell him something, trying to protect him from something?

Anthea had been big on trying to get him to listen to his subconscious, his gut feeling, his intuition, and acting on what it told him. He still struggled with it, truthfully; he wasn't sure he really got what she was on about. For instance, had it been his heart or his head telling him to go to Ballarat? Plenty would say it was probably the small head residing in his pants, but he knew that wasn't right. That had led him astray plenty of times in the past, but definitely wasn't now or recently. He hugged the dog closer, hoping she wouldn't feel too trapped – especially for a dog not used to such affection – and get up and leave him. Right then she felt like his rock, his life buoy, and he didn't want to let her go.

'Good dog,' he whispered. She moaned quietly in response.

'Timmy,' he muttered quietly. Then he felt a little startled. *Who's Timmy?* This dog was called Jess. The others were Ernie and Bert. Where had the name Timmy come from? He cast his mind back over the years. Nope. None of the Peterson dogs had been called Timmy. Another thread of memory tugged and while he tried to concentrate hard on it, pull it so it came free, he failed and it slid slowly from his mental grasp, the fragment of nothing much disappearing, leaving him helpless and frustrated.

'Rick!'

He lifted his head. Had he just heard his name called? Yes, there it was again. He didn't want to move. But he had to, didn't he? He sighed.

'Sorry, girl,' he said, patting the dog as he eased himself away from her and up. He really didn't want to go, but more importantly he didn't want to be found looking like he'd completely lost the plot and most of his dignity.

He left the small shelter and picked his way past the other two sleeping dogs sprawled out in the sun, trying to dust himself off. As he went, he thought about how Jess had come into the shaded, cool area to be with him rather than stay out in the sun. Just dogs and not part of the family, were they?

Outside of the compound, he turned to glance back. Seeing Jess standing there behind the wire with her head tilted, her tail waving from side to side, nearly sliced his heart open again. Tears rushed into his eyes. He longed to take her with him but knew it was probably the last time he'd ever see her again. He was most likely going to the city. She belonged on the farm – a farm. They all did. And right then he wasn't sure he could take care of himself, let alone a large work dog too. If his sisters decided to sell, their kids would love and make a fuss of the dogs. They might not be on a farm, but they would be cared for. Or maybe another farmer would want them – they were well bred and pretty good with sheep.

'There you are! Are you okay? Sorry, silly question. Of course you're not, but …' Matilda's voice trailed off and she shrugged a little helplessly.

'It's okay, Matilda, it's not your fault. It was Mum's decision,' he said as he followed her back inside.

'It's a lot to take in. We took a break to make some lunch – empty the fridge. Christ, what a day.'

'Ah, there you are,' Danni said from the sink when they came in.

'Can I just have a look at the Will? It's not that I don't believe you, it's just, something's bugging me.'

They followed him into the office.

'Just on top there,' Danni said, pointing.

'Actually, can you just read the bit about me?' Rick didn't think he could read anything, let alone comprehend it. 'Does it say Rick Peterson, "my son", or not?' *Am I imagining it, being paranoid?* On his way back to the house, a couple of the dots had connected.

'Huh?' Matilda said.

'Hang on, I know what you mean,' Danni said. She flipped the pages and read.

'Oh. Shit.'

'It's just plain Rick, isn't it – not "my son"?'

'Yes,' Danni said, clearly reluctantly.

'They must have made a mistake.'

'Lawyers don't make mistakes like that, Matilda,' Danni said.

'No,' Rick said, sinking to the floor.

'Is it that big a deal?' Matilda said, clearly baffled.

'It's a legal document, Matilda. Of course it's a big deal.'

'But what does it mean? No, surely not. But that means … No. It can't …'

Rick wanted to snap at her that it could be, because it clearly was and to stop babbling. Her chatter wasn't helping. He tried to remain calm and speak neutrally.

He picked up his birth certificate and silently handed it over. Danni took it.

'Oh,' she said.

'What? Let me see,' Matilda said. 'Hang on, that's weird. The parents' names on yours are different from ours,' she said, thinking aloud. 'What the fuck?' she said, her eyes growing enormous. 'How come you didn't notice that before?'

'I did, sort of, but I just thought maybe they were using different names – you know, people do …' He shrugged a little helplessly.

'Shortened versions, nicknames, maybe, but not completely different names,' Danni said, rolling her eyes. 'Hang on. I'm not listed as his sibling. You wouldn't be, Matilda, because you were born after, but …'

'Well, der, Danni. Anyway, the sibling section's optional. A couple of friends said they didn't bother. And, anyway, it could be different in other states. Sorry, getting bogged down in detail. Shut up, Matilda. Um, so he's not our brother? Like, seriously?'

'Hey, I'm right here. And, no, apparently not. Not your brother, not Joseph and Maureen's son.' Rick felt strangely calm.

'Then whose son are you?' Matilda said, frowning.

'These people – Beatrice Eleanor and Bartholomew Thomas Peterson,' Danni said, tapping Rick's birth certificate with her finger.

'So, who *are* you?'

'Stuffed if I know.' He glanced at Danni. She was always the one to take charge of things, when silence needed filling with practical things like instructions and sensible solutions or comments. She could be cold and blunt, but she could be relied on to tell the truth and not waste time or energy. They'd never really got on but he'd respected her as his bossy older sister.

There was silence while they all checked their phones. Rick figured they were running the names Beatrice Eleanor Peterson and Bartholomew Thomas Peterson through Google, just like he was.

'Nope, nobody who looks like it could be them,' Matilda said, putting her phone down.

Danni silently did the same.

'Though I'm not surprised,' Matilda continued. 'Earlier this year I was helping one of the kids in my class search online for information about some interstate relatives who were quite famous in the early nineties. He'd had the actual articles in a scrapbook, but a new puppy had got into them. Anyway, so we had really specific things to search for and still we found nothing. It was really frustrating. The National Library's online archives site, Trove, is brilliant, but there are gaps – whole decades of newspapers are still waiting to be digitised. And the newspapers we were looking at only had online searchable obituaries going back five years. Thankfully my student was going to Adelaide so could go into the state library and get what he needed off the microfilm version. We think *everything* is online, but it really isn't. Hard to believe there was a time before the internet, but apparently there was.'

Rick kept hold of his phone, turning it over in his hands as he wondered if he was more disappointed or relieved to find no mention of them on social media. He'd have been devastated to know they'd been going on happily all these years without him. He did another quick search specifically for Ballarat obituary notices. Nothing. So they'd died before the online records began? Or could they be still alive? Jesus, he hoped not: he wanted to believe he'd been here through no fault of his real parents. They were good, faultless; Joseph was the arsehole.

'Oh my god,' Danni said, and went over to the chair behind the desk and slumped into it. She was as white as a sheet – worse than at any time previously on this awful day. She ran her hands over her face and hair, over and over. 'I can't believe Mum would drop this bombshell and just leave us.'

'Well, technically she didn't drop ...' Matilda started, but one shrivelling look from Danni and she shut her mouth. Then she opened it again. 'Yes, sorry, not helpful,' she babbled, with an almost hysterical edge to her voice.

'But why wouldn't they have said anything? Why keep it a secret? It's not like adoption has the same connotations it did in the sixties and seventies?' Danni said. As Rick sat in the silence in the room that felt like all the air was being sucked out of it again, a strange calm came over him. Well not calm, exactly, he realised, trying to channel Anthea and put words to his feelings. Vindication? No that wasn't quite right either. Or maybe it was, but it wasn't exactly a feeling. Finally, there was a reason why he'd always felt like he didn't quite fit, didn't belong.

Christ, who the hell am I? His head began to pound as another thought tumbled in: *Do I want to know? What if it's bad? What if there's a reason they've kept this secret all these years – a reason beyond being secretive arseholes.* That thought hurt, made him feel a twinge of guilt. What if they'd done the right thing in adopting him? Had they, though? The girls clearly hadn't found any adoption papers. Rick felt a part of him trying to retreat – the part that wanted to know more. Maybe it was best to let sleeping dogs lie. That had been one of his father's – who was not his father, actually, as it turned out – favourite quotes. Was that a clue? But the stronger part of him was throbbing with the need to know. The cork was well and truly out of the bottle. He leant over and picked up the framed photo. And then the envelope that had the mice across the front around to the back where there was a Ballarat return address. He put his finger under the loose flap.

'That's private,' Matilda said as he pinched the letter and drew it out.

'It's a little late in the piece to be worried about that now, don't you think?' Rick said. Quite restrained, he thought, when what he really wanted to do was spray a heap of F words everywhere.

'I guess,' Matilda said with a shrug.

It was very short. The handwriting was large, looping but neat and clear on the thick cream paper. Rick noted the date and did a quick calculation. He must have been not quite born yet. Unless they'd somehow lied about his date of birth as well. God, where did it end? He shook it aside – there was only so much he could deal with right now. He read aloud: '*Dear Maureen, Please don't be like this. I miss you. We're family – they're brothers, for goodness' sake. We know you and Joseph don't agree with our choice of lifestyle, but we're happy. Why can't you be happy for us? What harm are we doing to you? Come for Christmas. Please! Let's talk about it. I'm begging you. Come on your own if Joseph won't. I'll pick you up from the airport – let me know. Please. Don't leave it like this. All my love always, B.* And some hugs and kisses.' *Jesus*, Rick thought.

'Oh god,' Matilda said. 'That's heart-wrenching. The poor woman is begging. Actually begging. I wonder what they fell out over. What do you reckon *lifestyle* means – that they're druggies or crooks, or something like that? Like, Dad was embarrassed or something? Though, it was his brother ...'

Rick almost scoffed aloud. Joseph Peterson had been a walking, talking pile of hypocrisy. Matilda was kidding herself if she thought family was like superglue.

'Hang on, that must have been around the time Dad's parents died. Maybe it's something to do with inheritance,' Danni said thoughtfully. 'Lifestyle *could* be referring to spending too much money.'

'I wish I'd known the Peterson grandparents,' Matilda said wistfully. 'I bet they'd have been nicer than Granny and Grandpa V.'

I doubt it, Rick thought.

'Where was the plane crash again?' Matilda asked.

'New Zealand,' Danni said. 'Queenstown. Before my time, too. Well, sort of. I think I was maybe one or nearly two, or something.'

'I reckon you're right. People only ever fall out over money or love.'

'Oh, honestly, Matilda. Generalising much?'

'Well, it's true,' Matilda said quietly.

'Okay, so whoever this *B* is, she's Dad's brother's wife,' Danni said carefully, clearly thinking it through as she spoke. 'Wow. I didn't even know he had a brother. And they clearly lived in Ballarat – well, they did in nineteen-eighty-six.'

'So are the photo and this letter related, do you think?' Matilda said.

Rick pushed back the clips holding the back on the photo frame in and took out the photo. On the back of it was more writing in the same large, round letters as the handwriting in the letter. He read it aloud: '*Bart and Beatrice all ready to start being responsible adults!*'

'I reckon they are. I think she must be Rick's mother – pregnant with him,' Danni said.

'So that makes us cousins, then, not siblings, doesn't it?' Matilda said, her forehead wrinkled tightly.

'Yeah, I guess so,' Rick said.

'It certainly seems that way,' Danni added.

'Well I'll still think of you as my brother!' Matilda declared.

Whatever that means, Rick thought.

'My whole life's been a lie,' he said quietly.

'It's not just about you, Rick,' Danni said. '*All* our lives have been a lie, really, when you think about it.'

But he didn't hit you when you were a kid and berate you for the rest of your life, did he, Danni? You got to go away to school and uni and …

There were so many things Rick wanted to argue, but his head was pounding too much. He badly wanted to go, get away from all the secrets and lies, learn the truth, start figuring himself out.

Because if they had hidden his real identity – as in the *facts* of his identity – then they'd also hidden his identity, as in his *personality*, too. All the cruelty he'd endured because he didn't behave right growing up, hadn't complied, had talked back, questioned things … He really liked the quirky outfits on the people in the photo – Bart and Beatrice. My parents. He stared at it. It might take him some time to start calling them that. And he reckoned the woman sounded like she'd been *fun*. Suddenly his whole being stopped as if dead. Were they still alive? And then his system started up again. *If they were, you wouldn't be here, silly.*

'I know I shouldn't say this, but Jesus I'm annoyed with Mum right now. And Dad,' Matilda said.

'I'm sure they had their reasons,' Danni said. And there was the Danni Rick knew and had told himself, convinced himself, he loved. The familiarity was a little reassuring.

Matilda repeated: 'You're our cousin? You were born in Ballarat? And your dad is, was, our uncle – Dad's brother – who we never knew about?' Rick could almost see the social media post composing itself.

'That's about it,' Danni said.

'So, are you going to go to Ballarat?' Matilda asked.

'God, what do we do about the farms?' asked Danni.

Rick looked at her with an expression he hoped conveyed his thought without him having to utter the words. *Not my problem.* He shrugged in order to make it clearer.

'You're just going to leave us, aren't you?' Matilda said, sounding a little scared.

'I'm not named in the Will as an executor. I have no owner-ship, which is fair enough given I'm not actually a blood son. It's nothing to do with me now.' *I've wasted my whole fucking life here: I'm not staying another day!*

'But we don't know where to start,' Danni said. 'We found the rainfall records, but that's about it. All those little red notebooks are just jottings and gobbledegook.'

'I can probably write a list of what's planted where at the moment, but that would be about it. The accountants might be able to help you with the money side of things. Call Warren Smith. He rang Mum about doing harvest and she was going to get back to him. He might even want more land to lease or buy, but that's up to you.'

'Jesus, what a fucking mess,' Danni said, running her hands through her hair.

Yup. It doesn't get much more fucked up than this, Rick thought. But at the same time, he could see himself fighting clear of it. He might have been cast adrift, but he was also being released. He could damned well do some art now if he wanted to. And he had a hundred grand – well, he would have eventually when that side of things got sorted out. Would they have to sell a farm to pay him out? He ignored the guilt that ripped through him. Perhaps they'd get away with just refinancing, depending how much equity they held. Or maybe Joseph had been sitting on a shitload of cash and it suited him to cry poor. Whatever. Meanwhile he had enough in his own account to tide him over for a bit.

'If it's too hard, you could always just put everything up for sale,' he said.

'God, Dad and Mum would have a fit. Turn in their graves.'

Had they both forgotten that it was just that morning their mother had died?

'Well, they should have planned things better – or differently, then. It's yours to do with as you want – the two of you.' While he didn't like seeing them stressed, he couldn't help feeling a little relieved that when he left it would no longer be his problem.

'Can you at least just write down the crop stuff you said?' Danni said.

'Okay,' he said, opening the drawer of the printer and pulling out a wad of plain paper. He drew a quick map of each of the farms with the paddocks and major landmarks and types of crop planted and where the three mobs of sheep were located.

'Here you go,' he eventually said, handing the pages over. 'You'd better take the dogs with you now and remember to feed the chooks until you decide what to do.'

'You're really going, aren't you – to Ballarat?' Matilda said.

'Yup.'

'You're not even going to help us with the funeral, are you?' Danni said quietly. That tugged at Rick's heart. How the day had started was clearly beginning to come back to her.

'Are you going to come back for it, at least?' she asked.

'I don't know. Probably not.' Rick thought he was more erring towards definitely not, but saying that wouldn't help anything.

'What about your place – all your stuff? You'll have to come back some time to sort that out.'

Nope. 'Yeah, I guess. There's not much – just my car and clothes, really, which I'll take. Everything else is yours now – furniture, the ute. I'll tip the milk out, but don't forget to empty the freezer.'

'Oh, don't be like that,' Danni said.

'Like what? I'm not being anything, Danni. I'll lock up and leave the key in the meter box. Okay?'

'No. Nothing about this is okay.'

'Could we pay *you* as a consultant? Can we do that, Danni?' Matilda asked, looking from Rick to Danni.

Rick shook his head. 'I need to go. I've wasted nearly my whole life here without knowing it, waiting to be rewarded, having my strings pulled. I can't do it any more, especially now I know the truth – well, a bit of it. I'm sorry, but don't be mad at me.' *Be mad at your parents*.

'I'm not mad. Well, not mad with you,' Danni said. 'I understand.'

'Thanks.'

'Well I'm mad!' Matilda said. 'How could Mum have done this – left us in the lurch like this?'

Now you might know a little of how I've felt all these years, Rick thought sadly. But he didn't say the words.

'There's always a place here for you if you decide to come back,' Danni said.

Maybe until you sell everything or the dust settles and you realise I mean nothing to you – even less than before – and you don't have to pretend.

'Thanks. I'd better get going.'

'At least have something to eat before you go,' Danni said. 'It's all out ready.'

'Thanks, but I'll keep moving. I'm sorry, but it is what it is. Look after yourselves.' Rick gave them each a brief hug – he was too close to falling apart to linger in their arms – and then gathered up his birth certificate, the framed picture of his parents and his mother's letter and its envelope.

When he left the room, Danni and Matilda were standing with their arms around each other. His heart twanged at seeing the tears rolling down their faces. *They'll be fine, they've got each other – they always did*, he thought as he strode through the kitchen and to the ute parked outside.

Chapter Twenty-three

Rick drove slowly, preoccupied with the jumble of thoughts racing through his brain. His name would be mud for leaving them in the lurch, but he couldn't help that. He just hoped Danni or Matilda might put the rumour mill to rest and tell the truth. Would they be too embarrassed by the actions of their parents and stay silent? That was up to them.

Rick felt like a big part of his soul had stayed at the house with them. He was hollow, completely empty. He supposed it should help to know the truth – well, part of it, anyway. Would he ever know any more? He couldn't answer that until he got to Ballarat.

His frustration turned him inside out as he thought of his mother – who was really his aunt – dying before telling him the truth. He really hoped she hadn't taken her own life. Why couldn't she have just finished writing her bloody note? Or, better yet, told him the other day? Jesus, how hard was it? 'Rick, you're not our biological son; you're our nephew on your father's side. This is what happened to your parents … blah, blah, blah and this is why you were living with us blah, blah, blah.' Stuff all the tiptoeing around. The silence. The lying by omission. For fuck's sake! They'd had more than thirty years to sit him down and gently tell him the truth! When he'd needed his birth certificate to get his driver's licence would have been the perfect opportunity.

The fury dug into him like a knife, twisting, turning, stabbing. *How could I have missed that? If only I'd been more observant.* Jesus, he was so annoyed at himself his mind was clouding red. If he'd known, he would have left. Got his licence and driven far, far away.

Oh, who was he kidding? He'd been as much under Joseph's control as he reckoned Maureen had been. They'd been his pawns. Arrogant arsehole. He probably only doted on the girls – well, other than the odd dig at Matilda about her weight. He had a gruff manner generally, but both of them had never really done any wrong in his eyes. Because they were blood. From his loins.

'Shit. Shit. Shit,' Rick muttered as the tail end of the ute swung out in the gravel on a corner and he fought to regain control. He'd taken it too wide in his haze, his inattention. *Concentrate, dickhead.* They were the words of his father. Jesus, he so badly wished he could stop referring to him as that – exile him in his mind and heart and soul. His heart was pounding. The last thing he needed was to have a crash and be stuck here longer. A part of him was a little sad to be leaving – disappointed, he supposed. But he really did feel cast out. Danni and Matilda would deny it until they turned blue, but theirs had been farewell hugs, not just saying goodbye to close the chapter of an awful day. And he wasn't being paranoid. It was the truth. He'd spent far too long ignoring how he felt inside, far too long telling himself he was wrong, giving excuses for what his parents and Danni and Matilda had said and done. Nope, when Danni and Matilda realised what they'd inherited they would only be in touch if they needed something from him – not that he had anything to give.

It would help that he wasn't around for any awkward meetings in the street by the post office or outside the supermarket. *Jesus. Supermarket.* God, wasn't he lucky his father hadn't left him money and he'd bought into the business Alice's family was selling? Not that he'd really taken the thought seriously. At the time, a part of him knew that maybe it was an attempt to raise the middle finger to the family by doing something different but staying in the district. It was mind-blowing how much could change so quickly.

Rick slowed as he came to the eighty-kilometre sign just outside of the town, for a fleeting moment wondering how he could be here already. He'd lost a chunk of time.

Oh. My. God. Rick was so busy staring at the *Welcome to Hope Springs* sign and fixated on his latest thought that he almost drove right through an intersection designated by a stop sign. He stopped just in time with a lurch, wheels partway across the line as new questions tumbled in, and the new realisation: how had this place kept a secret so big? All the oldies knew. They had to. They couldn't have not. What had been said? Had a whole town and district been capable of keeping this secret for three decades, when the reminder of it – Rick himself – was constantly on view? *This* community, when the moment someone so much as looked twice or for too long at someone else's significant other they were all over it, spreading the juicy rumour from the bank to the service station in a matter of minutes?

Had all the old ladies sitting behind the trading tables full of handmade jam, cakes, crocheted goods been smiling at him out of pity all these years, not genuine kindness? All the old family friends, churchgoers? Worse – had all the old barflies in the pub, sitting on the same stools they always had since he'd started drinking legally, known the truth too? Right then Rick thought he was as disappointed in the place as he was in Maureen and Joseph.

Fuck the lot of you, he thought. *You're supposed to be these lovely towns that are all kind and caring. Well, what about me? I'm one of your own.* The feeling of how he'd been duped, and for so long, how stupid he must have looked, made him feel physically ill. Where had been the gossip with the grains of truth being muttered about his origins so he'd get a whiff and begin asking questions? Why hadn't anyone got drunk and blurted out the truth? Even a hint would have been useful.

He checked for oncoming traffic and crawled across the intersection.

Oh. But, but of course. Maureen and Joseph. Two *of their own.* His parents – no, his aunt and uncle. *They* were theirs – the community's. And so had the older Petersons been. Bart might have been once, too, but he – Rick – was the ring-in because he'd been born outside. And for all he knew, the district had cast Bart out like Joseph had. Of course – that was how. That was why. Fuck.

And then he sighed. Maybe he wouldn't have been ready to hear it before this anyway. Just like Maureen hadn't been ready to tell it. He rubbed his face. *What a clusterfuck*, he thought as he drove out the other side of town, relieved to see no one he knew, not have to return any cheery waves.

Did the town know yet about Maureen's suicide? How long would it take? How long until word about his not being related was being openly talked about? At least he wouldn't be here to feel uncomfortable about whispers, mouths closing, knowing expressions, people looking down at his feet when he walked by, clasps to the shoulder by well-meaning but patronising old men who'd known the truth all along, but were now allowed to talk about it. Or, worse, would they blame him for her death – think he'd somehow made her do it? Would the police?

No. He had to let it go.

Anthea would say people don't give us as much thought or time as we think or worry they do. Though, maybe she'd never been part of a small district or target of a widespread conspiracy to keep a lie from one person. It wasn't her fault. And if it hadn't been for her, he'd probably be driving off the nearest cliff right about now, unable to handle what he'd learnt today.

Anthea was always a little cryptic, but he was beginning to see why that was important. If she'd told him straight instead of him figuring some of these things out for himself slowly, gradually – the puzzle pieces finally slotting into place after being pushed and prodded gently and turned around and looked at from several different angles first – then it wouldn't be the same. If he hadn't arrived at his own conclusions, which she'd stressed were his alone, then he might have got angry at being told things he didn't want to hear and refused to see what was behind the words.

Words on their own weren't all that much, he'd learnt. It was the emotion, the intention behind them that held so much weight. So much really was like a book report you had to do at school – not that he'd been very good at them – where you had to try and guess the meaning behind the author's words. At the time he'd thought, maybe the author meant to say that and just that. And maybe some did mean just that. But people often didn't. He could see that now. He thought he always had, but had tamped it down, told himself to trust more. Mainly because parents could be trusted. And they were there to teach. Now he could see where he'd gone wrong. If he'd continued to listen to his intuition – to those feelings good and bad, the warnings – he'd be in a completely different place.

He wouldn't have married Alice, wouldn't still have been on the farm with his dad – um, uncle.

Well, you're free now, mate. He was a bit scared about the future. But when he thought about it, peeled back that layer, he had to admit he felt a little excited too. He was going to go and find himself. Maybe he'd find his passion too – what he wanted to do with his life. He figured he couldn't find anything worse than who he'd been when he'd finally gone to Anthea for help. No, he certainly hadn't been strong enough to deal with all this back then, just a few short months ago. Oh how badly he wanted to tell her. It was going to hurt to cancel his appointment booked for the next week, but it would be crazy to come back for it. Would she do it by Skype or on the phone? But maybe there was a reason he couldn't have access to her, too. Maybe he didn't need her.

Chapter Twenty-four

Rick sat in his car idling at the gate just outside the house that had been his home for around the past eight years. It was four-thirty in the morning and still pitch dark. Google Maps told him he had twelve and a half hours ahead of him. He was taking a risk leaving at this hour, when the wildlife was still active on and around the roads, but it was a chance he'd have to take. He probably could have left late last night, too, if he'd put his mind to it. He'd had to consciously stop himself rushing, not throw things into bags and then the car, but take his time and do everything in a calculated, orderly manner. The urge to rush kept rising in him – he was both running away and running to – but he kept pushing it down. He'd tossed and turned a lot during the night and was a little tired, but the nervous energy and curiosity had him wired enough that he felt safe to drive. He had his swag on the back seat, so could unroll that along the way for a kip if need be.

He did a quick final inventory of what he'd packed and if there was anything he'd missed or forgotten to do. The ute was locked away in the shed, every other lock was secure, he'd made sure there was nothing in the fridge to stink the place out, and he'd remembered to put the keys in the meter box like he'd told Danni and Matilda. He'd packed his clothes – grateful as he did that he didn't possess many – toiletries and swag – the essentials. The only piece of furniture he'd taken was the small table he'd made all those years earlier in tech studies at school. It was the only thing in the house he felt truly belonged to him. He'd carefully protected each of his old bottles with plenty of newspaper and placed them in a box. He'd also wrapped up the sculpture – more so it didn't rattle against something and drive him mad than from any fear it would be damaged – and packed it in. The boot, back seat and floor were all full. He had a Thermos of coffee and some sandwiches in a small Esky on the passenger's seat beside him.

Okay. Time to go. He was both keen to get going, and apprehensive. *You can always turn around and come back.* He knew he'd probably never do that, but this gentle comment to himself did the trick. Rick took a deep breath, put the car into gear, and pulled away without a second glance.

He drove slowly, his eyes peeled for any sign of wildlife still out grazing or moving about, holding his breath a little until he was on the highway. The last thing he needed was to hit a roo and wreck the car.

Rick relaxed a bit as he got settled onto the open highway. He forced his shoulders down. If he didn't, he'd be exhausted by the time he'd driven to Ballarat. There really was no rush. And, anyway, he now had to take extra care to listen to his intuition. He'd realised along the way that it seemed to process things slower than his brain. Bustle drowned out instincts. He hadn't thought beyond simply getting there.

***

Rick arrived in Ballarat right at the time he'd calculated. In addition to stopping for fuel, he'd regularly pulled over to stretch his legs and sip from his flask and snack on the sandwiches. He was glad he'd taken the time to pack some sustenance. He wasn't sure his churning stomach could handle anything greasy, which he ordinarily enjoyed when on the road.

He'd tried not to think: had focussed on the white line in front of him and the music blaring from the radio all around him. But every time he stopped the car and walked around in the silence, the occasional car whizzing by, the questions started: Had he driven here with his parents – his real parents? Had they dropped him off? Had they promised to come back for him, but hadn't? Or had Joseph and Maureen driven over and collected him from Ballarat? How had he felt – scared, excited?

He wanted to feel some sort of connection with this journey – the landscape passing by the car – but it was all just a blur of unknown. Maybe he'd arrived by plane and they'd driven to Port Lincoln or Whyalla to pick him up. Or even the nearby town of Wattle Creek, which had still had a regular commercial air service then. If by plane, had he been unaccompanied or had someone travelled with him? Had he even still been living in Ballarat when he came into Maureen and Joseph's care?

So many questions had bubbled around in the back of his mind the whole way. He'd willed memories to come, but nothing had presented itself. He'd probably been too young, anyway. He'd most likely have been just a toddler – that was what the photos in the portrait gallery back at the house told him. How many of his questions would be answered? Any?

Rick found himself holding his breath every so often as he approached the centre of Ballarat with its old buildings and wide streets looming large in front and all around him. He hated city driving – he'd driven across and bypassed Adelaide today. It had taken longer, but it was worth it not to deal with the traffic. But now he had no choice. He was nervous, excited, curious – a mix of pretty much every emotion was running through him, he thought. He was being super careful to drive carefully, but couldn't help noticing his magnificent surroundings.

Waiting at the lights he let out a long breath and found himself relaxing again. Considering it was a city, the traffic didn't feel so bad. Not at all congested. Perhaps it was the width of the street he was on. Looking around, he saw people talking together outside their cars and on the footpaths. Others waving. He relaxed further. It didn't seem a whole lot different from Port Lincoln – still friendly, but just bigger and busier. Though, no trucks. Ah, that was the other reason – the bypass. All the larger places along the highway were now bypassed by main traffic. It was sad, because it meant a lot of the meandering traffic wouldn't bother getting off the main drag and pausing their journey beyond the basic rest stops.

He kept finding his mouth opening as he gazed around in awe at the buildings. He couldn't keep his eyes off them. They were incredible.

Shit! He'd just got honked. He looked up. The lights ahead were green. He put his foot on the accelerator. He thought to raise his hand in apology but didn't want it to be misconstrued as him giving the middle finger or something. His nerves started jangling – a little differently from before. The corner into the street he had memorised came up and he turned, and then pulled into an angle car space. He rubbed his face. The long day and many miles he'd covered were starting to catch up. He got out to stretch his legs. A blast of warm air hit him. He looked up at the parking sign in front and had to read it three times before he understood what it meant – two hours, metered, until six. It was four forty-five. He should only need fifteen minutes. He didn't know how often the parking inspectors came around – they didn't have paid parking in Hope Springs, let alone parking inspectors, or fines. He didn't want to do the wrong thing so leant back into the car and grabbed a handful of coins from the centre console. He stuffed enough of them in the meter to get him to six o'clock – just in case – and after double-checking what the other cars nearby had done, put the printed ticket on the dash under the windscreen on the passenger's side.

Now, Alice. He looked around to check his bearings. There was the building she worked in. Thanks to Google, he knew exactly where he was and what he was looking for. He probably should go and find somewhere to stay first – go over to the information centre across the way there. But suddenly he was too exhausted to deal with it. He didn't have Alice's home address. Thank goodness she'd included the name of the law firm where she was working on her Facebook profile. He didn't want to phone her – wanted to make contact in person. Suddenly it felt really important that he do that. Before he talked himself out of it, he rushed to the pedestrian crossing. Halfway across he felt his heart beginning to pound hard. Was he doing the right thing? He hoped so. Seconds later he was at a glass door with gold lettering between a pair of bay windows. He opened the door and walked to the reception desk directly in front, noting as he did that inside was a lot newer and sleeker than the outside had suggested.

'Hi, can I help you?' asked the receptionist, smiling up at him from her position behind the tall desk.

'Yes. Hi. My name's Rick Peterson. I'm wondering if Alice Hamilton is available. She's not expecting me,' he added.

'Okay. Just take a seat over there and I'll check.'

Rick watched as the young woman left the desk and went down a hallway behind it. He picked up a magazine from a small glass table. Something about homes or interiors, he thought, but he was having trouble focussing beyond his tired, distracted vision, hammering heart and quivering hands. Suddenly this felt like a really bad idea. But he'd given his name. He couldn't go now without it looking strange.

'Rick!?'

He looked up to see Alice standing by the end of the reception desk a few metres away. He put the magazine down and stood up.

'It *is* you! Wow.'

'Hi. Surprise,' he said, shrugging self-consciously. He was relieved she didn't look annoyed or disgusted. In fact, she was smiling broadly. And then somehow they'd both crossed the space and were hugging tightly. Rick found tears filling his eyes.

'Oh god,' he said, gulping, 'you've no idea how good it is to see you.' He felt all his defences leaving him, but he was relieved the tears stayed where they were and then disappeared. When they broke away, he said, 'I don't want to disturb you. Sorry if I stink – I've just arrived.' He knew he was babbling a bit. He suddenly felt the need to sit down, despite having been seated for most of the day. He tried to ignore it.

'You don't. Did you drive right through?'

'Yeah. Fuck, it's a bloody long way,' he said with a laugh. 'Language. Sorry.'

'Well, you have come from the arse end of the earth,' Alice said, grinning. Rick wanted to grab her again and tell her how relieved he was that she was just Alice – the Alice he'd once loved, still loved but in a different way. No airs and graces. Nothing like her mum or sister. 'Jesus, you must be exhausted.'

'I am a bit.'

'Where are you staying?'

He shrugged. 'I haven't got that far yet. But please don't think I'm expecting to stay at your place. I haven't come to impose on you. And, sorry, I'm happy to sit and wait until you've finished work. Do you finish at five or five-thirty?'

'It's fine, Rick. I can leave now. I just need to get my things. Come through and meet everyone – they're really lovely,' she said, grabbing his arm and giving it a gentle tug before letting it go again.

'Firstly, Kylie, this is Rick, my ex-husband.'

'Hi,' they both said, and shook hands over the top of the desk. Rick thought the poor young woman looked slightly perplexed.

'It's complicated,' he whispered conspiringly to her. But it wasn't, really. It was simple. They were exes who'd managed to become friends again.

Rick trailed along behind Alice as she made her way down the hall. She knocked on the frame beside the first open door they came to. Inside was an older couple. They got up from their chairs when Alice spoke. 'Lyn, Peter, this is my ex-husband, Rick.' She led Rick in. 'He's just driven over from Hope Springs, where I'm originally from. He's only this minute arrived.'

'Hello, Rick, lovely to meet you,' Lyn said, coming over with her hand extended. 'Welcome to Ballarat.'

'Thanks,' he said. 'It's lovely to meet you.' He became a little embarrassed at how untidy he might appear. Thank goodness Alice was giving the explanation upfront.

'Goodness me. That's quite a trip,' Peter said, also shaking hands.

'Yes, do you need to use the facilities?' Lyn asked. 'Or perhaps you'd like a glass of water?'

'That's very good of you, but I've had plenty of stops along the way. I'm fine. Thanks, though.'

Lyn went to the door and called out into the hallway. 'Ashley, can you come in here for a minute?'

'What's up? Oh. Hello there,' the young woman said from the doorway, grinning broadly at Rick and stretching out her hand.

Rick stared at her and had to remind himself to close his mouth. And breathe. She had literally just taken his breath away. His heart stretched and quivered, as if on the end of a bungy cord. *Oh my god, you're stunning*, he thought, taking in her features – the cutest button nose on a friendly, open, round face, not too tall, gorgeous curves enhanced by her tight skirt, hair pulled back into a low ponytail, huge round dark brown eyes surrounded by unbelievably long lashes – while hoping he didn't look like he was ogling her or staring to the point of rudeness. *Oh my god*. His knees went weak as he stretched forwards to accept her hand.

'Ashley, this is Rick, my ex-husband. Rick, this is Ashley,' Alice said.

'Hi,' he said, just managing to pull himself together in time. He didn't want to let go of her smooth, warm hand and firm grip. But he had to. As he eased back, he wondered what Alice had said about him to these people, if anything. Again, he thought of what Anthea said about the amount of time people bothered thinking about you.

'Oh my god. All the way from Hope Springs – *that* ex-husband?' Ashley said.

'I only have the one, Ash,' Alice said with a laugh.

'So, what brings you to our lovely city – other than our lovely Alice, of course?'

'Ah, well, that's a long story,' he said.

'Well, welcome. We're delighted to have you in our midst.'

'Thanks,' Rick said, blushing slightly. He had the sudden urge to hug them all, which was really strange considering how rarely he hugged people in general.

'God, you must be shattered,' Ashley continued.

'I am a bit.' He liked how he felt he could be honest.

'How long are you here for?' Ashley asked.

'I haven't decided yet. You could say I'm on a one-way ticket, if I'd flown, that is,' he said.

'Brilliant. Well, you'll have to come back for a decent chat and a proper welcome. Any excuse for a bottle of bubbly,' she added when she must have noticed his slightly confused frown.

'I look forward to it.'

'Ash, you'd better get cracking if you're not to keep your date waiting,' Alice said.

Rick felt his heart sink. Damn it, she's taken. Of course she is. But then he reminded himself that that was probably best – he had other things to concentrate on.

'Oh. Yes. Great to meet you, Rick. Alice, let me know if you need to cancel breakfast tomorrow. Bye, all,' she added, and left with her hand raised.

'Come on, we'd better give these good people their office back.'

'Yes, I've just got a couple of things to tidy up before I start my weekend,' Peter said. 'It was great to meet you. I hope you'll drop by again. Alice, have a lovely weekend.'

'Thank you. Yes, I will. And you,' Alice said.

'Excellent. Bye then,' Lyn said, already settling herself behind her desk.

'You're welcome to come back to my place for dinner, if you like,' Alice said.

'That would be nice, but I don't want to impose.'

'It's not a problem, Rick. If it was, I wouldn't have invited you. I'll just grab my things. This way,' Alice said, leading them out and to the right and further along the hall before turning into another, similar office though this one had more filing cabinets in it. And a dog bed in the corner with a small brown and white dog sitting upright in it.

'Oh, and this is Bill,' Alice said, bending down and scooping the dog up. She held him up for Rick to see and he put his hand out for the little dog to sniff. He received a lick. 'That's your seal of approval. Good dog, Bill,' Alice said, giving the dog's head a kiss before putting him back down again. She clipped a lead onto his collar and pulled her handbag out of a desk drawer. 'Right,' she said, 'we're good to go.' He followed her out of the room and back into the hallway.

Rick thought to say goodbye to the receptionist, but the lights were off and the desk unoccupied.

Once they were alone out on the street, Alice grabbed his arm. 'Oh my god, Rick, what are you doing here? I heard about your mum. I'm so sorry.'

'Thanks.'

'I didn't want to say anything inside and risk upsetting you. What's happened?'

'She …' He stopped. People, huddled in a group, were making their way up the street. He and Alice moved aside to let them pass. He opened his mouth. But closed it again. How would Alice react to the word suicide? He'd never known of her having an adverse reaction before, but then he couldn't remember them talking about her dad's death in any detail, or about anyone else they knew who'd taken their own life. What if today, for some reason, it upset her? She'd been dealing with a lot of emotional stuff with her mum lately. What else had that brought up? She might be feeling completely differently about her dad now.

'Rick, sorry if I'm out of line, and I can sort of understand why you don't want to be over there right now, but is it really a good idea for you to be *here*? Right now, I mean? What aren't you telling me?'

'Do you mind if we talk about it somewhere else? It's just …' He looked around, feigning self-consciousness.

'Yeah. Shit, sorry to be so pushy. I probably just sounded exactly like Dawn – demanding to know what you're up to and accusing you of shirking your family duties, blah, blah, blah. Another habit I'm trying to stop.' She shot him a gentle smile. 'Sorry.'

'It's okay. I'm not trying to be evasive, but you might want to be sitting down for what I have to say.'

'Oh. Okay. Right. Fair enough. Well, I usually walk home. It's only about ten minutes,' Alice explained, clearly a bit flustered. 'But I'm guessing if you've just arrived you've got the car somewhere,' she added, looking up the street.

'Yep. I'm parked just over there,' he said, pointing.

'Do you mind Bill coming in the car?'

'Of course not. As if.'

'Well, I don't like to presume.'

Rick smiled at Alice's exaggerated haughty tone and flick of hair – the attempt to lighten the heavy mood. He had to hurry to catch up as she raced off towards the pedestrian crossing, Bill running beside her.

'Sorry about all that back there in the office, too – the scrutiny,' Alice said, as they waited to cross at the lights.

'It's okay. Nothing to apologise for. I thought they were all lovely. And very welcoming.'

'They are. I'm so lucky to have met them – found the job. Wow, so this is weird. You being here. Nice, though.'

'Yeah.' Rick smiled. Her slight discomfort was cute. 'I was going to go to the information centre to look at accommodation,' he said, nodding in the direction of the signage. 'But I think I'm too tired to deal with it. I've got my swag in the car. Do you think I could unroll it on your floor, or would that be stretching the friendship too much? Seriously, say: I really didn't come to impose or be a burden.'

'It's fine, Rick. Honestly. Might be best to get a decent night's sleep and then deal with it.' They crossed the street towards his car. 'I can imagine it's all a bit daunting – as well as whatever else you've got going on.'

Oh, you have no idea. Do you? Has anything come up online yet? It had taken all of his willpower, but he hadn't looked once since he'd left the farm and the girls the previous day. He'd also put his phone on silent. He knew there were messages – texts and voicemails – but he was ignoring them for now.

'It really is so good to see you.'

'It's good to see you too, Alice. Shall we pick up some wine and something for dinner? I'm guessing there's every sort of takeaway you can imagine around here, right?' he said, looking around. This street seemed to be mainly business houses and a few swanky-looking restaurants. He didn't have the energy for that type of meal. Another night.

'Nope. All good. I've got everything we'll need. Oh, except wine. Or beer. I'm fine without. I don't drink much these days.'

'Same,' Rick said. 'I could do with keeping a clear head.' He hadn't meant to say the words out loud, but there they were. Still he wondered if she had an inkling about his sudden arrival. Though, maybe it wasn't sudden considering they'd discussed him visiting before.

'You okay to drive?' she asked as they settled themselves and Bill in the car. 'It's not far.'

'Yeah, I'm okay.' Rick put his key in the ignition and sat back and turned to look at Alice. 'Alice, it looks like Mum might have committed suicide.'

'What? Oh my god. Jesus. Hang on, might have?'

'Are you okay to talk about this? Because we don't have to.'

'I'm fine. Honestly. But god, how awful.'

'Yeah. Danni found her in the swimming pool, and apparently it's not obvious what, um, happened. Though, I didn't look. Gutless I know, but I didn't want to.'

'I think that's fair enough. What would it achieve?'

They sat in silence for a few moments. Rick wanted to let it sink into Alice and make sure she was really okay. A part of it was selfishness, too, because he couldn't bear it if she was distracted when he told her the rest.

'It'll take a few months to find out for sure what's what.'

He watched as Alice stared at her hands in her lap, nodding slowly and thoughtfully. The silence stretched.

And then she swallowed and took a deep breath before frowning and looking back up at him. 'But that doesn't explain why you're here and not there.'

'Yeah. There's a lot more to it. I know it must seem weird – really insensitive of me. But I'm not running away – well, not like how it probably looks. Danni and Matilda know where I am.'

'I saw Matilda's cryptic post. Something about everything being a lie. I almost called you last night to ask what she was on about.'

'I haven't seen it – been staying off social media as much as possible.' He couldn't tell Alice it wasn't because he was afraid of being overwhelmed, but because he was terrified of seeing no activity or that Matilda hadn't tagged him.

'What's going on, Rick? Sorry, I'm being pushy again. You don't have to tell me.'

'No, it's not that. But I warn you, there's a lot to get your head around.'

'Okay. Got it.'

'Actually, do you mind if we get the driving out of the way first? Then I'll be able to think better.'

'Sure. Back out and then straight ahead, get into the right lane as soon as you can and then take the second right,' she said. He followed the directions, and in just a few minutes she was declaring, 'Here we are. Welcome to my humble abode,' and leading the way to the door.

Rick deliberated over taking his swag and overnight bag in now or getting it later, but decided if he sat down he might never want to get up again, so took everything with him.

'Welcome,' Alice said, again, now they were inside. She opened her arms out wide. 'It's small, but it does the trick,' she said, with what Rick took to be an apologetic shrug. Or perhaps she was suddenly feeling nervous and awkward now they were here and alone together. Having your ex-husband turn up at your work unexpected was a bit unsettling, he could see that. Should he have phoned her instead? Oh well, she hadn't had to invite him to come for dinner. But of course she had. This was Alice, lovely Alice, who always put everyone else first. When he'd realised, it was too late. He'd probably forever regret taking her for granted and disrespecting her.

'Seriously, Alice, I don't need to stay. There are plenty of motels — I passed three on the way into the city centre before. If it's a bit too weird me being here — us, like this.'

'It is pretty weird,' she said. 'Who would have thought we'd ever be here?'

'Yeah.' He waited her out.

They were standing at either end of the small room. He noticed movement — heard a sort of scrabbling on the floor. He looked down and smiled. Bill was on his back presenting his belly for

Rick to rub, both ends of him wiggling in different directions. He squatted down to oblige. 'He's such a great little guy,' he said, smiling and looking up at Alice while stroking the dog's belly.

'Yeah. He's the best,' Alice said, visibly starting to relax. 'Look, you've clearly got the Bill's approval, so you can stay.'

'Honestly, Alice, it's okay to change your mind. As I said, I really didn't–'

'It's fine, Rick, really,' she said, waving a hand. 'Sorry I hesitated: it's just I've finally found my feet – alone. And I'm really enjoying the solitude. I need to spend time on my own. You know how I've gone from one serious relationship to the next, the why of which I'm just fully realising, so I'm a bit protective of me – a bit wary of sharing my space.'

Rick opened his mouth to speak, but he closed it again when she held up a hand.

'Sorry, can I just say this?'

He nodded.

'I don't want any mixed messages, so, sorry if I'm coming on too strong, or whatever. I just need to know. You didn't come here for me, did you? This isn't some knight-in-shining-armour crusade to rescue me from myself? You haven't been sent by my mother to sort me out, have you?'

He found himself laughing – at the quote marks she was using with her fingers each side of her head and the seriousness of her expression.

'Ha-ha no, definitely not. None of the above,' he said. 'While it is great to see you, Alice, my intentions are honourable and more about me saving me than anything to do with you. God, that makes me sound like an arrogant prick. I will always love and care about you in some way, but as far as wanting us to be together again, no. I think if we'd had this conversation eight-or-however-many-years-it-is ago and agreed to remain just friends – without benefits or any of that – we would have been much better off.'

'Okay. Great. Good to know,' Alice said.

He looked for a hint of anything but honesty, and relaxed when he saw none. 'I'm glad you asked the question and we know where we stand, though. Sorry if this sounds mean, but me being here isn't because you are. It might have been a week ago, but now it's a weird coincidence. Can we sit?'

Alice waved to indicate the whole room and sat on the chair at the end of the dining table. Not wanting to put a huge space between them, Rick chose a chair around the corner from her and sat down.

'I've just found out I was actually born here.' *Well, not quite true. Realised. I'm an idiot because I didn't notice, but still …*

'What? How could you have not known where you were born? It'll be on your birth certificate, which you needed –'

'Yeah, yeah, I know. I know,' he said, rubbing his face, letting his exasperation show. 'Turns out Maureen was not actually my mother. She's my aunt. Joseph was my uncle.'

'What?'

'Yup. Yesterday my whole life imploded. I can't believe it was only yesterday. Shit, I feel like it was a week ago or even longer. We were going through the office and found some things.'

'But why not tell you the truth? Adoption has been out in the open for, like, *years*. Even Hope Springs is not *that* far behind the times. That doesn't make sense. Who does that? Sorry, I don't mean *who* in that sense *obviously* … Fuck, Rick. I think you'd better start at the start. And tell me everything.'

Rick smiled to himself. He loved how Alice didn't mince words. He was so grateful to her for taking some of the weight of his load. She hadn't told him he was an idiot, hadn't dwelled on his failure in the situation. He was right where he was meant to be and with the right person to help him through this – whatever he found or didn't. He wasn't alone – he had a team-mate. It was a long time since he'd had one of those.

'I will, but do you mind if I get a drink of water and use the loo first?'

'I'm so sorry, here I am interrogating you when you're probably completely knackered. The facts aren't going to change in the next hour or so, are they? Why don't you have a shower while I get dinner organised?'

'I'm happy to order takeaway to save you the trouble,' he said.

'No, I made a lasagne last night – all I have to do is put it in the oven and make a salad. Come with me and I'll get you a towel and face washer.'

Rick picked up his overnight bag and followed Alice. Boy was he glad he'd thought ahead and brought it inside with him. 'You know,' he said, pausing with his hand on the doorknob to what Alice had indicated was the bathroom, 'you apologise a lot.'

'So do you. It's actually a result of emotional abuse, I've discovered,' she said, a little sadly, he thought.

'Oh?'

'True story. I'm trying to stop the habit, so feel free to tell me – gently – when I say it unnecessarily. Okay?'

'Right. Will do.'

'I'm also trying to curb the "yes" person part of my character, so watch out.'

He laughed as she did that haughty head-flick again.

'I'll leave you to it.'

'Thanks.'

'We also both say "thanks" a lot,' she said, pausing.

'Well, I don't personally see anything wrong with being polite,' Rick said, smiling.

'No. I agree.'

Rick waited until Alice had left before taking his bag and towel into the bathroom and closing the door. As he got undressed, ignoring the urge to just sit down and give in to his exhaustion, he thought again how good it was to be here – not just with Alice in her flat, but in Ballarat. He'd said he was happy to book into a motel, but he knew if he was sitting in a beige room with nondescript prints on the walls he could well be feeling really depressed by now. He really didn't want to be left alone with his meandering thoughts. And he'd never sat in a restaurant alone to eat, ever, and certainly didn't want to cross that particular bridge either.

Standing under the water felt so good Rick struggled to turn the taps off and get out. But he was mindful of not using all the hot water and causing Alice any discomfort. As he pulled his jocks and then socks on he found himself marvelling at how things had turned out – just how spooky coincidence was. Ballarat, of all the places in the world. And here they were. Together. As friends. Being kind and gentle. If he was going to find out more awful stuff about himself and his upbringing, he wanted her beside him.

'Better?'

'Yep. Much. Thanks.'

'Sorry about there being no beer or wine. You probably fancy something now,' she said.

'There's that word again,' he said, smiling. 'Honestly, though, it's fine. I really don't drink much these days. And, anyway, I could go and get something easily enough. So, don't worry about it.' He stood beside her in the kitchen. 'Now, I'm going to say this as your friend,' he said, surprised to find himself putting a hand on her shoulder, 'I'm a big boy, I don't need taking care of.' *Well, I kind of do, and, well, it could be nice, but it definitely wouldn't be right.*

'Sorry.'

'And there's that word again.'

'Damn it.'

They shared a laugh. He gave her shoulder a squeeze and hoped she didn't mind. He was getting better at this giving affection without any expectation of sex business.

'Let's take a seat. Dinner won't be too long. That's your glass of water there,' she said, leading the way to the table and sitting down.

He looked over at Bill snoozing on his bed. 'I'm going to own a dog one day – an inside, pampered pooch,' he declared. 'Once I've figured everything out and got settled, that is.'

'Sounds like a good idea to me. Until you experience true pet ownership, you can never know just how much they add to your life. So, I take it you didn't inherit the farms, then?' she added more quietly.

'No.'

'I'm sorry to hear that, I know you …'

'It doesn't matter now. And, that's the one thing that does make sense in all of this.'

'Oh, shit, of course. That's right. I forgot about that for a minute. You were going to tell me the whole story – but only if you want to. Do you think you'd seriously give up farming?'

'I don't know. Probably. It's never been me – I've always sort of felt that, and now I think it's probably true.'

Alice nodded thoughtfully.

'Hey, what's happening with your lot and the shop?' Rick took the opportunity to change the subject for a moment. When he got started, he didn't want her jumping up to organise dinner. Best to have a clear run with no interruptions.

'Frank said he was going to call you about it. Did he?'

'Yeah, we did have a chat. I don't really think it'd be my thing – even if I was able to find the money. Anyway, everything's changed now and I'm done with that place – Hope Springs. I feel completely betrayed and right now can't ever imagine living back there again.'

'Oh, I hear you. I just can't believe it took you so long. Everyone thinks small country towns are oh so lovely … The gossip – Jesus.'

'Yeah, I wonder what's being said about me right now.'

'None of that matters. You're here now. Ballarat is awesome. You're going to love it. I'll dish up dinner and then you can tell me everything.'

After complimenting Alice on her incredible lasagne, which it was, and the perfect meal for his troubled stomach, he told her all he'd learnt, which wasn't really much and didn't take very long. 'I think that's all. I don't think I've left anything out,' he finally said. 'I'm trying not to be angry at Mum – um, Maureen – but I kind of am.'

Alice was visibly shocked by the story, and she read the letter slowly when he got all the documents out to show her. She said, 'I understand that. And it's fair enough. But to us, in the age of everything being out in the open pretty much, I'm thinking they must have had a good reason, something hard to talk about. Maybe not hard for us, but hard for them. Maybe they meant to right back at the start and something happened and then they never found the right time. I'm not excusing them. I think it's a shit situation. But, let's face it, neither of them was into the deep and meaningful. And we might be the generation who plasters everything online for the world to see, but the olds aren't like that, don't forget. Maybe Maureen was under Joseph's thumb and he didn't want the truth out. She's not going to suddenly behave differently after so long, just because he's gone, is she? Like us saying sorry all the time and me being a people pleaser and all those things that you weren't really aware of. She did try to tell you – twice – at your place and in the letter. I'm not saying that what they did in not telling you was okay, but perhaps don't be too hard on her. I don't think it will help. What's done is done, as they say.'

'It just hurts.'

'Of course it does. Feel what you feel and own it, acknowledge it, but don't let it control you or define you going forwards. God, sor– I'm rambling. That's so weird about the birth certificate. Unbelievable.'

'Yes, I'm an idiot, we've established that.' That was still the bit that Rick thought frustrated him the most in all of this.

'Don't say that. I bet that creepy minister we had knew something. You don't know how much smoke and mirrors went on to protect the secret. Actually, about feeling betrayed by the town, don't get me wrong, I'm not defending their antics on plenty of other things, but maybe, just maybe they assumed you knew the truth right from the start. In that case, there'd be no need to mention it. Remember that gossip is really only ever spread to make the person spreading it feel important – that they know something other people might not. If there's no perception of a seedy little secret, then there is no gossip.'

'But how could there never be a mention that Joseph had a brother at all? Like, ever. In all this time. Even if somehow – no matter how ridiculously impossible – the town had been sworn to secrecy? How come not one person in the whole fucking district accidentally said I sounded or looked or whatever just like my grandad or Uncle Bart or said that whatever happened to him, or his life was such a shame?'

'I don't know. And I agree – it's fucking weird. Creepy even. I think if we can find the circumstances around how you came to be taken in by Joseph and Maureen, that'll go a long way to understanding that side of things as well as getting to know the real you.'

We. Rick liked that word in this context. How good to not be alone in this? And he could see that what she said made sense. 'I'm pretty sure I don't want to go back for the funeral.'

'And that's okay. You need to start doing what's right for you, Rick. Just don't make firm, life-changing decisions you might one day regret until you deal with the emotions a bit. You said the body won't be released for at least a week, so you've got time to think about that. One step at a time. You *might* feel like going back once the hurt and shock has worn off.'

'My name will be mud if I don't turn up for that, of all things.'

'And so what if it is? Maybe it's time to ditch being so bothered about what people think and letting it dictate your actions. It's bullshit. It's ruled so much of my life. And I'm sure yours too. And, anyway, if you wanted to go back for the funeral and didn't want to be alone – I'd go with you.'

'You would?' Rick's heart swelled as he looked up at Alice. Dear, sweet, Alice.

'Yes. So, don't not go because you're scared to turn up alone and face the looks and whispers. Okay?'

'Okay. Thanks. You've no idea how much just you offering means.'

'It's a genuine, unconditional offer, Rick. You'll never know how much seeing your face at Ruth's funeral meant to me.' Rick was surprised and saddened to see there were tears in her eyes. He reached across the table and clasped her hand and gave it a reassuring squeeze.

'It's okay. I'm okay,' she said, shaking her head. He removed his hand after a gentle pat before things got awkward. 'So, we know you were born here and your mum and dad are actually your aunt and uncle and that your real parents' names were Bart and Beatrice. Oh, and that they apparently lived some sort of completely different lifestyle that was somehow distasteful to Maureen and Joseph, but probably more so Joseph – because Beatrice was appealing to Maureen. Oh, and, we have an address, where they once lived – One Crabtree Lane. Is that about what we know for sure?' As she spoke, she was making notes in her phone. He probably should be too, but he was still avoiding looking at his.

'Yes. I think that's about it.' Rick was so glad Alice was remembering to not refer to Joseph and Maureen as his mum and dad, too.

'Maybe one of them was an artist, given the cute drawings on the envelope and paper inside, though I suppose the stationery could have been bought like that. And being an artist wouldn't be considered a distasteful lifestyle, would it?'

'Who would know? I got the impression Joseph thought I was distasteful for just existing. He was an arsehole. He hit me a few times when I was a kid and never really stopped putting me down. I can't believe I didn't tell anyone. Should have had his arse thrown in jail. I knew it was wrong. There were all those ads saying to tell someone.'

'Because you were brainwashed, Rick. Where we're from, especially, or maybe it's just our families, but family is meant to be everything, remember? And you have to be loyal and go back for more no matter how they treat you.'

'Yep, and not embarrass the family name,' he said, shaking his head. 'I bet lots of city people don't know what that's like.'

'I'm really sorry it's been so awful for you. I didn't know it was that bad.'

'I don't know why I said that just now.'

'Because it's time – *way* past time. I'm also sorry I wasn't there for you enough back then.'

'That's on me – I didn't let you.'

'It's not the same thing, but did you know that a woman leaves an abusive relationship an average of seven times before she manages to leave for good? I'm just saying, it's hard to stand up for yourself, even in what you can manage to tell yourself is a relatively benign situation. So, don't be too hard on yourself.'

'And don't you.' Because Rick knew why she was saying what she was. And while it could relate to their marriage – and he felt ashamed about that – he was sure right now she was referring to the stuff with her mother.

'That's pretty much everything, isn't it?' Alice said, putting her phone aside and picking up the photo again. 'They look lovely. Fun. Interesting. I love her smile.'

'Yes. Oh. Hang on. Back in a sec.' Rick got up and went out to his car. At the open boot, staring down at the wire sculpture, he wondered briefly if he was doing the right thing before deciding it didn't matter either way. This was Alice. And he couldn't suddenly get up like that and then go back in empty-handed – he'd look like a right tool.

'Oh, wow, that's awesome. Did you make it?'

He nodded. Thank goodness she didn't say something like 'what a mess' or 'what is it?'

'I made it for you, actually. Well, I was thinking about you and …' He stopped and looked up at her. 'In a non-creepy way, I can assure you. Remember how I used to like fossicking in that old dump?'

'I do.'

'Well, I went and sat there and started fiddling, and … voila. This came out.'

'It's awesome. I love it.'

'Well, it's yours if you want it.'

'Are you sure?'

'Yes, but no pressure, don't feel obligated. If you don't really like it.'

'Rick. I'm being honest. Thank you. I shall treasure it.' This time it was Alice who laid a hand on one of his. Rick glowed inside from the praise. Was there no greater feeling?

'I've got just the spot,' she said, after looking around the flat's tiny loungeroom. She got up, taking one of the placemats from the table with her, and sat the sculpture on it on the little wooden box against the wall. 'There. Perfect,' she said, standing back.

'I like that box,' Rick said. He'd been admiring it since he'd noticed it earlier, but he hadn't said anything. 'It looks handmade, too.'

'It is. It's a house-warming gift from a friend. Blair. You'll meet him tomorrow at the market for breakfast – if you want to come along. You're welcome to. He's a good guy.'

'Your guy?' Rick said, his eyebrows raised.

'No. Just friends. Actually, I'm trying to set him up with Ashley – we're all having breakfast tomorrow. Four would be even better but no pressure. Think about it.'

Oh. A jolt of pain ran through Rick, disconcerting him. It settled as a firm, heavy ball in his stomach.

'I thought Ashley was on a date tonight.'

Alice laughed. 'No, that's our little joke. Her "hot date" is with a book. She's not long ago finished her law studies, so she's making a committed effort to get back into reading for pleasure. And having been on a couple of speed-dating events, she's decided books are a much better idea.'

Rick felt his heart move – like an ember with a tiny flame coming out of it, he thought.

'Can I get you any more to eat? No dessert, I'm afraid.'

'No thanks, I'm all good. That was the best meal I've had for ages.'

'I'm glad.'

'The dishes – would you like me to wash or dry? Or both? I didn't see a dishwasher, did I?'

'No. I'll dry. That way you can't put everything in the wrong place – not that there are many places to put anything,' Alice said with a laugh.

'No, that is true,' he said, smiling as he got up and collected their plates from the table.

Chapter Twenty-five

Rick woke and for a moment wondered where he was. *In my swag. On the floor of Alice's flat. Oh, that's right.* He was about to roll from his side onto his back but realised there was a firm, warm patch against him. And then the patch moved, pressed into him harder. And groaned, as if to say, stay still and let me sleep. Bill. Rick smiled, reached his hand out and gently stroked the dog. The little dog stretched and gave what Rick took to be a contented groan. He put his arm around Bill. And then they both lifted their heads at hearing movement.

'Oh, there you are, Bill,' Alice said. 'I thought it was cats you couldn't trust to be loyal,' she added with a laugh.

'He's gorgeous,' Rick said, ruffling the dog's ears.

'You two are far too cute. Don't move.'

'What?' The next moment Alice had squatted down and was snapping photos of them with her phone. 'We're spooning.'

'I can see that.'

'Sorry.'

'Don't be. He clearly decided you needed him more than I did.'

291

Yes, I did, Rick thought. He frowned slightly. There was something déjà vu-ish about this scene. He felt he'd been here before – well, not *here* in this flat and probably not even in a swag, but curled up sleeping with a dog. And not the smelly farm dogs like the other day. Was a memory trying to get out? He stayed perfectly still in the hope he wouldn't burst the bubble. Too late.

'How did you sleep?' Alice said, now sitting on the couch and looking down at him.

'Good. But I think I always sleep well in my swag. And I was exhausted. I'm pretty sure I went straight out to it. I don't remember Bill joining me.'

'That's good. Can I get you a tea or a coffee?'

'Ooh, yes, please. Coffee would be great. And in bed – even better,' he said, giving her his cutest smile.

'Don't get used to it. It's only because it's about two feet from the table.'

'Just kidding. I'll get up.' He looked at Bill, who appeared to be very settled. He glanced back up at Alice, feigning helplessness. 'I don't think I can. I can't dislodge Bill, he's way too comfy.'

'Ha-ha. Welcome to my world. This will do the trick – come on, Bill, breakfast.'

Rick laughed as the dog sat up with his ears pricked and then looked back at him before jumping to his feet and running to Alice in the kitchen where she now stood by his bowls.

'Works every time,' she said.

'I think that's my cue to get up,' he said, easing his way out of his cocoon.

'So, are you okay to come to breakfast? It's entirely up to you.'

'Um. I do want to go and see what's at Crabtree Lane and whatever else I can find out.' Rick was anxious to get started on his quest, now he was up.

'Of course. We can do that afterwards. Unless you'd prefer to do it on your own?'

'No. I'd much rather to have you with me. But I don't want to upset your day.'

'We can do both. I promise it won't be an all-day thing – just breakfast at nine-thirty. Blair comes in to do his groceries and get his fresh fruit, veggies and meat at the market and then visits some family. He lives out on a farm.'

'As long as I won't be cramping your style.'

'Not at all. You'll make it a foursome, which will be a better number anyway.'

'Okay. Great. What time is it now, anyway?'

'Eight.'

'Seriously? I can't believe I slept that long.' He wondered if Alice had been stuck in her room for ages trying not to wake him. He hoped not.

***

Rick gazed around him as they walked to the mall. He missed Bill's presence already, but agreed it was best he stay back at the flat since they didn't know how long they'd be after breakfast and looking at Crabtree Lane, which was also within walking distance. It was cool in the shade of the buildings out of the warm sun. He was calm. Happy, even. Until he'd remind himself why he was here and of all that had gone on in the past few days – past week or so, really. What a bloody palaver. But at least he was doing something about putting things right inside him. He was a little apprehensive about what he might learn but felt his need to know weighed more heavily on him.

'Blair!' Alice called, waving to a well-dressed bloke standing in the sun, and increasing her pace. Rick caught up and held back as the bloke and Alice hugged. *Hmm. Interesting*, he thought, but was relieved to find no twinge of anything negative within him. 'Blair, this is Rick. My, um, ex-husband.' Rick shook hands and returned his warm smile.

'Pleasure to meet you,' Blair said.

'Me too.' Rick found himself relaxing even more. He had an instant liking for this guy, who was around his age, give or take a few years.

'And here's Ash,' he heard Alice say a moment later.

Rick's heart skipped a beat and then a second as if mimicking Ashley's trot over to them.

'Hey,' he said, and was stunned but happy to be embraced in a quick hug.

'Ash, this is Blair. Blair, this is Ash. Ashley.' They exchanged coy handshakes and smiles. Rick felt a hint of jealousy bite, damn it, as Ashley and Blair walked off together, already deep in conversation, leaving Rick and Alice to follow. He stole a look at Alice. She seemed pleased with herself. Rick forced his annoyance aside. He was silly for even thinking it – had decided last night romance was the last thing he needed messing with his head. He had bigger fish to fry.

They went into a café and Alice leant in behind Blair and Ashley to tell the guy behind the counter her name and that they had a booking for four. When had she done that? He was so grateful she had and he didn't have to stand there like an idiot waiting while someone bustled about setting another place.

'So, Rick, what brings you to our fair city, other than of course the lovely Alice?' Ashley asked.

'Oh, well, um, it's a bit of a long story, actually,' Rick stumbled, distracted by the way Blair was looking at Alice. And was the dreamy look being returned? *If you think you're not interested in each other, I'm a monkey's uncle*, he thought. Rick focussed on his menu, decided on the big breakfast, and then put his small clipboard back on the table while sneaking a glance at Ashley, who had her head bent down studying what was on offer to eat. There was his heart doing weird somersaults again. Damn it. Out of the corner of his eye he could see Blair and Alice leaning close, even bumping each other with their shoulders. *Okay*, Rick thought, *maybe you are just friends. Really close ones, but just friends.*

'Sooo, Rick, do you care to elaborate?'

'Oh. Yeah. Um,' Rick stammered, searched for the right words. He didn't want to lie. But he also didn't want to bring down the mood. He kind of hoped Alice might jump in and rescue him, but she was clearly distracted. Thankfully, right then the waiter who'd seated them reappeared with his pad and pencil. Rick gave his order, followed by Ashley, who also ordered the big breakfast. When she did, his heart seemed to become airborne in his chest – bumping against his ribs. The woman was real – an eater – not one of these pick-at-salad types. Hallelujah. *Stop it, Rick! You're being a sexist arsehole.*

'I'm a sucker for eggs and bacon,' Ashley said. Rick was thankful she'd ignored his earlier lame response.

'Hey, preaching to the converted here,' he said, holding up his hands in surrender.

'So, you're the farmer, aren't you?' Ashley asked.

'Nope, not any more.' *That's part of the long story.*

'Huh, but, Alice, didn't you say …? Oh, I'm confused. Is there a drought on over there, like so many other places – is that what you mean?'

'There is a drought on, yes, though not to the same extent as elsewhere. But, that's not what I meant. Sorry, I didn't mean to be cryptic. It's just …' *Oh hell. Here we go*, he thought, as the words tumbled out of him. Thankfully he managed to remain unemotional. 'Sorry I didn't answer you before. So, the truth is, I'm here because I've just found out – by accident, actually – that my parents aren't really my parents and that I was born here in Ballarat.'

'God. You poor thing. And, wow, though, what are the odds of that?' Ashley said. 'That you were born here, and Alice is here now and ...' She stopped. Rick noticed she'd gone a little red. 'I'll take my foot out of my mouth now,' she said, and took a sip of water. Rick smiled at how she'd said that aloud when she'd probably meant to keep it to herself. *Hmm, cute* and *funny*.

He found himself reaching across the table and touching her hand and saying, 'Don't worry about it; it *is* all pretty weird – the whole thing.' She looked up and he held her gaze. 'Really, it's fine,' he said, removing his hand and waving it about.

'Well, just know, I won't judge you. We all have our stuff to deal with,' Blair said with a shrug.

'No, we absolutely won't,' Ashley said. Rick felt something on his hand and looked down to find Ashley's was covering it.

'So, if you want to talk about it – if it would help to tell us the whole story – I, for one, would be happy to listen,' Blair said.

'And me,' Ashley said.

Rick had the sudden forceful thought pass through him of *look where secrets have got me. Right here, actually.* Maybe because he was meant to be right here right now, with these people. Maybe there really was no such thing as coincidence. Hell, if this was South Australia, he'd put money on being related to either Blair or Ashley. The thought about Ashley raced through him in a cold flash. There was only ever one degree in the whole of the state. One step at a time.

'Okay. But please don't think I'm telling you this so you feel sorry for me. And I really don't want to depress you all.'

'Mate, maybe you should leave that to us,' Blair said.

Rick opened his mouth, and just as he did, their coffees were placed in front of them. He felt a little disappointed but wondered if this was maybe a sign he wasn't meant to tell them after all.

'Right, you were saying,' Blair urged gently when the waiter had left.

Rick told his story. This time it was a little easier than when he'd told Alice. He ploughed on through the wide eyes and gasps of Blair and Ashley.

***

'Wow, that's one of those fact-is-stranger-than-fiction stories,' Blair said.

Yeah, Rick thought. He felt washed out.

'I really hope you find the answers or at least get some satisfactory closure,' Ashley said.

'Man, that's rough,' Blair said.

'But also a little exciting to see what turns up,' Alice prompted.

'Yeah, and I've never really felt connected to farming like I thought I should have been. So, maybe I'll find my groove, too,' he said, taking Alice's cue to cheer the group up again.

'Where are you going to stay – Alice's place is a bit small for two,' Blair said. *Oh, so you know Alice's flat, eh?* Rick thought. 'You'll want to be around longer than the weekend, won't you?'

'I'm going to check into a motel or maybe a cabin at the caravan park.' Rick didn't want to leave Alice's – if he was being honest, the thought of it frightened him a little – but he also didn't want to wear out his welcome.

'You can organise that when I go to work on Monday. I think we'll manage to not kill each other before then,' Alice said. Rick felt relief flood through him.

'You don't want to be paying for a motel if you don't have to. I've got two spare rooms at my place. You'd be welcome to stay with me,' Blair said. 'I'm a bit over half an hour out of town, but you've got a car, haven't you?'

'I have, but …'

'Seriously, it's a genuine offer. You don't want to be going back to a nondescript motel room each night with what you're going through. But, it's entirely up to you.'

'But you don't know me,' he said, the thought and his slight shock at the offer slipping out.

'You have Alice's ringing endorsement; that's enough for me, mate.'

'That's incredibly generous of you, Blair. I really appreciate it. And gratefully accept. Thank you so much,' he said, reaching across the table and shaking Blair's hand. He was warm inside. And comfortable – like he'd come home after being away for a long time, or something. 'That box you made for Alice is incredible. I'd love to see more of your work.'

'Thanks. I dabble in between running the farms.'

'Oh. You're a farmer? Alice said you lived on a farm, but I didn't realise you …'

'Yep. Don't hold it against me. And, don't worry, we've finished shearing. Just waiting for the crops to finish. Then if you're still here I might see if you want to do a few hours – paid of course. But if you're leaving all that behind, don't feel …'

'Honestly, mate, I don't know what the hell I'm doing. Or feeling, really, for that matter. But I'd be happy to help out.'

'Let's just play it by ear. Here's my number and address. Easier if you use Google Maps to find me than me explaining it. And you can always call if you get lost. I'll be around the place all day on Monday, so just rock up when you're ready.'

'Blair, Rick made me the most incredible wire sculpture,' Alice said.

Rick felt himself blush.

'Don't, Rick,' Alice said. 'You might not feel talented because of all the years of put-downs and all the other emotional bullshit, but you are. And even if you weren't then, you're allowed to do something that is fun now.'

'You're welcome to have a play in my shed-slash-studio,' Blair said.

'As in a man cave?' Ashley said.

'Nope, not a beer fridge or large-screen TV in sight. Just a place to scratch an itch.'

'Sounds perfect,' Rick said. He had the sudden urge to get serious about some art. The creative urge was beginning to burn inside of him.

'So, where are you going to start looking for answers, Rick?' Ashley said when their meals had been delivered and they'd taken a few bites.

'Well, I have an address – One Crabtree Lane – on the back of an envelope from a letter written by the person I think was my real mother.'

'We're going to go and check it out after breakfast. It's not far from here, actually,' Alice said.

'Good luck, Rick,' Ashley said when they'd paid and were standing outside the café in the mall. She gave him a quick hug. He wanted to hold on and drink in the floral scent of her hair, but reluctantly let her go.

'All the best. I'll see you Monday, then, right?' Blair said after shaking his hand.

'You sure will. I'll text when I know what time.'

Chapter Twenty-six

As he watched Blair and Ashley hug and say how nice it was to meet, Rick was annoyed to find himself feeling competitive towards Blair, who was clearly a really good bloke.

Damn. In the jumble of people around them trying to get past and into the café and his trying not to stare at gorgeous Ashley, he'd missed Alice and Blair's farewell. It didn't matter. He'd seen enough before.

He loved seeing Alice so happy and carefree. It was sort of strange seeing her away from Hope Springs. She was a completely different person. No, that wasn't fair. She was the same sensitive, caring person; she just seemed more sophisticated. Maybe. She'd never act as if she were better than Hope Springs, but she'd definitely outgrown the place.

Rick reckoned he'd suddenly outgrown the place, too, to a certain degree. Not just because right then he hated it and everyone in it. And not just because there were no decent cafés back there. Or people from different places and cultures. Purpose, opportunity and bigger thinking seemed to be all around him here. Perhaps that was the hope of those who'd come in search of gold seeping out of the buildings. *All too deep, mate*, he thought, chuckling to himself. All he did know was that Hope Springs and district was all about farming and grazing and industry to support farming and grazing. It was a very small world. Here, now, he could feel his mind expanding, ideas firing. Nothing specific, but the beginnings of him changing inside.

'Hey. You okay?' Alice asked beside him, jolting him from his thoughts with a little nudge.

He blinked to refocus his eyes. He looked down at his feet in an effort to stop staring after Ashley and Blair, who were walking side by side down the mall.

'She's great, isn't she?' Alice said.

'Who, Ashley? Yeah, awesome.' He tried to play down his enthusiasm. 'They both are. I can't believe Blair offered me a place to stay, just like that, without even knowing me.'

'Yeah, he's a good guy all right,' she said, looking after them.

'You two are so not *just* friends,' he said, doing quote marks either side of his head and grinning.

'We are, actually.'

'Me thinks the girl doth protest too much.' *What does that even mean? He'd heard it said before.*

'It's complicated.'

'Isn't it always? Fair enough, though.' *She'll tell me when she wants to, if she ever wants to*, he thought, when Alice didn't elaborate.

'You look happy,' she said. 'I'm glad.'

'Honestly, when I can forget for a minute that the two people I trusted most in the world betrayed me, it feels okay. I love this place already.'

'You know, I've come to realise anywhere is better than Hope Springs. Not necessarily the place, the people.'

'I'm sorry I didn't support you more or understand what you were going through with your mother and sister.'

'I didn't say that to make you feel bad, Rick; it's just a fact. And, anyway, I didn't realise the truth of it for ages myself either, remember? I guess it's just something I had to go through. Just like what you're going through now.'

'Yeah. I guess. For what it's worth, Alice, I'm really proud of you getting out and making a go of things.'

'Thanks. At the risk of sounding like a complete wanker, I'm actually starting to like who I am.'

Rick smiled at her. He put his arm around her shoulders and pulled her tight towards him and kissed her on the forehead. It seemed like the most natural thing in the world to do. He was beaming inside. And quivering a little with apprehension about what they were about to do …

'So, shall we go and see what we can find?' she said, smiling gently.

Rick took the beaming sun and still weather as a good omen. He was thinking this and trying not to think ahead when Alice suddenly stopped.

'Here it is. Crabtree Lane.'

Rick looked at the sign and then at the street. It seemed Crabtree Lane consisted of just one block. But this was it, because he recognised the corrugated iron warehouse-style building set way back with a gravel area – for car parking? – in front. His heart began to race.

Alice spoke, but her voice was a muffle in Rick's ears, like she was miles away. He was experiencing the same strange, unsettling experience of having been here before. Not just because he'd seen pictures online of this building. But he *felt* he'd been here before. Inside him. It definitely felt like the right place for answers, but now he was here he was afraid. The question running through his head now was, *Do you want those answers?* He frowned. And then looked at Alice. Had she just nudged him again?

'Sorry?'

'Do you think we should knock on the door?'

'Um. I don't know.' Suddenly Rick was struggling to think any thoughts at all.

'Or we could call the real estate agent.'

'What?'

'Look, there's a sign,' she said, pointing. 'It's up for lease.'

Rick was glued to the ground but wanted to run. He didn't want to be here. He didn't believe in ghosts or spirits – though actually he'd never had a need to consider the question at all before – but something about this place felt oppressive. He was right on the point of telling Alice he needed to leave when a small door within the large door opened and a man in bib and brace overalls stepped out into the light.

'Can I help you?' he said, shading his eyes with a hand.

'Oh, hi,' Alice said, rushing forwards with her hand outstretched. 'Sorry to bother you, but I'm Alice and this is Rick …'

'Jack,' the man said, looking and sounding a little wary. Rick forced himself to move towards them. He was slow, like walking through thigh-deep mud. He put his hand out, ignoring the pull to turn and run. In the back of his mind were the words of Anthea – *There is nothing to fear but fear itself. Yes, and I owe it to myself to be brave, don't I?*

'I think this is an address where my real parents once lived – about thirty years ago. I'm adopted, and I've only just found out.' Rick was surprised at how succinct he'd managed to be.

'Right. Wow. That's …'

'Hello.' A woman came out and stood beside the man. They were a few years younger than him and Alice.

'Hi,' Alice and Rick said together.

'Sorry to bother you. We're just being nosey,' Alice said.

'It's a great-looking place. Are you leaving?' Rick said.

'Yes. We're heading further out into the bush where it's cheaper and to see what living among nature does for the creative juices.'

'Are you artists?' Rick said.

'Trying to be.'

'Viewings are only by appointment,' the woman said with an apologetic shrug.

'That's okay, thanks. As I said, we were just curious,' Alice said. She looked at Rick. Rick cursed his sudden loss of voice. Thank Christ she was here.

'We'll leave you to it. Sorry to disturb you,' he finally stammered.

'Are you okay?' the young woman said, walking to him and putting a hand on his arm. 'You're really pale.'

'Yeah. You are. Are you okay?' Alice said, looking into his eyes. Rick could only nod.

He swallowed and then managed, 'We should go, Alice.'

'Okay. Yes, we should.' But she didn't move. Rick, through the strange haze engulfing him, saw her hand move. 'Actually, you wouldn't happen to know anything about this place – say, from thirty years ago? Would you?' she said. 'I know you couldn't have been here that long, but anything you could tell us would be really appreciated.'

'Sorry, but we've only been here a couple of years,' the young woman said.

'Oh, but hang on, the old woman behind us – back there,' Jack said, indicating, 'I bet she knows something. I think she's lived here, like, *forever*. Just go back to the side street and around. It's a weatherboard painted deep sea green. You can't miss it.'

'Thanks so much. Nice to meet you.'

'Are you sure you're okay, Rick?' Alice asked as they made their way back the way they'd come.

'No, not really. I felt something.'

'Like what? Ghosts or spirits, or something?' They waited for a couple of cars to pass.

'I don't know. I don't know what they feel like.'

'No, neither do I.'

'Kind of like déjà vu, I guess,' he said. 'Like I've been here before.' Rick's insides quivered weirdly.

'Wow.'

They walked along the next street, which didn't seem to Rick to have many houses. There was everything but, and, what's more, the collection of small flat-faced brick warehouses and corrugated iron sheds didn't seem overly new.

So lost in his inane thoughts, which he'd deliberately tried to keep at the forefront of his mind to stop himself from going crazy or thinking too far ahead, he bumped into Alice.

'Oh,' he said, looking up at a deep sea green weatherboard house that was just what Jack had described. It was between two blocks of flats. Rick found himself admiring the owner for holding out and not selling when he betted a developer had already come calling – probably several times.

He took a deep breath against the strange push/pull battle going on inside him – he wanted to run far, far away, but also stay and hopefully find out the truth. It was exhausting.

'Okay?' Alice asked, turning to look at him, her hand on the gate.

No. 'Yep, fine. Carry on.'

Is she a recluse? he found himself wondering as the hinges on the green-painted picket gate gave a loud squeak-squawk as Alice opened it and then another as he closed it behind him. This gate seemed hardly used. He liked that Alice was treading gently with him, giving him opportunities to back out. But he was too close or at least had come too far now.

He walked with Alice up onto the verandah and to the door. He heard Alice turn an old-fashioned doorknob, making a bell ring. Rick gasped against the sudden realisation gripping him. Could my mother live here? He'd assumed she was dead, but maybe she wasn't. Maybe there was some other explanation for why he'd been in Hope Springs. He felt tears welling up from right deep down inside of him. Despite waiting for it, he felt startled when the main door opened and an older woman peered out at them through a screen security door. He almost cried, 'Are you my mother?' The words were dangerously close to the tip of his tongue.

'Hello?' the woman said. They couldn't see her very well.

'Oh, hello. I'm Alice, this is Rick. The young couple at the warehouse around the back thought you might be able to help us.'

'What with?'

Rick was surprised to find himself touching Alice's arm gently to indicate he'd take over. She stepped aside a little to let him get closer to the door.

'We're really sorry to bother you, but I might have some connection – as a small child – to the warehouse. I've driven from Hope Springs in South Australia – it's a million miles from anywhere. Would you happen to know or have known anything about some people named Peterson? They might have been artists.'

'Peterson?' the woman said, still behind the door.

'Yes, is the name familiar?' Unlikely, Rick thought, time seeming to stand still.

Are you my mother?

'Did you say Hope Springs?'

'Yes, in South Australia,' Rick said, and he and Alice were forced to step back as the security screen door was opened out towards them. The woman came into the light of the verandah. Rick estimated she was only around sixty. She was the right age, but he knew from looking at her that she wasn't his mother. Relief and disappointment both snaked around inside him. But he was left thinking, *Jesus, am I now going to be one of those people who look at everyone around the right age and wonder if they're my parents? That'll send me mad.*

'Let me guess, they told you I was old, didn't they – the kids in the warehouse?' the woman said, grinning. 'I'm Sarah,' she said, not giving them time to answer. 'You'd better come in.' Rick heard her sigh as he passed, but he couldn't tell whether it might be due to weariness, frustration or pleasure.

'This way,' Sarah said, leading the way down the hall, their footsteps echoing in the quiet space.

They found themselves in a small, old-fashioned but tidy kitchen with a row of windows above the sink overlooking a large cottage garden. There were several established trees out there, and a gravel path meandered down towards the back and then passed through what looked to be a stand of bamboo. The weathered corrugated iron warehouse looming high above provided the perfect backdrop.

'Take a seat.'

Sarah sat down and Rick tried not to look impatient. She clearly knew something, otherwise why ask them in? No more secrets, he told himself.

'You have a lovely home,' Alice said, looking around, clearly picking up on his anxiety. Or experiencing some of her own.

Sarah looked up, a slightly startled expression on her face. 'Thank you. It's getting harder to resist the circling vultures.'

'Developers, you mean?' Rick said.

'That's them. They don't seem to understand one has an emotional connection to one's home.'

'Fair enough,' Alice said.

'So, are you two married?' Sarah asked.

'Um,' Alice said. Rick cringed as she looked at him – was she handballing this little grenade to him?

'We were once,' he said, looking sheepish.

'That's too bad. But, still, you're good friends now, and that's what matters.'

'Yeah, it's complicated.'

Sarah laughed. 'And isn't *that* the catch-cry of the century?'

'It certainly is,' Alice said.

Rick smiled on, becoming calmer with every beat of his slowing heart as he did. He liked Sarah.

Sarah looked away and out the window, took a few deep breaths and turned back to them. Rick was shocked to notice that her eyes were now red with tears glistening on the edges of her lids and ready to spill. His heart somersaulted, but something made him hold her gaze. He swallowed and took a silent but deep breath of his own.

'You're little Ricky Peterson, aren't you?'

'Yes, I think I might be,' he whispered. 'But I don't really know *who* I am. I've only just found out I'm adopted.'

'Oh dear.'

Tears rushed into Rick's own eyes and a hard, painful lump rose up in his throat. When Sarah put a hand over his, the dam of information and answers he'd been seeking broke. He let out a loud gasp that he only suspected had come from him because his mouth was open, and he began to sob. He couldn't stop himself: no matter how many times he tried to gulp it back, swallow it down, it just made things worse. He didn't notice Sarah or Alice get up, or any movement, but suddenly he felt arms wrapped around his shoulders and a head against his neck – he knew it wasn't Alice. And then words being whispered, quietly, calmly. Soothing words.

'It's okay. Let it out. You're home now.' Or perhaps he was mistaken. Perhaps that was what he wanted to hear. *Home?*

Chapter Twenty-seven

Somehow being told to let it out caused the opposite effect in Rick, and gradually his tears stopped, and he was left feeling raw and red-eyed and with a drippy nose. He searched his pockets for a tissue and came up empty. And then a box was being pushed across the table by Alice.

'Oh god, I'm so sorry about that,' he stammered. 'I don't know what happened.'

'Tears are healthy, tears are good,' Sarah said, sounding very much like Anthea. 'The real-men-don't-cry notion is so outdated. Do what you need to do. No one here minds. And I'm sorry, too. I hoped I'd see you again one day, but I'd given up.'

Suddenly Rick's mind was full of tumbling questions. He opened his mouth, but no words came out. He didn't know where or how to start.

'I can't believe Maureen and Joseph didn't tell you until now. Why now?'

'They didn't tell me. I found out.'

'Oh. Unfortunately, I can't say I'm surprised. Joseph was a strange cold one. So was Maureen to some extent, though I thought she would have … Sorry, I shouldn't have said that. You poor darling. So, I'm guessing you didn't get any of my letters, then?'

Rick shook his head as he pushed back the burst of renewed anger at Joseph and, to a lesser extent, Maureen.

'What did they tell you once you asked – after finding out?'

'Nothing. They've both just died. It was while going through their things that …'

'Oh, you poor thing. I'm so sorry for your loss. How awful. And then to be dealing with this on top of it.'

'Thanks. Yes, it's been …' Rick searched for the words but shrugged instead. He took a deep, fortifying breath.

'All we have is the details on his birth certificate, this photo and a letter from Beatrice to Maureen,' Alice said, bringing up the pictures on her phone. Sarah squinted and moved her head back and forth and lifted her chin up and down. 'Sorry, old person problems. Ah, I've got it now. Oh yes, I took that when your mum was pregnant. They'd just moved in.'

'What happened to them?' Rick heard himself whisper. 'They're both dead, aren't they?'

'Oh, pet. Yes. I'm so sorry. They died in a fire in the warehouse,' she said, looking up and out the window.

Rick's insides twisted and shrank. He pulled his lips together to try and stop the gathering tears. He'd known they were dead. He just had. But he hadn't let himself think of how that might have happened before now. Of course it would have been tragic; they had been young. How could he have not realised that? Oh god. He looked at the building rising out from behind the foliage and frowned.

'It didn't burn down,' Sarah said, pre-empting his next question. 'There was some water damage, but my Bobby – my husband, bless him – put it right again. I suppose it was meant to stay as a reminder ...' she added wistfully.

'So, if it didn't burn down, what happened to Bartholomew and Beatrice? And how come Rick was okay?' Rick was glad Alice had cut into the stretching silence.

'The three of them died from smoke inhalation.' She gulped and brought her hands to her face. 'Sorry.'

'Three of them?' Rick's brain was still trying to catch up when Alice asked the question.

'Oh god.' Sarah had her hands to her face, which caused her voice to be a muffle. 'You had a brother. A twin brother. Sebastian. How can you not have known that?'

Rick gaped at her. 'Sorry, what?'

'Your twin. Oh, Ricky–'

He shook his head, hard, remembering Matilda's blather back at the home farm. 'No, no, I didn't have a brother. There were no siblings on my birth certificate.'

Sarah shrugged helplessly. 'I don't know about that – you did have a twin, I promise. I mean, Sebastian was quite unwell when he was born, darling little thing, and had to stay in hospital for a few weeks. Perhaps Bea didn't want to have his name on your birth certificate as a reminder if he – I don't *know*,' she said again, dabbing at the tears rolling down her face.

It was as though Rick's blood was draining away out through his feet. He opened his mouth but couldn't speak. He stared at Sarah as the bit he knew he'd been trying to not think about, not let seep into his consciousness, seeped in. *I had a brother? A twin brother?* He began to ache, and then it was as if someone had taken a sharp instrument and scooped all of his insides out and left him completely empty. Hollow and limp.

And then, slowly, realisation began to dawn. Everything he'd been feeling all these years began to make sense. It hadn't been growing pains when he'd been a child complaining that he hurt all over. His loneliness despite being surrounded by people hadn't been all in his mind. He hadn't been being silly.

A montage of flickering visual memories flooded in and he found himself doubling over and holding his stomach, like he had all those times. Suddenly he desperately wanted to crawl under the table. He fought it. Reminded himself to breathe. A memory jolted free, bringing Rick back suddenly. Joseph dragging him out by the back of his pants, forcing him to be sociable, not be a baby. His heart quickened but he forced his breath to steady. He looked down, feeling Alice's hand on his. He looked up at her, the distraction bringing his mind back into focus.

'Are you okay?'

He nodded. *No. I'm not okay. But I need to know this. I need to know everything, no matter how much it hurts.*

'So how come Rick survived? Is it because Sebastian was weaker from when he was born?' Alice said.

'Timmy,' Rick said. The name had appeared from nowhere, just as it had the other day.

'You remember?' Sarah asked.

'No. Who was Timmy?' Rick said.

'Timmy was the family dog. Well, he was meant to be for the family but you two were practically glued to each other. They think you only survived because you were downstairs under the table together. It was Timmy who raised the alarm. He came around and into our front yard and kept barking and scratching at the door until we opened it. He just wouldn't let up until we came out to see what the matter was. As soon as we opened the door, we smelt the smoke, of course. And when we got there you were out the front sucking your thumb, looking for your dog, poor little mite. Your parents were found upstairs. Trying to rescue darling Sebastian. That was what they said – the assumption they made. Oh, it was awful.'

'What about Timmy? The dog?' he asked. He knew he was focussing on the wrong part, but he couldn't seem to help it. Suddenly it felt really important for him to know what had happened to the dog who had probably saved his life.

'The dear thing. He came and lived with us. He was touch and go, too, for a while from the smoke – so were you. You were in hospital for a week. Anyway, Timmy pulled through and lived here with us until he was, oh, about twelve.'

'What sort of dog was he?'

'I'm not exactly sure. He was a bitsa your parents went and got from the pound – a big hairy wolfhound type dog. Long legs, a bit goofy, but very well-mannered. It was as if he knew he'd been saved,' she said wistfully, smiling.

'I was devastated when Joseph and Maureen wouldn't let you take him to Hope Springs. You howled and howled. It broke my heart seeing you go. We would have taken you in, too, if we'd been allowed, pet. But your parents had chosen Maureen and Joseph as legal guardians – they were listed in their Wills.'

'How could they have done that to me?' He wasn't entirely sure if he'd spoken the words aloud, but if he hadn't Sarah must have seen the anguish in him because suddenly she was beside him and holding him tight.

'Oh, darling,' she whispered, kissing his head.

He let himself melt into her chest for a moment and shed a few more tears. *Oh why couldn't I have lived with you?* He knew it was ridiculous. He didn't even know this woman. But he allowed himself a moment of self-pity.

'So, are *we* related – you and I?' Rick said after they'd returned to their chairs and he was calmer again.

'No. But we were very dear friends with Bart and Beatrice. It all started when they bought Crabtree Lane from us. We instantly hit it off, just clicked,' she said dreamily. Then she shook her head. 'Sorry, there's me, getting all sentimental.'

I need sentimental. I love sentimental. He stayed silent in the hope she'd carry on. She didn't.

'What did Bart and Beatrice do in the building – or did they just live there?' Alice asked after a few moments.

'They were artists, absolutely brilliant artists.'

Rick's breath caught in his throat and he fought to swallow against the sudden dryness.

'Come with me,' Sarah said, getting up. She went to the door out into the garden and opened it. Alice followed Sarah. Rick took a moment to ease himself to his legs that were filled with a mixture of jelly and lead weights. 'They mainly worked with wire and steel and bits of metal. They especially loved anything rusty,' Sarah said, stopping on the path just beyond the back deck. On a neat square gravel area sat an egg-shaped sculpture, about chest height, made from rusty wire and assorted metal and with what looked like butterfly wings coming out of one side near the top. 'That's their work,' she said proudly, pointing. 'And this is my happy place.'

Wow. Icy fingers walked their way down Rick's back and up it again. His mouth was open. He looked wide-eyed at Alice, who was mirroring his expression. Sarah hadn't noticed – she'd closed her eyes.

'Oh my god,' Alice said beside him. 'It's like what you did for me.' Her voice was breathy.

He walked over to the object and laid both his palms on it. He was almost relieved to feel nothing but the cold, slightly rough metal. Anything else would be just too weird and he might lose the plot completely. He walked around it. On the other side, in the sun, it was warm. His parents had been artists, proper artists. *Good* artists. Rick brought his hands up to his face.

'It was the very first piece Bart and Beatrice made for their debut exhibition, which, I might add, was a sell-out. They called this one "Flight of Fancy". I'm not sure if I should say this, but its title – and I guess its form, too – is a bit of a dig at Joseph and Maureen, Joseph mainly. You see, he didn't approve of them and their choice of career at all. Not at all. Oh, but if you could have seen them working together – they made such a wonderful team … And they were so happy …

'Anyway,' Sarah said, clearly bringing herself back to the present, 'it's a depiction of the creative process. But they thought that didn't seem a clever enough title and was also a little too self-indulgent sounding. But see how there's a small empty egg inside and then around it, inside the large egg, are bits and pieces, random scraps – as if waiting to find their place. They were so clever. And ahead of their time, really. I know rusty metal is very popular now, but back then Bart and Beatrice were among the first to do it – certainly around here. It started with them using discarded scrap scrounged from wherever they could get it for free or very cheap.'

Rick nodded. *Wow.* He could feel his own creative juices starting to move around inside him and ping this way and that with ideas – almost like lightning in an electrical storm.

'Spooky,' Alice muttered beside him, taking the word out of his own mind. 'It's beautiful,' she continued thoughtfully, now back at normal volume, 'but there's something about it that's a little familiar to me.' Rick watched Alice walk around the egg.

'It is a popular medium; there are plenty of pieces around in people's gardens. Maybe that's why.'

'Hmm. Maybe.'

'Sorry, but I need to go back in. It's a little cold now that wind is picking up.'

Rick lifted his head into the breeze whipping around them and said silently, *I'm here, I've found you.* And then he experienced the strangest sense. He couldn't say it out loud, because he'd sound completely unhinged, but he felt that he'd been heard.

The breeze followed them until they were inside, but as Rick closed the door behind them, he noticed the trees were all completely still again. When he sat back down, he felt more at ease than he had for as long as he could remember.

'Ah, that's better,' Sarah said, hugging herself briefly.

'So, why didn't Joseph approve of Bart and Beatrice? The letter said *lifestyle*, so it can't just be about them being artists. Were they, um, into drugs or something else illegal?' Alice said when they were settled again.

'Oh no. They were just artists. Not *just* artists, I didn't mean it like that. What I meant was *they* weren't the problem. Joseph was. And I guess Maureen was dragged into it.

'Anyway, the Petersons didn't like Beatrice because she was arty-farty – their words, not mine – and they thought she was responsible for corrupting Bart. Because he left the family farm – near Hope Springs – to be with her. He told me the farm wasn't big enough for them both anyway, so couldn't see what their issue was other than some nonsense over what people would think about the older brother walking off the farm and leaving the district.

'Bart didn't care much about gossip or small-mindedness, but, oh, Joseph did. There was a hail of harsh words not long before Bart and Beatrice got married. Before your time. Bart thought maybe the reason behind Joseph's anger was that *he* – Joseph, that is – secretly wanted to leave the farm. To do what, Bart wasn't sure, but Bart leaving bound him there, or something. I'm not completely sure, but that's about the gist.

'I think there was also plenty of jealousy over the fact that Beatrice was from money – I'm not certain how well-off. Beatrice was too polite to discuss her family finances in detail, but they weren't short of a dollar. Middle to upper middle class maybe – not that we're meant to talk about there even being a class system here in Australia ... I think what bothered Joseph even more than them having money was that Beatrice's parents were supportive through and through – she had no limits placed on her, unlike Joseph and Bart.

'Anyway, as I said, I met them when we sold them the building. We called it The Barn. Anyway, they were happy. Really happy. Their wedding was simple and joyful and full of love – which basically sums them up. Dear, your parents were beautiful – kind, thoughtful, caring people. Two of the best. I'm really sorry you ended up with Joseph, because I didn't like him very much.'

'So, you met him – them – Joseph and Maureen, then?' Alice asked, just as Rick had opened his mouth to ask the same question.

'It was an occasion ... or some reason ... just let me think a moment ...'

Rick watched and became a little mesmerised as Sarah tapped the waterproof tablecloth with her index finger. It made a slightly hollow plasticky tack-tack sound. He could also hear the hollow click of the clock, which seemed to be keeping the same beat as Sarah.

'Nope, I don't recall. Maybe it was to talk Bart into going back to the farm. I know Joseph did tell his brother art was a waste of space and time and if he wasn't going to farm, he needed to at least get a real job and take proper care of his wife. Maybe she was pregnant then, I don't know. Oh! I remember now. Not *that*. But Bart leaving the farm meant being paid out a bit of money. Yes, that's right. Joseph was angry about giving his brother money. I don't remember how much it was, but at the time I'm sure I didn't think it seemed much to buy him out of the family company. But it was enough for a deposit on The Barn.'

'But he was so angry for so long – he took it out on Rick for decades. How could he have cared that much about someone else being an artist?' Alice scoffed. But Rick could believe it. Joseph had had a concrete heart. And plenty of other farming family bust-ups had been just as damaging, while appearing just as petty to the outside world.

'Dear, people do the darnedest things when their insecurities are jolted.'

'Because hurt people hurt people,' Alice said quietly. Out of the corner of his eye Rick could see her nodding thoughtfully.

'Yes, exactly. That's the conclusion we all came to. Bart and Beatrice got on with enjoying their lives and hoped Joseph would eventually come around. There wasn't much more they could do.

'Bart didn't even really want to take the money, but they were keen on being independent. Beatrice's parents would have helped them out in a heartbeat, and Beatrice was fine with asking them, but Bart wanted to provide for his family and I suppose prove something. And they sure did,' Sarah said, clearly proud.

Rick felt his own chest puff up a little in response, too. 'You said their debut exhibition was a sell-out – did they have any others?' he ventured.

'Oh yes. Several. And all sold out, to the best of my knowledge. Hang on there a moment. I put a scrapbook together of what bits and pieces I had,' she said, as she got up and left the room.

Rick sighed. It was so good but also sad to hear about Bart and Beatrice knowing he'd never have the chance to meet them and that there was only so much he could ever learn. Alice reached over and squeezed his hand and he returned her gentle smile.

A few moments later, Sarah came back with a photo album and handed it to Rick. He ran his fingers over the words BART AND BEATRICE written on the cover in thick black marker before carefully opening the album. On the first page was the photo he already had.

'They'd just moved into The Barn there,' Sarah said, leaning over his shoulder and pointing. 'I'd also just given her the stuffed monkeys – one for you and one for Sebastian. I can't remember why I chose monkeys. Maybe because they were so soft and cuddly and easy to hold and wouldn't show the dirt. There are photos of you and Sebastian in the back after the art.' Rick quickly turned the page, the desire to find out more – things he didn't already know – spurring him on. But did he want to see photos of his brother? Was he ready for that?

Over the next several pages were shots of his parents working in the huge space of The Barn – at a forge style set-up with coals glowing and Bart standing with an iron bar in them. Nearby Beatrice, her head wrapped in a bright floral scarf, sat on a stool with wire in her hands and a partially completed construction. Her position was just like his had been the other day. Again, icy fingers began creeping down his back, and then went up it again.

'Oh my god,' Alice said. He knew she had her hand over her mouth, because her voice was muffled. 'That's so much like what you made me.' He nodded and silently turned the page. In front of him was a large newspaper clipping with a photo and a lot of text beneath it – half a page, maybe, depending on the style of newspaper. The heading was: *Turning trash into treasures; local artists prepare for their debut exhibition*. It was hard for Rick to make out most of the detail of the few pieces they stood among. Alice leant in closer.

'What? What have you seen?' Sarah asked, clearly picking up on what Rick had.

'It's just the feeling again that it's somehow familiar. I think it's the butterfly wings, maybe,' she said. 'I've seen them somewhere.'

'Well, they're butterfly wings, but they also *aren't*, I should have explained.'

'Sorry?' Rick and Alice said at once.

'That's their signature. It's on all their pieces – sometimes small, sometimes really big. Bart and Beatrice. See, two Bs back-to-back. Clever, huh?'

'Oh, yes, I see. Yes, it is.'

Rick could see Alice frowning, like she was trying to remember something. He waited until she seemed to have given up before turning the next page.

'Aww, watching them work together was just like watching a beautifully choreographed dance routine,' Sarah said. 'They fed off each other, bantered, threw ideas around. And never a cross word, that I heard. But, of course, sadly, it was a short-lived partnership and career,' she added sadly.

Rick found himself torn between not wanting details but needing to know everything. He sat, unable, unwilling, to turn to the next page.

He heard Alice sniff and then a tissue being dragged from the box. 'Sorry. It's all so lovely, but it's making me sad,' she said. 'They were so clever.'

'It is sad. So much promise,' Sarah said. 'I'm so pleased to see you, to see that you fared okay,' she eventually said, breaking a long bout of silence.

Rick looked up at her and then back down at the book, which he didn't remember closing. He opened his mouth to correct Sarah – tell her the truth about Joseph. But what would it achieve? He *had* fared okay. Ultimately. Here he was with a new start and the courage to make it.

'Are you okay?' Alice said.

He nodded and swallowed as the thought, *He can't hurt you now,* ran through his mind several times.

'Oh. Hang on a sec,' Sarah said, when they heard the sound of a phone ringing. She hurried out into the hall.

Rick could hear her muffled voice, 'Oh. Yes, of course. I'll be there soon.' Well, that's what he thought he heard.

'Are you sure you're okay?' Alice said, looking closely at Rick, putting a hand on his arm again.

'Honestly, Alice, I have no idea. I feel like I've been dragged through one of those old washing machine wringers,' he said, and attempted to laugh.

'I'm sure. And, sorry, that was a silly question. It sounds like Sarah needs to be somewhere,' Alice said, tilting her head towards the hall. Rick copied her when she stood up. He reluctantly placed the scrapbook on the table, wishing he'd seen everything in it. Perhaps Sarah wouldn't mind if he came back some time.

'We've kept you long enough,' Alice said when Sarah came back in, looking a little flustered.

'Yes, I'm sorry to cut this short, but I do need to be somewhere soon. I didn't realise what the time was. It's got quite away from me.'

'Well, we really appreciate everything,' Rick said, finally managing to find his voice. He didn't want to leave. As they moved out into the hall, ushered by Sarah, he felt a bond to the artwork in the garden, the warehouse beyond, stretching painfully as if it was trying to keep him there.

'You haven't finished looking through the book. Take it with you,' Sarah said, ducking past them and back again.

'Are you sure?' Rick said, holding on tightly to the object now flat against his chest. It felt like the most valuable gift he'd ever been given.

'Yes, it's yours. As long as you promise to come and visit me again. And not leave it so long next time,' Sarah said, smiling at him and touching his cheek gently with a smooth finger.

Suddenly they were hugging. This time it was Rick making the first move.

He didn't want to let go. But he had to.

'I'll be on a cruise for the next couple of weeks, but after that, please visit any time. You know where I am now,' Sarah said as they made their way down the path to the squeaky gate. 'Oh, Ricky – little Ricky – that's what I called you, but you're not so little now – it's been wonderful, just wonderful. I've never stopped thinking about you, wondering, and hoping all was well. As I said, I did write. A lot, in the early years. I'm just so sorry your aunt and uncle chose not to tell you the truth.'

Rick nodded. He had no words. She must have caught a hint of the sudden spike of anger he was biting back, because next she said, 'Don't be too hard on them – they probably thought they were doing the right thing.'

Rick nodded again.

Alice opened the gate. It gave a long loud squeaking groan.

'Don't mind that, it's my security alarm – so I know when someone's in my yard,' she said.

Rick followed Alice. And then he thought of something. It really bothered him. The question turned itself inside out and a knot formed as options presented themselves to him and were discarded. He wasn't sure how to ask, but he had to know. He turned back. 'Um, Sarah?'

'Yes?'

'How do you know I'm Ricky?'

'Your features. You have your mother's eyes and your father's ears and nose, pet. It's very obvious to me.'

'No, how do you know which twin died, that I'm actually Ricky?' Rick almost choked on the words. *What if I'm actually Sebastian? Not Rick at all …*

'Oh, darling, I know. You were so different – you *looked* identical but were very different little boys.'

Tears suddenly filled Rick's eyes again. This time they were more out of frustration as he felt brought right back to the original question – who am I? He wasn't sure how else to ask.

'Oh. *Oh.* I see what you mean now,' Sarah said. She stood looking thoughtful, as if searching her memory. And then she said, sounding a little triumphant, 'Do you have a large, perfectly round brown mole on the top of your left foot? I guess it wouldn't be large now, would it, now you're so big?'

'Yes, yes I do.' *You remembered that?*

'Well, there you go, then. Little Sebastian didn't. You're little Ricky all grown up, I have no doubt about that.'

'Thank you.' Relief flooded through him.

'Come on, we'd better let Sarah go,' Alice said, tugging at his arm.

'Yes, I'd better. Again, I'm sorry to cut it short. But you're going to come back some time, aren't you?'

'Oh yes. Absolutely. Of course,' Rick said.

'Thanks again,' Alice said.

'Yes, thank you so much,' Rick said, though it was such an inadequate thing to say in light of what she'd given him. He let himself be gently dragged away as the gate squeaked closed again. He so badly didn't want to leave but reminded himself he'd be back. The gate was only closing on them for now. And he had the book, with more in it to discover.

He trailed along next to Alice for a few hundred metres until she stopped and leant on a low brick wall in front of a small group of flats. He settled beside her. He still had the scrapbook clutched hard to his chest with both hands wrapped around it.

'Wow,' Alice said. 'Phew.'

Rick nodded. He felt weird – light but heavy, fearful but calm. And also comforted, as if the missing and broken pieces of him that had been jangling about inside painfully all these years were gluing themselves back together and turning him into who he was really meant to be – not the person Joseph Peterson, aided by Maureen, had tried to force him to be. He was starting to think clearly, to see clearly.

'Crikey, what a morning,' he said eventually, needing to end the long silence.

'That's one way to describe it! I guess now we have some idea why you've felt abandoned, and like you don't belong, all these years. They say twins share a really strong, sometimes even psychic, bond. You've had half of yourself missing all this time,' Alice said sadly.

'Hmm. And probably why I hurt you so much. I'm really sorry, Alice. And even if it's a reason, it's still not an excuse. I was down-right horrible to you at times.'

'We've had this discussion, Rick. It's in the past. We're here now.'

He gripped her hand. 'Thank you. For everything.'

'And you need to stop thanking me, too. I'm your friend and I care about you. End of story. You don't owe me anything.'

Chapter Twenty-eight

Like each of the previous two mornings, Rick woke on Monday with Bill pressed against him. He would miss the little guy when he went out to stay with Blair. He got up and rolled his swag. He didn't want to linger and risk upsetting Alice's routine for getting herself and Bill to work on time.

He was also energised and keen to get on to the next clue. They'd sat up late Saturday evening and gone through the album Sarah had given them, and then again, looking for any hints of anything else Rick might find out about himself or his parents. And they'd found one – well, Alice had. He'd completely missed it, but she had spotted on the bottom of Bart and Beatrice's funeral notice a line about donating funds to help in the raising of their orphaned son in lieu of floral tributes. Rick had felt a little strange realising he was the orphaned son named.

He initially hadn't seen it as a clue to anything – was too busy chewing over why, if Beatrice had come from money – possibly quite a bit of money – and was an only child, would there have been a need to raise funds? Had Joseph's greed had something to do with it? But he forced that back, preferring to think it was more about a community rallying around his lost parents who, in his mind, wouldn't have flaunted any wealth they might have had. But then Alice had tapped her finger on the name of the law firm collecting any donations. 'That's where I reckon you need to go next. First thing on Monday,' she'd said.

So, after he saw Alice off at work, he was going to their office – which just happened to be down the street from hers – to see what they knew, if anything. Though, three decades was a long time. So, while he was hopeful, he tried to keep himself from expecting too much.

At the door to Alice's office they had a brief moment of awkwardness: they suddenly both didn't seem to quite know how to say goodbye after the intensity of their weekend. Alice stood in front of Rick looking a little bereft, he thought. He knew she hated goodbyes of any kind, so quickly pulled her to him in a hug, pecked her on the cheek and then held her back by the shoulders while he looked into her eyes. 'Thank you so much. For everything. I'll see you soon.' He bent down to give Bill some attention, rubbed his little head and quietly thanked him too.

'Good luck with the lawyer. Let me know how it goes.'

'Will do.' Rick then walked down the street with a wave. He was a few minutes early, but he wanted to give Alice the time and space to collect herself. He ran through what he was going to say, getting the order of words right in his mind.

Clear, concise, and stick to the point, he told himself as he walked up to the glass door of Taylor and Associates.

'Hello, can I help you?' a young man asked, looking up from his position behind the reception desk.

'Yes. Hello. My name is Rick Peterson. I was adopted after my parents and twin brother died in nineteen-eighty-seven and I understand there's a connection to this firm.'

'Oh. Right. Okay. Do you know who, which partner, handled your case?'

'I'm not sure it was a case, as such. I'm not sure of much about it at all, to be honest. Here, this might help.' He brought up the picture he'd taken of the funeral notice for his parents on his phone and handed it over.

'Ah, yes, okay. I think it best you speak to our longest-serving partner, William. But he's in court first thing this morning. He should be back at around ten, I believe. Unfortunately, he then has a client meeting,' he said, looking down and tapping on a keyboard.

'Would you mind if I wait, in case I can catch him between or something?' Rick didn't have anywhere else to be.

'Okay. That's fine.'

Rick took a seat in one of the five burgundy upholstered chairs with black steel arms placed in a row against the window.

Rick wasn't sure how long he'd been waiting – he hadn't wanted to look impatient by checking his watch or phone – when a tall, grey-haired man came in dressed in a dark blue pinstripe suit. He was carrying a brown leather satchel with scuff marks on the bottom corners. Rick wanted to leap up and accost him, but forced himself to remain seated. He tried not to look while the receptionist responded to the man's query about messages – no doubt a subtle question about who the man sitting waiting in the window was. There were hushed voices and then the man was standing in front of him.

'Rick Peterson, William Thomas,' the man said, holding out his hand.

'Yes, thank you,' Rick said, leaping to his feet and accepting the hand.

'Rick,' the man repeated.

Rick frowned slightly. 'Yes.' He nodded. He was surprised to find the man clasping him by the shoulder. They were still holding hands. It seemed a little more intimate, familiar, than merely shaking hands. But it was nice, not at all creepy. And it was over in not much more than a second or two.

'Come with me,' he said, turning around.

Rick followed. At the reception desk, William paused and spoke quietly. 'Michael, as you know, Isabell is often late. Please keep her here. If she doesn't want to wait, reschedule. I'm not sure how long I'll be tied up for. I'll let you know as soon as I have some idea.'

'Right, this way,' William said, leading the way into an office not far down a hall.

'Thanks so much for seeing me without an appointment,' Rick said, entering the room.

'No problem at all. Take a seat.' William sat behind a huge modern mahogany desk. 'So, what can I do for you? Michael said something about us handling an adoption or not actually an adoption, but something to do with one?'

'Yes. Do you know anything about this?' Rick said, bringing up the funeral notice picture again. 'It turns out I'm the orphan son. I've only very recently discovered I was even adopted.'

'Oh. Goodness me.'

'I'm not sure there was a formal adoption done, or if it was necessary – my aunt and uncle, who took me in, were named as legal guardians in my parents' Wills. My parents, Beatrice and Bartholomew, died in a warehouse fire here in Ballarat, along with my twin brother, Sebastian. We were eighteen months old. Nineteen-eighty-seven,' he added.

'Yes, that tragedy is ringing a bell. Very odd they wouldn't have told you, but when you've dealt with people as much as I have, unfortunately, nothing comes as much of a surprise any more.'

Rick pulled his wallet from his pocket, dragged out his driver's licence from behind the clear pocket and handed it over.

'Okay. Thank you,' William said, barely glancing at it before handing it back. He then began tapping on the keyboard on his desk.

Rick itched to fill the silence, but he waited. This man didn't need to know all the details.

'Ah, here we go.'

At that moment the receptionist, Michael, appeared and placed a piece of A4 paper, which Rick assumed must have come out of a printer in another room, on William's desk. He also placed a glass of water on the edge of the desk, an arm's length away from Rick.

'I might need to do some digging, but here's what I know right now,' William finally said, sitting back and clasping his hands in front of him on the desk. 'There is a trust fund in your name. We've been managing it since the year two thousand, having had to remove your aunt and uncle, Joseph and Maureen Peterson, after one or both of them made a fraudulent withdrawal of one hundred thousand dollars. We initially didn't query it because often boarding school fees or some such are needed by guardians, who may also take lump sums to reimburse for expenses over time.'

Rick's mind started searching for an explanation. No boarding school. Other expenses, then? And then his blood froze in his veins. The second farm? No. He tried to push it back, but it kept coming. Fuck. The farm he'd thought they'd bought to set him up on – *for* him – had been purchased around then, hadn't it?

He didn't know why and how he managed to sound so matter of fact, but he said, 'Maureen has just died. She left me exactly one hundred thousand dollars in her Will.'

'That will be to reimburse for that then, I imagine. There should really be interest.' *If they sell up everything, would Danni and Matilda pay the extra because it's the right thing to do?* 'You could try to sue the estate, of course, but I'd be inclined to let it go –' *Sue them? Christ, imagine the twist Hope Springs would get its knickers into over that, even if Danni and Matilda didn't freak out!* '– given the position you're in financially yourself.'

'Sorry? I'm not following.'

'That's understandable, it's a lot to take in. It says here a letter was sent to you just prior to your eighteenth birthday. It would have been by registered mail – to be signed for ...' He paused and looked up and must have noticed Rick's face, which he thought was probably very pale, going by the queasiness in his stomach.

'Unfortunately, there seems to have been a failure in the system somewhere along the line.'

Yeah, you could say that. Rick tried to blink away his confusion. 'What was the letter about?'

'Advising of your access to your trust and its balance and seeking instructions on how you wanted to proceed. Oh dear. You've really been let down all round, haven't you?'

'It seems that way.' Had he spoken the words out loud? 'So, um, what is the balance? Is that what you meant about my financial position?' he asked, finally gaining some clarity.

'You're the sole beneficiary of a trust which currently has a cash balance of a little over four-point-two million dollars, plus a building.'

'What? No. Really?' *Four million dollars? More than four million dollars?* Rick felt the blood rise into his face and then drain away again. As he found himself reaching for the glass he almost laughed.

'Yes. And the building.'

'What building?'

'Um. Let me see. Yes. You own a warehouse at One Crabtree Lane … It's managed by the real estate agency named Olsen and Owens. They're just in the next street over from here. They'd be the best people to speak with about that side of things. I know Gavin Owens well.'

So I have somewhere – of my own – to live? And I have my own money? And enough? More than enough? Oh wow. Rick's head started to spin as it tried to make plans. He brought himself back. One step at a time. The warehouse wasn't empty. He'd go and stay with Blair and take time to figure things out. *But, fuck!*

'Wow,' Rick now said aloud. 'I'm a bit stunned, to be honest. So, is this money – the cash portion, is that all because someone set up a fund for money to care for me? Who? You – as in the firm here managing the trust?'

'No, that wouldn't have been us that organised the fundraising – the trust was active well before then. From this, it looks as if your maternal grandparents, the Willoughbys, set it up. Unfortunately, they both pre-deceased your parents by, er, oh. Just a year or so,' he said, frowning slightly as he scrolled and peered at the screen. 'Yes. Here it is. We became managers, on your behalf, after your parents' deaths. I can't tell you who organised the fundraising, because I don't know. I could perhaps try to find out. Unfortunately, I would have to charge the trust for the time in searching, though …'

'I understand.' *Was it Sarah? No, she would have mentioned it – or at least directed him to the law firm. God, please don't tell me it was Joseph's doing.*

'Could I perhaps suggest it might be best for you to let the dust settle for a bit?' William said kindly. 'You're already dealing with an awful lot at the moment.'

'Mm, you could be right. I'll leave it for now.'

'Okay. You can always change your mind later.'

'Yes.'

Rick sighed. *Did it really matter? Well, did it?* Alice would say if he was meant to know, he would – in time. Anthea might agree.

'Their occupations are listed as artists, so perhaps they were part of a group or attached to a gallery. Someone is bound to know something.'

Rick nodded thoughtfully in response. He had the strange sensation that he was meant to visit the local galleries, that Bart and Beatrice were asking him to, guiding him.

'Hang on,' he said, something coming back to him, 'did you say the trust was started before my parents' deaths?'

'Yes. And there was already a reasonable balance. From an inheritance – your grandparents on your mother's side; Eleanor Anne and Richard Harrison Willoughby. I'll write their names down for you,' he said, pulling a notepad towards him and picking up a pen. 'Thankfully your parents were sensible and had reasonably up-to-date Wills. You inherited their assets and your brother Sebastian's assets – and then of course the fundraising proceeds as well. And the rent from the warehouse has been topping up the principal ever since, of course,' he added as he scribbled.

Rick found tears filling his eyes. He quickly wiped them away. 'Oh god. I'm sorry. This is such a shock – and a huge relief, actually.'

'I understand,' William said, pushing a box of tissues across towards Rick. He took one and wiped his eyes and blew his nose before stuffing the soggy item into his pocket.

'Why didn't they leave me with someone else – someone nice, then, if they were so organised?'

'I can't answer that. Perhaps they were the only remaining relatives and they thought it best you were with family. I'm sorry if it wasn't a happy experience for you.'

It really, really wasn't. But it wasn't all bad, was it? Rick tried to make himself think of some happy moments, but he failed. It was a montage of being told off, his ideas being ridiculed, and his dreams thwarted. He shook it aside. Anthea would probably say he needed to look to the future, not dwell on the past. Come to terms with it, not forgetting or dismissing its lessons, while focussing on the here and now. No, he couldn't let all that run into his future.

'But I do have a lot to be thankful for,' he said, thinking aloud, a little forcefully. For a start, he was alive and healthy. And he was young, with plenty of skills to fall back on. Farm life had been good for equipping him with practical skills. He would soon have a roof over his head – his own, rent free, mortgage free roof – and a sizeable bank balance. Plenty of people would kill for that. Money didn't buy happiness and couldn't make up for all the love he hadn't been shown. But it certainly helped him feel he'd be okay while he healed from that. It bought him time and gave him options. And of course the greatest gift in all this was realising he had a creative soul, which he was now allowed to use. He was free to pursue a new career.

'I'm going to study,' he blurted suddenly. 'Art. I'm going to be an artist.' Make up for all those years of school and tertiary education he'd been denied.

'That's great. Good for you,' William said. 'If there wasn't anything else, I'm afraid I had better be getting on.'

'Oh, yes. Sorry.' Rick wondered how long he'd been sitting silently musing on his thoughts and taking up this patient man's time. 'What happens now – with the trust?'

'That's up to you. We can organise for you to have full control or we can continue to manage it. It's entirely up to you.'

'Could we just leave it as it is? I need to figure a few things out.'

'Certainly. You know where we are now,' William said, getting up from his desk.

Rick stood up too. His legs were weak and quivering. He hoped they'd hold him.

'Actually, could you please let the real estate agent managing the warehouse know I might want to live there when the tenants leave?'

'Yes. I can do that. I'll let him know right away,' William said, leaning down and making a note on a pad on his desk.

'Thanks so much. For everything,' Rick said, holding out his hand.

'It's been my pleasure. Here's my card. Just let me know if there is anything you need. Whenever you're ready. Take care now.'

'Okay. Thanks. It's a lot to get my head around,' he said while staring at the card but not really seeing it.

Chapter Twenty-nine

In a daze, Rick somehow found his way back to Alice's flat and his car, which he'd packed ready to go before he left to walk to work with her. He hadn't wanted her to feel she had to give him a key. He unlocked the driver's door and got in. He sent Blair a text and waited for a response. Rick really hoped he was home and it was okay for him to go out there now. He knew he should probably be doing other things but didn't feel he had the energy. He'd had enough information for one day. His brain was full. He'd call Alice later. He didn't want to disturb her at work. And he didn't want to blurt out his news and be insensitive – she wasn't exactly flush with cash, so it might be a bit hurtful. Not that she wouldn't be glad for him, but still … *Oh! Hang on a sec. Technically I had this money when we were married, and when we divvied things up. So that means I definitely owe her something. Oh man. This could do my head in completely if I let it. Breathe, Ricky boy, breathe!*

Would he keep it all to himself or tell Blair? he wondered while he continued to wait. It might help to talk to a stranger. He felt he kind of needed to tell someone.

He found his thoughts straying to Ashley, as they had on and off over the weekend. Each time he'd sent them on their way. She was meant to be hooking up with Blair. But as a neutral person – an educated one at that: a lawyer – she might be useful. Should he ask her out for coffee? And ask her what? Ah, who was he kidding? He couldn't be around her on his own.

What about Blair and Alice? The whole thing was weird. But, god, he didn't want to find himself in the middle of a love triangle. Or was it a love square? Or maybe a circle. *God, too much for me*, he thought with a laugh, blinking and shaking his head.

When Rick's attention was caught by the movement of a curtain in the window of another flat in the group, he turned the car on. He didn't want to have to explain his lurking to the police. He reversed out and into the street and then around the corner where he parked again, this time under the shade of a tree. While he waited for a reply from Blair, he pulled up the details for the nearest bottle shop on his phone, and directions to it. He didn't want to drink anything, now or probably later, but he also didn't want to turn up to Blair's empty-handed and he couldn't immediately think of what else to take.

***

'Hey, there you are,' Blair said, appearing from around a corner of a corrugated iron shed. 'Found me okay, then?'

'Yep, no problems at all. Lovely spot you have here,' he said, looking around. And he meant it. He'd enjoyed the drive out, especially once the traffic had thinned. He had a soft spot for tall timber. Perhaps it was because he was away and his opinion was clouded, but this area seemed so much more beautiful than the country around Hope Springs.

'Thanks. It's home. Welcome,' he said, holding out his hand.

Rick accepted it with a firm grip. 'Here, this is for you. I wasn't sure what else to bring. Wine. I got one of each – red and white.'

'You didn't need to do that, but thank you,' Blair said, accepting the package he held out. 'I've made us an early lunch. This way,' and he picked up the handle of Rick's overnight bag with his other hand before Rick had a chance to.

'Great looking house, too,' Rick said on the way up a path towards the dark bluey-purple-painted weatherboard house.

'Yeah. Thanks. I love it. It's not huge and it's pretty basic but it does the trick. Even if I had ten million dollars, I'd probably still be here. You're just in here,' he said as they got inside, putting Rick's bag into a room off the hall to the right. 'Let's eat, and then I'll give you a proper tour.'

In the kitchen Rick was surprised and pleased to see two dogs – a large, lean black and white kelpie-border-collie-cross, he thought it was, and a smaller, slightly stockier red kelpie – lounging around on big mats in a strip of light shining through the glass sliding door. They got up and stretched and loped over to him. They stood, gazing up at him with their tails waving slowly back and forth. Rick's heart panged for Jess and the dog, Timmy, he couldn't remember having known. And then the next thought he had was that good people had dogs inside.

'Aren't you lovely?' he said, holding out his hands for them to sniff and then patting their heads.

'Meet Eric and Ruby – you can see who is who,' Blair said. 'Guys, this is Rick.'

'Great names,' Rick said.

'Sit, take a load off,' Blair said, waving towards the table where a small pile of sandwiches sat on a chopping board under a glass dome. There were two tall water glasses turned upside down on a tray and a jug of water under a crocheted cover with orange beads hanging down. Maureen had had one of those. Rick was pleased that thinking of her caused him to feel nothing much at all. She was gone. She was the past and he was looking to the future. He had the thought of what to do about the funeral lurking at the back of his mind, which he tried to keep back out of sight. 'Cup of tea or coffee? Or you can just help yourself to the water, or have a beer if you want. I don't tend to indulge until after five, but you feel free.'

'I'm right, thanks.'

The dogs walked away and lay back down in the sun.

'Help yourself,' Blair said, taking off the glass dome and setting it aside.

Rick took a couple of sandwich halves and put them on the small plate in front of him. He hadn't thought he was all that hungry until he smelt the egg filling.

'So, how was the rest of your weekend? Find out anything interesting in your search?' Blair asked, between mouthfuls and sips from his water.

'Huh?'

'You were going to check out the address you had when we said goodbye to you on Saturday,' Blair prompted.

'Oh yes. God.' Rick was again surprised at how much had happened, how much he'd learnt, in such a short space of time. 'Do I have a story for you …'

'Wow,' Blair said, his eyes wide, when Rick had caught him up on all his news. 'I'm not sure what to say about all that. Better late than never? So, what does Alice say?'

'I haven't told her what I found out at the lawyers. I didn't want to disturb her at work. I'll call her later.'

'Fair enough. I think she'll understand. She's a good sort.'

'Yep. The best.' Rick tried to imagine going through this without her and stopped. He did have her. And he didn't want to imagine his life without her in it again.

'Do you think you'll get back together?' Blair asked, breaking the silence a few moments later.

'What? God, no way. We're way beyond that.'

'Oh. Right.'

Rick thought he sensed a slight shift in Blair's demeanour towards relief. 'So, what's the story between you two?' he asked.

'No story.'

'Come on, mate, that's clearly not true. You can't even look me in the eye right now. I've spilt my guts. It's your turn now.'

Rick munched on his sandwich while staring Blair down.

'Yep. Okay. I like her. I *really* like her.' He lifted his hands and then dropped them again in a gesture of helplessness. 'But it's never going to work.'

'Why? Why not?'

'Because I stuffed up,' Blair said with a sigh.

'Did you sleep with someone else? Kill someone?' Rick asked with raised eyebrows.

'No. Nothing like that.'

'Well, then,' Rick said. 'She's a very forgiving person, given the right circumstances – not in a take-for-granted sort of way. So …?'

'We had a bit of an argument.'

'Can't have been that bad, the way she was with you at breakfast on Saturday. Come on, I know you want to tell me. Maybe it will help. Problem shared and all that. It's helped me.'

'Well, it seems so first-world-problems compared to what you're going through.'

'So? It's not a competition. And if it's important to you, then it's important. And I'm happy to listen.'

'Right. Um …' Blair began and stopped.

'From the beginning,' Rick prompted again.

'Okay. So …'

Rick listened to Blair telling his story. He died to cut in in a few places and give his opinion, but had managed to resist.

'… And, that's about it,' Blair finished with a shrug. 'At least we're friends – that's better than nothing. I guess.'

Rick wanted to laugh out loud, but instead said, 'You're more than just friends, mate. Stevie Wonder can see that. So, let me get this straight. You don't want kids and Alice has said she doesn't want kids, but you're worried she's going to change her mind, which will mean you have to split up and that will break your heart?'

'Yup, that's about the crux of it.'

'You're worrying about something that might not, probably won't, happen. You can see that, right?'

'Yes. I know. But I can't seem to dip my toe in. Once bitten, twice shy, and all that.'

'Ah, yes, but what about it's better to have loved and lost than to never have loved at all, or however it goes? Since we're tossing around classic sayings. Nothing ventured, nothing gained?' Rick said, grinning, but keeping his eyes on Blair across the table.

'Yeah, all right. You can stop now.'

'Not helpful?'

'No,' Blair said with a roll of his eyes, but grinning nonetheless.

'For the record, I don't think Alice is too fussed about kids – one way or the other. We talked about going down that path, obviously, because we were getting married.'

'And …?'

'We decided we'd wait and see how we felt later – agreed if it was meant to be it would be. I wasn't sure because of my parents, and look I don't think she'd realised she was doing it, but I reckon Alice might have been pushing back on family pressure too. Now she seems really focussed on getting her career as a lawyer up and running. For what it's worth, Alice isn't one to have regrets. She tends to think things through before making major decisions. You also need to know that out where we're from, it's still quite old-fashioned in some ways. Women get married and have kids, men run farms and are the breadwinners. That's the way it is. It's quite possible that any thoughts Alice has that she wants kids could well be a momentary insecurity, giving in to her upbringing and conditioning. Dawn was very controlling and manipulative – I'm only just seeing how much. That's my regret now – that I didn't support Alice more.'

'What do you think about kids – having them, that is?'

'Take it or leave it.' Rick then paused and let the question roll around in his mind for a moment. 'I think I could be an okay dad, especially now I know the truth about who raised me. But I get why you don't want them. I think good on you for being responsible in not wanting to pass on the cancer gene. Chemo and all that must have been terrible.'

'But …?'

'No but.' Rick searched his mind. 'Except. Okay, here's a but. *But* don't use that one fear and turn it into an even bigger fear.'

'Sorry, I don't follow.'

'If Alice has said she doesn't want kids, take her at her word. Like I said, she'll have thought it through. And I'd say if she ever changed her mind, then maybe that would be the universe taking it out of your hands.'

'Yeah, I guess. You've got a point. I'm over-thinking it, aren't I?'

'Quite possibly. But it is a big decision and an important one. You're just protecting yourself, but hurting yourself in the process is never ideal. Talk to her, mate, just don't assume anything.' Rick almost laughed at seeing Blair roll his eyes.

'Good advice, considering that's exactly what got me into this pickle in the first place.'

'Yeah, I think it's something they should tattoo on our forearms at birth: Never assume,' he said, holding his arm out and tracing his finger along it.

'Yeah, and we'd still ignore the advice …'

'Ha-ha, without a doubt.' They sipped silently from their glasses of water. Rick deliberated over whether to say what was now running through his mind. Ashley. Ah, to hell with it – they were past the point of being coy with each other.

'Hey, do you believe in love at first sight?' Rick ventured.

'Abso-bloody-lutely. I knew the moment I met Alice months ago at the Finmores' house. I run their farm for them and Alice is their daughter's best friend.'

'Lauren, right?'

'That's the one. She's a couple with Brett – he's a nice bloke, too. They were all at university together. In Melbourne. So, I take it it wasn't instant with you and Alice, then?'

'No, unfortunately not. It was more a friendship, hanging out at the pub, but again, out there, it's not at all the done thing to have a friend of the opposite sex – you get engaged after X months – or, say, a year – and then your parents organise a wedding, and then it's kids. Or maybe it was just us. Looking back, it's all very well-choreographed. Thank goodness we *didn't* have kids. There'd be worse people to be tied to for life, and thank goodness we've made up pretty well now, but I think the kids get pretty screwed up. If we'd had kids, Alice would never have left Hope Springs, and seeing who she's become, I reckon it's the best thing that could have happened to her.'

'If you love them, set them free, and all that?'

'Yeah, I guess, but I can't take any credit for setting her free. Not really. Not consciously. I was a fuck-up. No bones about it and no other way to put it. And I'm just beginning to see why. Not that it's an excuse for how I treated her, but it does go some way to explaining things.'

'It's good you're sorting through it. Hang on. Go back a bit. You've met someone. If you're over Alice romantically, then who is it you've fallen for at first sight?'

Rick took a deep breath. 'Ashley. It was instant. Bang. At the office Friday when I turned up. I thought I might have just been over-tired and delirious from driving so far.'

'Nah. I reckon you'd know the difference. And then you saw her at breakfast. Did that change your initial feelings?'

'No, but I really tried to not like her since Alice was busy setting her up with you.'

'I thought she was great. Smart and beautiful – the whole package.'

'But, just not Alice, right?'

'Exactly. It sounds like we need to organise a double-date sort of arrangement.'

'Hmm. Do you think all this upheaval I'm going through means it would be the wrong time to get involved in a relationship?'

'Have you just split up with someone – as in someone you were serious about?'

'Nope. I haven't been serious about anyone, really, since Alice, truth be told. A few casual attempts here and there, and a chick who moved in for about ten minutes a while ago – that's about it.'

'Then I'd say go for it – you're clearly not on a romantic rebound. That would be my only concern. Finding out your past is a lie and who you really are is a completely unrelated kettle of fish. I say go for it – not that you need my permission or approval.'

He leant back in his chair and stretched. 'Enough of this sitting around. Come on. I'll show you the place.' He pushed his chair back from the table and picked up the empty plates.

'Have you made most of this gorgeous furniture?' Rick asked in awe as they made their way through the cottage.

'Only the smaller pieces. I just did up the large ones. Okay, so that's the house,' he added when they were back in the kitchen.

'It's great. And feels like home.'

'I like it. It's rustic. You know, you're welcome to stay as long as you like – until the warehouse is free, or even longer. I don't mind. Take your time.'

'Thanks. But careful what you offer.' Rick laughed off Blair's generosity, though he felt very touched by it. He just didn't quite know how to express that. He had the overwhelming urge to hug the bloke. And where he was from, that sort of thing would get you smacked out. *Where I'm from*, Rick mused. *I'm from around here. I'm not Hope Springs. That wasn't me*, he thought as they stepped down two steps onto a path running between a back garden with neat raised beds.

'Awesome garden,' Rick said. 'I've never got there myself. I think it always felt a bit strange to be growing stuff, tending crops as a day job on the farm and then coming home and doing more of it.' He slowed his step. *God, I sound just like Joseph. Maybe it wasn't me who thought that at all, but it was another notion instilled in me.* Frustration rose as he wondered what was real and what wasn't.

'Each to his own,' Blair said with a shrug. 'Not very manly, but I like growing flowers – roses mainly. I like the colours and the smell.'

'Hey, who gives a shit if it's manly or not? I reckon I've spent my life – no, I *know* I've spent my life not doing things I loved because they weren't considered masculine.'

'The art, right?'

'Yeah. It makes my blood boil – at Maureen and Joseph, the people who raised me, but also myself for not having the guts to challenge it, fight back.'

'You were a kid, I'm betting, and I'm guessing you conformed for your own protection and wellbeing.'

'Yeah, but look how screwed up I am as a result. Thank goodness for Anthea – a counsellor I was seeing. Otherwise, I might not even be here at all.'

'So, there you go. I reckon it takes serious guts to seek help, to accept you don't like who you are and to change, or at least try to understand yourself and why you are the way you are.'

'Do you think I'm running away?' Rick asked as they went through the garden gate towards the sheds.

'Only you would know the answer to that, mate. I think we're probably all running away from something – big or small. And you're running towards something, too, remember? You could have stayed back there and buried your head in the sand and not grown as a person inside.'

'I couldn't have – I'd have gone mad. I already was, just didn't know it or why.'

'The fact you acted on it by going and seeing Anthea says a lot, I reckon.'

'I feel free, actually,' Rick found himself blurting. 'Still a bit scared, though.'

'Ah, I reckon just go with it. One step at a time. Now there's another tattoo we should all be given.'

'You know, society isn't geared for people to stop and think too much or for doing something different – following their hearts. We're meant to be on a hamster wheel.'

'True. It doesn't help that there's no value given to the arts and creativity by those in charge. Other than to make it into a money-making commodity of course, but that's a whole other thing.'

'You're right. There's no encouragement of people to find what makes them truly happy and then do that. Farming, I guess for most, is sort of like that, but still …'

'Yup, the world would be a better place if more people were happy, that's for sure. But I think the meaning of happiness has got a bit lost along the way, too, though.'

'Huh?'

'Well, I reckon back in the old days you were probably pretty happy if you had a full belly and a warm, safe and dry place to sleep, your brain had some stimulation but you also got plenty of R and R. These days it seems happiness is more about being entertained, busy socialising or playing on gadgets. It's all about being busy, always doing. And so many people are stressed out because of it. Sorry, I'm getting a bit deep and heavy,' he said, dragging open a heavy sliding corrugated iron door with a long metallic scrape.

'It's food for thought. I get where you're coming from. What you're saying is we've gone too far past the appreciation of the simple things in life.'

'Yup. That's about it. Though, don't get me wrong, I'm as much a capitalist as the next bloke – I like to drive a nice modern car – I just don't think it's worth selling your soul for. It's also about gratitude. Look how good we've got it compared to times in history like the Depression.'

'Hmm.' Rick nodded. His brain was firing with a million ideas for pieces of art he'd make – metal and wire sculptures, abstract paintings even.

His eyes opened wide as Blair flicked some switches and one by one rows of long fluorescent tube lights blinked and with a series of tink, tink, tink sounds fired up, lighting the space.

Wow. He walked forwards and did a three-sixty-degree turn, taking in the ordered, well-equipped space, letting out a whistle as he did. 'Oh, man, I'm jealous. You have all the toys. Again, I say, careful what you offer – I might never leave.'

Blair laughed. 'I am really grateful to have creative parents – they're not serious artists, just like to dabble and keep busy. It's one way of ignoring whatever the weather's doing outside.'

'Yeah. Near Hope Springs, where our farms are – were – was a windy shithole. I hate the wind.'

'Yeah, it's not too bad here – being in a gully with all the big gums out over the back helps.'

'What are you working on?' Rick asked, going to a large work bench in the centre of the space, where some pieces of timber were laid out. He noticed a hand-drawn plan nearby and went over to study it. 'Ah, a chair,' he said.

'That's right. It's a chair that folds up and can also be a small stepladder. It's for Alice. It's a surprise, though, so don't tell her.'

'Oh, man, you've got it bad,' he said, grinning over at Blair.

'Yep, I sure do.'

'Well, you'd better get your shit together and sort things out with her before she meets someone else.'

'That makes two of us. You need to tell Ashley how you feel, too.'

'Yeah.'

'I'm texting both of them right now to invite them for dinner Friday night. Okay with you?'

'Perfect.'

Chapter Thirty

Rick woke to the sound of movement beside the bed on the floor. In the dim light he could see the outline of one of Blair's dogs.

'Good morning,' he said, leaning over the side and peering down. The sleek black and white dog, Eric, stretched, yawned, groaned, stood up and licked the hand he held out. Rick smiled and patted the dog. 'You're a good dog, Eric,' he said. He sat on the edge of the bed patting the dog while looking at the set of work clothes he'd unpacked from his large suitcase and laid out ready the evening before. He didn't think he'd be working with sheep so soon, if ever again, really, but here they were.

He found himself thinking of Danni and Matilda back near Hope Springs. Neither had responded to the voicemails he'd left last night to tell each of them that he wouldn't be back for the funeral on Friday. He hoped they weren't avoiding him, but he was a bit grateful they hadn't answered, as it prevented him getting into any discussion. Every time Rick thought about it, he became angry. There was no way he was ready to have a rational, calm conversation with them about any of it – it was too raw, and he knew they'd only make him angrier by pretending they cared about him. They were in for a shock when he did. He might just sue their arses. Just out of principle. He still didn't entirely believe they hadn't known at least a little of the truth. He was trying to but hadn't got there yet. *What was so bloody scandalous about me being taken in by my aunt and uncle? Nothing! Exactly! I wasn't the scandal, Joseph and Maureen, you arseholes – your money-grabbing was. Church every fucking Sunday. All those Sunday bloody sermons, the fucking commandments! And, worse, you're not here to face the music, are you? I am.*

While Rick would never have proof, he was absolutely sure it had all been for the money. They could have had some, they'd only had to ask. He could have been a silent financial partner and gone off and done his own thing. But, of course, Joseph was too proud and too insecure for that. *Mean old prick*, he thought as an image of the man screaming at him made its way through his mind amid the red. Hurt people hurt people, Alice had said. *That about sums it up.* He shot an angry arrow towards Bart and Beatrice, too. How could they have let it happen when they'd already had a falling out? And then he softened. They'd also bought into the blood-thicker-than-water bullshit. Most people did until they had a major realisation. And right now Rick was hurting too, so being there wasn't a good plan. Time, he needed more time. He took several long, deep breaths.

'I know, I know, Eric, I need to let it go,' he said, patting the dog. A calmness gently wafted through him as he acknowledged that he couldn't control what people did or thought, especially when they only had part of the story – the part one person wanted to share for their own reasons. 'Best I'm right out of it, eh, pup?'

'Rick, breakfast,' he heard Blair call.

'Come on, that's us, mate,' he said, giving Eric's ears a final ruffle before leaving the room.

'Ah, there you are,' Blair said, looking up from the stove.

'Sorry if I'm late.'

'You're not. And I was actually talking to Eric,' Blair said with a laugh. 'My fault, I should have been clearer.'

'I hope you don't mind, but he as good as knocked on my door. He was quite insistent.'

'No worries. He's taken a shine to you. You're a sensitive chap, aren't you, mate?' he said. Both dogs were now sitting politely side by side next to their feed bowls at the far end of the kitchen bench.

'And he slept on the bed for part of the night. Sorry,' Rick said, cringing.

'No need to be sorry. I don't mind at all. If you can put up with them – at least they're reasonably clean at the moment. We'll see how they are tonight after being with the sheep.'

'I like that you treat them as part of the family.'

'Well, that's what they are,' Blair said, bending down and pouring dry food into the bowls.

'That's nice. We weren't allowed to have farm dogs in the house – apparently if they were pampered too much they'd forget their place and wouldn't work.'

'I have the opposite view. I reckon they'll work harder if they feel loved and respected, but I have no proof. I'm just a softy, I guess. Don't see why they can't be treated well after all they do.'

'Are they good with the sheep?'

'Yep, they're both pretty gifted – but in different ways. Eric's strength is out in the paddock – probably because he can cover a lot of ground with his long legs. And Ruby comes into her own in the yards – she can be really pushy and yappy when she needs to be, not nasty, but assertive. I think it's the clichéd red-headed feistiness. They make a great team. You'll see. Right, bacon and eggs and coffee before it gets cold,' Blair said, bringing two plates out of the oven and placing them on the table and then delivering two mugs of coffee.

'Sorry, I should have helped.'

'Stop apologising. It's no worries, mate. And I'm putting you to work, remember, when you could have said no. The least I can do is give you a decent feed.'

'I'm happy to help.'

'Did you sleep okay?' Blair asked when they were eating.

'Yes, thanks. It's a very comfortable bed.'

'It is. So, not too much churning going on upstairs in the brain, then?'

'Well, I wouldn't say that,' Rick said with a laugh. 'There's a lot of processing going on up there, that's for sure.'

As he matched Blair bite for bite, Rick found himself wondering how it was going to be working sheep with him. Much different, he wouldn't mind betting. It had always been a stressful experience with Joseph in charge. Rick shuddered as a shard of memory shot through him of his uncle screaming and kicking out at the dogs and them cowering and running off to hide beneath the ute.

***

'Okay, I'm not sure how you do it, so forgive me if I sound like I'm being patronising. I'm just used to doing it on my own and my way. I'm going to open the gates into the yards so Eric knows where to bring them,' Blair said once they were in the ute and backing out of the shed. Rick felt weird to be sitting there doing nothing – usually Joseph sat back and gave orders while Rick did all the work. And despite being on the farm for many years, he had never been left to his own devices.

As he sat with the sun streaming in the window, watching Blair opening and closing gates and organising the yards, he thought about how, thanks to Anthea, he'd begun to see there was nothing wrong with being quiet and sensitive. And since Anthea, he'd discovered where this nature of his had come from. He really was beginning to like who he was.

'Rightio, off we go,' Blair said poetically, and grinning, when he was back in the vehicle and putting it into gear.

'You're enjoying this?' Rick couldn't help himself asking, unable to keep his amazement to himself.

'Sure. Why not? The sheep need drenching, it's part of the program, part of the business. May as well accept that and get on. No point getting all stressed about it – that just puts everyone on edge and makes it take twice as long,' Blair said with a shrug.

Oh how I wish Joseph Peterson were here to hear this.

They drove, largely in silence, out on to a track, along it for a few minutes and then into a heavily wooded paddock. Blair drove into the paddock, did a large loop, then exited and backed up and parked parallel with, but back from, the gate they'd just used and facing the direction of the yards.

'Huh?' Rick said, when Blair turned the vehicle off and went to open his door to get out. He looked across Blair and out the window at the sheep dotted around the paddock.

'I take it you don't do it this way?' Blair said, pausing with his door half open.

'I don't know. I guess not, though I'm not sure what you're up to,' Rick said with a puzzled laugh.

'Watch and learn, my friend. Watch and learn,' he said.

Rick looked out the back window where Blair gave both dogs a lot of attention before unclipping Eric.

'Good boy, Eric. Off you go – go get 'em,' Rick heard Blair say, and then saw him wave his arm in the direction of the paddock. In a split second, Eric had leapt from the ute, over the fence, turned right, and raced off around the perimeter of the paddock. He turned back to the back window where he saw Ruby looking after Eric, straining on her chain for a few moments and giving a couple of barks before settling down.

'Now what?' Rick said, frowning, when Blair got back in and made no move to start the vehicle.

'We wait.'

'We wait? And do nothing?'

'Yep.'

'Wow. Okay, then,' Rick said, with big eyes, and sat back with his arms folded. But he kept looking past Blair to the paddock where Eric had been sent. The sheep were still scattered around, slowly grazing and all heading the same way – faces into the breeze – like sheep did. That was no different from their behaviour in his neck of the woods. Rick checked his watch. He was interested to see how long this took – as a comparison, too.

He looked back to the paddock. The grazing sheep were still undisturbed. He scanned the perimeter where Eric had gone. Over there it was heavily wooded. He couldn't tell from this far away if the trees were part of the paddock or fenced off. But then he saw several small white blobs moving out from under the timber. Soon a stream of white stretched out into the paddock, moving towards the middle. The grazing sheep stopped and looked. And then they turned and started coming in Rick and Blair's direction, too. Gradually, in just a few minutes, all the small and larger mobs and individual sheep that had been dotted around and hiding under the trees had become one big wave moving towards them.

'Wow,' Rick said, gazing with wonder at Blair. He looked proud and Rick thought he had every right to be.

'Yep. It's as easy as that.'

Rick nodded, feeling a little lost for words.

'And then what?' he finally managed.

'Because we went to the yards and drove the exact path, both dogs know where they need to go. Once we get them a bit closer, Ruby will do her bit and give Eric a break. As I said, they're a great team.'

'Are you a dog trainer, too?' *Is there nothing this bloke can't do?*

'Nope. They're mostly self-trained. It's in their genes apparently.'

Rick wondered what the three sleek dogs back at the Peterson property were capable of if left to do their own thing. 'And you can trust him to bring them all out – every last one?'

'Yep. Hasn't let me down in five years. In the early days I used to go in and check once Ruby took over. If he finds one back in there that can't walk for whatever reason, or any other problem, he'll stay put until I go and see. Or if I'm distracted and not looking, he'll get sick of waiting and come and get me. It's a bit embarrassing having your dog tell you off for being slack, I can tell you,' Blair said, laughing.

'Unbelievable.'

'Might seem that way. I think most animals are a lot smarter than we give them credit for. You can't make them do anything, just ask them to, really. That's my philosophy, anyway,' Blair said with a shrug. 'It seems to work. And it worked for Dad and his dad before that.'

'Back where I'm from working with sheep was always a shitfest. Stressful. Lots of yelling and slamming of gates, throwing things.'

'I've heard that from a lot of blokes. I just love sheep – they're really not as stupid as people like to think. Take it slow, is my motto. And have some respect. And keep them quiet. Too many people rush it and stir them up. Then they just scatter. Like most things in life – slow and steady is the key.'

'Yeah, we always seemed to be in a rush,' Rick mused. He felt a tug of yearning – to go back and do things differently, do things right. He pushed it back down. There were other ways he could challenge and prove himself. He felt disappointed in Joseph all over again. Stupid old bastard.

'Are you involved with live export – like, to the Middle East?' Rick ventured.

'Hell no. I'd never send my stock on a death ship to meet that sort of fate. The whole practice is barbaric. There is absolutely no need for it and the sooner they stop it, the better, in my opinion. Sorry, I'm a bit vocal about it.'

'Don't be. I completely agree. I was just sussing out where you stood. We weren't into it either, thank Christ – but I think that was more about distance and the cost of getting them to a port than any altruistic views on Joseph's part.'

'I've even gone to the protest rallies.'

'I've seen it all over social media, but I was never in the right place at the right time.'

'Fair enough. I don't share about it online because it's such an emotive topic. A lot of farmers are into it, obviously, and while I want to help the cause to shut it down, I do my best to avoid aggro all round. So much online starts off as a healthy debate but then gets completely derailed by people throwing their own, different, agendas into the mix or simply not knowing the facts of what they're talking about.'

'There are a lot of stupid, gullible people out there, that's for sure. The trouble is they jump on the bandwagon without inform-ing themselves. That's what pisses me off,' Rick said.

'That mob that tried to insinuate that shearing was the same as skinning a sheep alive just about did my head in,' Blair said, shaking his head. 'I eased up my time online significantly because of it. Right, here we are,' he added, as sheep began streaming out the gate, turning right and heading down the track towards the yards. When there were no more, Blair got out. Rick could hear him call Eric to the back and tell him to get up. Through the window he watched while Blair gave the heaving, panting dog plenty of attention and then clipped him to his chain and unclipped Ruby. He gave the red kelpie a good pat before waving his arm in the direction of the sheep. Back in the ute, Blair turned on the ignition and began to ease the vehicle forwards slowly. Ruby was trotting along behind the sheep, keeping well back and letting them pick their way.

Rick smiled when the dog paused and looked back, as if to check they were coming. To him she was saying, hurry up. But when he saw Blair wave his hand out of the open ute window and then Ruby carried on, he knew she was checking for instructions. Rick shook his head in amazement and respect.

As they inched along, they heard a ping from Blair's phone tucked in the console. He checked it. 'Oh. Brett and Lauren are going to come on Friday night too. I told you about them, didn't I?'

'Yep. Sounds good.'

'You'll like them. They're awesome people.'

As they closed the gate behind the last of the sheep at the yards, Rick noted it had taken under an hour to bring in a mob of around two thousand sheep. All without any stress or shouting. So far. He was impressed.

'Do they both work the yards?' Rick asked as they got out of the ute and Blair unclipped Eric.

'Yeah, but Eric doesn't like to push too hard – as a pup he got a fright from a cranky ram who tried to have a go at him. Thankfully, like I said, Ruby can get pretty assertive if she needs to.'

'Okay. So, what can I do to help?'

'Are you any good with a drenching gun?'

'Of course.'

'Great. We can run two races, then, and get it done in half the time.'

'Brilliant. But will they work for me?' he asked, nodding towards the dogs who were sprawled out in the shade of a tree panting, waiting, wet from taking a dip in the trough on their way past.

'Yep, should do. They know what's what. They've done this before. Just say, "bring 'em up", in an authoritative tone and they should fill your race for you. Then say, "good dogs, that's enough", and they should hang back. Unfortunately, they can't open and shut gates, so we'll have to walk back and do that ourselves.'

'Oh damn,' Rick said, grinning.

'Yeah, I'm working on how I can sort it, believe me. But, hey, we need a bit of exercise, so I guess it's only fair.'

Rick and Blair and the dogs were soon working as a well-oiled machine, with the only sounds being the bleating and shuffling of the sheep, the odd bark of the dogs, instructions from Rick and Blair, and the occasional word from Blair asking Rick if he was doing okay and his reply that he was. Rick was enjoying the calm repetitive toil of bending down, placing the long, thin metal gun-shaped apparatus carefully between the lips and into the mouth of the closest sheep, squeezing the trigger, then pulling it out, just as carefully, and then moving back to the next one in the line.

Rick was surprised when they stopped for lunch and said so. He was hungry, but he was used to ignoring it and pushing on.

'The dogs need a break, and so do we,' Blair said. 'No point pushing ourselves and them. That's when tempers can start to get frayed. Grandad taught me that taking a decent break can make you much more productive.'

They opened the gates and let the remaining sheep have plenty of space, which included a trough. Rick was further impressed. Peterson sheep had often spent all day in the yards panting, their flanks heaving and tucked up from lack of water. He'd once questioned Joseph about it and been yelled at – told to not be disrespectful. Rick cringed at the memory and thought of the stress all the sheep over the years had endured.

'It's coming in warm. We'll see after lunch, but we might leave them – give them some feed – and carry on in the morning. There's enough shade and shelter.'

'You wouldn't want to just get them dealt with and let back out?' Rick ventured carefully.

'No – because they're so quiet, being kept in doesn't seem to be causing them additional stress. It's another of the perks of having quiet stock.'

'Yeah. I see that. We always had to get it done in one hit, if possible – start early work late.'

'Whatever works,' Blair said, diplomatically, and shrugged.

'I reckon your way is the right way,' Rick said.

'I'm just all about the path of least resistance. I don't see the point in making it stressful if you can get around it. It's business, but it doesn't have to be hard. Life is to be enjoyed and, if it's not, for a lot of the time, change what you do. That's what I reckon, anyway.'

'Sounds good to me,' Rick said, as they made their way back to the house, the dogs trotting in front. 'A part of me wants to be a farmer again – do it better, properly, this time around,' he said, as they took off their boots outside and put them on the step.

'You can do whatever you like with yourself, and your money. It's yours, but for what it's worth, I reckon just living your life and being content in what you do is enough revenge, if that's what you're looking for. You'll be forever chasing your tail and unhappy if you try to compete or score points with or prove anything to anyone – especially dead people. Do what you want for yourself, inside here,' he said, poking himself in the chest. 'Being happy – which is the same thing as success, in my book – is the best revenge you can have.'

He looked at Blair, nodding, and his new mate looked steadily back. 'Yeah, I think you're right,' said Rick.

***

Rick and Blair finished the sheep Thursday afternoon, having stretched the job over two and a half days. They were muscle sore and weary from the activity and monotony of the task, but not frazzled or cranky. This was a first for Rick, and a very enlightening experience. He was really beginning to see how much better a different, calmer, approach from Joseph's bull-at-a-gate one could be. The frustrating thing was that it was too late to tell the people who had raised him. He marvelled at how different everything might have been – how different *he* might have been with a gentle approach. He told Blair of this inner turmoil while they were tidying everything up. Blair had said he thought perhaps there was a reason they weren't there to tell. Rick had frowned back, his confusion exacerbated by the weariness that had seeped right through him.

'Maybe *they* didn't have to learn it, Rick – maybe *you* did,' Blair explained.

'But …' Rick had begun to protest, but then realised Blair was right. And as Blair had said before, perhaps he was learning these things now because he was ready to – in a receptive frame of mind with his soul open.

'You can't help those who don't want to help themselves,' Blair had added.

Rick had nodded several times. No matter how much it made sense, the resentment remained. 'It's just so bloody frustrating,' he said, not meaning to utter the words aloud.

'Yep. That's why we have artists and art.'

'Sorry? What?' They'd been driving back to the house after closing the gate on the last of the sheep in their fresh paddock and Rick thought he was clearly more exhausted than he actually felt because this comment of Blair's had him completely stumped.

'To express the frustration, to make sense of the world around us – its stupidity, its loveliness ... the whole gamut,' he said, sweeping an arm around. 'They're the smart ones – artists, creatives. They take the time to sit and ponder, think, delve deep within and answer their own questions and how they fit into wider society. Fools simply get angry and become aggressive. Obviously, it's not so cut and dried as all that, but the fact is, in my opinion, not enough people in this busy society of ours are capable of just *being*. Being true to themselves. Being kind. Being gentle. Being at peace. It's all about activity and being constantly on the move these days. When did you last see someone under about fifty simply sitting and enjoying their surroundings – watching the world go by and not staring down at their phone?'

'Good point. I'm pretty addicted to mine, I have to admit,' Rick said, his cheeks burning a little with his embarrassment.

'Of course you are. We're part of the tech generation. It's as programmed into us as the apps in our phone. At least you're not posting a dozen selfies a day,' Blair said, looking at Rick.

'*That* I'm not doing, at least,' Rick said with a laugh. 'Why can't we all simply take a photo to remind ourselves later of where we've been? It's all too deep for me right now. I'm exhausted. I'm clearly very unfit.'

'Or just using different muscles than you have recently,' Blair pointed out.

'Maybe,' Rick agreed. 'And, anyway, forget selfies. I'm too busy figuring out the real me – the one that's hidden inside.'

'So, did your sisters, um, sorry, cousins, say anything more either way about you not going back to the funeral? And have you changed your mind? We could still make it if you wanted to go and fancied the company. Everyone would understand if we postponed dinner.'

'Thanks. I really appreciate the offer, Blair, but I'm done. I'm not going back. Ever, probably. And I'm at peace with that. Their communication – or lack of – has said it all, really. They haven't expressed a desire for me to be there – just asked if I will be and tried their best to make it look like they're including me. They're probably afraid me being there will turn their mother's funeral into a freak show. And rightly so. They'll most likely milk the he-left-us-in-our-hour-of-need factor, but so be it.'

'Fair enough. As long as you're sure you won't have any regrets later.'

'The only regret I'll have – have already – is that I was an idiot and didn't take proper notice of my birth certificate. If I'd uncovered all this back then …' he said, shaking his head. Suddenly it was overwhelming again. He could see how different everything would have been.

'And if you had, you wouldn't be here now and the person you are. And you might even have completely blown all that money if you'd got your hands on it back then, too. Plenty have in the past.'

'Hmm.' Rick wasn't ready to be grateful for Joseph and Maureen protecting him from that. 'I know you've said it, and I do believe on some level that it had to happen this, that, way. But it still hurts and frustrates me.'

'Of course it does. You're human. Now you just have to find a way to make peace with it, figure out how you're meant to use what you've learnt to have a better, more meaningful life going forwards.'

'You make it sound so easy,' Rick said with a tight laugh.

'Just follow your heart, be true to your soul, drown out the negative noise and I think you'll be perfectly fine,' Blair said.

Chapter Thirty-one

'I'm going to have a house-warming when I get settled,' Rick blurted. They'd gone into town earlier to do the shopping and were now in the kitchen getting everything ready for their dinner party that evening.

'Good for you,' Blair said from beside him at the bench.

'Oh, except I only know about four other people.'

'Then just make it a nice, civilised dinner party. Like tonight is going to be. So, you're going to move into the warehouse, do you think, when it's available?'

'Yep. You're right. I just need to settle, stop for a bit and think things through. Or not – as you say, just be. I have the luxury of time, thanks to the money in the trust. And I've spent my life under the shadow of worry about money and what we owe and all that. No matter what the year was, there was still negative talk of money. In good times it was all about not paying tax. In the bad times it was whingeing about the amount of debt. So, I'm just going to let the dust settle and see how I feel. But I do feel a bit of urgency to get organised, though, because I want to get a dog.'

'You can't go wrong with sharing your life with a dog or two – their therapeutic qualities are immeasurable. And if you're feeling really down, so bad you don't want to get out of bed, it's good to have someone who relies on you completely to survive – you know for food, water, et cetera.'

Rick looked at Blair. 'Have you ever been that depressed?'

'I certainly have. A few times. Mainly when I was sick. I have a great family, but we're scattered and sometimes you just can't help feeling lonely and sad and not like talking to anyone or sharing certain things. I struggled with being a burden and having them feel sorry for me, and of course feeling shit all round when I was having chemo. So, yes, there were certainly times when I might not have got out of bed of a morning if it weren't for the fact I had these two darlings telling me to get up and feed them. Or them just making me feel better by keeping me company.'

Rick nodded silently and thoughtfully, grateful he had something to do with his hands and pretend to be concentrating on. Blair was so wise, philosophical and upbeat, Rick struggled to imagine him in a really low state. Maybe there was hope for him too. No, there definitely was – he felt he'd come a long way already. Just throwing off the heavy chains of his upbringing and starting to think for himself had produced real results. Now he had to focus on not stuffing things up with the lovely Ashley. *Concentrate, big fella, concentrate.*

'Here they are,' Blair called at hearing the knock on the door and voices. He wiped his hands on the nearest hand towel.

Rick did the same, took a deep breath, and followed him out of the kitchen and down the hall. As he stood next to Blair, ready to welcome the guests, he almost laughed. For anyone who didn't know them, they might look like a *couple* couple – two gay men. The old him would have been terrified of this potential misunderstanding. The new Rick wasn't bothered at all. And if he had been that way inclined, there'd be few people better than Blair to make a life with.

His heart tumbled three times at seeing Ashley. *Yup, love at first sight. Again,* he thought. And this time he knew it had nothing to do with lust – there was no stirring going on in his pants. The only filling up going on here was in his heart, which was expanding, as if stretching out to grab her – just like his hands were actually reaching out to her shoulders. He pecked her on the cheek and caught a whiff of freshness tinged with roses and maybe jasmine. He knew roses well, but only recognised jasmine because Blair had pointed it out in the garden the other day. Ashley was beaming at him, just as, he noticed out of the corner of his eye, Alice was beaming at Blair. Rick almost sighed with relief and contentment. Imagine his hurt if both women had been interested in Blair. And Ashley definitely wasn't, because she'd just tucked her hand through Rick's arm. His jittering heart steadied. He found himself lifting her hand and bringing it to his lips for a gentle kiss. He didn't think he'd ever done anything so corny in his life. He didn't care. He was happy. And he didn't want there to be any confusion around his intentions. They beamed at each other – in their own little bubble. Rick was glad Lauren and Brett hadn't arrived at the same time.

Here they were now. He turned to await the arrival of the car behind the headlights making their way up the driveway, his arm slipping neatly around Ashley as naturally as could be. He felt her lean into him and thought she let out a contented sigh, but that could have been his wishful thinking. He looked up at the stars shining in the clear, dark sky beyond the lights of the verandah, thinking this night would still be perfect if the wind was howling and thunder and lightning raged around them. He had the feeling that no matter what happened, with Ashley by his side, he could get through it. A little voice inside him tried to tell him that was being ridiculous – he'd probably spoken less than a hundred words to the woman in total, so how could he possibly know? *Oh, I know*, Rick thought. *I know. This is it. Ashley is the one.* His chest expanded and he became taller. Right then, he could have taken on the world – slayed any dragon, real or imagined, that came anywhere near him and his girl.

'Lauren, Brett, this is Rick Peterson,' Blair was now saying to the newcomers.

'Alice's ex-husband, right? Brilliant to meet you,' Lauren said, not waiting for an answer, or accepting his hand – instead throwing her arms around him.

'Yes,' Rick said.

'Great to meet you, mate,' Brett said when Rick had been released, and offering his own hand.

'Okay, people,' Blair said when they'd all made their way through to the kitchen. 'Rick, you sort out drinks while I get dinner prep finished.'

'No problem.' They'd discussed how things would go, so he was all over it. 'We have beer, sparkling white, red or non-alcoholic sparkling apple juice, water or tea or coffee, if you prefer.' He was thrilled when Ashley stood beside him and pretended to help. He chose the apple juice, wanting to keep his head clear. And he was impressed to see Ashley sticking to the soft stuff as well.

'I'm not a big drinker ordinarily, but I don't like to have anything at all if I'm driving,' she explained. And Rick thought he fell in love with her just a little bit more, if that were possible.

'Sounds like a good idea to me,' he said as he filled their glasses and the others', having to remind himself to watch what he was doing and not get distracted by the lovely vision that was Ashley.

'Ah, a mighty fine drop,' he said after they'd all clinked glasses, cried, 'Cheers!' and taken a sip. Rick and Ashley remained by the bench, Blair moved to the fridge and Lauren, Brett and Alice drifted over to the end of the table where their platter of nibbles had been placed. The tightknit trio was standing close, clearly catching up on what had gone on since they'd last met. He leant over to Blair.

'Do you mind if I take Ashley over and show her the studio?' he whispered.

'Sure. No problem. Here, you'll need keys. It's locked,' he said, opening a drawer and taking a set out and handing them over.

'Come on, I want to show you something,' he said to Ashley, putting an arm around her and gently guiding her towards the back door. If he'd been doing this back at Hope Springs he could imagine someone yelling out, 'Don't do anything I wouldn't do,' or 'If you can't be good, be careful,' or the sound of loud, derisive cheers following them outside. He was beginning to see how uncomfortable his friends back there had been with affection and intimacy. No opportunity to make fun of someone or humiliate rarely went to waste. Rick hadn't really understood what a true friend was, he didn't think, until he'd arrived in Ballarat and Alice had taken him under her wing. And then Blair. *God, how lucky am I?* he thought, shaking his head slowly. *Coming here.*

He suddenly remembered Ashley beside him and squeezed her closer. The breeze whipped her scent around him.

'God, you smell good,' he found himself saying, in a slow, drawn-out voice.

'Thanks,' she said.

'Sorry, was that sleazy?'

'No, not at all.'

'I'm very out of practice with, um, all this,' he said.

'Me too. But don't worry, I don't think there are any rules beyond having basic good manners and respect,' she said, smiling.

As he turned to hold the gate back to let her pass first, he leant in and kissed her – deeply, lingering. But no tongues. He didn't want her to be in any doubt how he felt, but also didn't want her to think he was after the one thing blokes were well known for being after. Their height difference was irrelevant as they gazed intently into each other's eyes. The glow from the moonlight and string of soft solar lights across the back verandah gave them a gentle sheen.

'God, you're beautiful,' he said, pushing a loose strand of hair back from her face. *Jesus, you sound like a bloody Hallmark card or a soppy movie.* But he didn't care. He kissed her again, deeper. Her lips parted and she leant into him; their chests were hot against each other.

Suddenly Rick pulled back and released her. He didn't want to cheapen this, and she'd been almost bent backwards over the wire and steel fence. They had their whole lives ahead of them, however long that might be. He didn't want to rush this.

He almost gasped: he finally really got the meaning of delayed gratification. The anticipation of what might be to come, later, much later. That if he took this easy, they might spend months, years getting to fully know each other, inside and out – piece by piece. Instead of a quick roll in the hay and satisfying a basic, urgent need in one hit and not having anything left to look forward to.

'Oh my god, Ashley,' he groaned. It would be hard to resist. She smelt and felt so good he couldn't get close enough to her. He wanted to climb inside her and join their souls together. *Creepy much?* he found himself thinking, as he held her tight. 'Oh,' he said, pulling back as he felt something bump his leg. He looked down. Eric and Ruby stood in front of them, peering up, their tails wagging.

'Hello, you guys,' he said, bending down and giving them each a pat. Ashley bent down beside him.

'Aww, aren't you lovely?' she said, ruffling their ears.

'Ashley, this is Eric and this is Ruby.'

'Cute names.'

'Well, I can't take any credit for that. So, you like dogs, then?'

'Oh yes. I have a miniature poodle called Max. He and Alice's Bill get on famously – they hang out at the office with us.'

'I'm sure Alice might have mentioned that. Sorry, I forgot.'

'No worries. But, yes, I'm a huge dog lover. All animals, really.'

Rick relaxed, surprised to find he'd even been tense in the first place. But now he thought, *You're lovely. You really are.*

'Are poodles the ones that have the hair that people don't get allergic to?' He thought he'd heard that somewhere before. *Most probably online and it was complete BS. Oh well, too late now.*

'I'm not sure. I'm not allergic to any dogs, that I know of. He was at the shelter and we had a connection. That's all. And he's an awesome little guy. You'll love him.'

Rick soared. 'I'm going to get a greyhound – you know, from the adoption program?'

'That's great.'

'I haven't looked into it fully yet. I like the idea that they don't need a lot of exercise and apparently are happy to just hang out. They seem really chilled. And there must be a lot who need homes.'

'Yes. It's hard to believe they call them couch potatoes, to look at them.'

'Yeah.'

'So, Alice tells me your parents were artists and you've inherited their warehouse-slash-studio? She updated me after you called her. Are you going to stay? In Ballarat? And become an artist?'

'Yes. Definitely – to staying. And, maybe, if I can figure out if I have any talent or not.'

'Are you kidding?'

'What?' Rick was genuinely perplexed.

'Alice showed me a picture of the sculpture you made her. And the ones from your scrapbook of your parents' work – they're on her phone. You've clearly inherited their talent.'

'Thanks. It's a little daunting, to be honest.'

'Why? What is? I mean, god, of course everything would be. What am I saying? I hope you don't mind, but Alice has told me everything. It started with her being so shocked that she blurted it out. And then, well …'

'No problem. You know, I'm learning how much help talking about things is. I was raised by people and in a place where that was a no-no and counselling was practically something you could go to hell for. Not that I'm religious – that's a topic for another day. I'm cool with people knowing. I've realised just how unlikeable guarded people are, to be honest. I've been surrounded by them my whole life without knowing. Including Alice's lot.'

'Yes, her sister and her mother sound like real pieces of work.'

'Yep. I was an idiot and didn't see it, though.'

'Well, that's the whole thing about narcissists, so don't feel too bad.'

'Um, do you think we can *not* talk about my ex-wife on our first date,' Rick said, and gently turned Ashley towards him to look her in the eye so she'd know he was being more playful than serious. Though, he did also mean it. They were all friends, but he didn't want to get caught on that path.

Ashley surprised him by leaning in, teetering on her tippy-toes, and kissing him on the cheek. He wrapped his arms around her again. Their bodies were practically fused, their hearts beating fast together – thumpity thump, thumpity thump. The thought, *Easy, tiger, you don't want to scare the girl off*, rolled through him and with a slight groan he reluctantly stopped kissing Ashley and gently eased them apart.

'Come on, I wanted to show you Blair's studio and I don't want to hold up dinner.' He kissed her on the lips, took her by the hand and led her out the gate, shutting it behind them, checking over her shoulder as he did that the dogs were on the house side. As they walked in silence, still hand in hand, Rick wondered if Ashley had a big goofy grin on her face like he did.

He pulled the door open and flicked on the lights. Gradually the place was illuminated. 'That's a chair-slash-stepladder for Alice that Blair's making.'

'God, he's got it bad, too,' she said, going over and running her hands over the timber.

'Yep. Too?'

'She's smitten. And, I meant us.'

He came up behind her, wrapped his arms around her and nuzzled her hair. She leant back into him. Right then he'd have given every cent of the trust fund to stay like this forever.

'Okay, so tell me more about the very lovely Ashley Baker,' he said. 'Is it too early to be talking deal-breakers? I don't have any, but you might. Probably good to know from the beginning. Like, do you only date bad boys and do I have to get some tatts? I don't have any, by the way. But, seriously, if I'm coming on too strong and freaking you out, just say.' *Stop babbling. Give the poor girl a chance to answer.*

'No, all good. I much prefer to be upfront. Bad boys? No way. Um, okay, well, this might be a deal-breaker …' she said, tensing up a little in his arms. 'I'm pretty sure I don't want kids.'

He shook his head. 'Nope, not a deal-breaker. I'm pretty sure I don't want kids, either,' he said, giving her neck a reassuring kiss. It worked. The tension was gone again. 'Next.'

'Um. I probably won't ever want to leave Ballarat – holidays are fine, just not permanently.'

'Good with me. I've just arrived, and I'm not going anywhere without you. Do you think you could be okay with being with a crazy artist?'

'What form would the crazy bit take?'

'I'm not sure yet,' he muttered. 'Still figuring it all out. But I can promise I won't be a miserable drunk or mean.'

'A happy drunk, then?' Ashley muttered.

'No. Not a drunk at all.'

'Same goes from me – all of the above. Do you think you can live with a lawyer?'

'I think I'll take my chances. And you might be useful.'

'Oh really?'

'Yup,' he said, hugging her tightly and giving her head a kiss. 'Anything else?'

'Nope, that's all for now. But I'm not going anywhere, so you can ask whatever you want anytime you like going forwards.'

'Yes please! I like the sound of that.' Rick gently turned her to face him and looking intently into her eyes said, 'I *really, really* like you, Ashley Baker.'

'And I really, really like you, Rick Peterson.'

'Good.'

'So, do you think we'd better get back before they send a search party or the steaks are ruined?'

'Yeah,' he said, flicking off the lights and closing the door. He held her hand tightly.

Back inside, looking around the group, the warm sensation flowing through Rick told him he belonged – really belonged. These people who he'd known barely a week – and Lauren and Brett, less than an hour – felt like the family he'd never had. Tears filled his eyes and he quickly wiped them away. But he wasn't quick enough for Alice and Ashley, who happened to look at him at that moment.

'Are you okay?' they both whispered, each patting his leg.

'Yep. Thanks. Just having a moment.'

***

Alice appeared beside Rick at the bench, startling him slightly. He'd been absently staring at the marbling in the Laminex bench top while waiting for the bread rolls to cook in the oven – one of his set tasks for the evening.

'Hey,' he said.

'Hey. Just getting a tea towel. I spilt some water,' Alice said.

'Right. I'm watching the bread rolls cook.'

'I can see.'

'Could have set a timer or alarm on my phone or something, but, hey …' he said with a shrug. Suddenly he was worried about what Alice thought about him and Ashley. Was she hurting? *Oh, please, no.* He swallowed before speaking again. But Alice got in first.

'Wow, what a great night,' she said. 'So, you and Ashley have really hit it off, hey?'

'Yeah, I really like her, Alice,' he said, feeling a little wary. 'Um, is that okay with you?'

'You don't need my permission, Rick.'

'I know, but …'

'I'm happy for you.'

'Really?'

'Really. Truly.' She touched his arm as if to make the point more clearly. He looked down at her hand.

'I'm going to marry her one day,' he whispered.

'Good for you.'

'You don't mind?'

'Why would I mind? Oh. Because you're so clearly smitten and it took you over twelve months to realise you liked *me* that much? And that might make me jealous or something?' she said with her eyebrows raised.

'Well, yeah,' he said, shrugging. This was getting awkward.

'You're two of my favourite people. If you're happy I'm happy. Seriously. You and I weren't right from the start, remember? We wanted to be, tried so hard to fit together. For our own reasons, because of our own insecurities, the damaged bits inside. Ashley isn't screwed up like I was, like I now know I was. She's all-round awesome. And you'll be great together.'

He opened his mouth to protest but wasn't sure what to say.

'It's okay, Rick, it is what it is. I'm just saying it, and not to make you feel bad. I'll always love you and be disappointed we went through all we did and hurt each other so much. But look where we are now. Not many divorces end in friendship. And I consider you a dear, forever friend.'

'I love you too, Alice,' he said, pulling her into a hug. 'You really are the best, you know that? You're all-round awesome, too,' he whispered into her hair before releasing her. 'How lucky was I to find you again?'

'About as lucky as I was.'

There was a beat of silence before Alice continued. 'So, on a more sombre note,' she said, 'I don't want to bring you down, but I just wanted to know how you are about today – the funeral. I know you don't feel a part of things and you've probably got all the closure you need in terms of facts, but still … It must be weighing on you a bit.'

'Yeah. It's the weirdest thing. I'm torn between wanting to be part of it – acknowledged and not cast out, and to set people straight – but I also don't want to know or be a part of it. And also I'm a bit sad. I know I shouldn't be, but I am.'

'Of course you are, Rick. We don't just grieve people we loved and lost. You're grieving the loss of all you knew, who you thought you and your family were. You'll be grieving knowing you can never confront them and get full closure in that sense. And even unhappy situations can feel safe and secure. There's a certain amount of comfort to be found in certainty. And upheaval and the unknown are scary. That's a big part of why abused people struggle to leave and keep going back, remember? And maybe the little voice telling you you have to be loyal and not make waves is creeping in – the upbringing, the small-town factor, talking?'

'Yup. Thank god you get it.'

'I do. Unfortunately, I don't have any answers. It's such an individual thing. We all handle grief differently. The only way through it is bit by bit. Slow and steady. And getting to a place inside you where you feel okay takes as long as it takes. And, really, it all happened mere seconds ago in the scheme of things. So just be kind to you. Time doesn't heal all wounds, but it helps.'

'I guess. It just all hurts so much,' he added in a whisper.

'I know. But that's because you're human and a kind person. And that's a good thing. I've learnt that no matter how hard it hurts, be grateful that it does. For me it means I'm nothing like my mother.'

'Hmm. You know you're not, right? Not at all. Or anything like Olivia.'

'Thanks. I'm still working my way through it all.'

'Jesus, aren't we a fine pair?' Rick said with a laugh.

'Well, at least we have each other. And Ashley and Blair and Lauren and Brett. Safety in numbers,' she said, looking around.

'Yeah, they all seem pretty awesome,' Rick said, following her gaze. 'I'm glad you've sorted everything out with Blair. Properly. You have, haven't you?'

'Yep. I'm all loved up, too,' Alice said a little coyly.

'I'm glad.'

'Thanks for talking to him. He didn't say, but I know you must have.'

'Guilty as charged. But nothing off limits. I promise.'

'I know. You know, Rick, I would trust you with my life,' Alice said thoughtfully, looking at him.

'And I you with mine,' he said, matching her tone and returning her slightly intense gaze. Again he felt tears rush into his eyes. 'Oh god. No,' he said, brushing them away with his sleeve. 'Come on, let's get back before they think we're going to run off together.'

'The bread rolls. You're here to stop them burning, remember?'

'Oh yeah. Shit. I completely lost track of time,' he said, peering through the glass into the oven.

'Usually when you can smell them, they're done,' Alice said, sniffing the air. 'Give them a minute more, maybe two.'

Chapter Thirty-two

They all oohed and aahed at the platter of succulent meat placed in front of them in the middle of the table and helped themselves to salads and condiments. They'd settled into their meals when Lauren spoke through the clatter and scrape of cutlery on plates.

'Okay, so we want to hear all about you, Rick. Why you're here, how long you're staying …'

'Oh, well …' Panic rose in Rick briefly. But he'd seen no evidence tonight that these were the type of people to tease or ridicule.

'I'm a nosey bugger. Don't tell me if you don't want to.'

'She blames it on being a writer, but she really is just a nosey bugger,' Brett said, putting his arm around Lauren, who pretended to shrug him off but then kissed him.

'Guilty as charged,' she said happily, taking a sip of wine. 'Seriously, though, if it's too personal …'

'No, it's okay.' He wondered what she wanted to know. 'What has Alice told you?'

'Practically nothing at all.'

Rick realised Lauren was a little tipsy.

'It wasn't my story to tell,' Alice said.

'And, seriously, Rick, don't mind me. If you don't want to say, don't,' Lauren said, waving her glass before taking another sip of wine.

'It's okay. I've decided: no more secrets. I'm just not sure where to start,' he said, scrolling through everything in his mind's eye in case there was anything he shouldn't share. *No. And, anyway, it's my story.*

'At the beginning,' said a chorus of voices.

'Are you sure? I don't want to monopolise the whole evening.' It was Blair's dinner party, after all.

'Go on, if you want to. The night is still young,' Blair said.

'Well, okay, then. So, once upon a time, there was a little boy ...' he began, causing everyone to chuckle before falling silent.

Every time Rick paused for too long or attempted to stop, feeling he'd hogged the limelight for too long, the others urged him to keep going, including Ashley, who also nudged his knee.

'And here I am,' he finally said, feeling a little exhausted. He picked up his water glass and took a long slug.

'Wow,' Brett said.

'If I wrote that my lecturer would probably say it wasn't believable,' Lauren said with awe.

'I have the scrapbook with the articles and photos and everything, so ...'

'Oh no, I'm not saying I don't believe you, it's just ...'

'I know. Sometimes just thinking about some of the bits does my head in,' he said.

Everyone lapsed into thoughtful silence and Rick was suddenly concerned he'd brought down the mood.

'Hang on a minute,' Lauren said, holding up her hand. Rick thought she seemed suddenly very sober and very serious.

Lauren looked up at Rick, her eyes boring into him. 'What were your grandparents' names again – Willoughby?' she asked.

Rick had the feeling Lauren wasn't just asking to show polite curiosity. 'Yes, Willoughby,' he said. His heart rate started to rise.

'But what were their first names? You didn't tell us just now, did you?'

'Oh. No, I didn't. Because I can't remember. Oh god. Hang on. Um.' Rick searched his brain. He felt awful at not recalling them straight away. They were his grandparents.

'Was it Richard and Eleanor by any chance?'

'Yes. That's them. Richard Harrison and Eleanor Anne,' Rick said. 'Why?'

'Oh my god. I know them! Well, obviously I don't know them personally – I know *of* them.'

A chorus of 'how?', 'why?' and 'what?' ran around the table.

'They owned our house. They were the people before the people before us.'

Rick thought if he wasn't sitting down, he might have passed out. His mouth dropped open and he had to force it shut.

'Oh my god,' Alice said. 'I've just realised.' They all turned to look at her. Rick thought she looked as pale as he probably was.

'What?' they all demanded. 'Realised what?'

'The mailbox.'

Mailbox? Rick wondered, but waited.

'Rick,' Alice said, 'remember at Sarah's how I said I thought your parents' signature was familiar ...?' Her eyes were wide and darting around a little with excitement.

Yes? He thought he'd spoken the word aloud but couldn't be sure. He wasn't aware of anything but Alice and the silence around them. He nodded. Or he might have imagined he'd done that, too.

'Is anybody else completely lost here?' Lauren said, looking around, blinking. 'Alice, you're not making sense. Oh. *Our* mailbox?' Lauren still looked perplexed.

'Yes! You said, that day, you thought your gorgeous mailbox, that was there when you bought the house, was made by a local artist?'

'Yes.'

'The curls you think are butterfly wings aren't actually that at all.'

'Sorry, you've lost me again.'

'That's their signature – two Bs back to back! I think your letterbox might have been made by Rick's parents.'

'Oh. Oh. My. God,' Lauren said.

'How cool would that be?' Alice said, squirming a little on her chair.

'And pretty bloody spooky,' Brett said.

'Wow,' said Ashley, 'I thought you said it was South Australians who were only ever one degree of separation, Alice. Man oh man.'

'So, does anyone have a photo of it or do we have to do a quick road trip to check?' Brett asked, looking around the group.

'It wasn't in the album,' Rick said.

'I bet it was the first piece they ever made. How romantic would that be?' Alice mused. 'I thought I had a photo of it on my phone, but I can't find it,' she said, scrolling. 'I hope you don't mind, Rick, but I do have the others – from the album.'

'No, not at all.'

'Oh. Hang on. I do,' Lauren said. 'After you mentioned it, Alice, I took a pic in the hope it would provide some inspiration. I separated everything into albums the other day,' she said, scrolling through her phone.

'Of course you did,' Alice said with a laugh.

'I was procrastinating,' Lauren said, not looking up from her phone.

'Of course you were,' Brett said.

'Ah, here it is!' Lauren said, practically leaping out of her chair.

Rick's heart stopped and then skipped two beats as he held his hand out and then stared at the mailbox, which did indeed share characteristics with Sarah's piece and the pictures in the album.

'Oh. Wow. It's incredible,' he said.

'It's even more beautiful in real life,' Alice said. 'And here, Lauren, here's some of their other work – see, it's unmistakeably theirs.'

'Oh my god. It is. Well, Rick, you'd better come over tomorrow and see it for yourself. Impromptu lunch at Mum and Dad's, anyone?' Lauren looked around the group.

'I'd love to,' Rick said. He looked at Ashley and Alice with his eyebrows raised.

'Oh no! We can't,' Ashley said. 'I have a friend's wedding.'

'And I'm Ashley's plus one. Oh. Or maybe you should be now, Rick!' Alice said.

'No offence, Rick, but I wouldn't want to make it about us – all the questions we'd be asked would take it a bit away from the bride and groom,' Ashley said. She squeezed his leg, where her hand had been all night. 'Sorry.'

'None taken. Not at all. You're absolutely right. It would be a bit rude of us, I think. I was just figuring out how to say exactly what you so eloquently did. Although I will wish I was there with you,' he said, gazing into her eyes.

'Well, you can have fun with us instead. We are very fun people, actually,' Lauren said, feigning huffiness. 'And while we can't compete with wedding cake and terrible dancing, we do have possibly the most gorgeous mailbox on the planet.'

'Get ready to have your mind blown, Rick – again – because their house is amazing,' Alice said.

'Oh my god. What a coincidence. Well, it would be if I believed in coincidences,' Lauren said, waving her hand again.

Rick smiled.

'Okay, everyone, just hold that thought. I'm going to get our dessert while there's a lull in proceedings,' Blair said, standing up. Alice leapt up and began helping him collect the plates. Rick thought he'd be more useful staying put and leaving them to have some alone time. He wasn't sure his legs would hold him up anyway just yet. And his brain wasn't thinking very well – it was stuck on, *What are the odds of that?* running around and around on a loop.

'Yum, this looks good,' Lauren said, as a large platter laden with several different cheeses, crackers, nuts and a variety of dried and fresh fruits was placed in the centre of the table.

'Tuck in, people,' Blair said. 'More wine, or anything else, anyone, while I'm up? Shall I open another bottle? I thought I'd put the kettle on later. Call me an old fogey, but I love a pepper-mint tea after a big meal.'

The alcohol drinkers around the table agreed they'd had enough wine and there was a general consensus that water now and peppermint tea later sounded like a good plan.

'So, Lauren, tell me about being a writer,' Rick said, breaking into the looming silence. He felt a bit bad about how much airtime he'd taken up during the night.

'Oh, I wish,' Lauren said, rolling her eyes.

'Do I have that wrong? You're not a writer?' Rick frowned. He looked at Alice, who had just returned and sat down, for help.

'Lauren, stop it. She is, Rick. She's really talented and has even won an award and been published,' Alice said.

'That's brilliant. Wow. Congratulations.'

'Only with short stories.'

'So, what's wrong with that – short stories, that is?' he asked.

'Exactly! Darling Lauren here thinks the be-all-and-end-all is a novel, and she hasn't found her groove there yet. So she continues to put her talents down.'

'Well … I …' Lauren began to protest.

'Stop it,' Alice said gently. 'She has a Masters in Creative Writing with all high distinctions.'

'And I'm resorting to teaching to at least bring in some money and stop sponging off Mum and Dad so much, bless them,' Lauren said.

'Brett, please tell her teaching is not resorting – she'll be bloody brilliant,' Alice said.

'Oh I've tried, believe me, as have both Charles and Melissa. Her parents,' he added, looking at Rick and then Ashley. 'Who are both teachers, I might add – though in different areas. Shall we tell them our other news, darling?'

'Yes. Let's.'

'What are you talking about? What other news?' Alice said, looking quizzically from Lauren to Brett.

'We're moving back to Ballarat. We're going to live with Lauren's parents,' Brett said.

'Oh my god, that's *awesome*,' Alice said.

'Well, that's not the half of it. Don't worry, Rick and Ashley, the house is huge, so it's not as weird as it sounds,' Brett added.

'Huuuuge. And has a separate cottage, anyway,' Alice added. 'And Lauren's parents are fantastic, so it wouldn't matter either way.'

'I've got an interview on Monday with an engineering firm – I'm a civil engineer.'

'That's great. Good luck,' Rick said.

'Thanks.'

'Oh, come on, that's not the interesting bit,' Lauren said. 'He's taken up photography, too. Is doing a course. Because, Alice, you know how I said Mum wants to do events at the house? Well, we're doing it. Seriously going to give it a crack. Weddings, birthdays, corporate rah-rah offsite thingies, the whole shebang.'

'Ah, I get the photography now,' Alice said. 'In order to provide a whole package, right?'

'Exactly!'

'We're going to offer a whole deal – accommodation for a few couples, catering, gorgeous premises with awesome photo opps. And a photographer. We're going to start with focussing on mainly smaller weddings, but we'll see,' she finished.

'I think the whole idea is fantastic,' Alice said. 'And you'd do a brilliant job. And the place really is incredibly beautiful.'

'And what I mean by the whole package is making it so the bride and groom will barely have to organise anything but their outfits and guest list.'

'Listen to you, saleswoman extraordinaire,' Alice said.

'Well, you can help too, missy: you're part of the family, too, you know. It's a whole family affair. No shirking.'

Soon after they'd enjoyed mugs of peppermint tea, a series of yawns made its way around the table, and then exclamations about the time being one o'clock. Mere moments later the three couples had all wandered, entwined, outside to the cars.

'I might be drunk, but I was serious about lunch tomorrow,' Lauren said to Blair and Rick, hugging them both. 'I'm sure it'll be fine with Mum and Dad, but I'll check and send a confirmation text tomorrow. Er, later. Shit,' she said, getting into the car.

'Okay, sounds like a plan,' Blair said.

'Great. I'm looking forward to seeing your home,' Rick said.

They said their goodbyes to Lauren and Brett, hugged them, and then watched as their car drove off.

'I don't want to leave,' Alice said, nuzzling Blair.

'No, neither do I,' Ashley said.

'Well, I'm going to be a true gentleman and terrible host and kick you both out. How about that?' Blair said, gently prising himself away from Alice.

'Probably best,' Alice said.

Rick kissed Ashley and then holding her said, 'Talk to you tomorrow,' reluctantly peeling himself away.

'Is that a promise?' Ashley asked.

'It sure is.'

They drove off, their hands waving out of the windows. Blair and Rick stood there silently watching them go until they turned out the gate a hundred or so metres away.

'Wow, what a night,' Blair said, putting his hand on Rick's shoulder.

'That's one word for it, mate,' Rick said. 'Good to see you and Alice are back on track.'

'Yep, couldn't be better. Is it weird that I'm in love with your ex-wife?'

'Nope. Is it weird if I say I'm going to marry that woman one day – Ashley, that is – and we probably haven't even had a proper first date?'

'Yep. That is weird. But, seriously, good for you. You wait until you see the Finmores' house – you're going to shit yourself. Come on, I need to go to bed,' he said, slapping Rick's back.

'What about the dishes?'

'Ah, leave them until the morning. Deal with everything then.'

'You sure?' Rick was surprised. He'd never seen anything out of place for longer than about two seconds in Blair's house.

'Yep. I never do dishes the night of a party – too easy to break something.'

'Okay. Fair enough.'

Chapter Thirty-three

'Okay, so here's the apparently famous mailbox,' Blair said, bringing his ute to a stop and opening the door. 'I can't believe we've all been looking at it for years, none the wiser,' he said, walking around it. 'I check their mail most days.' He opened it now and peered inside before shutting it again.

'Apparently Toilichte means happy in Scots Gaelic,' Blair said as he moved away a little.

'That's nice. I wonder who named it.'

'I don't know. I think Lauren would have said if she knew. Your parents do, did, beautiful work,' Blair said with awe, shading his eyes against the sun.

'Yep, they sure did,' Rick said, tracing the back-to-back Bs with his finger. He'd expected a rush of emotion, but he was completely calm. How would he do his own signature? He really wanted something similarly stylish. After a few moments he joined Blair and they walked the few steps back to the vehicle.

'Okay?' Blair asked as they got in.

'Yep. All good.'

'I was half-expecting you to get emotional,' Blair said, turning the key and then putting the vehicle back into gear. 'You're clearly coming to terms with everything. That's great.'

'Hmm.' He kept thinking about Ashley and wondering when he'd get the chance to see her again. He didn't want a relationship confined to huge chains of texts for too long. He missed her already, had started to the instant she'd left his side.

'Are you serious?' Rick asked as they came out of a tree-lined driveway and saw an enormous stately home looming up ahead. He knew his eyes were bugging out of his head and his mouth was open, but he didn't care. He turned to Blair, who laughed.

'Yep. Deadly serious. Welcome to Toilichte House.'

Rick had to keep reminding himself to close his mouth, which kept dropping open as he gazed around at the massive old stone two-storey house with sweeping tapering steps joining it to a huge expanse of white gravel. 'It could be out of *Downton Abbey* or something. It's incredible. Man oh man.'

'That's what everyone says. Isn't it awesome? And it's just as stunning inside.'

They'd just pulled up and got out and Rick was still gazing up and around, taking in the detail of the magnificent building now they were close up, when the huge front door opened.

A woman and a man, both with dark hair and both dressed in jeans, sneakers and purple polo tops, came down the steps to where Rick and Blair stood on the gravel. Rick assumed they were Mr and Mrs Finmore, but thought they could almost pass as Lauren's older siblings.

'Melissa, Charles, this is Rick Peterson. Rick, meet Melissa and Charles Finmore,' Blair said.

'Hello. Welcome,' Charles said.

'Yes, welcome, welcome,' Melissa said, bundling Rick into a hug. It was the type of warm, all-encompassing hug that he imagined might come from a much larger, more voluptuous person. Hugs must come from inside, he found himself thinking as he clung to her, taking in her scent, which he took to be most likely lavender. It was subtle, but definitely there. He was surprised at how much more observant he was these days – it was as if a switch had been flipped. Like he was suddenly allowed to think for himself … *I really am an artist at heart*, he thought.

'It's wonderful to meet you,' Charles said, pumping Rick's hand.

'Yes, likewise. Thanks so much for having me. Your home is gorgeous,' he said.

'Thank you. We love it,' Charles and Melissa said at once.

They've clearly had to respond to this comment plenty of times before, Rick thought.

Brett appeared on the steps, making his way down. 'Hi, Rick, great to see you,' he said, holding out his hand.

'Hey, Brett,' Rick said. 'Where's Lauren?'

'Writing.'

'Oh. Great. That's good, isn't it? For a writer, right.' He let out a slightly self-conscious laugh.

'Yes, it sure is,' Brett said. 'Although, she hasn't stopped since we got home. From last night. Well, technically, this morning.'

'Right. Wow,' Rick said.

'So, we're going to be very quiet and do the full inside tour later,' Melissa said, taking him gently by the elbow. 'Come in, though,' she said, speaking quietly while guiding him.

'Shoes off?' Rick asked when they were inside the incredible vestibule and about to step onto a magnificent Persian carpet. He took his dress Akubra off his head.

'No, no. Please, come on through. Lunch is ready, but we're going to hold off in case Lauren surfaces. Meanwhile, would you like a cool drink or a hot drink, perhaps?' Melissa said, as they made their way through and into an enormous kitchen with a stone bench the size of a small country. 'I'm having tea. Anyone else fancy one?'

'Actually, a cup of tea sounds perfect, thank you.' Rick was surprised to hear himself making the request. Until recently, the only time he ever drank tea was in the shearing shed.

He watched while Blair got a glass from a cupboard and went to a filter tap at the sink and helped himself.

'Settle yourselves down,' Charles said, taking a seat at the bench. 'No formalities here. So, how are you enjoying Ballarat and surrounds, Rick? We hope you don't mind, but we were up last night when the kids came home and did get some of the details. Sincere condolences for your losses.'

'Yes, it must have been a very difficult time for you lately,' Melissa chimed in. 'Here you are,' she said, placing in front of him a mug of black tea and a tray with a teaspoon, a pot of sugar and a small jug of milk on it.

'Thanks. Yes. It's been a bit confronting. But I'm getting there,' he said.

'And Brett tells us you actually have a connection here, specifically, too,' Charles said. 'That's incredible.'

'Yes …' Rick wasn't sure what else to say.

He was relieved when it looked like he wasn't going to be quizzed further on that or have to tell the story again. 'Your plans sound exciting, too,' he said. 'I can see why you'd want to do weddings here. It's perfect.'

'Yes, thank you. It's early days. We're still getting our heads around how it'll work. But we're keen to give it a damned good shot,' Charles said.

'Blair, darling, speaking of love, have you properly sorted things out with our dear Alice yet?' Melissa said. 'We love her like our own,' she said to Rick.

'I have,' Blair said. 'We're back on track.'

'Oh, I'm so pleased.'

'Yes. Jolly good,' Charles said.

'We might just hit you up to have a wedding here before too long.'

'Sounds like we'd better get our skates on, dear,' Charles said.

'Yes. Rick, darling, is all this a bit odd, given Alice is your ex-wife?'

'Not really. She's great. Actually, if Ashley and I work out and get married, I'd ask her to be my best man – well, best person, I guess I should say.'

'That's fantastic,' Charles said.

'Yes, it's wonderful when divorced couples can eventually become friends, let alone as close as you sound like you are,' Melissa said. 'She's been through a lot, too, poor thing.'

'Don't let Alice hear you call her "poor thing",' Blair said, smiling. 'She's quite okay, as she'll be very quick to tell you.'

'Yes, thank goodness she got away from her family by the sounds of things,' Charles said.

'She'll only really get away from them when she goes no contact, if she decides to,' Brett said sagely.

'Yes, well, it's complicated I'm sure,' Charles said.

'It's just sad when families don't support you,' Melissa said. 'So, changing the subject. Come on, Rick, let's give you a tour of the outside and outbuildings, unless you're starving?'

'Oh, no, I'm good, thanks,' he said, vacating his seat and following Melissa out. Blair, Brett and Charles fell in behind them.

Again, Rick had to tell himself to close his mouth several times. The yard was a series of various sized, solid red brick outbuildings arranged around a large courtyard, like a small village. All neat and in perfect repair. Not a blade of grass was to be seen in the gravel and not a flake of paint peeling anywhere. Nothing was out of place. Everything was pristine. He sighed with contentment. Another thing he'd learnt since being away from Hope Springs was that the notion that Anthea, and Alice, too, had spoken of a lot was so true – tidy life, tidy mind. Here, with everything in its place and ordered, he felt clear to think, to not just take in what he was seeing but to feel it seeping into him at a soul or cellular level. He had the comforting feeling that right here right now was where he was meant to be and that somehow this was going to be instrumental to his future.

'It's so neat,' he found himself uttering with wonder.

'Yes, we might be a little OTT on that front, but we do like things just so,' Charles said.

'Never ...' Rick said, the word coming out like a long breath.

'I must say,' Melissa said, 'we're very excited to have another creative in our midst. We do so love being surrounded by clever people with vivid imaginations who use their gifts for good.'

'Did you tell them about the mailbox, Brett?'

'No. I haven't got that far, yet.'

'What about it?' Melissa asked.

'It looks like it's the work of Rick's parents – the bit that looks like butterfly wings is actually their signature – two Bs back-to-back.'

'Oh. How interesting,' she said, tapping her lip with her finger. 'See what I mean about clever, creative people.'

'I'm not sure I'm there yet,' Rick said quietly.

'Ah, but you will be before too long. You've got creative written all over you.'

'I do?' Rick found himself looking down his front. Obviously she knew his history, but how could she say he looked creative? He was in jeans and a T-shirt.

'It's in your eyes and your expressive hands,' Melissa said.

Rick turned his hands over and inspected them.

'You don't have to have purple hair or shaved bits or tattoos to look like an artist, my boy,' Charles said. 'It's about what's inside – the depth and breadth to which you think and interpret and then what you will create with all that thought that sets you apart. I won't say from *normal* people, because I don't think there is such a thing as normal.'

Rick's heart stretched and he glowed inside. He felt like he'd spent his whole life waiting to meet these people, to feel so welcome, so understood. And for the first time since he'd left Hope Springs, he didn't mind that it had taken him thirty-odd years to figure out who and what he really was. *Better late than never, indeed.*

Blair must have sensed his thoughtfulness because he clasped Rick by the shoulder. 'You okay, mate?' he whispered.

'Yep. Just a lot to take in. Sort of like a lifetime's worth.'

'You'll be right.'

'I know I will.'

They waited while Charles pulled open a pair of large swinging barn doors.

'We're thinking of turning this one – old stables – into accommodation that is a little more rustic. It'll be perfect for Lauren's writers when we add a large table in here for them to work around.'

'Oh, I think we forgot to mention that last night,' Brett said. 'That Lauren's going to be doing writing workshops – we're organising a week-long one for, hopefully, soon.'

Rick looked around the space, which was paved in red bricks. He found himself frowning slightly at something above them in the rafters in the far corner that looked a little out of place – not exactly untidy, but …

'Oh, yes. Darling, the furniture!' Melissa said, looking in the same direction as Rick. They must have noticed his gaze.

'Yes, I'd quite forgotten it was there. Can you bring the ladder, please, Blair?'

Moments later Blair had positioned a large A-frame ladder under the rafters.

'Would you rather do it later after lunch – we might all get covered in dust,' Melissa said.

'We can shake our clothes out later if we do,' Charles said.

What are they up to?

'Okay, but I'll get a towel to give them a wipe over,' Melissa said, and disappeared, only to reappear moments later. Rick figured there must be a washroom in here, too. *Of course there is!*

'Everything?' Blair asked, ascending the ladder while Brett held onto the bottom to keep it steady.

'Yes,' Charles said.

Oh. 'Don't bother on my account,' Rick said, as he finally realised what they were doing.

'No, no, you see, these bits and pieces have been here since before us, and before the previous owners,' Melissa explained. 'We thought they'd been accidentally left but, when we got in touch with them, they said they'd thought the same – about the previous owners. We don't need them and maybe they belonged to your grandparents. Either way, you'd be very welcome to have them if they'd be useful to you. Unless of course you're already fully sorted in that department.'

'Rick, please don't feel badgered. My darling wife can be a bit, um, passionate at times.'

'Yes, I can, so please do be honest. There's absolutely no obligation. They can just as easily stay where they are or go back up again.'

'Right, here we go,' Blair said.

Together Brett, Rick and Charles lowered the several pieces of timber furniture down to the ground. A few moments later they were staring at a rocking chair and what looked like a wooden federation-style slatted bed in pieces. *Oh wow*, Rick thought, staring.

'Well, I'm not sure you'll want a rocking chair,' Charles said with a laugh.

'Oh no, but I do. I love it.' Rick ran his hand over the curved timber of the arms. He knew it, felt it – these pieces had been owned by, used by, his grandparents. He told himself they had – he felt it.

'The bed looks like it's probably only a double, unfortunately. That's why it's still here – we prefer kings, or queen at a minimum. That's a shame,' Melissa said.

But Rick didn't think it was at all. He preferred king or queen-sized, too, but he was seeing how he could expand the timber bed head and foot to suit. He became excited, watching it unfold in his mind as clear as if he was watching a YouTube video. He'd cut the timber and inset a fancy iron design in the middle – maybe entwine his and Ashley's initials if things went well …

'Ah, there you guys are!' They all turned towards Lauren's voice coming from the open doorway. She raced up to them. Rick was so taken aback when she threw herself into his arms for a hug he let out an, 'Oh'. Then, 'Hello there,' and a little awkward laugh.

'How did you go?' Charles asked.

'Oh my god, Dad, it's awesome!'

'Wonderful. That's so good to hear, Lauren,' Melissa said.

'Brilliant,' Blair and Brett said.

'I do believe I have a sound idea for my novel.'

'Oh, wow, that's fantastic,' Rick said.

'Well, it's thanks to you, actually,' she said, looking a little sheepish.

'Me?' he said.

'I hope you don't mind, but I'm going to steal your life. Well, not *steal* your life – I'm not a complete psycho. Borrow some bits, maybe?'

'Oh. Right. Okay. I think.'

'Don't worry, I won't use your name – it'll be fiction. But your journey, your discovery of who you really are. So physically and emotionally far from how and where you were raised … Sorry, I'm probably not making sense. It does to me.'

'Well, that's the main thing,' Brett said, putting his arm around her.

'You don't mind, though, do you?' she said.

Rick could see the pleading in her eyes. At any moment she might drop to her knees and beg him. He could see it meant *that* much to her. 'Why would I mind? I'd be flattered to think my story is interesting enough. And no one will know it's me, anyway. Go for it, I say.'

'Oh, thank you, thank you,' she said, hugging him again.

'But didn't you say it was "stranger than fiction" last night?'

'Yeah, probably,' Lauren said with a laugh. 'I'll cross the believability bridge later. But for now, I've got it all planned out – pretty much every scene down to a dot point.'

'Since when are you a planner for your writing?' Brett asked.

'Since now, apparently. Who knew?'

'You must be exhausted. Have you slept at all?' Melissa said.

'Nope. But god, I'm suddenly starving.'

'Come on, then, let's come back to this after lunch,' Melissa said.

Rick smiled the whole way through their lunch of assorted sandwiches. Lauren was practically bouncing off the walls with her excitement. And not one person told her to sit still or be quiet. He again had the overwhelming sense that he'd found his tribe. They were all very different people, but there was a collective similarity between them – kindness, generosity and honesty.

Epilogue

Around six months later ...

Rick stood beside Alice under the small gazebo, now decorated with green foliage and white roses, that he'd made as a gift for the Finmores. They'd got there twenty minutes earlier than the scheduled time of eleven a.m.: Alice had assured him Ashley would be ten minutes early – there would be no fashionably late for this bride! Rick didn't mind at all – left to his own devices, he'd have been here hours ago, he was so keen to get married and get on with spending the rest of his life with Ashley. And he wanted to soak everything up. He looked around.

He was chuffed with how his steel and wire construction had come together, particularly the entwined initials of T and H he'd placed at the front to signify Toilichte House. The Finmores had loved the design he'd drawn of the initials so much they'd used it for their business's logo. He'd checked they were also happy with the gazebo being rusty – perhaps for a wedding venue it might be better painted, he'd suggested – but they'd assured him they were. It was a bit new-looking at the moment – Mother Nature still had to do her work and turn it properly red-brown. He agreed with them that the colour would go perfectly with the surroundings. When it was just right, he'd seal it to keep it that way and prevent it staining anything in the future.

He was as proud of the design as he was of his welding and decorative metal work. It was open, but with plenty of support – unrecognisable as part of the decoration – to hold fabric for shade or protection in case of rain. The many hidden hooks he'd incorporated would also secure strands of lights for evening events. It would be stunning when lit up. He looked forward to seeing that some time soon. Charles and Melissa had gushed and told him he'd thought of everything. He was pleased – that's what he'd been hoping for. It had taken him several days to figure out how to make the whole thing sturdy yet collapsible for storage and easy transportation. Far from becoming frustrated, he'd loved every moment of it. At the last minute he'd added loops at the bottom for pegs to hold it down in case they loved the finished product as much as he did and decided they wanted to leave it up somewhere on the property on a more permanent basis.

He'd had plenty of time to devote to the project – day and night, when he chose – thanks to living and working in the same space. He couldn't wait to start studying fine arts and see what other mediums he enjoyed working with. It was exciting not knowing what was inside him to be unleashed and being free to explore whatever took his fancy.

As well as knowing he'd found his calling, Rick felt more comfortable and at peace in the warehouse than he'd ever thought possible. Jeff and Leon, both shiny black greyhounds – the only way to tell them apart being Leon's spot of white on his chest – had come already named and with a bag of goofy antics. He couldn't wait for Ashley and Max to move in permanently next week.

The dogs had been as good as chosen by Ashley's Max and Alice's Bill. Sometimes it was pure chaos in the warehouse with them all tearing around. The greyhounds might like to snooze for hours on end, but they seemed to enjoy the odd burst of energy occasionally, too – usually spurred on by Max. Rick loved sharing his space with so much life and positive energy.

He'd thought he might feel the presence somehow of his parents and twin brother Sebastian in the warehouse, but he didn't think he had. Yet. Or perhaps all the good energy he felt there *was* them. He didn't know, and had decided it didn't matter. He was at peace. They were in his heart, even if he didn't remember them. Sometimes he thought he did have glimpses of partial memories, but he couldn't be sure if they were real or he was conjuring them up by trying too hard.

It had only been the day before yesterday that he'd gone to see their graves for the first time. He hadn't wanted to before then, despite Ashley and Alice quizzing him on it regularly. They'd been right about it being the last unresolved thing in this whole journey.

Anthea, who he'd continued to work with via Skype, and who had arrived during the week for the wedding, had quietly agreed, but said it was entirely up to him. He'd started with asking if she would join him and Ashley and her parents on the cemetery visit. And then he'd decided it wouldn't be right without Alice too. Or Blair. Or Lauren or Brett. And of course he couldn't then not have Charles and Melissa there too – they, along with Lyn and Peter Baker had become his new surrogate parents. And so it had wonderfully snowballed, until finally Sarah and Frank and Anthea's husband Tom had also joined the pilgrimage. Far from being a sad occasion and cutting him up all over again, it had been fun. Poignant, too, but not depressingly sad, because he had all the people who now mattered most to him right there providing support. It helped that afterwards they'd all gone to a café for lunch and he hadn't had a chance to become morose. The only tears he'd shed had been later when Sarah had pulled him aside and told him how proud Bart and Beatrice would be of him. Her comment had touched him the most out of everything everyone said that day because Sarah had actually known them.

'Look,' Rick said, gently giving Alice a bump. He nodded towards the front row of chairs where Sarah and Frank were the first guests seated. They were sitting tall, looking expectant. He'd just noticed Frank reach across and clasp Sarah's hand. Now they were looking into each other's eyes.

Rick and Alice had both seen their instant connection the previous day. Rick was pleased for Alice that Frank had come back to Ballarat a week early, and now it seems he might stay permanently, if Sarah had anything to do with it. He'd heard her offering him a room at her house and saying she was tired of rattling around on her own.

'Aww,' Alice said. 'That's beautiful.'

Gradually the group of approximately sixty chairs began to fill. Up the back he could see his cousins-once-sisters Danni and Matilda. He was pleased they'd come. A part of Rick had hoped they might bring their husbands and kids and make a bit of a holiday of their visit to Ballarat. It really was a lovely place and well worth seeing. But they'd come alone and had arrived late yesterday and were leaving tomorrow morning. Perhaps it was best. They'd never been close, but now they seemed to have nothing to talk about, nothing at all to bind them. He'd asked if they wanted to be seated down the front, but they'd insisted on being up the back. Ashley had said it was a pretty awkward situation and it might take time for them to thaw. She'd suggested they might be feeling ashamed about what their parents had done and not really know quite how to face him. He was glad Maureen's death had been ruled a heart attack and not suicide, and they had that burden removed, if it had been a factor. But at least Rick had reached out and they'd accepted. That was something. After today who knew what would happen – he figured it was up to them.

'I'm half-expecting to have Dawn and Olivia make a grand entrance,' Alice whispered beside him.

'Don't worry, Charles has studied their photos and is all ready to escort them off the premises if they do,' Rick whispered back. Alice had told him how her mother had rung and practically demanded she and Olivia be invited to the wedding, despite it being none of their business. Alice hadn't even told anyone she was being his best man, er, person. She barely spoke to them at all these days and had gone to the Gold Coast for Christmas with Blair and his family so she couldn't be dropped in on. You just never knew with Dawn. Why they would want to be at the wedding of their ex-son-in-law or ex-brother-in-law to another woman was just plain bizarre – and summed up their insecurity and need for attention pretty well, he thought. Alice's mother really just couldn't seem to grasp the concept 'it's not all about you'. And poor Frank – that would be all he needed after having finally escaped.

'All good?' Lauren asked, ducking in behind them.

'Yep. Perfect, thanks,' Rick said.

'Nothing you need?'

'Nope. You've done an awesome job,' he said, smiling.

'Brilliant. Anthea is just coming down and Ashley will be five minutes.' And then Lauren was gone.

Rick sighed. The whole thing had been brought together so smoothly. Everything, down to the finest detail, had been

organised with precision. And calmly. That was the thing that
had blown him away the most – how the Finmores and Brett,
Alice and Blair, had been so busy, so efficient, but never seemed
stressed. He hadn't been aware of one snapped word or frown.
The whole day was going to be perfect, he just knew it.

'How are we, folks?' Anthea said, appearing from behind them
and touching Rick and Alice on the shoulder. They all beamed
at each other.

'Perfect. Now you're here, it's all perfect,' Rick said, sighing
contentedly again.

'Aww, bless you. I'm so pleased to be here.'

Rick thought he would never get over the intense rush
of feeling he'd experienced at hearing Anthea's voice on the
phone when she'd rung to tell him she would love to, would be
honoured to, officiate at his wedding. When they'd started their
Skype sessions, she mentioned she'd recently gone off and done
the course to become a qualified, registered celebrant. Ashley had
agreed they absolutely had to ask if she'd come over and marry
them. Rick had written to her, hadn't trusted himself to call in
case he'd begged – he knew his day wouldn't be complete or
completely perfect without her presence. He knew it might sound
melodramatic, but he knew he really wouldn't be here or who he
had become if it hadn't been for her. She'd tried several times to
rebuff his effusive gratitude in recent days by saying he'd simply
have found someone else to talk to. Because he'd been ready. But
Rick knew the truth in his heart. He'd been thrilled to hear her
husband would be coming with her and that they were making a
holiday of it. They would be around for a few days yet.

When he'd heard that, Rick had again been glad he and Ashley
had decided they would wait to have a honeymoon – until when,
no one knew. They hadn't been able to think of anywhere they

wanted to go – were both too content and busy with their lives here in Ballarat. Perhaps when he started studying fine arts, he would find he'd like to visit some of the homes of the old masters overseas. Until then they would enjoy settling down together.

'Not too nervous?' Anthea said.

'Never. I can't wait.'

'Excellent. Well, not long now,' she said, cocking her head and putting a hand to her ear.

The string quartet had just started playing. The sea of chairs was almost full. Rick nodded and smiled at Lyn, his soon-to-be-mother-in-law, as she sat down with a big grin of her own and a double-thumbs-up gesture. Rick smiled and gave a little wave as Blair, Charles and Melissa slipped into their reserved chairs in the front row. Beside them remained Brett and Lauren's empty seats. Brett was off taking photos. The only other space was beside Lyn, for Peter, who was walking his daughter down the aisle between the two rows of chairs.

And there she is. Oh wow! Rick gasped as Ashley appeared in the gap in the green foliage, her arm looped into her father's. She'd chosen not to have a bridesmaid because she hadn't been able to choose between her group of friends, so it was Lauren who was now crouched behind her straightening and fanning out her beautiful but simple ivory dress and train. He loved that her shoulders were bare – they were one of his favourite parts of her. The tune of the string music changed and became louder and more vibrant.

'Okay, folks?' Anthea said.

Rick nodded and swallowed down the lump in his throat and blinked back the rush of tears.

'I hope they're happy tears, mister!' Alice whispered, giving him a nudge. She grinned at him. He grinned back.

'Yep. They sure are.'

'And don't forget to breathe.'

He took a deep breath. 'Thanks for being here, Alice,' he whispered.

'I always will be, Rick,' she whispered back, reaching out and giving his hand a quick squeeze.

Acknowledgements

Many thanks to:

James, Sue, Annabel, Adam, and everyone at Harlequin and HarperCollins Australia for turning my manuscripts into beautiful books and for continuing to make my dreams come true.

Kate O'Donnell for her expertise and guidance to bring out the best in my writing and this story.

Amy Milne at AM Publicity for getting the word out with previous titles and for her kindness and generosity of spirit. A beautiful soul tragically taken far too soon. Rest in peace, lovely lady.

The media outlets, bloggers, reviewers, librarians, booksellers and readers for all the amazing support. It really does mean so much to me to hear of people enjoying my stories and connecting with my characters.

Special thanks to Brevet Sergeant Sean Patton of South Australia Police for his assistance with country policing and to Ben Price for updating me on some snippets of contemporary rural life. Any errors or inaccuracies are my own or due to taking creative liberties.

And, finally, to my dear friends who provide so much love, support and encouragement – especially Mel Sabeeney, Julie Ditrich, Bernadette Foley, NEL, WTC and LMR. I am truly blessed to have you in my life.

Turn over for a sneak peek.

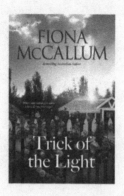

Trick of the Light

by

FIONA McCALLUM

Available April 2021

Prologue

Erica arranged slices of buttered date loaf on a plate and placed it on the coffee table. She'd got up early to bake despite there still being plenty of other offerings in the freezer from Stuart's wake ten days earlier.

Having something to focus on that wasn't her sadness and the great gaping hole in her life was important, even though baking, like so many other everyday tasks, was also a horrible reminder that life just carried on, regardless of the assault on normality she had just endured. When she let her mind go there … Erica tried hard to not think too deeply about anything much because no one thought ever completely stood alone. Most things were connected, with one idle ponderance linking to or prompting another. Before grief, thoughts and memories tied together had been comfortable and comforting. She longed for the occasional isolated memory, a single grain of sand, but instead got pulled into quicksand, the darkness and drag of which took a lot of effort to resist. Today she hoped baking from scratch instead of taking out some cake and watching it defrost on the bench would distract from the quicksand. (And she would have watched because all too often lately she was having to drag her attention away from something after losing chunks of time staring mindlessly.)

Erica wished there were only so many tears a person could shed. Her bouts left her wrecked – completely exhausted – as if they'd been wrung from her, like someone had put a hand around her top and her bottom sections and twisted in opposite directions to painfully extract every last drop.

She longed to laugh properly again with her girls and reminisce without eventually dissolving into tears. And actually *be* strong without pretending or working so hard to be. They'd get there. It would happen: she had to believe that.

She'd also thought grief would be easier this time around, having lost her mother six years before and her brother many more years before that – though that was different because she'd been a kid and didn't think she'd properly understood or processed it. Even now. With her mum, it had taken her a good – or bad, really – two years to not burst into tears whenever her father, a dear old soul battling dementia, uttered her mother's name. And it only twisted the knife that he still didn't realise she'd departed, and relayed memories and chatted to whoever happened to be beside him as if that person were his wife or as if she had just popped off to the loo or the kitchen to get another cuppa. She was thankful he wasn't as upset as she was, but, Christ, it hurt. Physically. It was a deep punch into her side on top of the all-over ache that was already there as another appendage. She'd thought, hoped, the practice she'd already had would help. But it didn't. If anything, it was harder, more painful. And she didn't think it had anything to do with the fact that Stuart hadn't had a long life, or that he'd had a lot more living and contributing to do. No, Erica found her grief compounded. Thoughts of her mother sometimes set her off now as strongly as thoughts of Stuart, gone just days before.

Not even the fact she'd had time with Stuart to say goodbye, come to terms with it, helped. Those callous enough to suggest someone dying of cancer – slowly – was easier to deal with than sudden loss were wrong. Well, in her case, anyway. Regardless of the fact she truly hadn't believed he'd die – had thought he would get through this like the previous two episodes – she'd thought it a matter of staying positive. She hadn't sat beside him, acknowledging his prognosis and offering final words. Though, what did you say?

Some things you only could say to the dead, not the living. And they hadn't been a very gushy, emotionally or physically demonstrative couple, anyway. Yes, they were strong and supportive, said 'I love you', held hands occasionally – usually when crossing the road – but they'd had more of a quiet contentment about them. She hadn't sat there stroking his hair and cooing that she'd be fine if he left – *Just go, slip away, my love.* She had sat beside him thinking positively, reading a magazine. Being quiet and keeping him company. Mackenzie and Issy had done the same. Right near the end, though she hadn't realised that it was, Erica had figured what Stuart needed was rest for his body to concentrate on fighting the beast within, not endless chatter. And if he'd wanted otherwise, Stuart would have said. He was the leader of their family.

They'd had a week to deal with the shock of losing him before the funeral, though planning the event took plenty of energy and had been a welcome distraction and source of momentum. In the time since, they'd cried together, watched lots of action movies – Stuart's favourite genre – and gorged on leftover sweet and savoury offerings friends and acquaintances had brought. Yesterday was the first day the three of them had been at home alone with no one dropping in.

Erica would have preferred to have the wake at the funeral home, but the three of them had reluctantly agreed that Stuart would have wanted to have everyone at the house – and this was their last chance to do anything for him. It wasn't about them. Stuart had been proud of their home, especially the massive renovation, the design of which he'd contributed to heavily. It wasn't entirely Erica's taste – a little too white and minimalist, especially the décor – but she did enjoy the features he'd incorporated to control the climate and keep the cost of running the home down, including double-glazing for all the glass in the windows and patio doors. It had probably cost a fortune, but Stuart had kept the details to himself, except to say it was paying dividends, along with the huge solar system on the roof.

While Erica had learnt with grieving over her mum that keeping busy was best, it was as much about keeping the mind active as about being physical. She was probably at risk of being considered a little hyperactive at times, but when she was still the memories came flooding back and the sadness began to pound sharply at her temples and under her ribs and bluntly inside her chest.

She was glad Stuart had been a stickler for having everything in order and had appointed his accountant and financial planner as executors of his estate, and of hers too. They were due here any second to tell her where things were at.

When she heard the doorbell, Erica habitually wiped her hands on the tea towel, pressed the button on the kettle to set it to boil and checked her watch as she went out into the long hall and made her way to the front door. They were right on time.

'Hi, Paul. Hi, Toby,' she said, giving the accountant and financial planner each a quick hug, made a little awkward by the briefcases they carried. She didn't know them very well. They'd been Stuart's advisers for probably a decade, or even much longer, but even so she'd only met them a handful of times. They hadn't crossed over into socialising together; theirs was a cordial professional relationship and Erica had never met either of their wives or partners or been to their homes. In fact, they might both have husbands – or be married to each other – for all she knew about them personally.

They'd been at the funeral and here afterwards and at most other open-house style functions Stuart had put on for his business – Christmas, major achievements and the like. Stuart had liked to celebrate publicly – well, as publicly as it got in a private home with professional caterers. Not many of those parties had been thrown of late due to Stuart's illness. He'd insisted on doing the usual Christmas shindig the previous year – though right at the beginning of December rather than the end – and had managed to be the epitome of an ebullient host. Not wanting to spark fear or a mass exodus of clients, he'd even had Erica use her professional makeup skills on his unhealthy pallor. No one had any idea he'd be dead in less than three months, including her.

'Come through,' she said, leading them down the hall into the large, white-tiled open space overlooking the back garden. Six panels of hinged glass doors when pushed open to one side literally brought the outside in. There was a slight chill to the early autumn air, otherwise she'd have opened them up and let the sunshine in. There was plenty of it casting shadows onto the lawn via the surrounding trees. A few of those had lost the first of their leaves overnight, though perhaps it was just the wind; it was a bit early in the season. Nonetheless, she'd rake them up later. 'I've just put the kettle on. Can I get you a tea or coffee?'

'No thanks, I'm fine,' Paul said.

'I'm all good, too, thanks, I've already had my morning quota,' Toby said.

'Okay. Take a seat.' It didn't feel right to have a cup of anything when they weren't, and something about their demeanour made her join them at the modern timber laminate dining table with high-backed chairs in cream leather that matched the large L-shaped couch.

The men seemed more sombre than usual, though, of course, she'd only ever seen them when socialising and at the funeral and wake – not quite socialising in the traditional sense, but still …

Erica watched as Paul, the accountant, unloaded a few files from his briefcase onto the table. But he didn't open the folders. Instead he sat with his hands on them as if they were simply props. Were they for reference later?

She ran her hands down her jeans-clad legs under the table, palms first and then the backs of her hands. Damn it, of all times to have a hot flush. Thankfully hers didn't make her red; they were just uncomfortable heat and sweat. Horrible. How fun was being forty-nine? Not at all! She really wished menopause and all its many and varied symptoms would bugger off.

Erica had experienced what others had described for six months but then the sweats and mood swings vanished for another six – she had thought they'd gone for good. Had hoped. Her best friend and cousin, Stephanie, had warned her they came back. She hadn't wanted to believe it, but now there was her upper lip sprinkled with beads of sweat along with the sides of her nose. Damn it. She pulled a tissue from her pocket and quickly and gently dabbed at it and then her brow and down the sides of her nose and around her eyes. She hoped the men hadn't noticed.

Menopause, while slowly being more openly talked about, still probably wasn't a topic for discussion with men beyond your own intimate partner. Perhaps in board rooms and businesses where menopausal woman ruled it came up. Regardless, and Erica wasn't quite sure why, but she was a little embarrassed at the thought of them thinking of her as menopausal. They might think she'd been wiping away tears – understandable – and averted their eyes, not wanting to acknowledge the emotion or not knowing how to.

But Erica didn't have any tears, not now she had her war paint on, as Stuart had referred to it. Just as well, given she thought she wasn't exactly a pretty crier. And displays of raw emotion usually made people in the vicinity feel decidedly awkward and not know where to look or what to do, not to mention the domino effect ...

They looked up at her with pursed lips. She smiled back at them in an attempt to disarm them, ease their clear discomfort.

Paul nodded to Toby and he nodded back. 'We're sorry we don't have better news. We're really sorry to have to tell you this, but Stuart's left the finances, your finances, in a bit of a mess,' Paul said.

'Sorry? Complicated, you mean? He was always muttering about this deal or other, moving money from here to there.' She demonstrated with her hands across the top of the sleek table. Anything to ease the stifling crowding-in feeling coming over her.

'Well, yes, there was that, which is part of the problem,' Paul said.

'Has he done something wrong?' Erica's heart slowed. Suddenly she found it very unsettling that they were both seated right across the table from her, side by side. It was hard to not see them as a united front with her on the outer.

'Not as such,' Paul said.

'Well, not in a fraudulent sense,' Toby added.

'Yes. More in a mismanagement sense,' Paul said.

'What are you talking about? Perhaps you'd better just tell me.' After the shock of losing Stuart, there was little else remaining to startle her. Or so she thought.

Paul took a deep breath, let out an audible sigh and said, 'You're almost broke, Erica.'

She stared and then blinked. 'What? Don't be ridiculous. He had a quarter of a million dollars in life insurance – just like I have.'

Both men shook their heads. 'He cancelled the policies several years ago,' Toby said. 'Without telling us.'

Um. Wow. 'Really? That's – But there's his superannuation ...'

They shook their heads again. Erica's pounding heart became slower and slower.

'He stopped contributing years ago and withdrew it, which he was allowed to do due to financial hardship because of his illness.'

'How much did he withdraw?'

'There's nothing left in his account,' Toby said.

There was silence. Erica tried to think, to understand, but just couldn't.

'What?'

'We're so sorry. This must be a huge shock. It was for us, too,' Paul said.

'But hang on. You're his accountant and financial adviser – where was your advice? How could you have let this happen? What the fuck were you doing?' Erica cursed her language and emotion but fear was bubbling up and teetering on uncontrollable. Her eyes burnt with frustration and anger. 'How could you have not known?'

'It was our role to advise, yes. We advised against plenty of things Stuart suggested, of course – but his affairs were his own. We can't, couldn't, *make* him do anything he didn't want to,' Toby said.

Erica took several deep breaths and tried to still her whirling mind and the shaking of her entire being from her organs inside right out to her skin. As much as she wanted to rant and rave at these two – blame them – they were the messengers. And she'd known Stuart. He was self-assured, at times arrogant even. His confidence was what had drawn her to him – especially his assurances that he'd take care of them. And he had. Very well. Or so she'd thought. Now Erica could see it might have been a case of 'I think he doth protest too much'.

'Okay. So, that's the bad news, what's the good news?' She was pleased she managed to sound a little upbeat.

'Sorry?' Toby said.

'There is no good news,' Paul said quietly.

Erica sat staring at them expectantly, her hands clasped in front of her on the table, the smile stuck on her face. And then her brain caught up. *They're being serious. There is no good news; nothing positive at all.*

'Sorry,' Paul said.

'Erica, we're both really sorry. About everything,' Toby added.

'Right. Okay. I get that. And I appreciate it. But what do I do about it? Am I going to lose the house?' Alarm gripped her. She watched as Paul averted his gaze to the files under his hands, and then began to fiddle with their edges.

Oh my god.

'Well that depends on you, really. We can see from the accounts that Stuart took care of all the mortgage and utility and other main expenses from his account – supplemented by his super since he hasn't been working. You need to start making all those payments now – from your own account: the one in your name that Stuart was signatory to. It'll be easier if you set up automatic direct deposits,' Paul said.

'But you'll have to make sure there's always enough to cover everything. Becoming overdrawn, even for just a few days, will incur hefty charges and could also do your credit rating serious damage,' Toby said.

'Yes. Look, people do owe Stuart money. We've submitted creditors' claims with several organisations that have gone into administration, and we're hoping for funds to come in there. But there are no guarantees we'll be successful, and even if we are, it's rare the full amount is achieved,' Paul explained. 'And there might even be claims to come in relating to Stuart's businesses,' he added quietly. 'But what it means right now is that wrapping up the estate is going to take a lot longer than usual.'

'Right,' Erica said, nodding slowly, despite most of this information not sinking into her spinning brain. Did she even *have* a credit rating if Stuart had taken care of all the finances? She had her account, where her salary was deposited and the board the girls paid, and which she used for groceries, eating out, and anything for herself or the girls before they'd become self-sufficient.

'You have a bit of a buffer on the home loan – you're a little ahead there – so you're keeping up with that, but it's tight. For your reference, here are the weekly, monthly and quarterly amounts I've calculated you need to come up with,' he said, sliding a page out of the file in front of him without opening it fully.

She blinked several times to try to stop her eyes from bugging as she attempted to calculate what she brought in as a full-time makeup artist running the counter of JPW Cosmetics at David Jones in town. It was a long way from minimum wage, but it wasn't a salary to get excited about. But that hadn't mattered; she'd never seen job satisfaction as just about the money, and being the family's secondary earner meant she hadn't needed to. There was so much she'd always loved about her job. She tried to tell herself that's how it should be to push back the wave of disappointment gathering inside her.

'Yes, you might want to tighten your belt a bit,' Toby said. 'Tighten the budget.'

'Unfortunately, it's probably going to require a serious adjustment on your part,' Paul said.

Right then Erica hated the idea that these men might know about every cent she earnt and spent and that they were as good as telling her – as if she were a child – to curb her spending. But that was the way Stuart had set everything up, including his appointment of them as executors. And she'd been grateful for not having to deal with the finances. Full stop. Ever. She'd asked to be included in their early days together – had assumed they were a joint venture in that sense, too, but clearly not. Stuart hadn't wanted a bar of her knowing and she'd been content to leave it at that.

She found her mind scrambling to where she could cut costs. Eating out was a biggie. Until the last few weeks, she'd socialised quite a bit – probably more than most. Stuart had encouraged her to keep it up, despite him being in hospital. She continued to have several café or restaurant meals out a week with friends. That was expensive, wasn't it? Probably. Especially when she always had at least one glass of decent wine. And she always bought her lunch in the city. She spent lots of small amounts on bits and pieces of makeup, expensive hair products, clothes, books, movie tickets, snacks, gifts with tap-and-go. But together they probably added up to quite a large sum each month ...

'I guess you could say the good news is that you live in Adelaide and not Melbourne or Sydney, where the cost of property and living generally is so much higher,' Toby offered with a slight shrug, breaking the looming silence. 'And you have Mackenzie and Isabella at an age where they can pay their way or at least aren't a major drain.'

Oh god, they might be the worst part of all of this. They'd adored their father – it would destroy them to know how much he'd let them down.

'Toby,' Paul warned.

'Sorry. That's not very helpful. But, honestly, things could be a lot worse, Erica. School fees, alone, if the kids hadn't already finished. Financially worse, that is. Obviously,' he said, blushing as he cleared his throat.

Erica knew they were trying, and in a very difficult position, but she was too caught up in her own head to either admonish or reassure.

A slow creep of realisation mixed with growing fear made her light-headed.

Oh fuck!

Mackenzie and Issy. Yesterday she'd transferred five thousand dollars to each of them for their overseas trip – their gap year. She hadn't thought they'd still go – had secretly hoped they wouldn't – or at least that they wouldn't be already talking about it so excitedly. But they were. Life went on. And apparently, they could save a bundle on Qantas's snap twenty-four-hour sale. They'd started saving a few years back, as soon as they secured their respective waitressing and retail jobs, both choosing to defer university. Of course, this was all before Stuart's cancer diagnosis had turned from hopeful with options to nothing more anyone can do now …

She'd come close to telling them it was too soon, or posing it as a question, but had reminded herself just in time that they had to do what was right for them. And, anyway, they might change their mind between now and when they left in a few months. The girls had saved nearly enough for their flights and didn't immediately need her contribution, but Erica had wanted to do the transfer right then and prevent any future awkwardness with them having to ask her. She'd also leapt at the chance to concentrate on the internet banking so she didn't dissolve into tears and beg them not to leave her. Her insides quivered. She began to sweat under her arms. Probably not a hot flush this time.

No, it'll be okay. She swallowed hard. *It has to be.* She tried to focus her attention on the solemn men in front of her, but couldn't. She thought she should ask if there was anything else she could or should do, but wouldn't they have said? She wanted them gone and to be left alone. She was probably even close to throwing up.

'There *is* the option of applying for hardship dispensation,' Paul said, as if reading her mind, 'but we think that's best to keep up your sleeve for now. See how you go for the next few weeks. Perhaps your employer might be open to increasing your salary?'

'I can only ask,' she said, trying to smile. The thought of doing that coated her insides with another layer of anxiety, but she conceded she didn't have many other choices.

'Unfortunately, that's about all you can do at this point,' Paul said. 'Cut out all non-essential spending, like eating out.'

'Yes,' Toby agreed, nodding. 'And takeaway coffee is another expense that really adds up over time.'

Erica was torn between accepting their wisdom and advice and telling them to piss off. How fucking embarrassing! She'd love to tell them she'd drink as many ginormous barista-made lattes as she liked, but reminded herself they were not the ones to blame. How were they being paid for the work they were clearly still doing for Stuart, anyway? She pushed that thought aside. She already had too much to deal with.

'Should I be, um ...' gulp, swallow '... putting the house up for sale?'

'You won't be able to sell until probate is granted and Stuart's estate wrapped up, which will be quite a few months in this case. And, anyway, the market isn't in your favour at the moment,' Paul said.

Erica held her tongue on telling them they'd proved themselves to be not very good advisers. At least she had them. She didn't want to alienate them.

She looked around the room and her gaze locked on the two huge modern canvases adorning the far white wall; she became a little buoyant. 'Could I sell them? They're originals by Olive Jasper,' she said, pointing towards the paintings. She loved them but could live without them if it meant keeping the house.

Out of the corner of her eye she noticed both Paul and Toby shift on their chairs. She turned back to face them. *Now what?*

'Unfortunately, they're not actually originals,' Toby said quietly. 'They're prints Stuart had done – printed directly onto canvas. The originals were sold several years ago.'

'What?' Erica longed to get up and go and check, but stayed where she was.

'You didn't know?' Paul said.

Erica shook her head. She was suddenly cold and shivering, as if her blood had left her. Beads of sweat prodded her forehead and heat rose up her throat.

Paul and Toby looked a little red-faced themselves. They ran their hands down their faces.

'We're so sorry, Erica, we thought you knew – at least about the art,' Paul said.

Erica couldn't take her eyes off the paintings and kept shifting her gaze from one to the other and back again. 'When?' she asked quietly.

'I'm not sure,' Paul said. 'Maybe just after the first round of chemo. Around six years ago?'

About the time Mum died. Erica could understand if Stuart hadn't wanted to put more onto her then. But the truth was it was bigger and had gone on for a lot longer than that. What possibly hurt her most about it was that he hadn't confided in her – hadn't trusted her enough. He hadn't valued her intelligence enough to seek her suggestions for alternative courses of action.

Erica had the discombobulating sensation that she didn't really, hadn't really, known Stuart at all. Her next thought was that she could imagine a parallel situation where she was a widow learning about a husband's whole other family. She loved film, had probably watched too many movies. It was a plot that popped up regularly. How often did it happen in real life? She shuddered and brought herself back to the here and now.

'Where did the money go?' she found herself asking, despite being unsure she wanted the answer.

'Not really anywhere, as such, other than living, really,' Toby said. 'It seems he was robbing Peter to pay Paul. Not this Paul, obviously,' he said and cleared his throat. 'It all started when he first became sick.'

You fool, Stuart, you stupid, stupid fool. I thought we were best friends, that we had each other's backs.

'We'd better get going. I'll leave these with you. They contain all the account login details and everything you need in order to see what's gone on and where things stand – if you can be bothered. That's up to you. And, of course, feel free to email or call us if you have any questions,' Paul said, sliding the small pile of folders towards Erica. 'And remember to keep the passwords secure, for obvious reasons,' he added, standing up. Toby followed suit. 'We'll also need to take Stuart's car.'

Erica nodded and got up to fetch both keys from the bench where she'd left them earlier and handed them to Paul. She'd known Stuart's BMW was leased. It's why she thought they were coming around today. So at least this part of things wasn't a shock.

'It's in the carport,' she said, pressing the remote on her own keys to activate the roller door as she walked them out. The groaning sound of the raising carport door outside was the only sound beyond their heavy footsteps on the plush red Persian hall runner over the floorboards.

'Again, we're really sorry,' Paul said when they were outside.

'Yes. Unfortunately, it really was out of our control,' Toby said.

'I'm sorry, too,' she said, forcing herself to give them each a quick, awkward hug.

'We'll be in touch with any progress,' Paul said.

And if you magically find some money stashed away, let me know. These words were on the tip of her tongue, but when she opened her mouth it was only the lump in her throat that came forwards.

She waited on the verandah while Paul backed Stuart's car out, activated the roller door to close, and remained standing while both navy blue BMWs drove down the street and then turned onto the main road at the end. She went back inside and sat down.

Fuck. Fuck, fuck, FUCK!

Her gaze rose to the paintings, which were not paintings but prints, and she shook her head at them.

A moment later her phone pinged with a message. She turned it over. It was a text from Mackenzie saying she was heading out after work and wouldn't be home for dinner. And then a message came through from Issy saying she wouldn't be home either. She sent them both a thumbs-up emoji, two kisses and a love heart, as usual. As she put her phone back down, she thought, *Thank Christ they aren't here.* And then: *How will I tell them? Can I just not? Yes, they don't have to know.* Thankfully the girls came and went a lot as young people with hectic social lives and jobs tended to.

Chapter One

Three months later ...

'Mum,' Mackenzie called from the other end of the long hallway.

'In here,' Erica called back from behind Stuart's desk in his study. She took her reading glasses off, laid them down with a clink on the enormous expanse of glass and rubbed her eyes. Spending time in here poring over online bank statements and spreadsheets and tweaking her budget had become a new hobby bordering on an obsession since the day Paul and Toby visited. She hadn't heard from them much since, as not much had changed.

Despite finding plenty of unnecessary expenses to cut, she was still chased to bed each night by thoughts of what could be – especially if the economy suddenly turned and interest rates shot up. She tried not to think about that, but it crept in over her while she was vulnerable, lying in bed in the dark trying to get to sleep. She was making great headway, and so far she was still floating. But there were some things she couldn't curb without the girls asking questions. And them not finding out the truth was another preoccupation, and was as much about upholding herself in their eyes as Stuart. She knew she shouldn't be – they were her daughters, for goodness' sake! – but she was too embarrassed to fess up that she'd left the money in his hands and not taken responsibility, like it was the 1950s or something!

She often sat there cursing her recently departed husband. *Damn it, Stuart, how could you have done this to me? To us?* And then the inevitable guilt and sorrow rose within her. He was gone. Dead. He hadn't meant to leave her and his daughters in such a dire financial situation. She had to believe that. Thankfully the house was in good repair, she thought, looking around. Her life might be like a big old wobbling house of cards, but at least he hadn't left them with a leaking roof.

'There you are!' Mackenzie said, appearing in the doorway, Isabella just behind her. They were only fourteen months apart in age, but often Issy seemed years behind Mackenzie in maturity – or perhaps it was just that she idolised her sister and being the quieter one made her seem a little less sure of herself. Mackenzie was bold and had the gift of the gab, the conviction and ability to convince that her father had had, and his dark brooding looks. Issy was more like Erica: quiet, thoughtful. They tended to sit back and observe, and like her mum when she spoke it tended to be after careful contemplation. Words were sprinkled carefully by Issy and splattered liberally by Mackenzie.

'What's up?' Erica said, looking up. She forced a smile and pushed back her concern, imagined herself running her hand over her face to physically smooth the worry lines.

'Are you busy?' Mackenzie said, hesitatingly, still by the door, practically wrapped around the frame.

'Never too busy for you,' she said, and her breath caught as she realised it was always exactly what Stuart had said to her whenever she'd knocked on his office door, which he'd always kept closed. Now she thought she knew why.

'Come in. Sit,' she said, indicating the two modern leather and steel chairs. She backed Stuart's luxurious leather chair away from the desk and swivelled around to face them, again struck by how similar, but also very different, this scenario was from the way it had always been previously. She could see why Stuart called this his power chair; he'd always laughed when he said it, but she saw the truth in it. She was a little higher than the girls, who were both fidgeting with their hands in their laps, just like Erica had tended to when in the same position. 'What is it?' she prompted and settled herself for a difficult conversation or request. She tensed in response to Mackenzie's taut demeanour and big eyes that were darting around the room. *Oh god. Please don't be here to ask me for more money – instead tell me you've changed your minds about going.* They were meant to be leaving in a bit over two weeks for their gap year – or their well-however-long-we-last-until-we-run-out-of-money year, as Issy had begun calling it.

Erica and Stuart had been very encouraging, agreeing the goal would keep them sane during their father's bouts of illness and treatment. Maps to pore over and countries to discuss whiled away the time with him in hospital and the long days and weeks when he was bed-ridden. Erica and Stuart had both done plenty of travel so had a lot to contribute, but Erica had recognised early the girls' need to have this one thing with their father, though plenty of times she'd cringed at the creep of jealousy and pain of being left out sneaking in. But she pushed it all aside, telling herself firmly that it wasn't about her.

Since Stuart's passing, when the girls spoke of where they would go and what they would see, she added an anecdote of her own. But while they were polite and entered into the discussion, they always quickly returned to remembering something Stuart had said and took off on that tangent. Each time Erica was left feeling flat, but told herself of course they had to keep their father alive – it was vital for their healing. And, anyway, there was no competing with a dead man for their affection.

The #metoo movement and renewed popular interest in feminism had got her wondering, though, if this was her being silenced, and allowing herself to be, as a woman – well beyond her marriage. She'd been happy with Stuart. Of course, they'd had their share of moments of gentle conflict. But what had been her role in that? Perhaps being the peacekeeper, the nurturer, wasn't really the best strategy long term. But she was easy-going. Not much really bothered her. Perhaps if she'd stomped her feet occasionally, though, insisted on certain things, she'd be in a whole different financial situation now …

'Sorry?' Erica said, forcing her attention back to the room. Mackenzie had spoken so quietly she'd almost missed what she'd said. And had she misheard anyway?

'Why don't you come with us?' Mackenzie said.

'Yeah. It'd be fun, Mum,' Issy added.

Erica's heart swelled. 'Oh, bless you, darling girls.' She wanted to gather them to her. Right then all the sacrifices she'd made were totally worth it to have raised two such thoughtful, gorgeous young women. 'But you don't want your old mum tagging along and spoiling your fun,' she finished breezily, desperate to hide the sudden wave of emotion that had gripped her insides.

'We're not going to be doing anything silly,' Mackenzie said.

'I know. But, still, it wouldn't be the same for you with your mother in tow.'

'We really wouldn't mind,' Issy said. The plaintive gaze she bestowed upon Erica made her wonder if – hope – they were actually having second thoughts about leaving the nest after all.

'Darlings, it's so lovely of you to ask – it really is – but I need to stay here. I have to work. And I had so much time off when your dad was sick that I don't have any leave left.'

'Oh. Yeah.' They both looked down at their hands lying in their laps.

Erica wasn't sure what was now going through their minds. 'Maybe I'll be able to join you along the way sometime for a quick visit,' she said.

'Yeah. That'd be good,' Issy said, brightening up.

'Sounds like a plan,' Mackenzie said.

'Are you having second thoughts about going?' Erica ventured. 'Because you can change your minds, you know. No one will think any less of you if you put it off for a bit. Or not go at all,' she added gently.

'Oh no,' Mackenzie said. 'We're going. In two weeks, as we planned, for sure. Well, I certainly am!' she said, her usually self-confident demeanour back.

'Me too,' Issy said, with a little less certainty.

'We just thought you deserved time away too,' Mackenzie said. 'You know,' she added with a shrug.

'I appreciate the thought, darling girls, but I'll be fine. I am fine. You don't need to worry about me,' Erica said brightly.

'Okay. I'm making a coffee if you want one,' Mackenzie said.

'Oh, yes, please.'

Alone again, Erica pulled her chair back up to the desk and rubbed her face with her hands in an effort to resist the building tears.

***

Erica cocked an ear and listened to the girls cheerfully fossicking in the kitchen. Everything was worth it to hear their grief being punctuated by a moment of happiness, of joy. Erica knew you had to grab those precious moments with both hands and hold on to them tightly for as long as you could. It was her main focus as a mother – to help navigate them through the grief of losing their dad with as little impact and scarring as possible. Not that she knew what she was doing. Did any parent ever? Really?

At eleven, she'd probably been too young to fully take in what losing her older brother had meant. Or perhaps it was the wonderful care her darling parents had bestowed upon her that meant she didn't know the true impact on her beyond sadness and the huge piece missing from her heart and life.

Mark was eighteen and they'd been close – well, as close as you could be as siblings with such an age gap. She'd been too young to hang out with him often and he wouldn't have wanted his younger sister tagging along anyway no matter how much she liked her. If they'd been together, would he have drowned in the murky water hole or would he not have been so keen to show off to his mates and dived in where it was too shallow? Might he have done a bomb instead of diving? Could she have saved him? She didn't like to think about it. Didn't tend to much. Tried very hard not to.

But losing Stuart had brought up all sorts of upsetting emotions and conflicting thoughts she'd successfully shut down after losing her mum. She now often found herself wondering if the care her parents had taken in protecting her and nurturing her, shepherding her away from the pain by wrapping her extra-tightly in their love, had come at the expense of their own mental and emotional health. While Erica remembered there being plenty of crying, neither parent had ceased functioning. Had they both ended up with dementia because they'd bottled up too many of their own feelings and put the stopper in? She was so grateful to them for everything, but especially showing her that tears were okay and also that life went on but in an altered state. She couldn't explain it, given that Mark's name was never mentioned, but he did remain a presence in the house and their lives. Not in the way some families kept a lost loved one's room intact as if they might walk in the door one day and take up occupancy again. Though, now she thought about it, Erica couldn't put her finger on why or how she thought they'd kept his name or memory alive. Perhaps unconsciously they'd done the right thing.

Erica didn't have a choice about keeping Stuart's memory alive – he was everywhere around them. This room with its minimalism was so him, as was the house itself. If left to her own devices, Erica might have chosen something a little smaller, less ostentatious. But when they'd moved back from the US they'd had plenty of money and Stuart had wanted something he could impress his clients with.

He was in venture capital; while she didn't know the ins and outs of the field and didn't care to, she did know it was all about convincing people to invest large amounts of money in various projects and industries. Basically, he was a salesman, he'd told her on their first date. And he was a good one – or was back then – because she'd bought him hook, line and sinker, as the saying went. And he'd done well throughout their marriage, because they'd had a great life, she thought sadly. But she'd have lived in a tent with him and eaten nothing but baked beans on toast.

And the rate she was going, it might just come to that. Tears stung.

If Stuart'd had a fault, it was that he believed in himself a little too much. Too confident. And his slightly crooked grin, the glint in his eye, could probably convince Eskimos to invest in a snow-making machine. And when he added a wink, people were putty in his hands. He'd made Erica literally go weak at the knees. Right to the end. Even still, really. In hospital, fighting for his life, he'd set those big brown eyes on her and she believed every word he said. She hadn't thought for a second he would die, despite seeing all the scans and talking to all the doctors and specialists. Stuart had her convinced he was going to beat it. She figured that was why she'd been in a complete state of shock for the entire first few months after his death. How could he have failed her like that? Physically and financially. She'd had moments of anger at him for leaving her. So many times she'd wanted to yell and scream at him. And then the guilt would cut in. And then the remorse. And the sadness.

Grief was one big ball of emotions swirling around inside of her. The physical pain was a layer on top of her overall exhaustion – a completely different type of tiredness from what she'd experienced with the girls as babies and getting up to them through the night and then the accompanying drag during the day. This sort went deeper and was all-encompassing: too big and too deep for coffee or a nap or glass of wine to have any effect on. It was not a gritty-eyed tiredness but a weight that tried to hold her down, and left her suffering regular bouts of inattention, even when she got plenty of sleep – though she hadn't slept well for more than the odd night here and there for years and couldn't imagine doing so again. It was deeper than that. Or that's what she thought. Maybe it was tiredness, but just too ingrained after going on for so long. She could function, and she did, but it was as if she was moving through thick mud surrounded by fog. And sometimes she didn't think you could really call it tiredness because she was quite perky and energetic. It was more like she just couldn't be bothered with certain things she had before. And time did weird things. She wouldn't be surprised to learn one day in the future this had all been a dream – or nightmare – and she'd been out to it for a year or on another planet. Or for one day.

Sometimes she found herself staring and frowning at a glass or a spoon with vague curiosity or wondering what it was for. And when she realised – came out of her trance-like state enough to put the object to use – doing so seemed an insurmountable task. All too often she found herself snapping back to attention after realising she'd been staring at the object in question for ages. Or it took Mackenzie and Issy reminding her she'd zoned out or a quip from them telling her what the object in her hand was for. 'Mum, you look like you've never seen a glass before. It's simple. Look, you pick it up and take a sip. Like this.' And Erica laughed along with them while they demonstrated. More and more she was having to laugh off moments of vagueness, but the truth was plenty of days she just wanted to curl up and die too. Or not die, but just not have to do anything or face up to anything. Give in to the fog around her pulling her down, smothering her. But she owed it to the girls to keep going. She was raising two young women into a world that despite commentary to the contrary was still dominated by men and their views. And she couldn't exactly declare herself strong and independent given her cosseted life with Stuart and letting his career take precedence over hers. She had some regrets, but being mother to Mackenzie and Isabella was not one of them.

Now she had to face them leaving her too. Her cousin and best friend, Steph – when she'd accidently let slip this concern – had said that Erica should be proud of herself for raising them to be ready and to want to leave, especially two siblings who had such a close relationship with each other and their mum. And especially after all they'd gone through in losing their father.

Erica hadn't been able to bring herself to admit that she desperately wanted to beg the girls to stay. Another friend, Michelle, had gently suggested that now she could have her time in the sun, get her own career back on track. She'd nodded in response, unable to tell them the truth about that either. She wondered how she'd go when the girls weren't there and she didn't have the impetus to keep herself together. That scared her too. And being alone. The girls weren't big on parties and going out at night – they'd been too busy working. One of them had always been home at some point. She couldn't remember ever having spent a whole night all alone in the house and the thought of it terrified her, but she didn't want to admit it to herself, let alone anyone else. *Stop it!* she told herself firmly. *Cross that bridge when we come to it. You've got this far.*

Her friend Renee told her to just focus on one day at a time, or one hour or even just five minute increments, when she was really struggling. Anything to keep from completely losing herself to the darkness constantly trying to swallow her.

At least when they went, she wouldn't have to hide how frugal she needed to be. If they'd realised she was cooking a lot more chicken and vegetarian meals and almost no beef and lamb, they hadn't commented. And they didn't seem to have noticed that Erica hadn't ordered in any takeaway or that they hadn't had a meal out together since Stuart's death. Nor that she hadn't raved about a movie she'd seen. Giving up going to see films was probably her greatest sacrifice. She loved escaping into a cinema and inside fictional characters and storylines and used to go at least several times a month. But doing so was expensive – and now a luxury, though not really in Erica's mind. She thought that had helped keep her sane – certainly while Stuart had been in hospital. Much better than pacing the house and feeling helpless when not with him. But she'd reluctantly cut them from the budget and made do with the online streaming subscriptions. The girls would certainly notice the cancellation of those, so that had to wait until they left.

It was taking some getting used to, but Erica was determined to win this battle – to become strong and independent herself. Perhaps she should be sharing more about their situation with the girls, not protecting them so much from things, but that was her choice. And in so much of life you were damned if you did and damned if you didn't. Right now, she was having enough trouble trying to keep her mind clear and climb out of the quicksand Stuart had dumped her in without having to answer a million questions from the girls. And risking them turning against her. She couldn't bear them leaving angry or disappointed in her. That would destroy her. They were all she had.

talk about it

Let's talk about books.

Join the conversation:

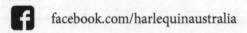 facebook.com/harlequinaustralia

 @harlequinaus

 @harlequinaus

harpercollins.com.au/hq

If you love reading and want to know about our
authors and titles, then let's talk about it.